Praise for Tom Avitabile:

"Frighteningly realistic. Most of Washington really works this way. Homeland Security had better read this one and take corrective action."
– U.S. Ambassador Michael Skol on *The Eighth Day*

"Awesome. I could not go to sleep last night because I couldn't put it down!"
– Donna Hanover, WOR Radio 710 on *The Eighth Day*

"*The Hammer of God* is a tightly plotted, fear-filled and all-too-realistic thriller that is finely written, in fact the best this reviewer has read in a long time. It should be a best seller and will make the reader anxiously awaiting the third and final novel in this thriller trilogy! Great job, Tom Avitabile!"
– Crystal Book Reviews

"Well done and ensuring that the reader will grab book three as soon as available."
– Bookbitch on *The Hammer of God*

The Devil's Quota

Tom Avitabile

Gramarye

Gramarye Media
1270 Caroline Street
Suite D120-381
Atlanta, GA 30307

Print ISBN-13: 978-1-61188-314-5
E-book ISBN: 978-1-936558-86-5

Visit our website at www.TheStoryPlant.com
Visit the author's website at www.TomAvitabile.com

First Story Plant paperback printing: October 2014
First Gramarye mass market paperback printing: February 2022

Printed in the United States of America

0 9 8 7 6 5 4 3 2 1

To the strong and the brave who protect us from tyranny in all its forms.

And to the special class of protector/warriors who volunteer to put themselves at risk in service to us all.

Prologue – The Naughty Lad

The crisp snap of an English bullwhip reverberated off the cold granite walls as it cracked over the shoulders of sixty-two-year-old "Lord of The Manor" Jenkins. The red rough flannel undergarment in which he was clad dulled the full sting. His round belly tested the strength of the buttons along the front. He winced as another lash thrashed his back. Matilda, the wretched wench, was particularly spirited this day, laying into her lord with much force. As he faced her on his hands and knees from the featherbed, he couldn't help but notice that her breasts jiggled and peeked out of her peasant dress with every lash.

He heard his own voice echo in the chamber as he pleaded with his cherished tormentor, "No more, Matilda, I will do as you say."

"Oh, so now ya decide to give me the uppa 'and. Well, runt, you can just taste my lash before you taste my..."

"Yes. Yes. Oh, Matilda."

Later, Jenkins propped himself up on his elbows and arched his back, his red garment now flayed open, its buttons torn off. Between gasps, he focused on the flickering candles of the wall sconces in the now quiet master chamber. Twice he averted his gaze from the piercing eyes of Oliver Cromwell's portrait that stood as a disapproving witness to the final act which all the previous theatrics had built up to – that of Matilda, now on her knees, bestowing upon Jenkins an oral gratification.

He moaned like a rutting elk. "I've been a bad lad, Matilda. Urgh. I stole the list. It's wrong but they are evil. Urgh. Urgh."

"Um-hmmmpppphhh,um-hmmmph,"   Matilda urged him on as he was close.

Jenkins groaned and grabbed his chest, tearing at the spreading tightness, and fell back.

Matilda was miffed. "C'mon Jenky, you were almost there this time... Jenkins?"

She rose and lightly slapped him on his cheek. "Mr. Jenkins? Mr. Jenkins?"

But the man just lay motionless looking straight up... forever.

"Oh shit!" She grabbed her cell phone from the nightstand and dialed feverishly.

1. The Fat Lady Sings

The flash that illuminated Jenkins' face cast momentary daylight into the dark, dingy, depressing room of the vacant apartment in which his body was now lying. The crime scene photographer's focus was interrupted by the unexpected entrance of NYPD Detective First Grade, Mike DiMaggio, dressed like he was going to the opera, his clip badge stuffed in his tuxedo pocket.

New York City Medical Examiner, Dr. Harvey Sussman, in a sport jacket more suited to the racetrack at Aqueduct, removed the thermometer from the small incision he had made above the dead man's liver. DiMaggio watched as the doctor squinted, trying to read the red line against the scale so he could calculate the time of death.

"Ninety point five degrees, that means the body's temperature cooled eight point one degrees since his heart stooped... I make the TOD three and a half to four hours ago," Sussman called out to his assistant, who recorded the finding.

DiMaggio cleared his throat to get Sussman's attention and was quickly rewarded. "Hey DiMadge! What the hell are you doing here? This one's natural causes!"

DiMaggio bent down to see the body. "No, it's a mercy killing."

"How do you figure that?"

"Got me out of sitting through Madame Butterfly."

"I'm no opera critic, but the fat lady sang in a natural key on this guy." The M.E. reached over to DiMag-

9

gio's lapel and rolled the satin between his thumb and forefinger. "Nice workmanship. So why is Manhattan homicide's finest here in his bar mitzvah suit?"

"When a federal circuit court judge dies, everybody's night gets ruined," DiMaggio said. He looked around, squinting from the glare of the portable work lights. From the looks of the place, it was an empty apartment. Dust was everywhere, and it smelled moldy and dank. "How much you figure a high-up judge like him makes?"

"Gotta clear one hundred fifty a year." He handed the thermometer to his assistant.

"I would have figured a buck seventy-five, maybe two hundred Gs."

"This guy? He was..." Sussman waited for his assistant to take one last shot of the body, and then he used a penlight to examine the eyes of the corpse for petechial hemorrhaging. "...he was already rich. Married well. Ever hear of the DuPont's of Chappaqua?"

"The dog peed all over my copy of the social register. But if you're telling me his old lady has cash up the wazoo, then this figures even less."

"What does?"

"What a guy like him was doing in an empty apartment like this."

The M.E. sighed. "I hate this part of the job. His Honor, Judge Jenkins, was having sex!" He pulled down the front of the dead man's underwear.

DiMaggio followed the M.E.'s look. "You already ran a test and found vaginal fluids around his unit? Fast work!"

"No, professor. He's got lipstick on his dipstick."

DiMaggio stood. "I would've seen that if I looked as closely at it as you, but I am a well-adjusted male."

The M.E. looked up and said, "Fuck you very large, Detective. Wanna be copied on all my reports?"

"I'm afraid the commissioner would insist." DiMaggio continued taking in the surroundings. Since the power wasn't turned on in the apartment, the M.E.

had battery-operated work lights all around the body. DiMaggio picked one up and traced the steps from the doorway to the body on the floor. "Something hits me wrong here."

The sixty-four year old, grey-haired doctor stood with a grunt, as he said to the fit, thirty-eight year old Italian with the dark head of hair, "Because you believe sex ends after sixty?"

"Because why would he be wearing this unflattering red flannel get up in the middle of sex? On top of that, what hooker would leave a wallet full of cash, not rifle through his attaché case, and leave no sign that she was even here, other than the lip lock?"

"She freaked out?" the M.E. said.

"No, I don't think so. The floor is dusty, except for our footprints and this clean swipe leading right up to the body."

The M.E. looked at DiMaggio with "Good point" written all over his face.

DiMaggio walked toward the feet and noticed one pristine, smaller footprint in the dust a few feet from the body. "Listen, nobody walk on this end of the body. Take a shot of this footprint here that's smaller than ours."

"So someone dragged the body in here? Maybe it's a good thing you missed the aria after all, my boy." The M.E. said.

ᴅᴏ.

Two minutes later, DiMaggio walked out of the brownstone and stood on the wide top step of the stoop. He inhaled deeply, enjoying the sweet, fresh air of the mild summer evening. There was a young, black uniformed officer across the step, also clearing his lungs. DiMaggio asked, "First on scene?"

"Yes, sir!" the kid, who looked like he was right out of the academy, responded.

"You see anyone leaving as you pulled up" – DiMaggio glanced at his nameplate – "Towne?"

"No, sir."

"First death?"

"Does it show?"

"Unfortunately, you'll get used to it." Looking around, DiMaggio observed the small crowd of neighbors, who were drawn by the police car's flashing lights. Another detective's car pulled up and Maggie Reade, a detective from his squad, got out with two crime scene techs lugging forensic kits. He hitched his head in the direction of the first-floor apartment. "I'm very interested in the footprints in the dust at the foot of the body," he said as he continued down the stone steps.

On the sidewalk, he approached the building superintendent, a skinny, Middle-Eastern man who immediately started backing away.

"C'm'ere, I need to ask you some questions. What's your name?" DiMaggio said.

"Hafiz Haffad. I know nothing."

"How long have you worked here?"

"Three years but I don't see nothing."

"Three years and you've never seen the owner?" DiMaggio said.

"I don't see nothing. I never see. It's company apartments." By this time, Haffad was breathing heavily, his eyes shifting back and forth, looking for a way out.

"Calm down, take a deep breath." Stepping closer to block the only escape route, DiMaggio noticed that the man smelled of some kind of seasoned lamb dish. "Now, what's that mean? Company? You mean corporate? No tenants?"

"Yes, no tenants... always different people, every two, three weeks. But this apartment, no people for months."

"What's a place like that rent for?"

"Much money. Very not nice people. Always yelling 'Clean here; this not clean enough; smell like barn...'"

DiMaggio was about to tell him to calm down again when a statuesque, impeccably dressed woman exited the brownstone and descended the eight steps to the street. The woman was model-perfect with long legs, shoulder-length blonde hair, and minimum jewelry – a pearl necklace with matching earrings. She didn't even glance at DiMaggio or Haffad. DiMaggio watched every move she made as she stepped to a waiting Lincoln Town car, which was across the street from all the commotion and police cars...without ever, DiMaggio noticed, turning her head or looking around to see what it was all about.

"Who is she?"

"She doctor. Very big. Very smart. Her office top two floors."

Her driver hustled around and opened the passenger-side rear door. The hem of her pencil skirt flirted a little when it rode up slightly as she swiveled into the sedan.

"...Very big." Hassad said, swallowing a gulp of dry air.

DiMaggio realized they were both acting like high school freshmen drooling over the prom queen. "What company?"

"Who?"

"What company owns the apartment?"

$$\text{ID}_\blacktriangleleft$$

When the door locks on the town car clunked and the driver pulled away, Dr. Cassandra Cassidy finally let out a deep breath. She fished through her Gucci bag and found her phone. She held down the button on her iPhone and said to Siri, "Call Miles."

She had an urge to look behind her to see if she was being followed, but Miles got on the line before she could turn around.

"What's up?"

"Are you busy? Can I come over?"

"Well, actually, I'm still working. I got two cases I'm reviewing, and then I got a late conference call with the coast."

The doctor's heart sunk as she realized he was still mad. "I just need a minute or two. I've had a rough day and I thought..."

"Hold on, I have a call."

She threw up her hands and the phone hit the rear passenger-side window. She brought it back to her ear. She became conscious of biting her bottom lip and stopped herself just as he came back on.

"Sorry, it's crazy here. What were you saying? Hello? Come on, I'm busy."

"Are we seeing each other tonight?"

"Look. We went over that this morning. Today's a real bear and you're insisting we go to the Met tomorrow night, so I've got to do double duty tonight. Geez. What the hell's gotten into you?"

"I'm just, I'm just... I've had a really bad day, that's all, and I thought..."

"Dammit, hold on." She heard his muffled voice as he called out to his secretary, "Tell him to hold."

Speaking clearly through the phone again, he said, "Now what's the matter?"

"I need... I ... Never mind. We'll see each other tomorrow night?"

"Sure, but only because you're blackmailing me about the Boys' Club dinner Wednesday night... we still have a deal, right? I do Puccini and you show up for my table, my ten-thousand-dollar table! And don't be so emotional. Have a drink and relax. Whatever's bothering you can't be all that bad. I gotta go."

She was startled by the way she was so quickly dispatched. Not even a simple pleasantry; no "Miss you", no "Love you" – nothing. She would have even settled for the dreaded, "Love ya." Instead, she was hanging on the phone with a dead connection. In the silence, she realized she had been fooling herself; she had no connection with him either. With all her accomplishments and professional standing, she was still, in the end, alone – all alone. Blinking and widening her eyes to stave off the tears she felt forming, she looked out onto the New York City night and suddenly wished she could call her mom.

IQ

"Amalgamated Holdings," Detective Second Grade Maggie Reade said as she handed DiMaggio a printout back at the station house.

He scanned the page. "And Amalgamated is holding the bag for who?"

"Dunno, but the five corporate directors of the company that owns the brownstone are all doctors. It looks like just an investment thing."

"Damn, I got to get some investment thing going. That's where you make the real money."

"Invest? On a cop's salary? DiMadge, you kill me."

An administrative clerk, Julio Hernandez, walked over with a stack of folders. "Maggie, here's all they had on Jenkins downtown."

"Thanks Hernandez. Put 'em on the chair."

"Please Maggie, call me Julio."

DiMaggio smiled; Julio had been trying to play a little search and seizure with the five-foot-ten-inch curly redhead ever since he was hired to help out the squad. DiMaggio felt bad for the guy because he knew Julio was not a person of interest to Reade. He watched as Julio left with sunken shoulders.

DiMaggio gave Reade a questioning look, but she just rolled her eyes.

Her reaction prompted him to say, "What's wrong with Julio?"

"He's a nerd! I once let him bore me to death about bugs... and then the elevator reached my floor."

"I'm guessing it wasn't a tall building," DiMaggio said as he grabbed a few of the folders.

"He's got some kind of master's degree in insects. That's why he's good for digging up files and reports.

Maybe a little too good. Will ya look at this stack? It's taller than he is."

DiMaggio grabbed a folder from the pile on Reade's desk and sat at his own desk.

"How did we get involved in this in the first place?" Reade said.

"Nine-one-one got an anonymous tip about a dead body. Delaney was supposed to cover but he was on his knees, praying at the porcelain altar – bad sushi or something – so I got the beep. By the time I got there, the M.E. had it figured for a natural."

"So then why did you ruin my night, and why are we still involved?"

"One, I outrank you, and two, I think the body was moved."

"From where?"

"Ah, that will be the first question the chief asks tomorrow morning, and the answer may be in this stack of stuff."

"It's after ten and there's hours of work here," Reade said, pointing at the pile that had toppled over across her desk.

"I'm thinking pizza."

"Why not? But look, I know you outrank me and all, but just once couldn't you be thinking salad?"

"Hmmp." DiMaggio's eyebrows went up as he scanned the contents of the folder from the top of the pile.

"What?"

"Nothing. It's just that I could have sworn the super of the building, Haffad, was from Iran, but it says here he's from Afghanistan."

2. The Devil's Farmer

Setara froze mid-breath. From the sounds she heard outside, the man from northern Afghanistan, Dehqan, "The Devil's Farmer," had returned. Just as he had told her he would. She had feared this day for the last six months. She couldn't let the man find her. But what if someone in the village betrayed her; told the man from the north where she was hiding?

She had brought this on herself. If she hadn't made a deal with this devil out of fear and uncertainty, she wouldn't be suffocating in a pocket of the remains of a burned down hut right now.

IOL

At the center of the dirt-poor village, Dehqan, "The Devil's Farmer" approached an old man who kept starvation and death at bay by selling water bottles. "Have you seen Setara?"

"No."

He glared down into the old man's eyes, which appeared like slits in his leathery, cracked skin. "You are lying."

"Why would I lie of such a thing?"

"You know why I am here?"

"Yes."

"You do not approve?"

"It is not my place to approve, but that of Allah."

Disgusted, Dehqan placed his hand on the old man's face and pushed him back so hard the man and his chair fell on the ground.

$$\mathbb{Q}_\blacktriangle$$

The few village people who witnessed this act of disrespect to an elder said nothing. Nor did they protest in the slightest, for they knew the tall man from the north to be ruthless and cold. In fact, they now quietly cursed Setara for bringing the vile man back to their quiet Afghan village.

$$\mathbb{Q}_\blacktriangle$$

It took ten minutes, but eventually DiMaggio trekked through Bellevue Hospital's massive complex until he reached the Van Nagel Clinic. In small type on the doorframe was the nameplate, Dr. C. Cassidy, M.D. Ph.d.

DiMaggio noticed only older male patients in the sterile, blue-and-white-themed waiting room. He approached the nurse at the desk. "Is Doctor Cassidy in?"

"I am sorry. Doctor Cassidy is very busy, so if you don't have an appointment, there's just no way."

DiMaggio flashed his gold shield. "Ask her to take a break." He knew the nurse saw his point when she reluctantly got up and walked into the inner office.

DiMaggio picked up a pamphlet entitled "What you should know about PENILE IMPLANTS – the benefits and risks." He shuddered as an unwelcome picture flashed through his mind.

"Officer, the doctor will see you now," the nurse said as she returned to the waiting room.

Glad for the interruption, DiMaggio passed her and the elderly, overweight man she was escorting out of the office. He looked eerily like Judge Jenkins.

In marked contrast to the antiseptic quality of the clinic's waiting room, Doctor Cassidy's office was a study in white and red. The furnishings included a white lacquer Japanese desk, two low-slung red chairs, three large paintings adorning the walls, each a simple geometric shape in red on a white field, and two large ornamental jars – one white, one red – big enough for a small child to hide in. But all that quickly receded to the back of DiMaggio's mind, as he focused on the doctor herself. Even in a plain white non-designer lab coat, she was still stunning as she came around her desk and offered her hand. "Officer...?"

"Detective, ma'am. Detective Michael DiMaggio, ma'am."

"Doctor, Detective."

"'Scuse me?"

"I don't hold an M.D.-Ph.D. in 'ma'am'."

"Huh?"

"Let's drop it. What can I do for you, Detective?"

"Ma'am, you were observed leaving Five Twenty-Three East Fifty-Fourth Street shortly after one Horace Jenkins was declared dead at the scene the night before last."

"Who observed me?"

"Well, I did, ma'am."

"Please stop calling me ma'am."

"Oh, right. You didn't study that. Gotcha. I observed you leaving the premises, Doctor."

"I saw the commotion but I was in a hurry."

"What were you doing there?"

"I have my offices there."

DiMaggio looked around and opened his palms saying, "What's this?"

"These are my clinical offices. The offices where I have my practice, where I see my private patients, are uptown on Fifty Fourth."

"What do you do ma... Doctor... Cassidy?"

"I am a clinical sexual psychiatrist."

"Come again?"

She sighed. "I help people who have diagnosed psychosexual complications."

"You mean they can't get it up?"

"That is an essentially correct however evolution-arily-challenged description."

"Two floors?" DiMaggio said.

"Is that relevant to your investigation? Which, by the way, is what exactly?"

"Excuse me, Doc. But I get to retire with half pay after twenty years for asking the questions."

DiMaggio noticed the doctor glancing at her watch. To him, this was a classic "my time is more valuable than yours" move. He stared at her, clenching his teeth in anger at her arrogance. Her looks didn't matter anymore. He couldn't stand her now. "I could call you down to the precinct if you'd like, and we can continue there."

"No, let's not make this take any longer than it has to. I need two floors because I have five treatment rooms, four consultation rooms, and an office staff of ten, so I need the space."

"Wow. Lotta bucks in psychosexual complica-tions."

"Is there anything else, Detective?"

"No, that's all for now. Thank you for your time." He waited for her response, but she had already forgot-ten him. As she sat down in her matching red, tufted, soft leather chair behind her desk, it audibly exhaled a sound like a comfortable sigh, and she picked up her phone. "Roberta, send Mr. Wells back in."

"I'll just let myself out," DiMaggio said, hitching his thumb over his shoulder.

"Did you say something?" she asked over the rim of her just-donned Fendi frames.

"Yes. Have you heard of Amalgamated Holdings?"

"Of course; they're the landlords of the brown-stone."

IQ.

DiMaggio stopped off at his apartment to change into his tuxedo for the redo of the operatic evening interrupted by Jenkins' death two nights ago. He lived on the second floor-back of an old rooming house on St. Mark's Place, which had been converted to apartments after World War II. He lived alone, so the unimpeded male décor ensured it was not a place that was likely to be found in an issue of *Good Housekeeping*, much less have a stick of furniture in it that ever got within a mile of Japanese lacquer. It was, however, a great place to watch football with a few guys from the squad or host their weekly poker nights.

The apartment smelled heavy with the ashes from the logs he had burned in the fireplace the night before. He opened the door leading out to his deck to let in some fresh air. He had a momentary urge to go down the wood stairs to the small backyard and just sit on the metal chair for a while, but there was no time. However, he did take a moment to admire the flower garden.

DiMaggio's downstairs neighbor, a widow, spent most of her days planting "time bombs," as DiMaggio thought of them. A series of flowers timed so that some were blooming every month of the year, except in the dead of winter. He had to admit it was nice to see flowers out the back as he had his morning coffee. On the occasions when he had a female overnight guest, the "flower power" was not lost on them, either.

There was a cold half-cup of coffee sitting on the deck railing, which must have been there since yesterday morning. A fly had committed suicide in the murky brown remainder, and the cup had a red lipstick tattoo around the rim. DiMaggio's mind instantly went to the dead judge's red-ringed unit, and he immediately flushed the image from his head. DiMaggio grabbed the mug and gently traced the red imprint left by the sultry lower lip of the woman who had been sipping from it two mornings before, Susan Milani.

After dating on and off for several years, recently they had begun seeing each other once or twice a week. That was practically "going steady," given their busy schedules. Susan was good-looking, street smart, and knew how to make him feel appreciated. She wasn't clingy or insistent on defining their relationship every other day, which was what made her unique among the women in his life.

Nobody got more tail than cops. Back when DiMaggio was in patrol, he was never without a woman trying to capture him as a boyfriend. DiMaggio had a rugged male look and one other thing going for him – women fell for his eyes. It was almost certain that at some point in the courtship, a woman would compliment him on his eyes. Not so much the deep-green color or his long eyelashes, but the way they said he looked at them. They way they wanted a man to look at them. Some even said they felt that he could look right through them to their soul. He took it all with a grain of salt, as he figured they mostly commented like that after they'd had a few drinks.

At first the women in his life were mostly waitresses, secretaries, and nurses – working women who liked a guy in uniform. Even after he made detective and met Park Avenue divorcees or dynamic career women, he never found the "one." The one female he wanted to stay with, make a life with, have a family with.

He met Susan at, of all places, his niece's wedding. They had so much fun dancing and laughing that it wasn't until the end of the night, after they already liked one another, that he even mentioned he was a cop. Now it rarely came up as Susan was focused on her career. She was an Executive Office Manager at the corporate headquarters of CitiBank in Long Island City, and she had her sights set on VP of Facilities. The odds were in her favor in that she had seventeen years with the bank and she was on track to be promoted to the coveted position.

When they were together, there was no starting gun, no trapeze; they were there to relax and relax each other. He had gotten to the point that over-energetic sex, or the *Cosmopolitan Magazine* hyped-up expectations of most females, wasn't any fun for him anymore, leaving him feeling more like a competing athlete than a partner. With Susan it was blessedly different; she was 'traditional'; the sex was just as good as the "swinging from the chandelier" shit he had put up with in the past, but more satisfying.

In the past, they saw other people on occasion, but now he and Susan were just about to move into an exclusive relationship. She was the woman he wanted on his arm at important events – the detectives' holiday dinner or a family wedding. She was comfortable to be with and she was fun but, more importantly, she knew how to act. She had class but not in a snobby *I'm a Park Avenue doctor and you're a schlub*, way. Susan was warm and gracious and had a genuine interest in everyone she met, which made men and women alike instantly charmed in her presence. Now that it was turning into a serious relationship, he even dared to imagine that once she made VP, he might buy her a ring. *Maybe*.

He came inside and placed the cup in the sink, aimed the faucet at it, and hit it with enough water to fill it once over. Then he left it there and headed to his bedroom; he'd load the dishwasher tonight.

At this time of day the low sun came through the back windows and glinted off his prized possession. Above the mantle, in a display case was an ivory-handled Colt Single Action Army or as it was also known, 1873 Peacemaker .45, "The Gun That Won The West." He had inherited the U.S. Cavalry standard issue firearm from his grandfather. A similar gun, in slightly better condition, recently fetched six hundred and ten thousand dollars at auction. Bill thought of the gun as his retirement fund. By then it should be worth well over a million.

Standing at the dresser mirror, he finally got the bow tie that Susan had bought him tied right after three tries. It was 4:15 p.m. when he left his apartment for the precinct in his tux.

IOQ

As DiMaggio approached Reade's desk, where she was reviewing a report, he saw her glance briefly at him before returning to her work.

"Really sucks... that a decorated NYPD detective, first grade, has to moonlight as a freaking headwaiter," she said.

"Trying not to be a headless waiter, 'cause if we miss Ma'am Butterfly again, Susan will chop mine off," DiMaggio said.

"Not Ma'am Butterfly, Ma-dame Butterfly!"

"Don't you start now! Anything new?

"Nothing except we confirmed your 'Doctor Flynn, Medicine Woman' pays rent to Amalgamated."

"I know. She told me."

"You interviewed... her?" Reade held up the Journal of the American Medical Association and pointed to a picture of Cassidy at a conference. "Here, look under the picture and read the caption." She handed it to him.

"Clinical Psychiatrist Cassandra Cassidy... Cassandra! Accepts the Browning Fellowship Award... yada yada yada. No wonder she's so full of herself." DiMaggio tossed it down.

Reade picked up the journal. "I dunno Mike, says here that she was an honors graduate, she interned with prestigious doctors at some equally prestigious hospitals, then she opened her own clinic... She does pro-bono work for the poor and indigent... If she's full of it, then get me a couple of gallons of whatever she's drinking."

"Pro bono, right. More like pro *boner*," DiMaggio said.

"Well, oakie doakie then... by the way, dead end on the doctors of Amalgamated. They are all clean to Judge Jenkins' cases," Reade said.

"What about the door to door?"

"Nobody saw nuthin'," she said, holding up a plastic evidence bag with a zip disk inside and dangling it, "but looky what we found in the lining of the judge's briefcase!"

"Hello. Well, what's on it?"

"Don't know; this disk's only fifteen years old and our computers are twenty five, so we ain't got the little thingy this goes into. I was going to send it to the lab."

"Check it for prints first. Then take it yourself and leave with it."

"You know that I'm a second grade dick around here, not a clueless probie, don't cha?" Reade said with her hand on her hip.

"Look, just do me the favor. Don't send it normal – walk it in yourself, wait for it and sign it back into the evidence locker."

"Okay, why the precaution?"

"I don't know yet, but something about this is off kilter."

"Right. Well, then sign me out will ya? I gotta leave a little early to pick up LaShana. The techies will get it first thing tomorrow."

"You still manage to find time to volunteer?"

"Yeah, when I am not being your over-paid delivery girl. Hey, Big Sisters is a good program and I get a lot back."

"Maybe I should check out Big Brothers," DiMaggio said, looking down and arranging the papers that were dropped on his desk, just missing the old in-basket.

That made Reade smile as she slid the disk in her backpack and swung it over her shoulder.

The disturbing text message on Kevin Grimes' phone reminded him of a famous quote atop a calendar page from an old day planner. *"Trouble is never a welcomed guest and always arrives at the most inconvenient time."*

"Make a wish!" his wife of ten years suggested for the tenth year in a row. She set his candle-obliterated cake before him, accompanied by the usual strained tones of people who sing out loud only at such occasions.

He took a deep breath but intentionally held back on blowing out all the candles so his eight-year-old son next to him could help "Daddy" blow out the forest fire of sixty candles raging over the custom-decorated icing. His only wish was that the text was a mistake.

His wife quickly took the cake away to the kitchen to remove the dripping candles. While waiting for her to return, he shook hands with their guests and received a few gifts, which by family tradition were only to be opened once the coffee was served. He hazarded another glance down at his personal cell phone. It just read "Jenkins."

So it was that right in the middle of his birthday celebration, one of the most powerful men in the city, a trusted public figure who had quietly garnered a ground swell of big donor support to fuel his run for City Hall, was inwardly shaken. He focused on the pinkish remnant of a red wine blot on his brother-in-law's shirt, and it reminded him of a stubborn bloodstain from an old wound that wouldn't wash out.

Like all men of achievement, he didn't arrive to his current position in virginal white, but in the stained drab gray that one dons by slaying the dragons and crossing the muddy waters on the way to the top. His best path to mayor was to keep his head down for now because he was still serving the current occupant. He didn't want to roil the waters and give his boss, and soon-to-be political enemy, an advance warning and a possible advantage.

Tonight, however, celebrating his birthday with his friends and family around him, the last thing he wanted to see was that text. He was opening his third "Old Fart" card when his wife brought the cake back and set it on the table.

"I'm sorry, honey, but the candles messed up the pretty design. Do you still like it, Kevin?" his wife said.

He glanced down at the cake. The sixty candles had been removed, leaving holes in the custom air-brushed marzipan sheet that made it look like it had been sprayed with a Tommy gun. As he looked at the "bullet-riddled" icing, he hoped it was not an omen.

He kissed her on the cheek, forced a smile, and said, "I don't know how you managed to make it look so real... I love it." Chief Kevin Grimes then took the big knife and cut the first piece right out of the punctured, yet picture-perfect, rendering of the three-star badge of the NYPD Chief of Detectives.

3. The Invisible Man

Marc Chagall's two larger-than-life murals stood thirty-six feet high, creating a surrealistic bracketing of the "center" of Lincoln Center, namely the Metropolitan Opera House. The large, sweeping plaza, spread out before its one-hundred-yard setback location, insulated these works composed in the major key of primary color from the yellow cab-dotted dissonant gray of New York City traffic. The plaza was elevated by seven steps that literally raised its patrons above street level and the prosaic commonplace performing arts that animate the soul of Manhattan.

On this night, however, DiMaggio could see that Lincoln Center's trademark fountain was only half as bubbly as Susan Milani who – wrapped in an office manager's monthly salary worth of slit-to-the-thigh blue velvet – looked fantastic on the arm of his "head-waiter" get up.

She twirled around taking in the night and the sights. "This is what life is about, Mike. The fine arts, sophisticated people, so transporting..."

DiMaggio beamed as her "Susan in Wonderland" trance infected him.

They found their way upstairs to the bar on the Grand Tier level. DiMaggio ordered and then watched as one strawberry each was dropped into two tall champagne glasses with a bubbly fizz. He handed over a fifty to the bartender and waited for change... and waited and waited. When he realized he just spent half a C-note on six ounces of booze and some fruit, he reluctantly pulled out a five-dollar bill and stuffed it into the tip jar. He turned and handed one flute to Susan and tipped his own toward hers. "To the little Miss Caterpillar who became...?"

"...Madame Butterfly!"

They clinked, kissed, and looked around as they sipped.

"Nice to be here isn't it?" a wide-eyed Susan said.

"Look at these people," DiMaggio said as he gazed upon the "upper crust" engaging in casual, wine-glass-punctuated conversation, their feet shifting in the lush, deep pile carpet that made their Manolo Blahniks, Bruno Maglis, and Louboutins that much more comfortable. "How much do you have to make in a year to afford this all the time? Not to mention the Fifth Avenue apartment, the place in the Hamptons, the ski chalet and the villa in Tuscany."

"Mike, we're supposed to be having a nice time..."

"Then the Beamer in the garage... the nine hundred dollar a month garage! And the Land Rover out at the country house. God, how much do you have to make?"

Susan grabbed her man and kissed him. His tension relaxed and he engulfed her in his arms in a dizzying embrace.

The champagne in Susan's hand was dangerously close to spilling down DiMaggio's back as an usher, playing a little bell chime, walked through. As they broke their embrace, DiMaggio saw Dr. Cassidy and Miles Bennett pass by. He was a tanned, handsome, and rich accident attorney who looked just like he did on his incessant late-night TV commercials. Yet it was Cassidy who was turning heads in an off-the-shoulder white gown, which caressed and gently revealed the Pilates-honed figure beneath. DiMaggio figured that little frock must have carried a price tag in excess of a "Scratch Off and Win" lottery prize.

Susan misinterpreted DiMaggio's stare. "Take a picture; it'll last longer."

"Sorry; she's someone I questioned about the judge's death."

"She doesn't look like a killer to me, not in Versace anyway," Susan said, nibbling on the champagne-soaked strawberry.

"She's a head doctor... for people who don't get any..."

"Don't get any what?"

"Head!"

Dr. Cassidy's and DiMaggio's eyes met for a second. DiMaggio nodded but the good doctor seemed to look right through him and continued on without showing even the barest glimmer of recognition.

Susan smirked. "Yeah, nice try Mike. You almost sold me but that woman's never seen you before in her life."

DiMaggio was about to protest when the usher walked through a second time playing the chimes and everyone headed to their seats.

DQ.

"Oh, and happy birthday by the way," the man said.

Chief Grimes caught his ironic tone of voice and would have typically answered him with a sarcastic comment like, "thanks a lump." This was no time for any kind of levity, however, so he just responded with a dry, "Thank you."

As he left the federal building, his mind reeled from what he had just been told. The text he'd received last night simply stating "Jenkins" was an understatement. As it turned out, the judge didn't make seemingly idle threats; this old coot actually went active. Somehow, he got hold of evidence damaging enough to sink half the politicians, business leaders, and media elite in the country. This little do-gooder could wreck the entire city – hell, the whole country – leaving it rudderless in the stormy seas ahead.

The fact that this black-robed traitor managed to get the evidence in the first place was sheer incompetence. In contrast, the assurances of the powerful man he had just seen that the evidence would be "handled" were nipping at his brain. This was all too much intrigue, too much drama for him right now. He was in a delicate political position. Reluctantly, however, he concurred, providing he was not implicated.

In the beginning he had agreed to go along with any minor administrative manipulation of a few of the issues surrounding the M.E.'s investigation into the judge's death, which, thankfully, by all indications was looking more like natural causes everyday. To his relief, his intervention to defuse or divert any possible criminal inquiry might never be needed. Although if it was necessary to tweak certain clerical items, he would do it to guard against anything that might threaten himself or his family. But now, now that there was damning evidence on a disk somewhere out there, he felt less sure...

The morning after his night at the opera, DiMaggio entered the squad room and found several cops waiting for him. Reade was the first to interrogate him, saying, "So?"

DiMaggio tried to ignore her, but seeing her raised eyebrows and shoulders, he realized she wasn't going to give up. Reluctantly, he said, "Okay, so I nodded out during the second act."

"Diaz, was it you who had second act?" Reade called out.

A smiling Detective Diaz walked over to the bulletin board and pulled a stickpin out of six five-dollar bills.

"I had you figured for the aria," Reade said.

"I'll try harder next time. Anything on the disk?"

Reade grabbed her backpack and felt around inside. "Aw, crap! You're gonna kill me; I forgot it at home. I'll run it over first thing tomorrow morning."

"You've got to be kidding me, Maggie," DiMaggio said as he pushed back from his desk, slapping his hands on the top in frustration.

"Hey, you were the one who wanted to do this outside normal procedure."

"You're right," DiMaggio said with a sharp exhale. "Let's turn the page and try to dig up any connection between Miles Bennett and our judge."

"Miles Bennett? The stuffed shirt ambulance chaser guy on TV?" She grabbed her cell phone and walked toward the ladies room, muttering under her breath, "How did you connect him to this?"

ID.

In the ladies room, Reade dialed a number and spoke in low tones. "It's Maggie; can I speak to her?" She started biting a hangnail, caught herself, and stopped. "Hi, did you find it?"

At the end of the call she let out a sigh of relief, checked her hair, and went back out into the squad room.

ID.

All day long, the chief kept thinking about the dead judge and how one of his best detectives had drawn the case. Mike DiMaggio wasn't going to write this off as a death by natural causes. DiMaggio was an honest cop and the chief had nothing on him. In fact, he could be like a dog with a bone. But tomorrow he'd make Mike an offer that would surely allow him to lay the case to rest. The chief's thoughts were churning until the clink of the brandy snifter against the shot glasses brought his attention back to his present surroundings.

After putting their son to bed, the Grimes' settled into a little tradition of sorts that had emerged over the years. As they did most nights, they retired to the den for their brandy nightcap. As he settled back into the embrace of his recliner, he began sipping the Rémy Martin V.S.O.P., hoping it would help him relax. He studied his wife's face, bathed in the soft orange glow of the fire, as she watched the flames dancing about below the mantle. She was younger than him by seventeen years and she always made it clear she wanted a family. He kept up his end of the bargain, although not in the usual way.

He looked at the far-too-many photos of their little family crowded onto the stone ledge – a family he'd risked much to have and that cost him 10 million dollars. Of course, that didn't matter, now. What did matter was that she was happy and being happy, she didn't need to know the unpleasant details. *Does the end indeed justify the means?* he wondered. *Even if those means include murder?*

4. A Higher Power

Scanning the pockmarked and scarred Afghan terrain through the crosshairs of his Leupold Mark 4 high-powered sniper's scope, Sergeant Eric Ronson removed his finger from the rifle's trigger. He watched in amazement as two little boys played in and around the mangled chassis of an up-ended truck jutting out of the crater left by an exploded IED. As it was in most war-torn regions of the world, life found a way to continue and take root in even the most acidic soil. Glancing down at his boots, he mindlessly toed the dirt. Afghanistan loam was tilled by decades of what the invaders called war but the indigenous tribes called survival. A devil's aggregate consisting of sand, dead dirt, TNT, shrapnel, gunpowder, and blood: a fallow field that left little hope for, or faith in, the renewal of nature. Yet, the fact that children were born and played, flowers bloomed, and animal life progressed was a miracle that he knew belonged to no particular religion.

Curfews, bombings, and skirmishes had greatly diminished his interaction with the locals... all except one. Only the barest necessities brought people out from the relative safety of cover just as now the most compelling need forced him to risk sticking his neck out as well.

During his tour of duty, he had witnessed that, in spite of all the ardor and human capital wasted in warfare, including the occasional spasmodic release of enormous amounts of concentrated, lethal energy in anger, the norm of this embattled land tended to be quiet and still.

On the other hand, the U.S. Forward Operating Base, or FOB, was a busy and hot place. Not the infra-

34

red Afghan summer "cook you alive" kind of hot, but the kind of hot that came from the reality of constantly being forward deployed.

He lived with the possibility of awakening from his bunk in the middle of a firefight. At the FOB, he had to be war-ready for anything from a fire-fight to incoming mortars, 24/7. There was no need to travel to a distant field of battle – the war was right at his front door.

The Forward Operating Base itself was a huge target and needed its own perimeter patrol to keep the camp secured. That's where he and his spotter, Ortiz, came in. The commanding officer of the FOB liked to have a sniper like Eric out covering these patrols. If something got hot, he wanted a strategic weapon, which he considered Eric to be, picking off enemy leaders at half of a mile out.

He looked at the setting sun's afterglow behind the far off mountains. *We're scheduled to return to base at zero-three hundred*, he thought. *That's when I'll do it.* No one ever worried about counting heads on a returning patrol at three in the morning, especially if the unit met no resistance during the night. With no moonlight tonight, he knew the cover of darkness and general routine of the regular patrols would buy him at least four hours before anyone, including his spotter, Ortiz, would realize what he had done. Tonight had to be the night; by the next occurrence of a moonless night, he could be stationed five hundred miles away.

I can't believe I'm actually going to go through with this. He shook his head. That he, Eric Ronson, a trusted soldier and battle-hardened warrior, would even consider this act was simply inconceivable. *I just can't live with myself another day. No matter what happens, I can't screw up tonight. I can't blow my one chance.*

5. Mike on the Menu

DiMaggio could count on one hand the number of times during his career when he had briefed the mayor at City Hall. This whole "dead judge" affair smelled funny and this was just another whiff of the weirdness. Although this judge was a Fed, it wasn't like he was a Supreme Court guy. Yet the mayor wanted to be personally briefed by the lead detective on the case. Weird.

DiMaggio was in the middle of making his preliminary report. The conference room was packed with suits and brass. A huge portrait of LaGuardia, before he was an airport, loomed over the conference table, his beefy countenance reflected in the furniture's highly polished surface. The mayor was not pleased and made that known to the room. "Not a single lead?"

DiMaggio was confused by the question; he looked to one of the multi-starred uniforms and got the go-ahead nod. "A lead, sir? So far, there isn't anything solid to suggest foul play. As best as we can piece it together, the judge suffered a myocardial infraction while involved in coital relations, resulting in his expiring."

The mayor, who was showing something on his cell phone to his chief of staff, perked up. "He what now?"

"He was having a matinee when his pump stopped."

Grimes rolled his eyes, but the mayor got it. "Oh... jeez, what a way to go. Thank you for clarifying. Go on."

"Well, that's about it, sir."

The mayor's chief of staff, Walters, hadn't been paying attention to who was talking either, but put the mayor's iPhone down and suddenly spoke up. "Who are you, again?" He looked at Grimes with a subtle sneer.

"I am Michael DiMaggio, Manhattan Homicide, lead senior detective on the Jenkins' death."

"Senior? What grade?" probed Walters in an unfriendly tone.

"Made first grade with fourteen years in, sir."

The mayor then asked, "Does this whole affair make sense to you, Detective?"

The brass shifted in their chairs, as looks of consternation to control DiMaggio's answer flew at him.

DiMaggio looked up at old Fiorello LaGuardia, an immigrant Italian and his dad's favorite mayor. The "Little Flower's" eyes were soft and friendly, seemingly urging him to be brave. Since it was still a free country, he ignored the enlarged eyeballs underneath the scrambled-egg brimmed hats of his superior officers that were trying to will him to silence. Instead, he opted in favor of LaGuardia's. "Honestly, sir, no. But I have no idea which part is out of whack. The room we found him in was, to be kind, a shit hole. There's evidence of a sex act, which may have contributed to his cardiac arrest. If Jenkins paid for it, we may have a case against the hooker, if we can find her, on a possible leaving the scene charge."

That got an eyeball conversation going with Chief of Detectives Grimes and another man in a black suit sitting by the wall behind him.

"Anything else?" Walters said.

"I am also looking into the doctor's offices on the top floors above the room where the body was found. There's some inconclusive evidence the body may have been moved from another location. I am waiting for the M.E.'s report as we speak."

The unknown man then leaned over and spoke in low tones to Grimes. To DiMaggio, it looked as if they were debating whether to have steak or fish at a restaurant. Suddenly, Grimes addressed the room. "Well, that's all there is for now. Thank you, gentlemen, for your time. We'll convene again next week if the situation warrants."

Everyone got up to go. There were handshakes and small conversations. Grimes caught DiMaggio leaving. "My office in five minutes."

DiMaggio let out a deep breath as he thought, *looks like they decided on skewered pig.*

IQ

DiMaggio stepped out of City Hall into a beautiful crisp day. The kind of day that, years back, would have instinctively triggered a reach into his pocket to pull out a Marlboro and light up. Instead, he folded a stick of spearmint gum into his mouth and decided to walk over to One Police Plaza.

Six minutes later, he entered Grimes' office. It was obvious to him that Grimes and the man in the black suit had been driven over in the chief's car, because they were already seated at the small table to the right of the chief's desk. DiMaggio noticed a single birthday card on the credenza behind the desk – the large, flowery kind with sentiments of love usually sent by a wife to her husband next to a picture of Grimes with his young pretty wife and kid.

"Take a seat, Mike," Grimes said.

"Wow, how old is your son now, Chief?"

"Eight." Grimes turned to the picture. "That was taken last year when he was seven."

"He's almost got the height advantage on you already. He's going be a ballplayer, maybe B-ball." Looking at the photo, DiMaggio couldn't see where the kid got his height from; the Chief was maybe 5'5" and his wife was a peanut. *Maybe the milkman was tall.*

"Kid's got a good arm."

"He's eight years old; sign him up for little league," DiMaggio said.

The other man in the office cleared his throat, obviously not interested in the pleasantries of the moment. DiMaggio waited to be introduced to the other guy but it never happened.

DiMaggio took his cue. "What did you want to see me about, Chief?"

"Mike, do you really think the doctor's office upstairs is linked to this in anyway?"

"Just a hunch, Chief."

"A hunch?" The man in the black suit asked.

DiMaggio offered his hand. "We haven't been introduced, Mike DiMaggio."

His hand stayed on the tabletop. "Smith."

The chief continued, "So you have nothing solid linking the offices upstairs?"

DiMaggio was thrown off guard. *What is the agenda here?* he thought. *Why are they interested in this doctor?* Even though he knew that bristling the chief of detectives was a surefire way to suddenly find yourself working for the chief of patrol pounding a beat in the Far Rockaway precinct, he decided to throw career caution to the wind. "What's this about? Why are you so interested in where I am going?"

"Mike, Mike. Listen. All we are saying is if you don't have to go there, DON'T GO THERE! Copy?"

"Is that an order?"

"Mike, consider it strongly suggested."

DiMaggio looked over at Smith. "I think I understand, sir."

"Good, good. By the way, there's a joint anti-terrorism task force in Paris looking for a liaison officer... in Paris, coming up soon. I'd like to award that to someone I can trust." Then the Chief just sat there, and DiMaggio could almost feel his eyes bore right through him. DiMaggio knew that last bone he threw him was supposed to make this all go away, but Mike had never liked French cooking all that much.

The moment stretched on until it became uncomfortable, so DiMaggio said, "Well, if there is nothing else, I'd better get back to the squad." He then turned and walked out. In the elevator, just one thought kept reverberating off the walls of his brain: *they care more about the live shrink than the dead judge.*

IOQ

"You have almost filled your quota but are short by one. And I might say the most prized one of all," the tribal chief said as he poured two cups of chai with his right hand, which had the stub of a missing little finger.

As the chief's father, his father's father, and his father before him had done, he offered the utmost hospitality to anyone who came under the roof of his tent, be they friend or enemy. His current occupant lay somewhere in between.

"Our customer grows impatient. I do not wish to inform him of any interruptions."

Dehqan had surmised the customer was someone of great power in the west. Which is why the correct racial and ethnic blend as well as the physical appearance of the merchandise was so important. "A little matter of some small resistance, but I assure you by the end of this week the package will be delivered," Dehqan said.

The chief grunted. His guest had gained a passive/aggressive notoriety as "The Devil's Farmer." At times, he was the very charitable essence of Allah, bestowing food and water on unfortunate camps and villages, always in an effort to control the swayable with a bribe of the imperative. Yet he could turn at a moment's flash into a Mongolian-like figure who'd shock those same people with extremely swift violence to which a common man had no defense, no answer, and no alternative except submission. Or death. His methods made the Devil's Farmer's "reaping" very effective. For he farmed everything from gold to human organs, and lately, humans themselves.

"I take no pleasure in reminding you that you have guaranteed delivery on the heads of your grand-children," the man said matter-of-factly as he handed the guest in his tent a cup of the brew.

Dehqan gave a nod of his head in appreciation as he took the cup. "It will be done, Khan, as I have said."

ऀ

A day later, the village awoke to screams of the wash-erwoman, who on her early morning trip to the well was startled by the horror before her. The villagers came running, many in their bedclothes; some even came with ax handles or knives to ward off whatever thievery or crime was in progress. When they drew close, they stopped dead in their tracks.

The pitchfork was a clear sign. This was a warn-ing left by the Devil's Farmer. Twenty folks just stood as one in shock. Not one villager moved. Then the imam of their small, local mosque separated the crowd and gazed upon the atrocity. He was confused and speechless. Beheadings were as old as their religion, almost a rite, but one to be practiced with care and observance to Shariah law. Even against an infidel, the propriety of the act was in adherence to tradition and ultimately God. It was simply the vanquishing of an enemy in a "humane" manner. But this... This was almost blasphemy. The death was careless and sloppy. The blade had severed the head above the jaw line, leaving the lower teeth and tongue exposed as the body hung from the well han-dle. The head, minus the jaw, was impaled on the end of the upright handle of the pitchfork driven hard into the ground. Without anything ceremonial or even ritual about the slaying, all the imam could do was offer a prayer for the old seller of water bottles.

As the prayer ended, the crowd started murmuring, "Setara."

"It's her fault..."

"Let's find Setara!"

"Yes, it's the only way to stop this evil."

And thus, the mob was formed with one goal – search every house, shack and tent until this godless female was found.

IQ

Heading up the FDR, DiMaggio kept replaying the strange meeting with the mayor over and over in his head. There was a lot of high-priced city payroll warming the seats in that room. Why? Especially if the judge's death was by natural cause. A train rumbled over the Manhattan Bridge as he sat below it, bumper to bumper on the three-lane FDR drive. He was tempted to flip on the dash light and hit the siren, but nobody could move anyway. He'd just be pissing people off. Resigned, he called the office. "It's DiMadge; get me Reade."

"How do you do it?" Reade said over the phone.

"Naked like everybody else... what the hell are you talking about?"

"Your tip on Bennett paid off big. He and the judge are directors of the same stodgy, paneled-wall, high-backed chair, stinky cigar, good-old-boys' club. The Walden Club."

"Bingo! I want you to put some people on an unofficial stakeout of the doctor's office. Everyone who goes in and out."

"Unofficial?"

"Yeah, write it up as the Amato case, address and everything, and then brief the troops in person only."

"You're signing this one, Mike."

"I will. Oh, and Reade, forget to tell anyone else, okay."

"So, ready for the latest gossip?" Reade spoke in a tone usually reserved for a dish session with her girlfriend.

"Bennett and Cassidy are an item?" DiMaggio said dryly.

"How do you do it? Amazing."

6. Playland of the Rich

As DiMaggio turned off the New England Thruway, his mind wandered back to a time when he was a kid and his dad took him and his cousins up to Rye Playland. It was an amusement park with caramel candied apples, a midway with all kinds of games and prizes, and a huge rollercoaster – The Dragon, he seemed to remember them calling it. There was also The Crazy Mouse, which was a single-car rollercoaster that made sudden jerks right and left and up and down. There were even rowboats you could rent to go out into Long Island Sound. It wasn't until he got older that he realized Rye was also a community of well-to-dos. The proof was in the multi-million dollar mansions he passed on the picturesque tree-lined lane.

His GPS informed him he had arrived at the Mansuring Island home of the judge. But all could see was an ornate gate intersecting the ten-foot-high wall surrounding the grounds. He was about to ring the intercom button outside his driver's side window when the gate opened automatically. A landscaping truck pulled out and DiMaggio quickly pulled through before it closed.

He pulled his unmarked Ford around the elliptical drive encircling an elaborate fountain, which could have been transplanted from Rome. He got out and surveyed the well-manicured terrain. *Gotta cost at least a hundred grand a year to keep all this lush and trim,* he calculated in his mind as he pressed the pineapple-shaped doorbell... *Gold-plated pineapple!*

The carved oak, twelve-foot-high front door opened and a butler, right out of Central Casting in a day coat and white vest, answered. "Sorry, sir, the family is in a period of mourning."

DiMaggio flashed his tin. "Official police business, I'm afraid."

The butler was about to protest, but DiMaggio tapped his finger on the 18-karat badge. "Ah, Ah, Ah! It's gold, you know."

The condescending look on the face of the butler, who DiMaggio assumed made more in one month than his meager civil service salary amounted to in a year, turned to resignation as he led DiMaggio into a paneled room which seemed to hold more books than a small-town library. DiMaggio had to tilt his head to see the tops of the huge floor-to-ceiling bookshelves completely filled with books that appeared to be meticulously organized by author. He didn't recognize any names as he tried to figure how much all the editions in the room could be worth. He gave up the mental exercise as a fortyish blonde entered.

The flawlessly coifed and impeccably dressed blonde stood there for a few seconds before speaking. "Are you a policeman?"

"I'm just waiting for Mrs. Jenkins." He added a forced smile as punctuation.

She walked over to the martini shaker and poured the contents into a frosted glass that just seemed to be waiting there.

The butler returned. "Oh, I see you've already met. Sorry, Mrs. Jenkins, I thought you were upstairs in the library."

Library? DiMaggio said to himself looking around. *Then what the hell is all this?* "I'm Detective DiMaggio. I'm sorry to bother you at a time like this but I have to ask you a few questions. I am afraid they are rather indelicate."

"Save the tap dance, Detective. I am no grieving widow."

"Oh...?"

"No, I didn't kill him. But he's been dead for days now and there's no difference around here." She gestured around the room with the liquor dangerously sloshing around the Baccarat cut-crystal glass.

"Do you know why your husband was on Fifty Fourth Street?"

"The papers are saying it was sex, some call-girl thing? Impossible."

"Why would you say that?"

"My husband is... was impotent. And not interested."

"That's hard to believe..." He caught himself looking at her.

"Thank you, Detective. Aside from what you read in the columns, he married me for my looks, not my money, but after the first year..." She was quiet for a few seconds and then just blurted out, "We have been celibate for ten years." She brought the glass to her lips and before she took a sip said into it, "Well, he has anyway."

"Was your husband seeing anyone about this? A doctor or psychiatrist?" He could see she didn't expect that question and was actually thinking about her answer this time.

"A doctor? I don't think so," she said. Her brow furrowed as if her mind double-checked her answer.

"One last question. If you don't believe your husband was there for sex, what was he doing there?"

"Isn't it your job to figure that out?"

ID

As he drove back to Manhattan, DiMaggio called Reade. "I just left the grieving widow. Rich people are really fucked up. Anything shaking?"

"Yeah, my knees. You'd better get back here quick."

This time he hit the lights and siren and took off in the passing lane.

ID.

At the precinct, Reade had taken over Interrogation Room Four. Along the wall next to a poster of "Big Sisters" were day and night surveillance photos.

"What did you get us into, DiMadge?" she asked as her hand waved across several eight-by-ten pictures pinned to the soundproof-tiled walls.

DiMaggio scanned the pictures up close. Recognizing all the faces, he said, "This is unbelievable."

Detective Pankin, who had helped Reade assemble the photo wall, was uncomfortable with the whole situation. "Mike, I think we are going out a little too far on a limb here. It's going to take two seconds before everyone realizes this isn't the Amato case."

"Don, I'm signing everything; you were just following my orders."

Pankin still didn't like it but he acquiesced. "Yes, mein Führer."

Just then, the chief of detectives walked in.

"Glad you came down chief... look at what we found..."

Looking at the wall, the chief screamed, "Everybody out! NOW!"

Reade and Pankin hurriedly left, with questioning looks.

"God dammit DiMaggio, you were ordered not to pursue this. What am I supposed to do now?"

"Look, I see now why the stuffed suit wanted us off this and the doctor. Jenkins was upstairs when he croaked."

"You're not getting this, are you? You disobeyed a direct order from me. Are you on drugs?"

"Hey, hey, I followed the leads and this is where it got me!" He tapped the pictures on the wall.

Grimes reached into his jacket pocket, retrieved a tri-folded sheet of paper, and slapped it on DiMaggio's chest. "No, *this* is where it got you – suspended without pay and up on departmental charges for disobedience and, I am sure when I look, misappropriating manpower to do unlawful surveillance!"

"Chief, what are you talking about?"

"Listen, fuckhead, you dug this grave yourself. You were warned. You got over twenty in, so you are either going to put your papers in and resign or I'm going have you pulling midnight watch at the morgue or manning the gate at One PP. You have an hour to decide which way you want to go."

"You're weirding me out, Chief."

"One fucking hour!" He walked out and slammed the door.

A few moments later, Reade gingerly opened the door and walked in. She was silent for about thirty seconds and then said, "Wanna talk about it?"

"He's fucking insane."

"He's... a little rattled." She turned toward the photo wall and walked by every picture. "The D.A., a senator, the head of the Machessi crime family, a network executive, and the guy that owns the ball team. That's not to mention the mayor and the chief of police! There are very powerful men, Mike, visiting your lady doctor. Playing hide the salami with a ... what did they call them?"

"Sexual surrogates."

"Health plan hookers," Reade said.

The argument raging in DiMaggio's head finally exploded and he ordered, "Pack up everything here. Get it out of the building... and burn all the time sheets."

"Whoa, hold it cowboy. That's a career buster. I ain't burning anything."

"Can they just get lost for a while?"

She hesitated briefly and then said, "Got some room in my basement at home."

"Do it right now."

ID.

An hour later, true to his word, Chief Grimes showed up at DiMaggio's desk with a captain and two uni-

forms. "Detective DiMaggio, you are relieved of duty."
He nodded to the uniformed captain, who then held
out his hand. "Your badge, gun, and ID card please."

"What is this?"

"It's my bureau and you serve at my pleasure, and
now I want you out," the chief said.

DiMaggio looked around the squad room at all the
faces in shock. He decided not to press the issue and
started to collect his things.

"Touch nothing." The chief turned to the uniforms. "I want everything impounded: all his notes,
phone messages, and personal effects. And I want
everything on the Jenkins case. Every DB-5 and all
physical evidence."

DiMaggio stood up and glared at the chief.

Grimes continued, "I can't take away your civil service rank, but I am having a word with the chief of patrol."

Just then, Detective Bernstein arrived. "What's
going on here?"

"I am exercising my discretion as chief of detectives and relieving this man of his post as a detective."

"As the precinct shop steward for the Detectives
Endowment Association, I protest this treatment of
my brother officer," Bernstein said, reciting the book.

The taller uniformed officer handed DiMaggio's
phone log to Grimes.

"I am touched. You wanna drag your brother officer here into a messy departmental trial, be my guest.
For now, get out of the way."

"Thanks, but it's okay Bernstein. We'll talk tomorrow," DiMaggio said as he walked out of the room.

DiMaggio unceremoniously blasted into the brownstone's treatment center and caught a man being
scolded by a woman dressed like a teacher in a low-
cut schoolmarm dress. She was leaning over in front of
him, rapping his hands with a pointer, her cleavage in

full view and jiggling with every hit. He stormed into the doctor's inner office.

Cassidy was startled and hit the stop button on the VHS tape she was reviewing. "Who let you in here?"

He got right in her face. "Time to come clean! Who the hell are you and what exactly do you do here and to whom?"

"Don't you ever get tired of this Neanderthal act? I do." She tried to dismiss him by turning her attention to some folders on her desk.

DiMaggio spun her around, locking her in her chair with his hands on the armrests. "I'll tell you what I'm tired of! Losing my job! Whoever you're fucking or whoever's head you're fucking with, has enough juice to get me canned. I deserve to know who!"

"You don't think this type of harassment had anything to do with your current problem?"

"Cut the shit... Wanda Bertowsky!"

"I don't know who you are talking about."

"I am talking about a high school fuck up who got suspended for a little incident with half the swim team. They remember you real good at Evander Childs High School in da Bronx, Wanda."

"You never stop amazing me with the ingenious ways you come up with for me to despise you."

"Aw, too bad! But I despise having eighteen years of my life flushed down the toilet."

"Are you arresting me? Wait – you can't – you aren't a detective anymore. That means you are an intruder. I'll have Regina call a real cop."

"I am going to be all over you like cheap perfume on a five-dollar-a-go hooker."

"Colorful... Did Robert Mitchum say that to Rita Hayworth or something?"

"Look lady, don't trip, don't sneeze, don't even fart, because I'll hear you and expose you, this fucking high-end whore house, and all your 'patients.' He grabbed the remote control and pushed play to start the video again. It only took DiMaggio a few seconds to recognize the chained man in the video who was being whipped by a shapely, latex-clad woman. "Well, well, Joey "The Mule" DiCicco. Look how he spends his free periods. Boy would the guys in his crew down on West Street love to see this."

"Get out of here!" she screamed, snatching the remote with trembling hands. He glared at her and left. Nervously, she rummaged through the drawer and found an old cigarette. She lit it and puffed away anxiously.

7. Puzzled

Police Officer Marcus Towne entered the Midtown North Precinct on west Fifty-fourth Street twenty minutes before muster. He'd have liked to be there ten minutes earlier but he'd been burning the midnight oil lately playing catch up on a forensics class at John Jay. Although just barely a new cop, he wanted to make detective at the earliest possible opportunity, so he accelerated his academic trajectory taking advanced courses for a probationary officer. His life-long desire to be a first-rate crime fighter wouldn't really start until he earned his Detective Third Grade shield. Even though he was later getting to his locker than he had wanted, he was crisply uniformed with his shoes spit-shined as he headed to the morning's roll call.

The muster room was an off-yellow-tile walled room that reminded Towne of his high school gymnasium. But instead of smelling like old socks and sneakers, this assembly room was ripe with the pungent smell of shoe polish, leather, gun oil, aftershave and coffee. The muster at shift change was the time and place that the NYPD imprinted onto its 34,000-plus officers the cohesiveness of tradition and procedures. Order among the ranks was inculcated through inspections, reminders, and bulletins that made the blue flock a whole. Every eight hours, all across the city, the ranks were infused with the tenets of the fraternity. It was an important part of the chemistry, a shot of authority, the notion that someone was watching and you were responsible to a clan larger than yourself. All this was necessary because after the muster, each was on his or her own as a guardian, ambassador, negotiator, and, more importantly, the sharp end of the stick of law.

So it was that the watch commander pointed out a few opened buttons, a loose gun belt, an unsecured holster strap or even a stain on a shirt, officially called a tunic. This was the moment and the place where the standards were upheld.

Then there was the reading of the blotter; today it was the usual morning list of what happened overnight and any international or domestic threats to the most famous city in the world. When it was over, the duty sergeant called his name, "Towne."

He hustled up to the podium, "Yes, sir."

"At the end of your shift, you are to report to Room One Twenty at the Puzzle Palace."

"Yes sir," he said and walked away, not sure where or what the Puzzle Palace was.

ℚ

At 4:30 p.m., after an uneventful day, Police Officer Towne reported to Room 120 in the building, which, as he learned from his veteran cop partner, had many names. Puzzle Palace was the endearing name for One PP, which itself was cop speak for One Police Plaza, which was yet another name for NYPD Headquarters.

A civilian worker escorted him into an elevator and slid a card through a magnetic reader. The button for the top floor lit up and she then stepped off before the doors closed. When the elevator doors opened, he was met by another person who escorted him through the halls. Towne looked around and immediately noticed a big difference in this part of the building when compared to the lower floors. The expensive, plush carpeting under his feet was a far cry from the dingy linoleum on the first floor. As they walked down the hallway, he noticed the glow from the warm soffit lighting. It was a welcome change from the garish fluorescent glare of the normal department facilities.

At the end of the hall, just before two huge doors, each with a hand-carved crest of the city of New York in relief, his escort stopped and opened a single door on the right, which led into a very small, windowless office with a round table surrounded by six chairs. The escort silently gestured for him to enter, which he did, and the escort closed the door and left.

Towne looked around the room. There was a teleconference mic in the middle of the table, a huge flat-panel display on one wall. He was drawn to an enlarged black and white photograph on the opposite wall. The old photo was from a time when men wore hats and long trench coats. Looking closer at the picture, he saw that the photo was of five men standing on the front steps of a building with an old stone facade. To their right, a sign was hanging from a pipe with an arrow pointing toward the building and the words "Detective Division."

The newbie police officer's heart skipped a beat when the chief of detectives walked into the room through the connecting door, as sunlight from his larger office blasted in behind him. "Towne?"

"Here, er, yes. Yes, sir. That's me." He shot up like a rocket and stood at attention, fumbling his hat and squinting his eyes at the glare behind the Chief.

"At ease, Towne." The Chief sat, closing the door and unplugging the wire to the spider-like teleconference gizmo on the table. "I understand you've got your eyes on a gold shield?"

Towne's heart was about to bust out of his chest as he sat. He actually felt lightheaded. "That's all I ever wanted to be, sir. Even as a kid."

"Well, as you know, you only make detective by appointment. Do good work, make some solid collars, play ball with your bosses, don't ever get written up and you'll get your shot."

"Thank you, sir. I will follow that advice." The moment hung. Neither man talked. Finally, Towne asked, "Is there anything else, sir?"

"Yes, you were first on scene the five nights ago on the Jenkins case?"

"Yes. My partner and I responded to the call for the ambulance."

"But you were first through the door?"

"Yes, Officer Curtis was clearing the street so the bus could get through."

"Did you find anything there?"

"You mean besides the deceased, sir?"

"Yes. Anything out of the ordinary or something of a personal effects nature that might have been in that room?"

"No, nothing odd, just what we logged in." He looked up trying to remember his written report. "A pair of pants, belt, shorts, shirt, not on the body. Flannel pajamas on the deceased. An attaché case. Phone. Shoes. Watch, wallet, and keys."

"Nothing computer?"

"You mean like a laptop?"

"Anything."

"No. Just an old-school flip phone, probably analog from the..."

"Did you open the attaché?

"No sir, it was locked. We left it to the detectives."

"Remember which one?"

"A female. Manhattan Homicide. Reese or Rears? I'd have to check the case sheet."

"No need. She works for me. Okay, you've done well, Officer. From time to time, I like to ask patrol officers about my detectives in the field. It helps me evaluate our bureau. And I like to be quiet about it, so let's keep this chat between us, okay? It's also a good way for me to meet officers on the way up. Keep your nose clean and you'll have that gold shield someday, son." With that, the chief abruptly stood and left.

Towne sat for a moment, his mind reeling. *Did I do okay? What was he looking for? Why didn't I see the thing he wanted to know about?* he thought. *"Officers on the way up!"* That thought made him smile.

8. Accelerant

DiMaggio sat on a bench facing the water with the sun setting behind the Palisade cliffs of Jersey and watched
the tugs and commuter ferries chugging up and down
the Hudson. Two young boys playing cops and robbers
brandishing yellow toy guns with red tipped barrels
were running around using the big iron tie offs, now
painted light blue as decoration, to hide behind as
they shot it out.

"Bang, bang you're dead, you crook!"

"No, I'm not! You had blanks in that gun."

"Did not."

"Did too."

It went on like that. DiMaggio tuned it out as a big
ship made its way down river. He replayed in his mind
how he got here, with nothing to do in the middle of a
workday but sip coffee. Then it hit him – the end of the
movie *Serpico*. Al Pacino winds up right here, by the
docks looking at the water. *How fucking sad,* DiMaggio thought. *At least he had a friggin' dog.*

The bang-bang kids had moved on to killing zombies up by the aircraft carrier, Intrepid. Now the place
was quiet but it just made the noise in his head louder.
It was getting dark and he decided to leave and began
to walk toward his car.

He had parked in a temporary construction site
parking area on the pier, head-in and pointed toward
the water. As he neared his car, he saw that his driver's side window was smashed. "Shit. This is turning
into a real hemorrhoid of a day." He opened the door,
carefully swept the glass off the seat, and got into the

car. He was flicking some glass off the dashboard when a large truck loomed up behind him. It didn't stop. It rammed his car with a bang and he felt a violent lurch as the truck began to push the car toward the edge of the pier. He attempted to get out, but a white van pulled up tight along the driver's side, scraping the paint and locking him in. Another car was parked tight up against the passenger side. Realizing he was trapped, DiMaggio quickly started his car and threw it into reverse. He could smell the acrid smoke as the tires spun against the torque of the huge truck. The car slowed but didn't stop its advance toward the edge of the pier. DiMaggio pulled his leg piece, covered his face with his forearm, and rapidly fired six shots at the back window. The bullets destroyed the glass and punctured the radiator of the truck, which spouted steam, but the truck kept moving forward. The car's rear bumper collapsed and got ground up under the wheels of the large truck. The trunk started to fold in and collapse. All of a sudden, DiMaggio smelled gas and he knew the fuel tank had ruptured. *Crap!*

DiMaggio threw himself into the backseat of the car as it hopped over the last concrete parking curb, in place specifically to prevent vehicles from going off the dock, ripping off the front bumper. The front wheels rolled off the pier and the underside of the chassis started to spark as it scraped over the parking curb. At the last split second, just as the car rotated to fall off the edge, DiMaggio climbed through the blown-out rear window and, pushing off from the back of the falling car, did a swan dive into the river. The sparks ignited the fuel and flared up, but the fire was short lived as the car followed DiMaggio into the river, plummeting in and barely missing him. He frog-legged away, holding his breath so as not to let any air bubbles give him away. The murky water made it impossible to see, but he went in the direction he thought would bring him under the pier.

ɪꝒ.

The van driver got out to check. He had to be sure DiMaggio was gone. As he stood at the edge of the pier, the smoldering tail end of the Lincoln slid under the water. He waited a few more moments and then climbed into the dump truck as it pulled away, hissing steam from the radiator.

ɪꝒ.

"Creamsicle! Mommy's home." Maggie Reade closed her front door with a back swing of her right foot as her hands were full of grocery bags and her backpack strap was slipping off her shoulder. The orange and white tabby rescue cat came out with a sleepy face. "There you are," she said in that affected, wondrous voice that animal lovers use when the furry thing they love comes to them. Maggie put the bags on the counter, removed her jacket with her shield flip wallet in it, and bent down as the little cat did a half roll onto its back. She ran her fingers over its belly as the paws went straight up, its feline face a study in squinty-eyed ecstasy. "Hungry?"

Then she heard a noise. Her detached single-family house in Queens, where she lived alone with Creamsicle, creaked and popped a lot, especially during cold days when the heat came on. But this sound was different.

She reached around and pulled out her smaller, off-duty Glock, Model 26. With her weapon in a two-handed grip, stiff-armed in front of her, she continued in her "cat mommy" voice. "Okay, I'll feed you in a minute. Mommy has to go upstairs to the bathroom." Leading with her piece, turning fully at the waist as she came around the familiar doorways and walls of her home, she made her way to the cellar stairs where the noise came from.

ĪDQ.

DiMaggio exploded out of the murky water under the pier and gasped for air. He took a few minutes to steady himself against a creosote-tarred piling as he caught his breath and then swam over to a workboat tied off to a slip about twenty yards away.

He climbed onto the gangway wet and disheveled and his immediate thoughts were of Reade. He pulled out his cell phone, the waterproof Otter Box having done its job–the phone lit up–then thought twice about leaving a trail. He spotted a rare pay phone at the side of the construction trailer, fished through his pockets, and came up with a quarter. There was an automated message after two rings. "The number you have reached is not in service or experiencing technical difficulties at this time. Message number 2010234..." Annoyed, DiMaggio slammed the phone down as the chopping sound of an NYPD helicopter caught his attention. The distant sounds of sirens announced that someone had seen and called in the car crashing into the water. He looked up and saw the blue and white police aviation copter against the darkening sky start to circle the area off the pier with its bright searchlight beam bouncing off the pier and the water. In a short while, they'd bring in the divers and the cranes and retrieve his vehicle. By then they'd know he wasn't in the car. He decided he needed to be dead a little longer so he went out onto the West Side highway and hailed a cab. "One thirty-eight Jackson in Queens right through the tunnel, as fast as you can."

Just before they hit the tunnel, DiMaggio asked the driver if he could borrow his phone. He got the same "out of order" message.

As the cab turned the corner, it was met with red flashing lights cutting through the night, strewn hoses, and ambulances. Still dripping wet, DiMaggio got out of the cab and walked toward the trucks. He found the fire chief in the white hat.

"What do we got, Chief?"

"Got a possible arson on this thirty-by-fifty single-family dwelling. Fire started in the basement; marshals are tracing for an accelerant now at the point of origin. One fatality – female, mid-thirties; probably the owner. One Margaret Reade by the name on the mailbox; all ID and paper were consumed."

DiMaggio ran to the ambulance. Reade was on the stretcher, covered.

The EMT shook his head to confirm she was gone.

Dreading the truth, he went to pull back the shroud.

The EMT put his hand on the bag. "Sir, the fire was pretty intense; there are no identifiable features left."

DiMaggio made a fist as tears welled up. He pulled himself together and went back to the fire chief.

"Any chance of some files surviving the fire?"

"You sound like a cop but I don't see no tin," the Chief said challenging him.

"Detective Mike DiMaggio, Chief..." DiMaggio read his name from below his badge, "Helms. I ran here and left my stuff at home."

"You must have been in a hurry. What did you do? Shower in your clothes?"

"She was in my squad."

"That explains the gun."

"Her off duty weapon?"

"I guess, if you say."

"Can I see it?"

"Bagged and tagged over there."

The gun, what was left of it, was still hot but completely mangled. Softened by the extreme heat, the nylon polymer-based frame was hammered from the inside out by the bullets, which were cooked off in the fire. It looked like her 26, but its shape was too distorted to tell for sure. There was still a slim chance it wasn't Reade's.

Then the chief came over and said, "One of my men just found this." He handed DiMaggio a clear plastic evidence bag containing a charred, slightly melted gold shield, the numbers 1117 clearly evident in the deformed metal. DiMaggio remembered how lucky Reade had felt to get that shield number because it was her mother's birthday, November 17th.

He looked up from the badge and stared across the street at a woman, probably a neighbor judging from the robe and slippers she was wearing, who was kneeling on the sidewalk, brushing ash from the fur of what at first looked like a gray cat, but now he saw was an orange tabby. *Didn't Reade have a cat? Cream pie, cream cheese...*

The Chief waited until DiMaggio came back into the here and now from wherever the badge had taken him. "I'm sorry for your loss. The house was wood frame and totally engulfed; nothing but the foundation brick is left. Everything else is in ashes. That's why I think this fire had help."

"This is just a guess, but you won't be able to tell that to anyone."

The fire chief gave him a screwy look.

"You'll see." DiMaggio walked off.

The chief shrugged it off.

ॐ

"Shit. And you went through everything?" The man sitting in the dark office on the phone was starting to get agitated at the unwelcome news that was being reported. "Was it necessary to kill her?" He listened intently. "Well, I see your point... Totally consumed by fire? No trace of your presence?"

He listened as he flipped his pen on the blotter of his desk, "Well, her not having it on her means the detective must have it." He listened more and agreed, "Or the woman doctor." He felt no need to divulge the fact that he was well aware of Cassandra Cassidy's name. "I am going to take this to the Secretary and call you right back."

He ended the call and considered the recommendation coming from Wallace in New York whose job it was to recover the missing item and contain this whole affair. Somehow, to his dismay though, instead of being contained, it was growing. Although nothing that couldn't be managed with all his contacts and control over many of the powers that be, but still, invoking that kind of power was not without risk of exposure. He'd have to be careful. Being after hours, with no one else around, he pulled out a pack of cigarettes and lit one up. Violating the federal regulation banning smoking in the workplace was of no concern, as he was about to violate at least thirty federal statutes. He looked out across the window of his darkened office at the two red lights pulsing at the top of the Washington monument. He figured enough time had passed, so he called Wallace back, and as his alternate persona, Mr. Smith, he gave the order. "The Secretary is aware that this must be contained at all costs. Your plan is approved; you'll get the additional funds in the usual way." He hung up the pre-paid phone of which only the team leader on the other end had the number. Rodgers, a.k.a. Mr. Smith, would never use an office phone, not in this office anyway. He sat in stillness as he convinced himself that this decision, to escalate, would bring about a quick resolution to this annoyance created by the meddlesome judge.

Anger arose inside him that this insignificant old man, this interloper, could threaten everything he'd built, all the hard work, the systems, the deals he made with politicians, foreign government officials, even tribal leaders in shithole war-torn places. All of it threatened by this old fool. This couldn't be the end. He was smarter than this. He could beat this.

He unconsciously looked over at the oil painting, depicting the construction of the Erie Canal, with his private wall safe behind it, not noticing the slight tremor in his left arm as his body reacted to what his mind had denied.

9. Piece of Cake

DiMaggio watched as a sleek Mercedes C 63 AMG pulled in through the automatic gate of a mini-mansion, whose Antebellum-style façade was hidden by tall pines from the winding streets of this tony part of Westchester. He slipped between the closing gates as the coupe ascended the gently curved driveway. DiMaggio ran up the other side of the drive and positioned himself by the side patio doors. Through the glass, he could see an alarm system keypad on the wall. He reached into his pocket and pulled out a lock pick and tension bar and started working on the door. DiMaggio heard the electric garage door close. He had the lock picked but didn't open the door, keeping his eye on the red "armed" light on the rear-entry door keypad. As soon as the light turned green, DiMaggio slipped inside closing the door quickly with the slightest click behind him. A split second later, the light became red again as the system was re-armed.

With little more than a sliver of moonlight to guide him, he padded carefully through the sunroom. He walked toward a light that had been turned on down a hallway, his feet falling softly over the parquet floors. Hearing a noise ahead, he stopped and waited a few seconds before continuing. Pausing at the doorway, he hazarded a peek around the doorjamb into the lit room.

He smirked at the image of Dr. Cassandra Cassidy, illuminated by the open refrigerator door, stuffing chocolate cake into her mouth with a vengeance. He stepped up behind her. Startled, she let out a Duncan-Hines-muffled yelp as she whipped around spraying chocolate cake all over him.

"How the hell did you get in my house?"

"You don't remember inviting me over for a little cake?" DiMaggio said as he tried to wipe off his shirt but ended up just smearing the wet chocolate cake into a larger mess.

She ran for the phone. "I am calling the police."

DiMaggio beat her to the phone and held down the receiver. "I am out of here in one minute if you answer one question. I promise."

She glared at him.

Then as a gesture of good faith, he released his hand on the phone. "Or then you can call." His offer must have had the desired effect on her because she relaxed her stance.

"So what's your question?" she said.

He held up a picture of Reade in uniform. "Is whatever you are hiding worth her life?"

"What happened?"

"She was holding some pictures of your clients for me and she was killed when someone torched her house."

Cassidy breathed deeply and looked down and to the left. "I had nothing to do with any of that."

He grabbed her chin and brought her eyes back to him. "What's so damned important to cost me my job, her..." – he wagged the picture in Cassidy's face – "her life, and lord knows what else?"

"Look, why couldn't you leave this alone, leave me alone? It's none of your concern."

"This may not mean much to a phony baloney doctor like you, Waaaandah," DiMaggio said, drawing her name out sarcastically, "but I took an oath to uphold the law. And unless they changed it while I was in the crapper, MURDER is still against the law."

Watching her carefully, DiMaggio could almost see her mind finally collapse under the weight of the mess she was involved in. When she looked up, his eyes met hers, and as much as he tried, he couldn't look away. Even with devil's food crumbs on her chin, she was captivating.

Suddenly her eyes flashed with anger, replacing the short-lived regret. "Why are you really here?"

"To try and nail down this case."

"Nail the case or nail me?"

"Whoa! Look sister, don't get all carried away with yourself here. You got nothing I want except information."

"I know your type, the blue collar snob. You hear one Bruce Springsteen song and think any woman with a brain and money won't be able to resist you."

"You know, for a head doctor you're out of your gourd. Everything is not always about sex!" DiMaggio looked away from her for a second, then suddenly put his arms around her and pulled her down to the floor.

"See!" She started punching at his shoulders. "Get off me you goddamn maniac."

Bullets ripped into the space where they had just stood, puncturing the refrigerator, smashing jars on the counter and blowing the faucet off the kitchen sink. The windows in the front of the house were turned into a cascade of shattering glass. DiMaggio covered her from the debris with his body. When the shooting stopped, he pulled out a six-shooter from his waistband. He placed his hand on her in a gesture for her to remain on the floor and whispered, "You okay?"

She shook her head nervously, too terrified to speak.

"Stay down. Don't move," he said quietly.

More bullets ripped through the room. Cassidy's body spasmed with the sound of each loud impact.

DiMaggio waited for a break in the firing and then sprang up on one knee, held down the trigger and fanned the hammer, firing three shots in rapid succession, in the direction of the incoming rounds. The .45 caliber bullets booming like canon fire from the wide bore of the pearl handled revolver.

From outside the shattered window, DiMaggio heard, "Oh shit!"

He ducked as one last burst sprayed the room. In the dead silence that followed, he heard footsteps running away. A door slammed as a car's engine started, the tires peeling out as it quickly sped away. DiMaggio ran into the night, hoping for a license plate number or at the very least the make of the car.

On the floor, shaking with her arms over her head, Cassidy slowly lifted her head as the silence continued, save for the water gushing up from the broken faucet. She jumped when DiMaggio returned, his shoes crunching on the broken glass.

"We've got to get you out of here. He was probably a sub-contractor; wasn't in it for a fight."

"How... How... do you know, know that?"

"A real professional would have made sure you were dead. C'mon we gotta go."

"I need to change."

"Look this ain't no fashion show. We got about a minute before the place is swarming with cops."

"I've never been shot at before and I need to change my pants. Okay? Feel better now Mr. Tough Guy stupid cop?"

DiMaggio finally caught on. "Oh geez. Okay, but do it fast or whoever wants you dead will get a second chance."

Grabbing a new pair of "7" jeans with the tags still on them from her bedroom closet, Cassidy went into her bathroom to change.

DiMaggio pulled the antique Peacemaker from his waistband and, holding the gun in his left hand, half cocked the hammer and flicked open the Peacemaker's loading gate. He rotated the cylinder with his right thumb as he pulled back the ejector rod with his right index finger and ejected the three fired shell casings. Then he popped three new Long Colt cartridges from his pocket into the cylinder. Being manufactured before 1898 the gun was legal to own without a permit as it was classified as an antique... but the modern .45 cal. bullets didn't know that.

She was washed and dressed in two minutes and DiMaggio snuck her out the side door from which he entered on his way toward his car parked out back. From behind a low garden wall they saw a Chevy Suburban barrel through the front gates. Three men, armed to the teeth, jumped out of the back. The team leader exited the front, hand signaling to the three to take positions in a classic cross fire defense.

DiMaggio noticed one of them was using only his left hand, like his right arm was injured. The driver was gesturing with hand signals when suddenly three local police cars screeched to a halt in front of the house. The three men quickly scrambled back into the rear of the vehicle and the driver threw his Uzi onto the front seat.

"Come on, let's get out of here," DiMaggio said as he grabbed Cassidy's hand.

She tugged away saying, "But the police, they'll help us."

"That crew is a mop up squad. If you or I show our faces, they will kill all of us, including the cops." DiMaggio grabbed her hand again and firmly pulled her in the opposite direction.

Rounding the corner, the last thing DiMaggio saw was the driver pulling something from under his coat as he approached the cops.

They made it around back to where he had hidden his cousin's car in order to avoid tipping off Cassidy when she pulled up. He drove a short distance to a spot down the street, parked, killed the engine, and turned off the lights. "Get down."

"I thought we were going?" Cassidy was whispering, confused and scared as she ducked down lower than the windows.

"We are. Right after the car they'll send around back passes us," DiMaggio whispered back.

"What is a mop up squad?"

"The first guy they dispatched didn't expect any return fire. He called them in. Its standard procedure for wet work."

"Wet work?"

"Yeah, messy stuff that makes pains-in-the-asses like you disappear."

"And now you."

"They already think I'm dead. This little shindig was all for you, darling."

"Me?"

"With me gone, you are now a loose end."

A police car, lights flashing, silently raced by.

DiMaggio spoke in a normal voice. "That's it. They're taking up a position in the back. It's safe for us to go now."

As Cassidy got up, she said, "You smell like low tide."

He drove without lights until they were a block away; then he turned on the lights and made a right.

10

DiMaggio looked down at the car he had "borrowed" from his cousin Cartrecia tonight, who was in Seattle for a month and long-term parked it in a garage in his neighborhood. He had purposely parked the car in front of Room 112 of the Yonkers Motel. As he pulled the curtains closed in Room 236 upstairs and to the right, Cassidy was testing what was left of the springs in the bed.

"This sucks. What are we going to do?" she said.

"Let's start by you telling me how you got involved in all this?" DiMaggio saw the reticence in her eyes. Even after being shot at, she was more afraid of whatever she was hiding than bodily harm. "You know, the cat is way out of the bag here. Whatever deal you thought you had has been erased by bullets."

DiMaggio could see that the logic of his statement was eroding her reluctance. He had turned many perpetrators into collaborating witnesses with this "you are on your own" approach. She appeared to be frozen in thought. Unsure if she could trust him. He decided to try again. "Cassandra, someone did try to kill you; of that there can be no mistake."

She hesitated but then said, "You better be good at what you do, Detective."

"I promise I will protect you, but I need to know from what?"

She let out a deep breath. "One of my patients turned out to be a major government military contractor who was selling secrets to the Russians back when that mattered. The Feds approached me and asked me to help them."

"Which agency?"

"It started with the Defense Intelligence Agency. Then my 'contract' was picked up by the FBI."

"Why did they continue this after you helped them with the contractor?"

"Two reasons. They were blown away at what reasonably smart people would blab out while in the throes of passion. I mean, I am good. I could work you and get you to tell me things you wouldn't divulge under torture. And most times not even realize you told me."

"Okay little Miss Humility, and the second?"

"Look, you have no compunction about telling me what a good little cop you are. Show me the same professional courtesy."

"Professional? You're a high-class hooker."

"I am a medical doctor with a Ph.D in Psychiatry and you are a fucking asshole." She stalked off to the bathroom.

"Shit." He reached for the clicker and turned on the TV. He mindlessly changed the channel until he found the news.

Next to a picture of the judge, an anchorman spoke right to the camera. "Five days after his death, speculation is growing tonight that federal circuit court judge Horace Jenkins was taking bribes from organized crime. Judge Jenkins' widow, socialite Marla DuPont Jenkins, could not be reached for comment."

Cassidy came out of the bathroom and focused on the television. "Poor Jenky."

"It's all bullshit – mob connection my ass, it's a fed trick. They just make a federal case against someone to keep all his records and actions sealed and out of the press. Do you know anything about this?" He jerked the remote toward the screen.

"Yes. They were very interested in him."

"Who?"

"FBI, CIA, NSA, one of those federal agencies; it gets so they all become a blur."

A light bulb went off in DiMaggio's head. "That's who that guy in the chief's office was – a Fed. Did they tell you why they were interested in the judge?"

"Don't know. It's a one-way street. I give them any non-medical information they might blab during treatment, but the feds never tell me anything."

"How did the judge get to you? Did they send him to you?"

"He was referred by another one of my patients. When they found out he was under my care they approached me and gave me guidelines."

"By phone?".

"Always by phone."

"Do you tell them who you are treating?"

"No, they just seem to know."

"They are probably watching your office." He paused then said, "I am sorry for the crack I made before."

"Asshole."

"Hey, I said I was sorry."

"Look, all this shit is happening too fast. Why am I holed up with you in this dump? Oh yeah, you had to play Canadian Mountie and always get your man, even if it meant getting me killed. I remember now."

"Can we get back to the judge? I figured he checked out in your place and either you or someone else moved him downstairs."

"I guess it doesn't matter now, but yes, when Jenky suffered his cardiac arrest in the Castle Room, I panicked..."

"Hold it – wait – the Castle Room?"

"I have five treatment rooms that have escapist themes to help facilitate our treatments."

"Five?"

"Yes, Tropical, Castle, Dungeon, Locker Room, Conference Room."

"Conference Room? Let me guess, executive fantasies – take a letter and take off your blouse?"

Cassidy's eyes burned lasers of hate through DiMaggio's skull.

"I'm sorry, I just love the way all this is justified as some sort of therapy."

"Hey, I actually help people. This treatment meets the condition where it matters. You can't correct these neuroses on just a couch."

"No, it takes the Jungle Room..."

"Look, you sanctimonious, self-righteous son-of-a-bitch, I am published. My papers on this type of fundamental therapy and corrective methodology are accepted practice worldwide... Published three times! Shithead."

"I'm sorry, okay? Let's get back to 'you panicked.'"

"I called my contact and he told me what to do and said that they would fix the investigation. So I had Matilda, she was in shock, poor girl, and two of the surrogates help me carry him down to the empty apartment on the first floor."

"I figured that. The ME said it was fifty-fifty that the body had been moved. Who is your contact? The one who was going to fix my investigation into the judge's death."

"Mr. Smith."

"Yeah, there's a very common federal family name. Got the number?"

"It's disconnected. I tried yesterday but I remember it was a two-oh-two area code."

"Washington. Was Smith always your contact?"

"At first it was a guy from the justice department. Rodgers from the FBI?"

"An agent?"

"No, he was more an administrator. You know, contracts, releases and the like. But then he left. After that it's only been Smith. No one else and only on the phone. I never met him or Rodgers for that matter."

"What was the second reason?"

"Second reason for what?"

"Why you stayed on with the Feds after the first case?"

"Medicaid fraud, or at least that was the threat. They set me up. The lovely Hannah Faust, my dear, sweet, loyal administrative assistant padded bills after I approved them; she probably worked for them all along, the bitch. They sort of implied that if I didn't play ball they were going to ruin my career and throw me in prison for fraudulent billing. Sure enough, as soon as I went along, both the charges and eventually Hannah magically went away."

"So you played ball and they bought you a new stadium."

"The brownstone was their show of appreciation."

"And, of course, the brownstone came pre-wired for America's Weirdest Videos." DiMaggio said.

"Yes, but not the clinic downtown – that's where my real work gets done. They had to promise to leave it alone."

DiMaggio saw a different look on her face. She was dead serious about her clinic. It didn't make sense. Despite her "being published" bullshit she was still a high-class hooker, and they don't give a shit about anything but cash. Why was she trying to show him she actually cared about people in her clinic? He decided that it didn't matter; let her have her delusions. He needed to figure out how to survive the next few hours and days. "Get some sleep while you can. Tomorrow we are going to pay a little social call."

DiMaggio shut off the lamp and lay there looking up at the ceiling. He could hear a couple in the next room, and from the energy and frequency of the bed pounding the wall, he figured they were probably young and making the most of the three-hour short stay rate. One thing kept rolling around in his head – the hit team. Mob? CIA? Cartel? And how did they not get arrested or kill the cops. He and Cassidy managed to escape in the distraction, but there was nothing on the news about the shooting of the house or any gunfight with police. How could they squash that? One thing he knew for sure: *this was some deep shit!*

10. Road Kill

With luck it would be 0700 hours before they realized he was missing. By then, he'd be about an hour away from the village. This being his third tour, he had been promoted to sergeant in recognition of his valor, cutting the usual four-and-a-half-year time in half. Although his military career was set, his Ranger training was based on loyalty, courage, and fidelity. Now he was about to be in violation of the Uniform Code of Military Justice, but even more painful for him was the violation of the Ranger's Creed. However, he felt his actions were in total congruence to his own internal code of justice. He was morally obligated to do this. His word and his honor as a man were on the line. He'd taken the oath for the Army, and over the course of his three rotations, he felt he had lived up to and delivered on his obligation, but this was something between him and God.

Hearing what sounded like a truck, he ducked as lights came over the horizon. Crouching low behind a rock along the roadside, he could see it was coming right at him. In the dim, early light of dawn, he was barely able to make out the silhouette of a JERRV – a Navy EOD truck. As it drew closer, he realized it was uncharacteristically traveling alone.

Since the giant bomb disposal truck – crammed with robots, computers, sensors, explosives to clear unexploded ordinance and remotely fired machine guns – was heading back to the same Forward Operating Base he'd left hours earlier, there was a good chance he knew the Explosive Ordinance Disposal crew. He uncapped the glass on the telescopic sight of his sniper rifle and focused on the windshield, trying to see if he could recognize the unit or at least the driver. He adjusted his footing to stabilize his scope, and as he did so, his right foot snagged a wire. He froze and slowly looked down to see a green detonation cord over the dusty tip of his boot. He carefully put his rifle down and gently removed his KA-BAR knife. Leaning over, he slowly pulled the cord up just enough to scoot his boot out from under it. Following the cord with his eyes, he could see that only three feet from him, toward the road, the wire was spliced to five others. *Crap!* He had seen this before. He was sitting right on top of an IED. The Taliban had improvised this explosive device with five charges, usually high-explosive artillery shells, to be set off with a small amount of plastique.

The Joint EOD Rapid Response Vehicle rumbled closer and he knew what he had to do. There were three "crazy" bomb techs in that truck, men who risked their lives to disarm and recover IEDs, looking for evidence of who made them. This bomb was big enough to kill them all. He didn't hesitate for a minute; he didn't think of his own life or even the other "mission." He closed his eyes and just jerked the knife up and severed the cord.

He was still alive – still in one piece. He breathed deeply for the first time since he found the wire. He grabbed the end of the cord and gently tugged to get a sense of the direction it came from. He turned his head and followed it past the junction of the detcord wrapped around the primer then following the command detonated copper wire saw it emerged from the rocky non-arable soil behind him to his right. Rocks and stones were dislodged and nudged aside as he carefully pulled up the wire even higher. He picked up his rifle and turned the scope toward a stone wall about fifty yards back. Scanning the edge, he not only saw a head poke up briefly, but he also saw that the other end of the cord was lying over the top of the wall right next to it. He flipped off the safety and chambered a round. He waited, sights zeroed in on the edge of the wall. The truck rumbled by making a strange grinding noise and continued down the road without incident. He saw the head pop up again, obviously surprised that nothing happened. The muzzle suppressor spit and the top of the head rippled and disappeared.

His next concern was being discovered by the crew of the lumbering JERV because he was where he shouldn't have been and on his way to do something he wasn't supposed to do. Even if it meant a bronze star for saving the crew, a medal wasn't what was important to him right now. He relaxed as the JERV continued rocking down the road, unaware it had just dodged five big bullets buried right under the roadway. He turned to continue on his way when he felt a pang of guilt. He re-spliced the det cord, then hustled the fifty yards to the wall and cautiously approached with the business end of his rifle leading the way. The body of the man he shot lay motionless. Off in the distance, he could see three men running. *They must have freaked when their buddy caught a head full of lead*, he thought. He searched around and found the detonator a foot away from the body. Looking back to the road through his scope, he panned to make sure there was no one near or approaching. Then he ducked behind the wall and hit the plunger.

It was an instant hell. Flames and dirt exploded into the air and the shockwave slammed into the wall with so much force that he felt it shake.

He looked at his watch; he'd have to hustle to make up time if he wanted to reach the village early.

ICON

The crew of the JERV heard the explosion to the rear and called it in. They all felt lucky for the first time that day. Earlier, they had been separated from their convoy, hit a giant rock, and were now limping back in with a bum rear end.

11. Signal 10-10 Shots Fired

The next day, Towne saw the headline of the *New York Post* – *NYPD Detective Dies in House Fire* – with Reade's department ID picture of on the front page. As he read the article, he suddenly connected the name Margaret Reade to the Jenkins' case and then the inquiry by the chief of detectives, whom he held in the highest esteem. But he was personally ordered by that chief, a man who would, and could, make him a detective, not to breathe a word of his inquiry. *Ordered or asked?* he thought as he pondered the exact words the chief used. He had also said, "Keep your nose clean." Towne quashed an uneasy feeling starting to rise in his stomach. He decided to ask his partner, a cop with twenty-three years in, when the time was right.

ID

It had been a quiet shift and Towne and Vic decided to take their lunch at the Thai truck by the ball field at DeWitt Clinton park, on Five-Four and Eleventh, for lunch.

Towne grabbed the radio mic and called it in. "One-Eight-Adam to Central. We are ten sixty-three at Five-Four and Eleventh."

Victor looked at him.

"What?"

"You have to end each transmission with 'K' so they know your message is complete. They ain't gonna answer you, till you do. They are real sticklers for that shit."

"One-Eight-Adam, ten sixty-three at Five-Four and Eleventh... K."

"Central to One-Eight-Adam, roger that, ten sixty-three at Five-Four and Eleventh... K."

"You'll get the hang of it," Victor said in a very comforting way.

Towne had wanted to approach his partner about what was on his mind all morning. Sitting in their radio motor patrol car with styrofoam trays on their laps, Towne was twirling his Pad Thai noodles around his white plastic fork when he broached the subject.

"Vic, did'ya ever meet the chief of detectives?"

"Grimes? Nah. Saw him at a funeral once but just a nod. Why?"

"Do you think he's a... an honest kind of..."

"One-Eight-Adam. Ten-eleven in progress; silent alarm; seven-ten Ninth Avenue K." The dispatcher's voice crackled through the radio, splitting Towne's questions.

"One-Eight-Adam to Central K; responding; two minutes out... K. Hit the lights, Marcus."

The RMP accelerated down Fifty-Fourth Street, heading east to Ninth Avenue.

Towne's partner, Victor Curtis, pumped a shell into the Remington in case the perpetrators were trying to get away when they arrived at the scene of the armed robbery. Young Towne glanced over, and the sight of the shotgun suddenly made all of this hot and real, not a drill. *I hope I do well; I don't want to freeze up or miss something important,* he thought. Most of all, he didn't want to get himself or his partner, shot!

The radio started squawking with other radio motor patrol teams responding, but Towne figured that he and Victor would probably be first on scene since the others were farther away.

Inside Ninth Avenue Liquors, Sim Ken Yung, the slight-of-build clerk, had hit the foot switch alarm as soon as the larger of the two hooded black guys brandished the .32 cal revolver. Although he was behind bulletproof glass, his sister was in danger. The skinny one grabbed her as she was finding a bottle of French wine for a customer, who was now cowering behind the display on the floor.

"You no hurt her. What you want?" Sim said.

"Give – me – all – the – money – motherfucker!" Demond, the bigger one, punctuated each word by jutting the gun at him.

"All I got is register!" Sim opened the drawer, grabbed every bill in the till, and unceremoniously stuffed it in the cash tray under the glass shield just as the sirens ramped up louder and louder.

The wailing tones of the approaching cop cars started to accelerate Tyrell, the skinny one's, rapid eye movements and blinking as he was holding the now-screaming sister. He started to panic. "Shit! The cops! C'mon man, grab the cash and let's split."

"Fuck man, there's only a couple hundred here," the hooded thief protested, banging the butt of the gun on the glass.

"You take money. You go now!" Sim said over his sister's crying.

"Don't tell me what the fuck to do man..."

"Let's go, Demond. The motherfucking cops are going be all over our ass." Tyrell's slight tremors, stemming from lead poisoning as a result of eating paint chips as a two-year-old, were now randomly ticking his gun hand.

Sim's sister's screams continued and Tyrell shook her, trying to make her stop, but it just added vibrato to her aria of fear.

"This gook is holding out on us, Tyrell. Cap that noisy bitch! Maybe he'll give us the rest."

Fearing for his sister, Sim Ken Yung said, "No. There is no more! All in safe. I can't open. No key! Only owner. Not me." He reached into his pocket and pushed twelve dollars and some loose change under the glass into the pile and then pushed it out farther, causing some of the money to fall over the edge of the counter.

"Twelve dollars! You fuck! Twelve dollars!" Demond turned to Tyrell. "Cap that bitch."

Tyrell either didn't hear him over the screaming or else thought he was just saying it to get the jerk behind the glass to fork over the money.

Demond turned and said, "I told you to cap that bitch's ass." He raised his gun and fired twice. The sister stopped screaming and writhing instantly as one slug found her heart. The other lodged in her sternum.

Tyrell jumped back and freaked out as the girl's body slumped to the floor. "What the fuck D. You could have killed me!"

Ignoring Tyrell, he pressed his face to the glass, his breath fogging it. "Now give me all your money, man. I want it all!"

Sim started crying and screaming, banging on the thick glass, "Why? Why? Why you do it? My sister! Why? I got no more money. Why?" and then collapsed, breaking down in sobs.

"You crazy motherfucker, D. Why'd you do that?" Tyrell said as the screech of the first police car was heard outside.

Demond fired two shots in to the glass, aiming down trying to shoot Sim, but the bullets ricocheted. "Fuck it man, we gots to go! Now, T!"

Towne and Victor got out of their police car, Vic with the shotgun, Towne with his Glock, just as two men with guns were hitting the street.

"Freeze!" they said simultaneously to both armed men leaving the store.

IQ

Towne saw confusion in the thinner one's eyes as he instinctively turned in the direction of his and Vic's unison yells.

The heavier man aimed his weapon at the older cop who was holding the shotgun and yelled as he squeezed the trigger, "I ain't going back to prison, motherfucker!"

Out of the corner of his eye, Towne saw the muzzle flash of the big guy's gun and Victor go down. He only had a split second to figure out what to do first – shoot the thin one who had not fired yet but was drawing down on him and then try to shoot the other guy? Or open up on the big guy who just shot Victor?

The thinner one's gun hand twitched again and made Towne's decision for him as he reacted to the motion by pulling his double-action trigger three times in rapid succession. He saw Tyrell blur as he was spun around and down by the force of the 9 mm slugs hitting solid bone. To his own amazement, Towne instinctively stepped to his right and swept his Glock toward the bigger one as the pistol that he was pointing back at Towne spit flame. He could feel the pressure wave as the slug passed right by his left ear and he quickly fired off six shots this time. He was trying to remember the Quell system of shooting to kill and aimed for the vital areas of sinus, throat, esophagus or heart. But Demond was a moving target so he caught one in the eye and half of his head disappeared in a pink plume.

Two of Towne's bullets had cracked the window of the liquor store. Towne ran toward the downed crooks. He kicked away the gun from Tyrell's limp corpse and then stepped on the wrist of Demond's hand, which still held the gun. Glancing at the growing pool of blood gushing from Demond's partial skull on to the curb and down into the street, he realized this precaution was unnecessary and ran to help his partner.

He could see that Victor was in obvious pain and his breathing was labored. Towne hit the shoulder-clipped mic on his belt-slung radio and used the code for "officer down." "One-Eight-Adam Portable to Central K. Ten-thirteen! Ten-thirteen!

At that instant, several responding patrol units came screeching to a halt in front of the liquor store. Throwing their car doors open, the officers ran to Victor, ripping open his vest and uniform, checking him for wounds.

A sergeant placed his hands on Towne's shoulders. "We'll take it from here; are you hit?"

The question confused Towne at first. In the adrenaline rush, he hadn't even considered his own condition. He began feeling around to see if he was in any pain, patting himself with his gun still in his hand.

"Whoa. Here, let me have that," the sergeant said, lifting the still smoking gun from Towne's grip as the first ambulance pulled up.

"No, no, I think I'm okay." He patted himself down again. "Yeah, I'm good. How's Vic?"

"I see his legs are moving, so that's a good sign." The sergeant turned Towne around saying, "Come on, sit over here." The sarge led him over to the back of the ambulance and sat him on the protruding bumper. "Take deep breaths. Try to ease up; you did good. Breathe."

Marcus Towne hadn't realized how tightly wound he was until he started to uncoil. He noticed his right hand shaking and quickly grabbed it with his left to silence it. He was grateful that the sergeant apparently didn't notice.

An older cop came over and reported to the sergeant, "We got two dead guys on the pavement and one cop down, possibly saved by his vest. Luckily, no civilians on the street were caught in the crossfire, we got one girl down by gunshot, dead in the store, and you somehow managed to survive. I hope for your sake this was a righteous shoot, or your young career is as dead as these two skels decorating the sidewalk in sticky red."

85

It took a second, but the words finally registered in Towne's brain. He lunged forward and ran into the store. He skidded to a stop right in front of Sim's sister's body. Cops were pulling Sim, who was hysterical, off her. She had two large bloody holes still oozing. There was a lot of blood from one of them.

Towne, put his hand over his mouth, which muffled his voice when he said, "Oh, my God..."

The sergeant caught up to him and grabbed his arm. "Come on, you can't do anything in here. Let's go back outside."

"I... I... killed her?"

"Outside, now!" The sergeant said in a command voice that Towne instinctively followed.

He sat on the bumper of the ambulance again, only this time he was a million miles away. The words, *I killed that young girl*, repeatedly ran through his mind.

An unmarked car pulled up and he watched as two Manhattan North third grade detectives approached the scene.

Letting out a whistle, one detective said, "High noon! What do we got Sarge?"

"Just finding out, Wilson. This is Officer Marcus Towne, first on the scene. His partner caught two in the vest – the EMTs are on him now."

"Marcus, I'm Wilson; wanna tell me how it went down? Marcus?" He bent down a little to be in the young cop's eye line. "Marcus, tell me what happened."

Towne looked up with tears in his eyes...

"It's okay, son, you did the right thing, but I need to know right this second if there was anybody else. Is there anybody out there right now with a gun and a grievance? Marcus, were these the only two?"

Towne looked up and said in a weak voice, "Yeah, only two."

"Good, good. Now Towne, tell me how it went down."

"We rolled up and we were just getting out of the unit when those guys came through the door.

The one on the left started shooting at Vic right away. Er, my partner Victor Curtis. I saw him go down and I had the one on the right pointing straight at me. I didn't know what to do when Vic went down, but then the one in front of me went to fire, or almost fired or maybe his gun jammed. I don't know; it happened so fast but I fired. He went down and then I turned to the guy who shot Vic, and he was already firing at me so I side-stepped and returned fire. I think I hit him a few times. He's all messed up."

"Did you identify yourselves?"

"I know I said 'freeze,' but they started shooting a split second later. I don't know what Vic said. He okay?"

The sarge looked over to the side of the blue and white unit where Victor was still lying down as the techs worked on him. "The EMTs don't look too intense so I'm going to say he's good."

At that point, the other detective came over and said, "I recognize the big one down in the gutter there, Demond Williams. This would have been his third strike. No wonder he came out blasting."

The sergeant nodded to Towne. "That's good news for you, kid."

"I killed a girl in the store. How's that good news?"

The detective continued, "I count nine from the street toward the store. We got three in the guy on the right, four in our old friend Demond there, and two misses into the glass on the left. Were those all yours?"

"I don't know. I don't remember how many I got off," Towne said.

The sergeant popped the magazine on Towne's gun. "Did you have the regulation full magazine of fourteen and one in the chamber, prior to discharging your weapon?"

"Yes sir."

"Well, I count five still in the mag..." He pulled back the slide and caught the ejected unfired bullet,

"...and one in the chamber, so that means you got off nine."

"I had no idea," Town said, running his hand through his hair.

"It happens fast," Wilson said. "Towne, come with me."

They walked back to the storefront right up to the bullet holes in the glass. The detective took out a laser pointer. "Here, look." He pointed the laser through the hole and shined it on four broken bottles on the third shelf, now dripping with booze.

Towne was focused instead on the cops leading a distraught young Asian man out of the store. All he could see of the young girl's body, hidden by a rack, was her feet.

"Are you looking, Officer?"

Towne looked at where the pointer was making circles.

Wilson then put the laser in the second hole and pointed it at three smashed bottles on the second shelf, lower and to the right. "Your rounds entered the window and shattered bottles on two shelves. That's two for two."

Towne looked at him, "So what does that mean? I still hit the girl!"

"No, Officer Towne, you didn't."

"How do you know I didn't?"

"Her wounds are not through and through. She has no exit wounds. Plus she is all the way over there. She was dropped where she stood with a cardiac puncture. She didn't crawl all the way over there with a bullet in her heart. But most of all, the slugs that killed her are still in her."

Towne had a revelation, "That means..."

"Your shots did not go through her and smash those bottles."

"No, they couldn't have. I didn't shoot her. I didn't kill her! I didn't kill her, Detective!"

"No, you didn't. But you did put two very bad men in hell. That's a good day's work, Towne, and as far as I can tell, a damn clean shooting."

Towne wiped the tears from his eyes ...and stood a little straighter.

12. The Ugly Truth

The ride up to Rye was a silent affair. Cassidy just looked out of the window all the way. She was pissed that DiMaggio had taken away her phone. Even though he said it was so no one could track their whereabouts, she just knew it was about power. They pulled up to the gate and DiMaggio announced himself over the intercom box. The gate opened and he drove up the driveway and around the Roman fountain to park in front of the marble stepped entrance to the house. The opulence of the place made Cassidy slightly self-conscious about the clothes she was wearing. They were literally the clothes on her back when they escaped from her house last night.

Maybe it was the posh surroundings, but to her surprise, DiMaggio actually came around and opened Cassidy's door.

A butler greeted them at the entrance. "Ah, Detective... DiMaggio, isn't it? Do you have an appointment to see Mrs. Jenkins?"

"No, but I wonder if we could have a word with her?"

The servant looked at Cassidy.

"And this is Doctor Cassandra Cassidy," DiMaggio said.

She smiled.

"Would you mind waiting here in the 'foy-yea' while I see if Mrs. Jenkins is receiving guests?" He crisply turned and strode off.

"I see you can be polite; not having the badge must really put a dent in your caveman routine."

"Please respect the decorum of the foy-yea... or else I'll trow you outta dis here foyer!"

Even though she tried not to, the fractured English made her smile.

The butler returned and said, "Right this way, please."

Cassidy could see that this was a grand old house from the roaring twenties. She looked up at the domed-ceiling main reception hall with its nine-foot doors leading to the separate wings of the mansion. The original stucco walls were accented with smooth walls painted al fresco with a glaze and then stipple brushed in the same muted orange colors that she had seen on the garden walls of Tuscany. The brass hardware of the doors and the sconces was kept brilliantly polished. As she passed, Cassidy noticed an oil painting by Canaletto commanding the back wall of the large dining room. Four candelabra were stretched across the table that seated sixteen in large high-backed French chairs.

Although Cassidy was well off and her own home, before it was shot to hell, was a showplace, she was impressed. This house was as near perfect to its theme and core as she'd ever seen – and she was rarely impressed by anything.

They proceeded toward the rear of the mansion and walked through a Florida room appointed in 1950s bamboo chairs and a sofa cradling large puffy green cushions with white piping on the seams. A banana-leaf-styled ceiling fan made lazy circles as its current swayed the plants and orchids that thrived under the glass ceiling.

They found Marla Jenkins outside, next to the Roman-styled pool with its six cherub statues emptying vessels of water on each side. She was lounging on an Italian chaise, her flawlessly tanned skin contrasted by a white, one-piece Gottex swimsuit topped off with tortoise-framed Gucci sunglasses.

DiMaggio and Cassidy approached. "Thank you for seeing us. This is Dr. Cassidy."

"Charmed..."

"Mrs. Jenkins, was your husband involved in anything illegal?"

"That's pretty direct, Detective; shall I call my lawyer?"

"Why don't we avoid making you a co-conspirator for at least five minutes; then if you feel in any way threatened, you can call," DiMaggio said reassuringly.

"Very well, what's your question?"

"Do you know how your husband came to be in possession of a certain computer disk which we found among his personal effects?"

She appeared confused by the question. "I found no disk in his personal belongings that were returned to me."

"Yes, I know; we were holding it prior to having its contents revealed. Unfortunately, however, it is now lost. Do you know how he might..."

"Horace was an antiquarian; he couldn't use my smart phone without cursing the thing out. He'd never touch my computer, and I never saw him with one. He hated them. He loved books, paper and ink. Even his clerks complained that everything had to be on paper. My Horace was an anglophile – he loved all things old, English and dusty. Computers were well out of the time Horace lived in. So no, I wouldn't think he would even know what a disk was."

"Could he have been hiding his computer literacy from you?" DiMaggio gingerly added.

"What game is this Detective? My husband was well regarded in this community. I don't think he ever stiffed a waiter on a tip, much less do anything untoward. All that rubbish now about him and the mob... ridiculous! Why are you here, Doctor?"

DiMaggio jumped in. "Dr. Cassidy was treating your husband."

That raised her eyebrows. "For what?"

"Sexual impotency. I have a clinic, in which we utilize several different methodologies to help patients reconnect with their sexual drive," Cassidy said in a dry professional tone.

"Well, apparently you did your job really well! He was found dead after some hookup with a call girl."

"Actually, Mrs. Jenkins that's not entirely true..." DiMaggio said as he turned to Cassidy to urge her on.

"Your husband suffered a fatal cardiac arrest while in session with a sexual surrogate. She was following my prescription."

"Prescription? What a quaint way of putting it."

DiMaggio squatted down to her level. "Look, Mrs. Jenkins, I came here to let you know that in a weird way, your husband died trying to make himself a better husband for you."

DQ

She quickly turned her head in the direction of the pool. The catch in her throat was slight but perceptible when she said, "Well, thank you for letting me know. But why did it take so long to come out?" She shot a look toward Cassidy, "Of course, you must have been worried about a malpractice suit!" She again looked away from them toward the flower garden she had planted to fall in the sight line of anyone seated at the pool. "Anyway, you needn't be concerned about me, Doctor. I certainly don't need your money."

"Actually," DiMaggio said, interrupting, "I was hoping to convince you to sue."

"What?" Cassidy said, his statement catching her off guard.

13. Take Out

From outside, there wasn't a clue as to what was on the top floor of the former shirt factory on the Westside of Manhattan. In the basement, only a trained technician would have recognized the orange flexible fiber cable. It was recently added to the inside of the telephone junction box and well out of place and time with the old, color-coded copper wires that had served the building since the 40s. Same for the temporary satellite uplinks and microwave dishes, which cropped up on the elevator tower on the roof.

At the other end of the fiber on the sixth floor was a large room packed with computers, monitors, laptops, and all kinds of communications and surveillance equipment. Everything was temporary in rack-mounted, roll-around anvil cases set amidst the old sewing tables and pattern-cutting machines whose usefulness was long abandoned to China, along with fifty percent of all American manufacturing.

Two men sat at a bank of laptops, while others were reviewing surveillance camera videos. The man known to the team only as Burns, a slight-of-build man in his mid-thirties who set up and operated temporary mobile HQs like this in and out of the military, got a hit on one of the three screens in front of him. "Wait a minute! Shit!"

"What is it?" Wallace, the older of the two, looked over, squinting, trying to see the screen with middle-aged eyes.

"We are monitoring for the doctor's cell phone but I never shut down DiMaggio's scan and son of a bitch, he just used it."

"The bastard is still alive! That explains the lack of a body floating in the river."

"He just called a restaurant."

"What's the number?" Wallace asked as he picked up the phone near the computer.

As Burns read out the numbers, Wallace dialed. As he did, he considered the consternation he'd receive if the Secretary were to find out that this NYPD dick was still breathing. He didn't want to make that call to the Secretary's lackey, Smith. Hopefully this cop screwed up, and they'd be able to eliminate him in a few minutes.

ↀ

The unblinking red light bulbs that were the eyes of the twenty-five-foot-long papier-mâché Red Dragon peered down from the wall as Chinese waiters hustled Dim Sum trays around the room.

At the front, the maître d' answered the phone. "Thank you for calling Red Dragon; how may I help you?" He listened as he stapled a bill to a takeout bag. "We are at two-nineteen West Thirty-Ninth Street. Okay. How many you come with.... Hello. Hello. Aya!" He hung up the phone, annoyed.

ↀ

The Chevy Suburban with the front-end damage from breaking down Cassidy's driveway gate pulled up to the front of the Red Dragon restaurant. Wallace got out on the passenger side. He crossed the street and entered the restaurant.

95

The maître d' greeted him. "Good evening, how many please? One! You come this way."

The man led Wallace to a deuce. As he sat, he looked around the room while a waiter set noodles, duck sauce, and a menu in front of him. He paid no attention to the menu as he continued to scan the room in search of DiMaggio. He took out his cell phone and punched in the numbers.

Three tables away, a young man sat with his girl as they discussed their next date. "Okay, how's this? What if we went to the party after we stopped by Ed's..." His cell phone rang, interrupting their conversation. "Hello..." As he held the phone to his ear, he tried again. "Hello."

Wallace got up and walked over to the young man. "Excuse me. May I have a word with you?"

"Who are you?"

"Just a minute of your time, please."

"Look, I am busy here..."

Wallace rested his hand on the young man's arm and then squeezed, making him wince.

Shocked and annoyed, his date opened her mouth in protest. "Excuse me..."

Wallace interrupted. "It won't take but a second. I'm truly sorry."

In pain, the young man just nervously nodded and stood up, with Wallace still holding his wrist. Wallace led him off into the bathroom.

Once inside, Wallace was immediately in his face. "Who are you?"

"David... David Ramirez."

"Where did you get that phone?"

"Is that what...? I got it from a guy."

"What guy?"

"I don't know his name. He gave it to me yesterday and said that after five o'clock tonight, the calls were free and that it had a month's worth of calls on it. Said he hated the fucking things. I figured he got a bad call."

"What did this guy look like?"

"Wet."

"Wet?"

"Yeah he was soaking wet. He said something else too but you aren't going to like it."

"What?"

"He said that someone would probably come around asking about the phone and I was to tell them 'wrong number' or something like that..."

Wallace took the phone and before he left smashed it against the tile wall with so much force it shattered in its protective case.

IQ

Don Pankin dug his keys out of his pocket and pressed the button on the remote. Five spots down, a Chevy Blazer beeped, unlocked, and flashed its lights. As he approached it, DiMaggio stepped out from between two SUVs in the dimly lit municipal garage.

"Shit." Pankin said.

"Don. I need your help."

"I'd be crazy to help you. Thanks to you, I am on traffic duty. Twelve years in and I am writing up double-parkers. Cram it, DiMaggio."

"Look, this wasn't something I did. This is a big stink coming at all of us."

"I can't be seen talking to you." He turned and walked away.

DiMaggio called out. "Reade died because of this."

That stopped Pankin dead in his tracks. He spun around, quickly strode back, and got in DiMaggio's face. "Can you prove that?"

"No."

He turned away again but DiMaggio spun him back around. "The fire chief on the scene told me it was arson, that an accelerant was used to burn down Reade's house. Of course, the fire just happened to also destroy my case files..."

Surprise registered on Pankin's face.

"Yeah, Don, I asked Reade to hold them in her house while the heat was turned up at the office. Somehow, they found out. I need you to check with your brother."

"What am I asking him?" Pankin said in a resigned voice, his tone making it clear that he couldn't believe he was going along with this.

"I'm betting nothing about this case makes sense. Ask him to sniff around Nine Metro and see if anything clicks."

Pankin's brother was a supervising fire marshal at the Fire Department's main headquarters at Metro Tech in Brooklyn. Fire Marshals were essentially Fire Department detectives, armed and possessing the same arresting and legal authority as gold-shielded cops. Like many marshals, Don's brother, Mark, started as NYPD.

DiMaggio stuffed a piece of paper into Pankin's shirt pocket. "I got a new number, and it's a disposable cell. You are the only one who's got the number. And Don, you don't know this but I'm dead."

IQ.

Not all wounds from a shootout leave bullet holes. Often there are serious emotional scars that, if not handled properly, could result in the department unknowingly putting a ticking time bomb back out on the street. To prevent this, as well as the potential repercussions, the NPYD required every officer involved in a shooting to undergo a mandatory, thorough psychological analysis.

Doctor Felix Barnard, a psychiatrist with thirty years in the NYPD, was looking for a very specific issue with Officer Towne. He had to determine if Towne's mental state might be affected by black-on-black guilt. Although intellectually and professionally, Towne was BLUE, which practically speaking is a race of its own in this type of confrontation, there could still be some residual self-animosity for taking the lives of two black men. The worst-case scenario would be if Towne hesitated the next time he was confronted with a black perpetrator, and the guilt-based delay in reaction time proved fatal not only to him but to the public as well.

Towne sat in the examination room as Dr. Barnard consulted with his colleague, Dr. Lu, outside.

"Do you concur?" Barnard asked.

"Yes. He exhibits no ambiguity over the shooting incident. His current frame of mind appears to be clear, probably due to his own healthy sense of self-worth," Lu said.

"I believe his rationale is straightforward." Dr. Barnard flipped through the chart until he found what he was looking for. "Here is his statement from five hours after the shooting. 'As I see it, they drew down on me; they fired at me; they tried to hurt me, to kill me, violently. Had they been the lucky ones, then I would be dead.'" Dr. Barnard flipped some more pages. "Later in the interview he said, 'Just as dead as if they hated me from the old neighborhood or dead because I am black or because I was gay and they killed me for it. Dead is dead and I could have been just as dead as they are except for my training, luck and instinct.'"

Dr. Lu's eyebrows went up. "He's certainly got the right perspective. From what you just read, I do not detect any latent guilt, remorse, or cognitive distortions."

"That's the way I read it as well; would you like to speak with him?" Dr. Barnard said.

"Yes."

The two doctors entered the exam room.

"Officer Towne, this is my colleague, Dr. Henry Lu."

"Hello, Doctor Lu."

"Hello. Marcus, most officers go through their whole career without ever firing a shot in the line of duty. You've already had a multiple-death shooting and you are barely out of the academy, so I am interested in a couple of things. May I ask you a few questions?"

"Sure."

"How do you feel about the men you killed?" Dr. Lu said.

"How do I *feel* about them? Well... feel?"

"Yes, feel about them – those two men and what happened."

"In one way of thinking, I could have grown up with these guys and gone to school with 'em. Hell, they could even have been my cousins."

"So how do you feel about being responsible for their deaths?"

Towne's attitude changed from being reflective to assertive. "Those two men, the two dead perpetrators, they died by choice."

"Choice? You mean they chose to die?" Dr. Barnard said with a cautious look to Dr. Lu.

"No, they chose to rob, to kill that poor girl in cold blood. They chose not to surrender, and then they chose to try to kill me and my partner in order to avoid the consequence of *their* choices... but fate chose me to live." Towne said.

"Are you sorry you killed them?" Dr. Lu said.

"No... Wait, that sounds horrible. What I mean is that once they engaged, we could have all died. So given the choice, I am glad it's them and not Victor or me."

"You were almost hit," Dr. Lu said.

"Felt the bullet go right past my ear," Towne said as he swept his hand past his left ear.

"Do you think about that a lot?" Dr. Barnard said.

"It makes you think, that's for sure. Doc, can I ask you a question?"

"Sure."

"When can I get back on patrol?"

The department shrink was encouraged and felt confident enough in the young man's psyche to let him in on what was likely to happen next. "Although this procedure was necessary and every case takes its own time before a return to patrol is approved, your turn-around should be quick, Marcus," Dr. Barnard said

Dr. Lu added, "Admittedly, this period will go faster because in your case, the shooting was deemed 'righteous' and in accordance with procedure, with no undue risk to the public or other officers."

"So how long?" Towne said.

"You'll be on the desk for seven to ten days at the most. You can collect your things and we'll see you in six months for a routine check up," Dr. Barnard said.

IQ

When Towne left the shrink's office, he found Detective Wilson waiting for him with two venti Starbucks in his hands. "Cup of coffee, Marcus?"

Sitting in the break room, Wilson laid his cards out on the table. "Word is you came out clean on this shoot. That's a career builder, Marcus. There's going to be a 'Forty-Nine' commendation letter in your personnel jacket. With that, you might even be able to put in for a medal. You just halved your time to detective."

"What makes you think...?"

"Don't even try the modesty bit. Everyone in the department, down to the guy who just handed you that coffee, knows you are bucking for a gold shield."

"Okay. But..."

"But what?"

"Between us?"

"Sure."

"After sitting with Grimes, I'm having second thoughts..."

"You sat with Grimes? When?"

An alarm bell started ringing somewhere in the back of Towne's head. It was instinct that had served him well all through school, through the academy and even three days ago when they rolled up to the liquor store.

"Well maybe sat isn't the right word. As I recall, he was the only one sitting. I was on the edge of my chair and he just kind of gave me this snarly look."

"Yeah, he can be a real charmer that way, but look, one bad glance – that ain't enough to kill your career."

"I don't know. Is he a good guy?"

"You mean, as a boss?"

"You tell me."

"All I can tell you, and all you need to know, is that he's the chief. In fact, I am here today because he wanted me to let you know that he's watching you." Wilson said it with a smile.

"Is that how he said it, just like that?" Towne asked, trying not to reveal the shudder that rattled his spine at what, to him, sounded like a threat.

"That's how you go up the ladder, man, when the big boys take notice. And you are on your way."

Towne didn't react, his mind reeling.

Wilson noticed. "Did you hear what I just said?"

"Yeah...he's watching me..."

"Okay, try to restrain your enthusiasm here... what is it, man?"

"Did you know Maggie Reade?"

"Manhattan Homicide? Only by name. I think we responded once to a double on the Eastside. Tough break, flashing tin and facing down cretins for a dozen years, only to die burned up in bed. There's no justice my friend."

"So Grimes is a good guy?"

"Yes. And if you are even thinking of the gilded shield, you better stop asking that."

14. Open Season

At first sight, it was just a bucolic setting of trees and undergrowth. A red robin perched on a spindly branch of an Arrowwood bush snapped his head towards a rustle in the bushes. The non-moving shape of a man in camouflage was outlined against the movement of the brush behind him. His face was painted green and brown to match the terrain. A long rifle now apparent in his grip with his eye on the scope. He squeezed off a shot.

◻

Cassidy gave directions while DiMaggio drove along a lonely upstate New York road, winding through a dense, sun-dappled forest. CRACK! Startled, DiMaggio's foot hovered over the brake pedal.

"That sounded like a gun shot!" he said, as they both looked out the windows, trying to discover the source of the sound.

They saw a quarter mile away, a camouflaged man burst out of the undergrowth and run toward the slain buck.

"It's the start of deer season." Cassidy said.

DiMaggio pulled the car up to a small cabin nestled in the woods outside Margarettsville, a hunting community one hundred miles up from New York City. Hanging off the fence post on two rusting, squeaking chains was an old weather-beaten wood-cut sign that read BER-TOWSKY. They got out with a few bundles of essentials they had picked up at the IGA in town where Cassidy had an account, so all she had to do was sign for the goods from the food cooperative. Matches were number one on Cassidy's list. Beer, coffee, and sirloin topped off DiMaggio's.

"Did you hunt?" DiMaggio said.

"My father tried but my sympathies were always with the deer. After he died a few years ago, I started coming back here just to get away from everything."

He looked around at the thick brush surrounding the cabin with only one long road in. It was a good strategic position if anyone came after them. Except for the fact that there was no escape route to the rear.

Cassidy came out to open the shuttered windows from the outside. "Got to get some fresh air in there. I haven't been here for a year."

DiMaggio looked again at the sign. He hitched his head toward it as he said, "I don't know if it's smart for us to be here."

"Why?"

"Your real last name."

"I haven't used it for twenty years."

"I found out about it."

"Yeah, how did you manage find my last name?"

"When I first went to find out about you, the trail stopped twenty years ago, like you said. Then I played a hunch. When you got all riled up that day in your office – 'Please stop calling me ma'am' – your Bronx came out. You sounded like my sister and her girlfriends when I would hit 'em with a water balloon or steal one of their bikes. I got a friend at the Board of Ed. Did you know they keep every yearbook from every school? Since I had your age pegged, it only took an hour and there you were, cute little Wanda B. Then I spoke with the guidance office at Evander High School, and they filled in the blanks and told me about your peccadilloes."

DiMaggio left out the part about her cruel nickname around school, "Wanda Bread" because everyone had a slice of her.

"Well, you were lucky that I didn't go to a private school. But no one else would ever figure that out... water balloons..."

"Yeah, but how do you keep up the payments on this place? That could lead to you."

"No need. My dad paid off the mortgage long ago."

"Taxes? They're always current."

"It's silly but maybe not so much now." She stopped what she was doing to explain. "I kept my father's checkbook. He died with a lot in his account and I pay the taxes with his old checks. I had five boxes of them and I only write four a year. I don't know, but for those moments when I am writing the check, his name is in front of me on the face of the check and the return address on those little Easter Seal labels – he liked to use those... like I said it's silly."

DiMaggio stopped at the top of the porch step as he was bringing in another bag of groceries. "Yeah, but in a way he's still doing his job – protecting you by keeping us safe with no trail back to you." He went inside.

That sentiment made Cassidy look at DiMaggio in a different way as he walked inside. It was the first time in the three days since they were on the run that he had a civil, human moment toward her. She then looked at the old, weathered sign and smiled.

Inside the cabin, sheets covered a sofa and two chairs. Cassidy got matches off a shelf and lit a kerosene lamp on the table, adjusting the wick height as she did so.

"'Til we get the generator working. Then we can also put the groceries in the fridge."

There was a rifle rack on the wall. DiMaggio was impressed by the eight rifles and was particularly drawn to the classic, western lever-action Winchester. Feigning a cowboy drawl he said, "You want me to go on out and rustle us up some dinner?"

"How 'bout we just go to town for a pizza, 'til I get the propane turned on, Tex? Besides there are no bullets."

"Cartridges!" He admired the craftsmanship – the finish of the stock and the scrolling on the side of the breach. "In a fine old beauty like this, you load cartridges."

"Figures. You would have gotten along great with my old man."

He took a small, bolt action, .22 caliber short rifle off the rack. It looked like a toy in his hands. "This is cute."

"Most girls got a princess phone for their sixteenth birthday. That single shot 22 was my father's last hope for me to become Annie Oakley."

DiMaggio pulled the old western Peacemaker from his waistband and placed it on the rack next to "Winnie." A reunion of sorts that made him smile.

Later that evening, a pizza box lay open with three cold slices left. A fire was roaring in the fireplace and Cassidy was all snug in a throw and reading a book, while DiMaggio was cleaning the Winchester like it was a newborn baby. Rags, oil, and barrel cleaners and new boxes of ammo were spread out on his side of the table.

Cassidy finished a chapter, closed the book, and yawned, "So what's the plan, Sheriff?"

"When the widow Jenkins sues you, we'll get all this about your practice into the public record. And whoever is trying to kill us will either give up 'cause it's out in the open or..."

"Or what?"

"I dunno; haven't thought it out that far."

"Great." She threw the book at him.

DiMaggio looked up. "What?"

"When are you going to admit that you haven't the fucking faintest idea what you are doing?"

"Look, I don't hear you coming up with any ideas."

She got up and walked over to the corner. She moved a small table, got on her knees, and pried loose a floorboard. Then she stood up and walked away, settling back on the couch.

DiMaggio went over, looked into the secret stash and whistled. "Must be thirty videotapes here plus a small black book."

"I never trusted them to not turn on me, so I kept a little get-out-of-jail-free collection. Give me the book, would you?"

DiMaggio handed over the book, took out the old VHS tapes, and started reading the spine labels. "Hmmm, let's see, Senator Warrens, the police commissioner, Frankie the Shoe, the mayor – I walked out in the middle of that one. The governor's wife? Wow. That's a treasured part of anyone's collection." He got up and walked back to his chair.

The ensuing silence was deafening.

When the silence continued to drag on, DiMaggio finally relented and said, "Okay, it's a better idea." He saw a slight smirk cross Cassidy's face as she pretended to ignore his mini mea culpa.

𝕀ℚ

Don Pankin dialed the phone from his easy chair in the living room of his Howard Beach, Queens home. He told his kids who were playing pull toy with the dog, "Take Sparky into the other room, I'm making a call." He unconsciously fingered the papers inside the FDNY case jacket rested on his lap.

𝕀ℚ

A cell phone ring broke the stillness of the cabin. DiMaggio answered. "Don. What did you come up with?"

"The official ruling was, 'cause of fire accidental.'"

"But...?" DiMaggio said over the phone, "You wouldn't have called if there wasn't a 'but.'"

"But, my brother doesn't see how that's possible, since the on-the-scene assessments, usually attached to the files, are missing. It was all done as post analysis – after the fact."

"So does that convince you?"

"That usually only happens when new evidence or an inquiry determines the on-scene investigation was seriously fucked. But even then there is a notation of that. This is just a jump in logic."

"Or someone covering up an arson."

"That's where the deep breath comes in; we are talking a lot of juice to change an official inquiry."

"This whole thing's been nothing but one giant juice bath from the beginning."

"Well, here's the kicker. The chief on the scene, Helms, the one you talked to, went on sabbatical a day after the fire. I'm betting for the good of his career and pension, he was politely ordered to take six or ten months off."

The sound of barking assaulted DiMaggio's ear on the other end of the phone.

"Hey, Tommy, take Rags inside. I'm talking on the phone here. Sorry, Mike."

"You took the file home?" DiMaggio said as he sat forward.

"It was..."

"Don, tell your brother to forget all about this, and you just walk away from it."

"This is some deep shit, DiMaggio." Pankin said.

"Lose the file and make sure you cover your tracks. In fact, maybe send the wife and kids to the in-laws for a few days. Just make believe you never heard about this. Seriously, Don, lose the file or you might wind up like Maggie."

In the cabin, DiMaggio closed his phone and looked at Cassidy.

"Any way we can catch a movie here?"

IQ

The small Honda generator was humming outside the window with an extra extension cord leading under the sill and into the house. The cord ran to an old, top-loading Panasonic VCR from the late 70s, which in turn was hooked up to an old TV.

"Why such ancient shit? I mean even my grandfather didn't have a VCR when he died!" DiMaggio said.

"I guess they just recycled all the old equipment from another case. But anyway it works with my Dad's old VCR he parked up here thirty years ago." Cassidy said.

"Government issue." DiMaggio said as he slid in a tape labeled "H.D. Session 6." On the screen was a man in latex, suspended from wires, being whipped by two women as he yelped and cried, "I'm sorry."

DiMaggio dialed a number from Cassidy's black book and held his cell phone up to the speaker. After a few good cracks of the whip, he spoke into the phone. "I figure Fox Network would love to use it on their new show, 'When Deputy Mayors Go Bad.'"

DiMaggio's phone call caught Herman Delgado at the dinner table, seated with his kids, as his wife brought a sizzling roast to the table. Just seconds before, the smells had made his mouth water; now it was parched. A wave of nausea overtook him and his eyes were moving rapidly as if he were looking for a way out. He suddenly got up, swiped his son's glass of Kool-aid from the table, and walked out onto the porch with his cell.

"What do you want?" He took a nervous sip from a shaking glass.

"Answers," DiMaggio said over the phone.

"Not in my office."

"What kind of car do you have?"

"Blue caddy."

"Take a little trip up the Taconic Parkway at eleven o'clock tomorrow morning. Bring this phone; you'll get directions."

"Who is this?"

The receiver went dead and he closed his eyes as an involuntary shudder spilled the red Kool-aid onto the porch.

15. Going To Get Her

The smell was horrible. He had approached the village from the trench that provided sewage for the inhabitants. It was the least populated part and, for good reason, not visited much. He knew Setara and her family lived in the third hut from the goat pen. He entered and the sounds of snoring assured him the people in this one room shack were all still asleep. He only counted three though and he was expecting four. She wasn't here. He found the other young woman under netting to keep the bugs off her face. He gently lifted the net and, in one move, placed his hand over her mouth and held her down with his other. She startled awake, wide-eyed, but her scream was muffled by his gloved hand.

"Shhhhhhh. It's me. I need your help... We need your help." He whispered as he looked around; the snoring continued. When she realized who he was, she relaxed.

She quietly got up and they carefully walked outside, continuing to speak in hushed tones. Fortunately, the young girl's English was good enough.

"What are you doing here?"

"I came for her."

"She not here: the Devil's Farmer after her."

"Who is the Devil's Farmer?"

As Felba related some of the story of how her sister had been branded a curse on the village and was now being hunted by the Devil's Farmer, his blood started to boil.

"Where is she?"

"Somewhere safe."

"I need to go to her."

"You have done enough." It was not a compliment.

"Look, I am here to make it right."

"No! You only make worse. Leave us."

"I can't do that. Please help me get her out of here."

The young girl looked into the camouflage-painted face of this American, Ronson. Her aunt had left with a Russian soldier twenty years earlier. She wondered which nation would be invading her country and her family when her time came. This American had soft eyes. She could see what her sister saw in him. She also remembered how in love Setara was with this American. It made her think that maybe it was wrong for her to keep them apart.

"I take you to her; please, but need to dress. Will be long walking from here." She gave him a reassuring smile and went back into the house to change.

Sergeant Eric Ronson felt the heat of the rising sun and realized that right about now he was being missed back at the FOB. He decided to lay low until Felba came out. He found a quiet place to hide about twenty yards up the hill. He looked down and saw a red flower. His mind went back to how he met Felba's sister.

Bravo Company had been slogging through this part of the godforsaken landscape and jagged rocks known as Afghanistan for two weeks when they encamped near a small, poor village. Some of the merchants from the village were the first to make contact with the Americans in hopes of getting U.S. dollars for their hats, statues, horrible Russian cigarettes, bootlegged DVDs of Bollywood films, and the other scraps they managed to procure for sales. The commanding officer would have none of it and ordered the "beggars," as he saw them, away.

The local merchants were persistent and kept returning, only to be turned away. Finally, tired of the constant hassle, the CO turned to Eric and said, "Ronson, take Ortiz with you and escort these gentlemen back to their village and tell them in no uncertain terms to stay put."

"Yes, sir," he said. Ronson knew it was his command of Dari, the local Persian dialect, that won him this babysitting detail. With Ortiz taking up the rear with his M4A4 assault rifle, it left Eric open to the constant haranguing of these pushy salesmen, every step of the two klicks back to the village. By the time they arrived, he held his .50 caliber rifle in one hand and a hand-made in China, Afghan pakol hat and a fairly decent red flower that looked almost real, made of palm leaves and wool, in his other hand. He planned to throw them out on the way back, but he had also purchased some degree of trust along with the junky items. He could tell they were listening, but he knew they weren't paying attention to his admonishments. Still, he had to try.

"It's very dangerous to be near the American soldiers. We could be attacked at any moment. But also, any contact with us could

113

be bad for you and your families if the Taliban ever came through." He gave the warning half-heartedly, because he knew they were poor and would risk much to make the few "Afghanis" and U.S. dollars they wrenched away from the troops.

He returned the men to their village and was tempted to stay; someone in the village was cooking something that not only smelled good but, more importantly, smelled cooked. Instead, he turned and headed back to a bag of MRE whose internal heating agent captured the aroma of exit thirteen of the Jersey turnpike. Judging from the setting sun, if he double-timed it back he could make it before dark.

Then he saw her. It took all of one second for her incredibly vibrant eyes to lock on to his, and in two heartbeats, he knew he loved her. She was cooling herself by splashing water on her face and thus her hijab moved back behind her ears. When she looked at him and then turned away, he could tell she was embarrassed. However, when she gave him a barely perceptible second glance, he thought he detected a sparkle in her eyes as well.

A compulsion to say something, anything, to her arose as a flutter in his chest. He slowly moved toward her, shaking with nerves the likes of which he had never known – even through his three tours of duty, scores of firefights and dozens of raids, and despite his two purple hearts, three commendation medals with V's for valor and one bronze star. Not helping matters was the fact that she became ten times more beautiful with every inch as he drew closer. He spoke in his best Dari, hoping it was now infused with the local dialect he had just been exposed to. "Hi. My name is Eric."

He waited but she didn't offer up any response, not even her name. As his eyes took her in, his mouth actually dropped open and he forgot to breathe. Standing before him was perfection, all wrapped up in one young girl. He just knew that if there was any truth to the idea that there was only one perfect fit for each person on earth, she precisely fulfilled each and every parameter for him.

Thunderstruck, he snapped out of it long enough to ask, "What is your name?"

Looking away she said, "Setara."

"Setara," he said, as if that one word had the magic to unlock his soul. At that moment, he felt that the entire world and everything in it was absolutely perfect. Even in the hellhole of this mountain province, suddenly all he saw was beauty. Her beauty. His brain returned to him long enough to register that her name meant, "Star" or "The Stars" or "Celestial One." As he looked her up and down, the term "heavenly body" also seemed very appropriate.

Then he realized she was looking at him, taking him in. He watched as her expression softened, no longer guardedly cautious and she allowed a small smile to escape. When he smiled back, it was almost like an experience he had had as a boy scout, blowing on and rubbing two smoldering sticks together, trying to coax a spark into a full fledged flame. Her face ignited. It was nothing grand – just a full smile that lit up his world like the sun had pulled right up to the edge of the sky.

He didn't know whether they had been standing there, smiling at each other for three seconds, three minutes or three hours when their connection was broken.

"Setara!" was the bark of an older woman speaking in the tone of voice usually reserved for disobedient youngsters. The mother pulled her hand over and around her own head as a gesture to remind her daughter of her scandalous unveiled appearance. When she saw she was not listening she called to a young man a few feet away, "Behzad, get your sister, come with me."

The young man came to Setara and said, "We must go, now."

Although seemingly at least twenty, Setara obediently heeded her brother's words and with the smallest of apologetic smiles, covered her head with her hijab, and walked off in her direction.

Eric was floating about one hundred feet off the ground when he realized she was walking away. He hustled up and handed her the flower he had bought. He smiled and said in English, more to himself but also out loud, "I'm going to marry you one day, Setara."

He knew all she understood was her name at the end of the unintelligible English words, but he hoped she knew the music behind it.

And that would have to do for now, as her brother beckoned more emphatically. "Setara!" as he looked at Eric with hatred.

Sensing that he was the cause of her mother's growing irritation, he walked off, looking at her every few feet until he went over the foothill and back to the camp. All the way he thought of only her, trying to recall every pore of her beautiful skin, every lumen in her powerful, one-thousand-watt violet eyes, every perfect feature of her beautifully sculpted face. If there had been a Taliban fighter or enemy patrol nearby, he'd have been a sitting duck. Eric's head was still back with Setara until he heard his unit commander call him over to his tent.

Later that night, as Eric lay in a Gortex sleeping bag between two JERRVs for cover, he tried to find some much needed sleep but all he found was her – he kept seeing her. He ached with each new memory. He tossed and turned; he kept fleeing from the thought in his mind that he might not ever see her again. Finally exhausted he fell off only to dream of her and the look on her face when he gave her the red flower.

IOℚ

He snapped out of his reverie and looked down at the hut and the village below; everything seemed peaceful. He gazed out over the vast terrain of Afghanistan and wondered where she was.

IOℚ

In another village, not far away, a sliver of rising sunlight fell on Setara's face as she lay in the dark, dank space. She awoke with the wood and cloth red flower that she had clutched in her hand when she fell asleep and which was now at her side. She picked it up and spun it in her fingers as she thought of the day "her boy" gave it to her.

> That day at the well, she felt something profound. She thought he was beautiful. He was optimistic; he had a positive look to his eyes. What endeared her the most was that he let her see him as he was, as scared and excited as she. She had not known men or boys who didn't posture, didn't play the tough fighter, the master! She had no time for these males and found them silly and childlike in their make-believe machismo. But this boy, he was delicate. He had the strong outside of a soldier with all the dirt, grime, and sweat. But he showed her a part inside, beneath the role he was ordered to play. That flash of vulnerability appealed greatly to something deep inside her. For all the bluster and show most men made of being brave, here was someone of obvious courage who was also fragile, exposed, and not afraid to show it.

She remembered how her mother, seeing this reaction of her daughter and reading into it only trouble, tried to bring her down from her "hundred-foot perch" by snapping at her, "Setara, stop being foolish. There is work to be done and dinner to be made; your father will come home hungry. Setara!"

Setara saw the rage in her mother's eyes when she grabbed the flower out of Setara's hand and threw it into the brush by the side of the road, then led Setara back down to the well with the four buckets they were carrying to retrieve water for the evening meal.

In the middle of that night, Setara ever so quietly slipped out of her bed, wrapped her robe around her, and silently left the shack that was her home. Taliban law forbade women to go out unescorted at anytime of the day, and especially never, ever at night. One of Setara's childhood friends, Talia was her name, had fallen for a boy from the mountains and went to meet with him one night. On the way home, she crossed paths with some Taliban fighters who repeatedly raped and brutalized her and then carried her back to her family in disgrace. According to the local religious laws and customs, Talia was stoned to death for bringing shame to her family.

Setara kept low and stopped whenever she heard a noise. She got to a particular point along the road, and in the darkness dropped to her knees on the damp ground and started feeling around with her hands. Soon, she found what she had been looking for.

She heard them before she saw them. Men were coming toward her. She stopped and started walking backward, straining to see any outline or shape on the road ahead. The fighters had marched all the way back from a late afternoon raid and were celebrating as they walked. A glint of moonlight winked off something one of them was carrying and she had no choice but to seek cover in a filthy trench along the road. She buried her head under her robe-covered arms and listened to every footstep and human sound. The group of men walked down the middle of the road, passing just two meters from her. One might have been standing right over her and she wouldn't have known it. A beetle crawled on her cheek but she stayed still, not daring to move even a finger to flick it away. The sounds and occasional talking became softer with distance, but she remained motionless, the beetle's legs pinching her cheek. She waited long after there was only the sound of rustling grass and crickets before she rose, brushed away the insect, and ran the rest of the way home.

The flickering flame of a dim oil lamp was enough for her to see the flower she had hidden under her robe all the way home. She put it in the box where she kept her best hair band and a locket from her aunt.

ID

A cooing sound, which turned cranky, brought Setara out of her morning daydream back into the reality of her current situation. As she opened her top, she peered out of the narrow slit at the new day, hoping against hope, as she did every day, that her predicament would change before sunset.

ID

Two Jeep Cherokees appeared at the end of the row of huts where Felba lived, snapping Eric out of his own daydreaming state. They stopped right in front of the hovel. Five men got out and entered. Eric was up and running, skidding to a stop on the rough, rocky hillside as Felba was hustled to the street along with her mother, father, and brother, clad only in their bedclothes. Felba wore only her undergarments, having been interrupted in the middle of changing her clothes.

The tall one fired a three shot burst from his rifle up into the air and spoke in Dari, "You all have sixty seconds to hand over Setara or we will start with her family and end with yours. Do not be foolish. She is a whore and a blasphemer – an atrocity before God. Save your own lives, not hers!"

Eric was stunned. *This must be the Farmer*, he thought. Three of his men were holding weapons on the family as the Devil's Farmer walked down the muddy street, banging on doors to roust the villagers. The fifth man stood guard with his back to Eric. Quietly, he moved over to line up a shot he could only dream would work. The three gunmen, who were sure they were on their home turf, unwisely stood together and were all roughly the same height and, from Eric's position, all lined up in a row. He could cycle his weapon in 1.5 seconds with good accuracy. At three

121

seconds between shots, his accuracy improved to nine-ty-seven percent. But at this close range with civilians close by, three seconds was too long. He decided on his firing order. *The three stooges first, then the guard, and then the Farmer. He may be the farthest away but if I'm lucky, he won't even know the first four are dead before the bullet enters into the base of his skull.*

He steadied himself. Since he was higher, he cal-culated on spotting the first guy high on his head to create a downward trajectory. He waited for the small back and forth motion people do unconsciously to come into sync. When all three heads were lined up, he fired. The result was what is known in the sniper profession as a Quigley: two kills with one shot. The bullet went through the first two but due to deflec-tion, hit the third guy in the shoulder; as a spasm ran through his body, he fired off a short burst from his AK47. Eric reset on the guard who had his back turned and took him out with a center mass shot to his back, right behind his heart. Felba and her family were down, but he didn't know if they were cowering or had been shot. He hesitated a split second on lining up on the Farmer to see if number three was still a threat. Through his scope, he saw the man groaning and holding his shattered shoulder. He acquired the Farmer as the man was in a full run back to the Jeep, firing wildly in his direction. He decided he wanted him alive, so he dropped his sights and aimed at his right leg. The man stumbled and turned, going down just as the large caliber slug passed through his hip. Eric put another round in his gun arm and started running toward the Farmer. As he ran past the third guy, who was still on the ground holding his shattered shoulder but still trying to lift his gun, Eric pulled his 9 mm Beretta from his holster and, with his gun point-ing down as he ran, shot him three more times as he passed, without looking.

The Devil's Farmer was down and shuddering; the leg shot had cut through his hip, severing both femoral arteries, and he was bleeding out fast. Eric bent down and said, "Why were you looking for Setara?"

The older man, who knew he was dying, just looked at him with wide eyes.

Eric grabbed him by the collar of his coat and raised him up. "Why? God damn it! Why?"

The Farmer just kept staring in disbelief that he had failed. Finally, his eyes closed for the last time.

Eric just dropped him in disgust and ran to the family. They were unhurt. He took off his camo-poncho and covered Felba as the town's people started to come out after the shooting. Felba's brother, Behzad, stared at Eric as their mother put her arm around him and led him inside. It caused Eric to ask Felba, "Is there anyone here I need to worry about?"

"No. The Devil's Farmer was hated by all."

"We need to get Setara; can you still show me? We'll take their car."

While Felba finished dressing, Eric started piling the bodies into the Cherokee. The town's folk watched with no comment. As he struggled with the bulk of one of the dead guards, a man stepped forward. Eric dropped the guard and placed his hand on his holster. The man then grabbed the guard's feet and hitched his head in the direction of the truck with an eager smile. The "volunteer" also helped him retrieve the Devil's Farmer's body.

When they were done, Eric asked, "English?"

The man shook his head no.

Eric continued in Dari, "Is there a deep body of water, like a river with a bridge?" He made hand gestures to help describe a bridge over deep water.

"Yes, there is such a bridge, thirty kilometers out that way."

Eric just had to ask, "Why are you choosing to help me?"

At that second, Felba came out of her house and the look on the young woman's face said it all. "Kalhan."

"Felba."

Eric saw how the young man suddenly went all dopey looking and recognized his own reaction when he saw Setara, so he smiled and said, "Would you like to come with us?"

IQ

Kalhan drove with Felba in the front seat of the first Cherokee as Eric drove the second one filled with bodies. The long drive gave Eric a chance to think about what Setara had gone through.

> At that time, it had been four excruciating days since he had first set eyes upon her. He thought about her every waking minute, and she crept into the light, on-demand REM sleep ability he perfected being forward deployed in a conflict zone. The war, his unit, his job all receded as background noise behind the radiant image of her. Finally, he wrangled a day off from his CO. This wasn't hard to do since he was a fierce warrior and, in the past, had to actually be ordered to take time off. Naturally, his commanding officer was all too happy to let him have the day. The real trick for Eric was hitching a ride to the area where Setara lived. He managed by hopping a patrol convoy that was passing within three klicks of her village. The TC of the truck wasn't fond of the idea of a soldier out in "Injun Country" alone and without support, but Eric had a reputation as a predator and enough deployments that the Track Commander could see he had his "shit wired tight."

> As he was jostled in the back of the rocking, up-armored truck, he realized that, if

he had been on an actual mission, it would have been scrubbed for lack of "targetable intel", short for intelligence, which is what the Army required before committing troops. He was heading into a situation without ample intel; he had no idea if Setara would be glad to see him or even if she would be there at all. This was a total crapshoot. But he had no other choice. Every aspect of his being drove him to see her one more time.

He jumped off the truck and watched as it rumbled on down the road. The men on the truck were on their way to reconnoiter a valley where a local tribal leader was said to have amassed weapons. Eric had done this long enough to know that of all the fire power on the truck, it was a sure bet that the most used weapon would be the strongbox, filled with U.S. greenbacks craved by the tribal leaders. Under the air-cooled barrels of American .50 caliber machine guns and squad automatic weapons, a few thousand dollars would change hands and the hidden weapons would be revealed. They would be mostly junk with a couple of artillery shells and a few old Russian land mines thrown in for "value." The really good stuff would have already been sold off to the cretins who made IEDs to set roadside traps and blew up tanks, trucks, and troops. Still, the bounty that paid for the almost useless items that remained kept the lid on things and cooled the temperature of this leader and his band of three hundred men.

He came upon Setara's village just as it was awakening. He found a high perch at one end of the small dirt street and used his sniper scope to try to find her. After about a half hour of enduring a few citizens, including a few women, relieving themselves around the backs of their shacks, he finally saw her. His heart physically throbbed; he could feel it in his chest. She wore a hijab and her breath was visible in the morning chill. He watched her as she headed for the well that was the center of town because the town centered itself around it centuries before. He hustled down from his high spot. He was suddenly conscious of his fatigues and wished he blended in better. He caught a few stares, and one older woman gasped out loud when she was startled to see a fully armed American on her street.

IOQ

When Setara turned toward the woman's outburst, she saw him. Actually, she saw concern in his eyes. He had an expression like a small boy wanting to grab a sweet from the table but playing the game of projecting his desire and guilt at the same time, intending to make his mother give in.

IOQ

He froze as he scrutinized her face, looking for the smallest sign of a smile or some facial clue that she wasn't going to turn and run from him. Without missing a beat, Setara put her finger to her lips, the universal code for silence and then pointed to some high bushes beyond the well. She turned away and continued carrying her pails of well water home, not looking back.

Eric was relieved; they had *communication*. He also immediately admired how quick thinking she was. How she hid whatever shock or surprise she had felt and immediately went tactical; Eric was, after all, a soldier and saw things in a military way. He went directly to the high brush area and plopped down and waited. He would wait all day if it came to that, just to see her again. As he sat, looking at a bug inch up a blade of tall switch grass, he had a smile on his face that could have best been described as... dopey.

IQ⌐

Back in her hut, Setara filled the washbasin and the pitcher beside it with the water from the well. With the remaining water, she flushed the indoor commode-like device, which was what passed for plumbing in this ramshackle shack. Her father left for the field and her mother melted into a throng of woman headed for the river. She finally saw her chance when her sister, Felba, went to a home across the way to help a woman with twins, a task for which her sister received the American equivalent of one dollar a week.

Setara wished she had a mirror, but her mother forbade them. She placed the dark-colored basin under the windowsill and with the sunlight on her face, she could see her reflection on the surface of the dark water. She smoothed her eyebrows, brushed her hair and pinched her cheeks as a way to bring some blush to them. She then opened her little treasure box and lightly touched the flower as she removed her prized hair band. She pinched two leaves off of a plant and chewed them. She cupped some water in her hand and sipped it in. After swishing it around in her mouth, she swallowed it all with another drawn sip from her hand. Setara then covered herself and spirited out of the hut. At first she ran, but then caught herself and walked, albeit with a little bounce, toward the area just beyond the well.

Eric heard the rustle in the brush. Instinctively he reached for his KA-BAR knife, but quickly released all his warrior tension as he saw her. Of course, it was replaced by a new tension, the one as old as men and women. She was looking behind her as she came to the little clearing. She turned slowly and their eyes met. She was wary and Eric read many things in her expression at once: *I hope you are not a maniac; I can't believe I'm doing this;* and *I hope you like the way I look.*

They both sat without breaking the lock on one another's eyes, amazed and comforted by the excitement on their faces. A bird chirped a few minutes later and they broke their stares. Eric patted his uniform and came up with the only thing he could find – his iPod. He unwrapped the ear buds and gave her one; she followed his lead as he slipped it into his ear. She slid the bud under her hijab and into her ear. He then hit play. It was loud and made her jump; he quickly lowered the volume and smiled; she smiled back. *Communion*. It was an Adele song. Setara listened at first with curiosity and then she started nodding with the beat. Eric smiled; he tried to speak but was so nervous that nothing came out. On the second try, he succeeded to speak and in Dari he said, "Do you like it?"

The softness in her eyes, her smile, and the way her eyes lit up was something he knew he would never forget if he lived to be a hundred and five. When she spoke, it was like he heard the voice of an angel. "I do like it, very much." She said it without ever looking away from his eyes, as if she were saying, "I do like YOU very much." Eric's mind was now somewhere out in orbit around Jupiter, so the rustling in the bush escaped him. Only when he saw Setara's eyes divert did he come crashing back through the atmosphere. She took it as a sign she'd been there too long. Eric didn't want her to go and he reached out and grabbed her hand. He saw her instinctively look down at his hand on hers. He did the same. *Contact. Touch. Connection.* Their first touch. He tried to memorize what he saw and what he felt. His hand on hers, the pounding in his ears. The slight tremble in her arm. He looked at her in time to see her eyes come up from their hands and catch his. That look was charged with the energy of the sun. Eric felt like he was falling and enjoying the trip, unafraid of the end. The stare devolved into a broad smile on both their faces. She motioned that she had to go and he resisted. But he had no option. Reluctantly he released her hand, slowly, until all that remained was his fingertip on her fingertip. He rolled up his iPod and handed it to her. "Here..." She looked at the offering but shook her head, "No."

Eric immediately understood. He pulled out his knife. Setara didn't react, which spoke volumes as to how much she already trusted him. He dug the point into the corner of the plastic case and chipped off an edge. He then placed the iPod on the ground and applied enough pressure with his boot to grind some dirt into the plastic case. He picked it up and suddenly it looked like it had gone through hell. He then listened to the ear bud and made sure it was still working. He handed it to her again, "Here. Now you can tell them you found it on the road. It's all my favorite music, so maybe you'll learn a little about me from it."

Setara took the device and clutched it to her chest. "When will I see you again?"

"In three days, I can come back, but I don't want to go now."

She smiled. "Three days." With that, she looked down at the beat-up iPod she "found," turned, and made her way back to the well.

They both looked back three different times, smiled, and waved like kids as they walked away from each other, until the terrain made seeing each other impossible.

Eric was smiling at the memory of Setara waving and holding the iPod, when the cars reached the middle of the bridge. Eric pulled to a spot where the side rail was damaged by the war. He got out and put the Farmer in the driver's seat and, with the gearshift in neutral, placed the dead man's foot hard down on the accelerator. Then reaching in with the butt of his rifle, he slammed the gearshift into first and the Jeep took off with a lunge, over the side of the bridge, and flipped as it crashed into the water below. The top of the car flattened upon impact and it sank greasy side up in a matter of seconds. Given the stillness of the surface, Eric figured it was at least fifty feet deep.

As he looked over the railing at the sparkling river valley below and the towering mountains off in a distant violet haze, he tried to assess his position. The villagers would never admit to even seeing the Devil's Farmer, and since the man was a privateer, no government follow-up was expected. In fact, the only ones who might care would be a few random tribal leaders who were doing business with him.

Eric got in the backseat of the car saying, "Take me to Setara, please," and Kalhan drove off.

16. Town and Country

A kerosene lantern illuminated the rustic interior of the cabin. It was getting late. Cassidy was reading a dog-eared paperback copy of Catch 22 with mild indifference. DiMaggio was nosing around the hunting rifle cabinet.

"Your dad must have been quite a hunter."

"Actually, my mom was a better shot."

"Really now, you are just full of surprises. What did your dad do?"

"He was a lawyer."

"Oh, that explains it."

She put down her book. "Explains what?"

"You and that TV shyster lawyer, Bennett."

"Can't you manage to go for fifteen minutes without insulting me or intruding in my life."

"Sorrr...reee. Wooo, touchy aren't we."

The paperback book came careening at DiMaggio's head.

IQ

In the room atop the factory, Wallace and Burns were off in a corner around a small worktable. A laptop and some papers were in front of them.

"We have a silent level four alert through NCIC and twenty-five guys on loan from various agencies at airports, as well as bus and train stations," Wallace said.

"That's a little risky, ain't it?" Burns said.

"We got cover out of Washington, the Secretary arranged for a federal writ."

"What's the writ?" Burns asked.

"DiMaggio and Cassidy, persons of interest in the death of Judge Jenkins." Wallace would have preferred only his selected men handle this, but the Secretary in D.C. was getting more dissatisfied with the team's results. The fact that he wanted it to be multi-juris-dictional was just a load of political cover horseshit to Wallace. "What about that fiasco at the river?" The pressure he was getting from the man in D.C. at their inability to "clean this up" was showing in his derisive tone.

"We got lucky and got two of our guys in on the ini-tial response. They changed the VIN of DiMaggio's car on the report to a similar one we found in the Brooklyn junkyard. They made sure they lost the plates at the scene, claiming they must have gone with the bum-pers that were stripped off the car when it impacted the water."

"Good, so with the Vehicle Identification Number changed, nobody knows there was a 'failed' attempt on DiMaggio's life. Anything on the whereabouts of the disk yet?"

"No, but it wasn't at the doctor's house or his, or his office or that police woman's house. I am sure they have it with them," Burns offered.

"The woman detective? That was a major fuck up."

"She came home when our team was there and she pulled her piece. They had to neutralize her."

"She winged Billings." Wallace said.

Burns pointed out, "But then Hayes nailed her, through and through, from behind. Even retrieved the slug from the wall."

"Still, three combat-hardened assets against one cop and she got a shot off." Wallace said, holding up three fingers.

"She didn't have the disk; they trashed the whole house so good they had to burn it down. The cop and the doc have got to have the disk with them, if they know what it is," he said with an air of confidence that gave Wallace no such comfort.

"How would they know what it is? I thought it was encrypted." Burns almost lost it.

"The encryption wasn't very sophisticated because it was never going to be out of departmental hands. Just enough encoding to fool the curious pain in the ass. It's still very possible they have no idea what they have."

"Either way, they're history," Wallace said as he walked away.

"Let's hope so for our sake."

Wallace didn't add, *your sake.*

17. Strange Bedfellows

Between the owls, the crickets, wolves, flocks of geese and bats, the forest was a pretty noisy place. Although still not Broadway, it had a din all its own as various species communicated under the starry blanket. Blue moonlight poured through the window of the cabin that was nestled beneath these conversations, as both DiMaggio and Cassidy were looking up at the ceiling from separate bunk beds that smelled of mothballs from the blankets that had been in a cedar chest until they arrived at the cabin earlier today.

"Where did you grow up?" she asked.

"The Bronx, like you."

"Was your dad a cop?"

"No, a fireman. In my family, you either ate smoke or chased bad guys. No doctors, no lawyers, heck even my sister is a detective in Hoboken."

"Lots of guns at Thanksgiving?"

DiMaggio laughed. "Yeah, made my mom nuts."

"My mom left us five Thanksgivings into my life."

DiMaggio rolled over on his side facing her bunk across the room. "Must have been tough."

"Yeah, first you blame yourself, then your father and then the whole world."

"Well, you seem to have done pretty good for yourself."

"I learned to lie at an early age to get what I wanted. It gets so I don't know what's true. My practice, my career – sometimes it all seems as fake as a showgirl's boobs."

"Colorful analogy."

The moment hung. "What you just said – you never give off any clue that you are a normal person with insecurities. I would have never guessed it," he said.

"Why, because you never took the time to talk to me, just accuse and insinuate?"

"I was going to go with ice-queen, but now that you mentioned it, cut me some slack. It was my job. You were a person of interest if not a perpetrator. I had to keep the pressure up to see if you'd slip."

"I hope you can give me the same slack and realize I am a healthcare professional and I specialize in very delicate afflictions."

"Fair enough; how did you get into this line of work?"

"I had no choice if I was going to get control of my life. I was sexually addicted. There wasn't anything I wouldn't do, and anybody I wouldn't do it with - all to get back at my parents. I was angry at my mom for deserting me and angry at my dad because he wasn't my mom and angry at life because of the shit sandwich it handed me. I was knee deep in men when I figured that part out."

"But you are not a sex addict anymore?"

"No. I was my own first patient. Then I got interested in the psychology of dysfunction and ended up specializing in sexual dysfunction in college when the boyfriend of my roommate was suffering from impotence."

"Wait, a guy in college was impotent? You never hear that one."

"Well, it turned out through my work that we revealed a lifelong denial of his homosexuality."

"So wait... he wasn't impotent, he just wasn't interested in your girlfriend, or any girl?"

"Correct. I saved them both a lot of anguish and him lots of recrimination over not living up being to the man his father wanted him to be."

"Okay, I get that, but I remember reading that you were a pretty fast-rising star in clinical psychology. How did you get into treatment rooms and sexual surrogates?"

"I'm impressed; you read up on me?"

"Go on." DiMaggio didn't want to confess that Reade read it to him.

"After my internship at Johns-Hopkins, I came back to New York and opened my clinic. At first, the phone was ringing off the hook, but from men looking for physical rather than mental treatment. After a year in practice and only a handful of patients, the debt became insurmountable. Rather than close up shop, I relented and expanded my practice to include physical treatment, which provided an immediate and lucrative influx of cash."

"So you are not a sex addict anymore."

"Out of all that, that's your take-away? Well, Jerry Springer, no I am not a sex addict anymore."

"Figures."

"What does?"

"I get locked up alone with a woman in a log cabin and she is no longer a sex maniac. Story of my life."

"Hold on, where did that come from?"

"Sorry, I regressed there for a second and forgot how much I don't like you."

"Well Michael, we almost had a genuine moment there, but you saved us from actually relating to one another. So good night and fuck you."

"Okay, so this is not Barbie's dream date... Look, I'm sorry. It's just... it's just..."

"Just what? Do you even know what you are trying to say, what you are feeling?"

"Feeling? Hey I ain't feeling anything. Don't even start with that feelings crap."

"Why are you so pissed off at me?"

"You mean besides you getting my partner killed and me almost dead. No job."

"No, that I know about, but there's something more. What's bugging you about me?"

DiMaggio swung around, slammed his feet on the floor, and slapped his hands on top of his legs. "Okay you wanna know? You really wanna know?"

"Think up something good now."

"No need. Here it is – you are the worst waste of beauty and brains God ever put on this green earth. I break my ass, deal with the dregs of the earth, get not one thank you ever, and I can't put together enough cash to put a down payment on your Mercedes baby, and here you are, swimming in dough because you are a slut with a degree?"

"Don't hold back now."

"You got everything going for you and you do what you do."

"Do what I do? Hey, I am a healthcare professional. I help people."

"You are a classy high-end madam and probably a jump-in-anytime, utility infielder for your whole team."

Now she sat up and faced him. "So what if I am? What the hell do you care? Why do you care?"

"It's just a waste, that's all. You should be... should be..."

"What? Popping out babies, married to a cop, pregnant and cooking. Waiting to service my man every night." She made a loose fist and jerked it up and down for emphasis.

"Where did that come from?"

"Oh knock off the shit. You want me and you want me bad."

"You are nuts, lady. I got a girlfriend, and I am just starting to figure her out. It's just beginning to get good. So no, I don't want you, bad or good. So get off that horse right now, sister."

They both lay back down, turning their backs toward one another. They lay silently for a few minutes.

"What's her name?"

There was no response.

"What's her name?"

"Susan."

"She the one at the opera?"

"You saw us?"

"Let's just say you clean up pretty well in your tux and bow tie."

"So why did you look right through me?"

"Yeah, I perfected that look long ago. It stops them cold – you know, the perverts and 'true soul mates' that I meet on the street. Worked on you too, I see."

"You didn't work on me... Not one bit."

She rolled over facing him, "Then answer the question, why do you care what I do?"

He rolled over and faced her, "Cause until we get out of this, you are either my get-out-of-jail-free card or my bargaining chip. So that means we are tied at the hip. And I don't want to catch the syph or some shit."

"You are a schmuck!"

"And you are a slut."

"Fuck you."

"In your dreams baby."

"My nightmares."

"Shut up."

"You shut up."

"I'm going to sleep on the porch."

"Fine."

He grabbed his pillow and blanket and stalked out.

IQ

Towne couldn't decide what to do. He had been elevated in the eyes of the department due to his dramatic take-down of the liquor store robbers. A street-cam video of the incident was posted on YouTube and went viral, with sixteen million worldwide views. The brass was all too relieved that Towne, who shot two black men in the act of robbery, was also black. It quelled the usual suspects and their demonstrations of rage. In fact, it was a daily double of sorts for the department's public image. The more Towne got patted on the back, the more the department got kudos for it's non-discriminatory practices.

That was the main reason why he was now sitting in a booth having an early breakfast at The Westway Diner on the westside, across from the vice-president of NOBLE, or The National Organization of Blacks in Law Enforcement. It was called a "line organization," and the Irish, Italian, Hispanic and Asian cops had them as well. Bill Owens had made his grade with only eight years in on a similar meteoric arc as Towne was now experiencing. This was probably why, at the department's "suggestion," he was administering sage wisdom to Towne on getting ahead in the formerly Irish-dominated force.

"You know, you are now a standard bearer."

"I know I am suddenly a political pawn. Practically every politician has tried to get a picture with me, and I am getting invitations just to be introduced at fundraisers and the like."

"That's the way it goes. Soon somebody will refer to you as a clean and articulate black man. It will be a politician, and somehow he'll try connect you to his social programs, that you've never heard of, but he'll want everyone to think they are the reason you are a hero. Welcome to the celebrity black cop club."

"I don't want to be in it."

"Unfortunately, the only way to cancel your membership is to quit being a cop."

"That's maybe easier than I thought."

The older cop, who had battled racism, double standards and uncomfortable compliments just to be a cop, reacted to this blasphemy. "Don't even think that. All this political crap will pass, but you are a good cop and you'll make a good detective. Don't let this horseshit take you away from that."

Towne looked at the six-foot-two, two-hundred-fifteen-pound mass of veteran cop and tried to look into his soul. The man had expressive eyes, which Towne was sure could freeze a perpetrator's blood cold, but there was an understanding there right now. It made Towne risk trusting him. "It's not that; it's something else."

"What is it, son?"

"I am not sure I could or would share it with you."

For his part, Owens thought he knew where this was going, but being gay wasn't a deal breaker neither in his book nor for the brass. So far, no one had gone there. *That was one group the blacks had passed on the discrimination ladder,* Owens thought. Don't ask don't tell was how everybody liked it, for now. "Try me; we can go off the record if you'd like."

"Just you and me?"

"Whatever it is can't be that bad," Owens said as he swirled his orange juice around the glass.

"Wanna bet?"

"Somebody pressuring you? Some chuckle-head don't like cops of color?" Owens was leading him to ease the moment.

"Nah, that shit I can deal with... this is... well that's just it. I don't know what this is. It could just be me, or it could be a really big scandal."

"Whoa! What are we talking here?"

"How well do you know Grimes?"

"I'm in his office or in his face at least twice a week."

"Is he a good guy?"

"He's been good for us. His biggest fear is ruining his chance to run for office someday. He don't want no pissed off blacks or Hispanics or Asians popping up on TV, so he gives us a little more leeway. But he's no soft touch either. On balance, I'd say he's pretty fair." *Oh kid, please don't tell me he's gay and he made a pass at you. Please don't.*

"See, now I am even more confused." Towne said as sat back and dropped his hands into his lap.

Owens tried to understand what he was getting at.

"Did you ever meet Maggie Reade?" Towne said.

"No, and now I never will 'cause she's dead."

"You think she died natural?" Towne said.

"Fire... unless the fire marshal declares it arson; then, no."

"Right before she died, Grimes was asking about her..."

Towne went on to tell his tale of Grimes and his quiet warnings.

Owens remained expressionless, although inside he was relieved he was wrong about Towne's secret.

When the young officer finished, they both sat in silence for a minute.

"You got nothing," Owens said.

"Yeah, I know. Nothing but a bad feeling. But let me ask you, does he really ask patrol personnel questions to check up on his detectives?"

"I never heard of it, but if he did do it, maybe he covered his tracks well."

"Covering tracks. I'm afraid that could be what I am dealing with here."

"I got a buddy at Manhattan Homicide, Reade's squad. I'll go pay him a visit."

"Thanks, just between us, right?"

"You have my word." Owens said as he was about to get up, but it seemed like Towne was still bothered. "What?"

"The truth?"

"Life's too short for anything else."

"I don't know if I just stuck a pin in your balloon, sir, or pulled one out of a grenade."

IQ

A sleeping, snoring DiMaggio was startled out of the porch's Adirondack chair by the slam of the rickety screen door.

Cassidy walked over to the car. "There's eggs on the stove. Don't choke on 'em."

"Where you going?" DiMaggio asked as he rubbed his eyes with the back of his hand.

"Where you go-in? Geez, you are such a lunk-head."

"Okay. Thank you, Cassandra, for making the eggs, but where are you going? ...dear?"

"We are out of coffee."

He looked at his watch. "It's just nine. Give me a minute. It's just about time for our deputy mayor to show his well-whipped fanny. So we'll go together."

He went inside, grabbed a rifle and binoculars, and then exited the cabin and went to the passenger side.

"Oh, is Mr. Macho going to let me drive?"

"I am a better shot than you. In case it comes up."

"Gee, now I feel all comfy."

The low layer of morning fog was burning off as DiMaggio caught a glimpse of a buck and two does grazing in a field as he drove by. "You played me like a fiddle last night."

"Did I?"

"You know you did and I fell for it."

"Oh, so you think I was saying one thing but meaning another?"

"No. I think you were playing me to see if I'd jump your bones."

"Yes, that's it! All I ever wanted was for you to jump my bones. What a romantic notion. Get over yourself, Mikey. You ain't all that hot and you ain't all that smart."

"Good, as long as we understand each other."

"Clear as day."

IQ

Owens entered the homicide squad room at 9:15 a.m. and spoke to the first shield he found. "DiMaggio in the house?"

"No more. Suspended. Pending disciplinary action."

"For what?"

"Getting up Grimes' ass, if you ask me."

"Who's in charge?"

He hitched his thumb over his shoulder at the inner office. "Henry's senior."

Owens walked into Henry's office. "Hey, Hank!"

"Owie. How the hell are ya?"

"Good, man. You're keeping up with the gym, I see."

"Don't tell anyone – yoga!"

"No shit. I'd have never figured you for the preying mantis type."

"What brings you to 'man-happy'-homicide?"

"I was looking for DiMadge."

"Yeah. He pissed on somebody's Cheerios."

"Grimes?"

"Grimes was the hammer but I think he crossed a line in an investigation and some 'grand fromage' way up the line got his feathers ruffled."

"The judge thing?"

"Most likely."

"You mind if I look through his stuff?"

"Got two problems with that."

"First?" Owens said.

"All his stuff was impounded."

"Second?"

"See number one."

"So you have no official work-up, no paper?"

"Not even a DD-5."

"DB-5!" Owens corrected.

"Yeah right, new thinking. Detective Division is too off-putting, too military."

"Detective Bureau makes us as innocuous and as harmless as a piece of bedroom furniture."

"Got a number for Mike?"

"Won't do you any good. Been calling him to pick up his check. No answer, no show. He's either totally in the bottle on some stupor..."

"Or gone to ground!" Owens said.

"Very dramatic."

"Maybe, maybe not. Was he working any CIs you know of?"

"No idea. He could have ten confidential informants and I wouldn't know."

"He married yet?"

"Mike? Who would marry him?"

"Still with Susan?"

"Last I heard. Ever had the pleasure?" Harry said.

"I met her at Joe McCormick's gold watcher – nice lady – we talked opera all night."

"Never got into that. It all sounds like wailing cats to me. See ya tomorrow, I guess."

At first, Owens was thrown but then he remembered why there was a black drape over the squad's logo painted on the wall. "Maybe Mike will show?"

"They was close, him and Reade," Harry said.

18. Reunion

Felba went first. She approached the old burnt out lean-to calling out, "Setara... Setara." Then she disappeared under the rickety shack.

Eric could barely hide his anticipation of seeing her again as he stood with Kalhan.

Felba reemerged and waved him in.

It was uncanny how even in the dim light of this crawl space he could see how brilliantly her eyes shone. He bent over low and rushed to her, hitting the ground where she lay. He kissed her with the kiss of a thousand years and then he heard it – a muffled cry. He pulled back and there at Setara's breast was their son. He was all at once shocked and elated. He looked at her in amazement and disbelief. She looked back with a smile and a nod of excitement. He kissed her again and then looked at his son.

My son! The first thing he noticed was he had her eyes. His were filling with tears as the wonder of the moment sunk in. It was like Jesus in the manger. His "Mary" was angelic and the baby, already with full head of dark hair, was picture perfect.

Felba also cried at the scene, and when Kalhan entered, he watched silently, taking it all in.

ID.

Bill decided not to make it an official call so he kept his tin in his pocket as he approached the receptionist. "Mr. Owens to see Susan Milani. "

"Regarding?"

"Actually it's a personal call."

The receptionist rang Susan and announced Bill. She hung up and said, "Ms. Milani is very busy right now; what is this in reference to?"

Bill reached into his pocket and produced his shield. "Ask her if she could spare a few minutes, please."

The receptionist's eyes opened wide and she picked up the phone. "Susan, he's a detective and needs to speak with you. I'll move your ten to ten thirty. Okay, will do." She got up and gestured for Bill to follow "Right this way, Detective," she said and opened a door to a small conference room, waving him in. "Susan will be in shortly. Can I get you something? Coffee, water?"

"No, thank you." Bill looked around the conference room. On the walls of the room were large poster-like photos of office buildings, skyscrapers, and factories that made it look more like an architectural art gallery. He figured since he was in a bank, these must be buildings they financed or owned. He was examining one where he thought he might have made a collar once. When Susan entered, she recognized him immediately on sight. "Bill, right? I am so sorry but I didn't remember your last name. Forgive me."

"I'm impressed that you remembered me at all."

"Actually, you impressed me. I thought cops and opera didn't mix, but you really know your librettos."

"My mom's hero was Leontyne Price and she dragged me to every performance she could afford on a cleaning lady's salary. I guess a lot of it stuck."

"Sounds like my kind of woman. What can I do for you, Bill?"

"I wanted to see you and talk face to face."

"Oh God, is Mike alright?"

"Yeah, it's not that kind of call."

"I haven't seen him." Her whole facial mask stiffened.

"When was the last time?"

"At the opera. Well, that whole night. He left for work in the morning, and then he called me to say

147

he'd be out of touch for awhile but that everything was okay."

"When was that?"

"Four days ago. I haven't talked to him since."

"Did he say why?"

"No, but now I am worried."

"Do you know what he was working on?"

"No. Yes. He was talking about a doctor."

"Got his name?"

"Her name. I can't remember it but I do remember she was with that lawyer on TV. Miles somebody. Is Mike all right? Since I heard about poor Maggie – how horrible – I've been worried sick."

"I'm sure he's fine."

"Why did you want to know what he was working on then?" Susan asked.

"I was following up a lead on something I'm working on and it crossed one of Mike's old cases. Nothing really."

"If you see him, please tell him he's got me going crazy with worry," Susan said, placing her hand on Bill's arm.

"Will do."

IΩ

From a spot high over the parkway, which allowed for a good vantage point, DiMaggio watched the approaching northbound traffic through binoculars. When a blue Cadillac came down the ramp, DiMaggio spoke into the disposable cell phone. "Pull over. Right this second. Don't go another ten feet."

He observed as the Caddy hastily pulled over, grinding over the gravel on the side of the road as it stopped and other cars continued on past. He looked up to make sure there was no airborne surveillance. "Good; you're not being followed. You just continue playing this real smart, Herman, and no one's ever going to know what a sick, twisted, little man you really are."

ID

At a roadside picnic table, DiMaggio and Delgado sat on one side, while Cassidy sat on the opposite side.

The deputy mayor was nervously looking all around as he handed DiMaggio a folder of papers. "Oh boy. I can't believe I am doing this."

"I can't believe this whole fucking thing. Who's behind this?" DiMaggio said.

"I just know who we contacted once. The rest is in there. Some of the copies are a little fuzzy cause I had to move fast. I was so nervous..."

"Yeah, yeah. Look, I need to know how far up this goes. Who is Mr. Smith?"

"Who?"

"Some government type sniffing around the chief of detectives' office when I was called on the carpet. He seemed like the four-hundred-pound gorilla that made him come down hard on me. I want to know where he lives."

"Why? Don't you know?"

"If I knew, I wouldn't have asked you?"

"What kind of game are you and the Secretary playing?"

"What secretary?"

Suddenly, Delgado's spine stiffened. "Hold it. Where did you get that tape?"

"Don't worry about that. What secretary?"

"Whoa. If you aren't working for the Secretary... then..." He turned to Cassidy. "You kept copies? You sneaky bitch."

DiMaggio's hand slammed across Delgado's face full-force, knocking him over. "Hey fuck-face, you don't get to call her names. Or the next hit will take your teeth with it."

Delgado sat up again, hesitantly touching his stinging cheek.

DiMaggio grabbed him by his neck. "You got five seconds to tell about this secretary or that tape goes to channel two!"

"I'm going to wait in the car," Cassidy said as she got up and left the table.

"All I know is that the Secretary is out of Washington D.C. and has all of us on tape. When somebody calls and uses the phrase 'the Secretary is aware,' then we know we better do what the Secretary says or exactly what you are threatening me with will happen."

"He's using her analysis tapes for... for blackmail?"

"I don't know if it's a he or she. But yeah, just like you are doing to me now."

"What have you done for this secretary?"

"Are you wearing a wire?"

"What? No..."

"Different things. Sometimes it's get some U.N. official out of the drunk tank quietly. Or make certain city records, medical records, even birth certificates disappear or appear."

"Do you get paid from this secretary?"

"No. It's all under threat, although sometimes there's a delivery of money. But I never ask for it."

"How much?"

"Last time it was $5,000."

"What did you do to earn that?"

"I don't know."

"You have twenty-four hours to find out who this Mr. Smith is..."

"Hey, I'm only a dep mayor, how – "

"Hey, you are only the guy with a lot to lose and my only way in. You find out about him or everybody else finds out about you."

"I can't see how I am going to do this."

DiMaggio lunged across the wooden table, grabbed him by his shirt collar, and got in his face. "You are going to be my eyes and ears. You fuck up and you don't get me an answer, or you make one person suspicious, and the tape goes straight to the papers and TV news."

"How do I know that if I do everything you want, that you'll destroy the tape?"

DiMaggio released his grip, "Well, you don't know. But I ain't interested in ruining your life; I am only trying to save ours. You play ball and you'll still be able to retire and pull in six figures a year consulting big companies on how to screw the city that's paying you right now."

"I'll try for tomorrow, but no promises."

"I hope we live that long. Here hold this." He handed him an empty glass.

"What's this?" he said as he grabbed it.

"Evidence." DiMaggio pulled out a hanky and took the glass back. "Fingerprints. Yours. Now, that I've got them, there's no telling where they'll turn up if you double cross me."

Delgado got up and left, and as he did, he gave Dr. Cassidy sitting in the car a dirty look.

Cassidy turned away.

DiMaggio noticed as he got behind the driver's seat. "What?"

"I hate this."

"Which part? Being shot at and pissing your pants? Or the guilt for getting my partner killed and me fired?"

"You still don't get it, you schmuck! I am a doctor and I just violated every tenet of doctor-patient confidentiality."

DiMaggio's mouth was stuck wide open. He blinked a few times as if the enormity of what he was about to say had gotten stuck in his throat. Finally, he spit it out. "Well, big whoop-de-fucking-do there, doc. I've got my partner of eight years burned beyond recognition. She had her whole fucking life ahead of her. She never got to spank a bad boy CEO, mayor, or senator. She never had a chance to live in a mini-mansion or have a three-hundred-fifty-thousand-dollar AMG or ski St. Moritz. But tomorrow, what's left of her, of this vibrant young woman, goes in the ground, and I can't even be there because I am somehow stuck running for my life for the last 4 days with you... so shut the fuck up!"

19. Ashes to Ashes

A small group of family and friends stood graveside at Calvary Cemetery as a white casket with brass handles was lowered into eternity. Surrounding the grave were over fifty police officers, most of them detectives with their black-banded gold badges hung on their regulation blue uniforms. Because she hadn't died in the line of duty, this was not an inspector's funeral, so the officers and detectives were there on their own time and out of their own sense of loyalty.

Grimes was also there but not purely out of loyalty. His attention was more focused on who else was there rather than the proceedings. Actually, who specifically was not there. "DiMaggio didn't have the guts to show." he said to Henry, a member of DiMaggio's squad.

Henry turned his head, first looking left and then right. "I can't believe Mike's not here either; they were so close."

"He's a cold man." Grimes walked away, confident that he had accomplished his mini-mission to cast suspicion on DiMaggio.

IQ.

As he watched the Chief pick up a rose and walked to the line of mourners, Henry held back what he was thinking, because he hoped he was wrong. For many cops, "the life" was all there was, and losing their job was sometimes the kick in the pants that made a few go over the edge – get lost in the bottle or worse. DiMaggio could have gone that way. He tried to erase the chill that the imagined taste of the oiled, cold steel of a gun barrel gave him and instead focus on the sniffling, teary-eyed Julio Hernandez, the admin clerk for the squad, as he approached Maggie's grave.

The immediate family lined up and started placing roses in the grave. A crying, older woman kissed a black shrouded picture of Officer Reade that was on an easel next to the grave. Since it was a closed-casket funeral, this was the only way for them to see her.

Bill Owens stood in line three behind Grimes and watched as the chief placed a rose near the picture of Reade and left in a waiting car.

Later as the mourners were filing past the parked cars on one of the little roads that wound through the cemetery, Bill caught up to Henry. "So, Grimes stayed for the whole thing."

"Yeah, go figure. All the other brass just showed at the church."

"So why do you think he came here?"

"He was hoping Mike showed," Henry said.

"Why do you think he would hope that?"

"We're all worried about him. Grimes just has a funny way of showing it, I guess."

Eric decided it was time to convert his appearance from U.S. Army to tribesman. As they passed the carcass of a goat lying on the side of the road, he had an idea. He pulled over, got out of the Wagoneer, and drew his knife.

Ten minutes later, Kalhan was negotiating with a local merchant in a small town, while the rest waited in the car. He returned with the traditional Shalwar baggy pants, Kaftan, and a Khapol hat. Eric went around the back of the car and changed into the local garb but kept his uniform with the goat-blood-soaked knife hole in the chest. That way if he needed to be a soldier again, to get through U.S. checkpoints or blend in to a patrol, he could. On the other hand, if locals searched the car, they would think the uniform was a prized souvenir from killing an American invader, which would enhance his stature in their eyes. His weapons – the sniper rifle, M4, and 9 mm – would be seen as further spoils of his victory.

Kalhan was driving them to a place in Khost where one could get passage to Qatar. From there, Eric figured he could wrangle passage for himself, Setara, and their son back to America or, more probably as he was now a deserter, Canada, where they could stake out a life. Felba slept as Kalhan drove through the night on the off-road terrain of Kandahar province to the Pakistani border. Setara had the baby in a sling-like swaddle and they both slept with her head on Eric's shoulder. As he closed his eyes, his cheek on the top of her head, his arm coming all the way around and holding Setara's hand on the baby's bottom in the sling, he couldn't help but think of the last time he had seen her.

IDL

It was after dark when Eric reached the village. Up until now he and Setara had "courted" during stolen minutes of daylight with each encounter finding more and more resonance between them. By this point nine months ago, their physical relationship had advanced to hugs and kisses. As "junior high school" as it should have been for Eric, who had soldier's leaves and liberties in some of the tawdriest cities in the world, where a fist full of fifties got you anything you wanted, it was a world of difference with Setara. Even the most innocent touch and platonic hug was supercharged and electric.

They both knew that the reason for this clandestine meeting at night, well after everyone went to sleep, was to delve deeper into their urges.

"Eric," was all she said as she grabbed him and kissed him. It surprised him, but he loved it. He held her tight and kissed her deeply and for a very long time.

It was far from a romantic setting but Setara watched, often stroking his arm or leg as Eric laid out a bedroll and placed a "buddy bag" sleeping bag over it. They nestled down in the clearing in the high bush that had become their Garden of Eden. Instinctively, Setara shed her clothes in a manner that did the impossible – her sudden sensuality made Eric even more excited than he had been.

Many times, each of them took turns trying to muffle the sighs and moans coming from the other. Usually with a gentle hand but most times with a full, Hollywood-style kiss.

For Eric, just looking at her while they were making love was almost too much for him. He couldn't get as close as he wanted to her, even when they were well entangled and not even air could get between their passion-pressed bodies. And then for those few moments, they both abandoned themselves in total release, becoming one, feeling as one and breathing as one.

They were both filled with throbbing excitement and couldn't wait to experience their passion again and again, using every opportunity to achieve that oneness before the break of dawn.

As their afterglow was met by the predawn glow of early sunrise, they reluctantly parted. "I do not want to leave you," Setara said, stroking his cheek.

"I will be back the day after tomorrow."

She smiled and kissed him once again.

"Setara, I said this to you once, when we first met, but in English. Now..." Even though it was something he had always thought was corny, suddenly it seemed like the most perfect way to honor her. He got down on one knee, grabbed her hand, and looked into her eyes. "Will you marry me and let me take you home with me as my wife?"

Her eyes opened wide and she pulled him into her, his face against her breasts. "Yes, yes Eric, I will be your wife and I will follow you anywhere you want to go, forever."

Although neither had planned on it, they were soon making love one last time.

Finally completely dressed, they agreed to one more hug and then this time, they would both walk off in opposite directions. On their last two tries, one of them calling back to the other had foiled this parting and they ran and embraced each other. The third time they resisted the urge and they were both off.

A minute later, the sniper returned to the love nest. In the emerging morning light, he had one task left to do. As a sniper, he instinctively policed his brass when he left a shooting perch. His current policing action was satisfied when he retrieved three used condoms. *Only three?* was his brief thought as he walked away, actually stopping himself from whistling as he walked.

IQ

Over the next two days when Eric's unit was out on patrol, not much happened except for one instance that had a profound effect on him. It was the moment when he finally understood the reason why, somewhere back in ancient history, back in the sixties, the peaceniks' rallying cry was "Make Love Not War."

His love for Setara was affecting his every thought, every action, and every deed on this patrol. Having had sex with his soulmate did not abate his urges, but in fact, it made his desire to be with her more intense than before. Try as he might, he just couldn't focus on the war.

On point during this very mission, he was scanning the area through his scope looking for enemy operatives who might be trying to infiltrate his patrol's perimeter. That was his job – unit security. The long reach. He could kill a bad guy at two thousand yards, over a mile. A distance too far for the enemy to be able to inflict harm on him and his men.

He found two targets at seven-hundred-fifty yards out, scurrying through the underbrush, one of them carrying a satchel. Experience had taught him that the satchel was probably an Improvised Explosive Device. The jihadist was probably going to sneak close enough to the American troops for either a suicide attack or else remote detonation of the IED at a moment chosen for the greatest body count.

As his spotter Ortiz zeroed in on the intruders, he challenged Eric. "Bet you a beer you can't get 'em both with a two-second recycle."

Eric lined up the one with the bag in the crosshairs of his very narrow field-of-view scope. "Ready. You count it off."

"One..."

Eric fired and hit the target dead center. He quickly acquired the second rag head, who instinctively turned to see where the shot came from.

"Two..." Ortiz called out.

Eric caught sight of his face as the young man turned and instinctively dropped his aim down and to the right and fired. The young man was spooked by the high-caliber bullet pulverizing the rock so near his face. With the grit stinging his cheeks, he was motivated to leave quickly. A few seconds later, Eric hit the satchel center mass and it exploded harmlessly.

His spotter just looked at him in disbelief. "What the fuck Eric?" It was one of the few times Eric had ever missed!

They walked away in silence. Ortiz was still shaking his head in disbelief. For his part, Eric kept picturing the stunned face of Setara's brother Behzad he saw through the scope and worked to calm his nerves over almost killing him.

10

The incident with Setara's brother and the way his love for her was affecting his work was something he had never experienced before. Nothing had ever gotten between him and job. So, the first thing he did when he returned to camp was approach his commanding officer.

"Sir, the end of my third tour is coming up, and I'd like to ask permission to request to be transferred stateside, sir."

"Eric, you are one of the best men in my unit. You've volunteered for many 'one way' jobs. Hell, soldier if anyone has enough tours and time in theater to rotate out, it's you."

"Thank you, sir. I was thinking that with your recommendation, I could serve at Fort Benning as a sniper instructor or assigned to the Army Marksmanship unit, since I already have the President's 100 tab." *And marry Setara and bring her home with me.* He did not verbalize that last thought.

"Ronson, nobody deserves a ticket home more than you, but request denied. I'm sorry."

Put off, but still at attention, Eric pushed. "Sir, may I ask why, sir."

"I'm sorry but the Pentagon is ratcheting up operations in this area. In fact, effective immediately and until further notice, all leaves, transfers, and furloughs are canceled, Sergeant," was all the light colonel said, but to Eric's heart it was a virtual death sentence.

What he didn't know was that it was going to get worse. His whole unit was being reassigned to the other side of Afghanistan, as far from Setara as he could get. Furthermore, there wasn't time to get word to her before they bugged out. He went into an immediate depression. He could only hope she would hear of the Americans pulling out. Or at minimum understand, or as Eric would have it, "know" that he would never just up and abandon her.

The Jeep Wagoneer bounced over a shell hole and took Eric out of his thoughts. The baby cooed. He cooed back and then adjusted his grip on the woman who was the center of his life. He did a conscious check that this moment, the one he was in right now, wasn't a dream. Satisfied, he felt the warm security of having his whole world, wife-to-be and baby, in his arms. From that safe vantage point, he returned to his thoughts, remembering when he wasn't sure he'd ever see her again.

10

The two weeks he had spent on the far edge of Afghanistan at the new FOB was already a living hell for Eric. He thought of Setara constantly. One night he was summoned to the command post and found a contractor standing with the colonel. Most of these private contractors worked for logistical supply and operations companies that had contracts with the DOD, or at least that was their cover story and they stuck to it. In fact, they were really representatives of three letter agancies or black ops units like "Delta" or the SEALS. This one was no exception.

"Ronson, this is Otterman." The colonel said.

Since he was not in uniform, Eric shook Otterman's hand.

"Eric, do you know what Otterman does?"

"Sir, his main job is to fill in all the behind-the-scenes aspects of the war, freeing up the canon fodder, like me, to earn my hazardous duty pay, sir."

Since most contractors were ex-military, Otterman knew exactly how Ronson felt. "That's the way I felt when I was recon." He turned to the CO saying, "He'll do fine, Colonel."

Not that he had a say in it, but Eric didn't really mind. He had been on many joint operations. In fact, a year ago he had made friends with another kind of "contractor" like this fellow on a "Spook Op" when they got pinned down by lots of bad guys. Luck was with them that night and he and the mission runner, Brad, made it out alive.

"So, Mr. Otterman, what's got a private security contractor with a cushy job like yours risking his butt at a Forward Operating Base this evening?" Eric said.

"I'm here to enlist you and your spotter to help clear an area where our trucks are getting harassed, hijacked, and blown up."

"Sounds like a fun few days out in the country; when do we bug out, sir?"

"One hour, Sergeant!" The Colonel said.

The patrol was uneventful, and that gave the men time to talk. At one point, Eric found out that this Otterman often went to the area near Setara's village. As soon as he had time, Eric sat down and wrote the note of his life. He poured his heart, his dreams, and his soul into the smudgy-penciled missive in passable written Dari. The contractor promised to deliver the message if he got to within five klicks of the village. "As long as it is not in enemy hands, that is," he added.

⚰

The shooting of an episode of *Law and Order, CSI,* or *Special Victims Unit* or some such version – with all the necessary trucks, trailers, and lights – was tying up traffic in Federal Circle as Owens navigated through the gawking crowd watching the TV lawyers and cops do a scene on the steps of the state courthouse. Presumably, the characters had just left a courtroom in the building in the background. In reality, the show couldn't get within one hundred feet of an actual courtroom. The courtroom interior sets were located in studios that had originally been shipping company offices on a Hudson River pier. But every episode had a "walk and talk" segment somewhere in the court district to make it seem like the intrepid cops and lawyers are right there in the real heart of the criminal justice system.

Away from the crowds, Bill Owens approached the only TV lawyer who was actually a real lawyer. One whose commercials ran on all the cable station reruns of the *Law and Order* shows. Still, he did have the kind of sharp, distinguished features and classic frat boy waspy-ness that could have landed him a role in Hollywood. As Owens approached the man in the Armani suit, he noticed the man had perfectly styled hair and a white shirt so crisp you could cut yourself on it, which brought out his Florida tan, "Miles Bennett?" He flashed his badge.

"Yes. What can I do for you, Detective...?"

"Owens, Bill Owens. Just like to ask you a few questions about a Doctor Cassandra Cassidy."

"I don't represent Dr. Cassidy and therefore cannot speak as her attorney."

"I know, but I love the gossip columns and you two are quite the hot item."

"And why is that any concern of yours, Detective?"

"Well sir, I actually need to talk to her, and her office and staff haven't heard from her in days. I thought due to the nature of your relationship with Dr. Cassidy, you might know how I can contact her."

Owens knew Miles was a sharp cookie of a lawyer and that his radar was always beeping whenever he was close to a cop. It was understandable; they were usually his adversaries in most criminal cases where he took up the defense of the accused. Owens expected some kind of tactical diversion to his question, like Miles demanding a warrant or what the basis of the question was, but Owens read a trace of concern on the man's face.

"You know, I am a lawyer and I don't give testimony outside the proper venue."

"Yeah, I got that, but you are also her boyfriend... so if you have personal knowledge of her whereabouts, that would make you a material witness if this were a case..."

"But it's not, so why should I cooperate?"

"Because you are also an officer of the court. You are high profile and we can make this all kinds of official, but what with all the publicity and everything..."

"That's you trying to get me to cooperate?"

"I am betting that maybe you are as concerned as I am, unless of course you know that she is safe and sound."

Miles looked away. To Owens it looked as though he had requested a sidebar with his conscience. A moment later he turned and Owens saw a different, more relaxed expression on the counselor's face. "I haven't seen her in five days."

"Where and when?"

"The night of the opera. We went to Trattoria Del'Arte afterwards and then back to my penthouse. She left at seven a.m. after we spoke about the charity event we were supposed to attend that evening."

"That was the last time you talked to her?"

"Yes."

"Do you usually leave separately?"

"I'm divorced, Detective, and I make no secret of our relationship. We don't sneak around."

"Not what I am implying, Mr. Bennett, but both your offices are downtown from your penthouse... and your doorman said you usually share a town car in the morning."

"I'll make sure to remember him when it comes time to stuff the Christmas tips envelopes."

"Don't be too hard on Julio. I flashed tin and he cooperated with the law. So once again, why leave separately on the last day anyone saw her?"

"It was her uptown day."

"Uptown?"

"She has two offices, one midtown, one down in Murray Hill."

"Are you concerned?"

"Truth be told, we didn't so much discuss the upcoming charity event as argue over it. She didn't want to go, and I had already bought a ten-thousand-dollar table."

"Ouch."

"It got pretty heated. I just figured she was pissed and giving me the silent treatment, you know. Besides, I was on the West Coast for three days. Just red-eyed in this morning. But now that you say her office doesn't know where she is, I admit you have me worried." Bennett furrowed his brow.

"Anything else?" Owens could see that volunteering information was not in the lawyer's make up. "Look, I'm trying to find her. She may be in trouble."

"What do you mean 'trouble'?"

"Not with the law. She may be in hiding, in need of help." Owens saw the man capitulate as the counselor's whole body language changed as he took a deep breath.

"Well, a few days before, she called me late at the office, which never happens. She said she had a bad day. She sounded pretty upset and that wasn't like her at all. She is normally like a rock. So I thought she was just looking for sympathy – you know, to bury the hatchet – but we had said some pretty nasty things that morning. I wasn't ready to capitulate, so I kind of blew her off. Maybe now, I'm thinking, it was something else."

"But..." Owens referred to his notes. "But you said you went to the opera, did you also go to the event?"

"No, the Boys Club dinner was what we fought about. She was still pissed... no, not as much pissed as... as... pre-occupied. In any event, she must have gone back to her place in Westchester that night."

"Been in that dog house myself... Do you know the address of the uptown clinic?"

"I was only there once, over on East Fifty-Fourth, between East End and the river I think, red brick, white stoop."

Owens took out his card. "If you hear from her or find out where she is..."

"Certainly; now may I ask a question? What is this about?"

"She may have some information about a missing detective. Do you know a Judge Jenkins?"

"Yes. Obviously from court and he was also a member of my club."

"Did you know he is deceased?"

"Yes. A tawdry affair if you can believe the headlines in the papers."

"Was Dr. Cassidy treating the judge?"

"No. I don't think so. At least she never mentioned it. But if he were her patient she wouldn't have; her work demanded extreme confidentiality, but it's possible."

"Why possible?"

"I introduced them once at a bar association dinner. They chatted and he asked what she did. He may have decided to see her professionally from that discussion."

"Did Doctor Cassidy know Mrs. Jenkins?"

"I don't think so. His wife never attended business things like that; she only came out for charity events, so no, I don't think Cassandra knew her. What does she have to do with your missing detective?"

"That's what I am trying to figure out. It could be just a coincidence that they have both been out of reach. If I hear anything, I'll let you know. Thanks for your time."

ᴅ᷉

Owens made it back to his desk a half hour later; Marcus Towne was already there. Owens hitched his head toward the interrogation room and they both went in. "Did you bring your notebook?"

Towne took his pad out of his back pocket and flipped the pages.

Owens filled the young officer in. "All the records of the Jenkins case were impounded by the chief of detectives as some kind of evidence against Mike, so what you have there is the only record. First, at what address was the judge found?"

Towne flipped to his notes from his ambulance call response.

"Let's see, responded to the call at 8:01 p.m. 10 days ago, at five twenty three East Fifty Fourth Street. We rolled up and the ambulance was already..."

Owens took out his notebook, "Hold it; what was that address again?"

"Five two three East Five Four; why?"

"That's the doctor's office. So, that's why Mike was interested in her. And now they are both missing."

"That wasn't any doctor's office; the place was empty."

"It was a multi-story building wasn't it?"

"Yeah, five floor brownstone. So who's missing again?"

168

"Detective DiMaggio, and a doctor – a psychiatrist – from that location."

"When did they disappear?"

"Five days ago."

"And Reade died five days ago!" Towne added as he closed his notebook.

"Marcus, I want you to go back to your job. Don't think about this; don't ask around; just drop it. I got this. I'll let you know what's going on as I find out. But I want you to keep your nose clean."

"Wait a minute. I can't just turn this off. Something's not right here. I came to you with this. How can I just walk away?"

"Look, I can take this further than you. I know more people and have more favors owed me. Besides if I wind up dead, I'll need you unconnected to me to find out who or what got me killed."

IID.

As he walked out of the interrogation room, Towne still didn't like the idea of handing over his investigation, but he reluctantly agreed because Owens had a way about him. Probably the same thing that made him the most decorated black detective ever on the NYPD, he thought as he smacked his notebook against the palm of his left hand.

20. Deal with the Devil

As they drove the rocky, uneven road, being jostled side by side, Felba and Setara told Eric stories of the last nine months. Eric found out that Otterman didn't get to Setara's village until a week ago, eight months late.

Eric couldn't fault the man though. For all Otterman knew, Eric might have already been re-billeted through there and had seen Setara in person. But Eric also understood that this was covered under the Soldier's Creed; that you never let your buddy down. This was especially true with battlefield promises, which carried with them the weight of imminent death, raising any promise to the potential level of "granting of a last wish," so he delivered the message, even as overdue as it was.

"I didn't want to talk to him, but when he mentioned that he was a friend of yours, Eric, I brought him to her." Felba said from the front seat.

Eric now knew Otterman found Setara pregnant, about to pop and in hiding. He probably surmised that it was Eric's kid, which would have also explained why she was living in the cold, damp root cellar of a dilapidated lean-to. Otherwise, due to the strict culture, either she would have already been married or else she would have been killed by her father or brothers, the victim of an honor killing.

"The man, this Otter Man handed me the piece of paper and left. Felba stayed with me and my heart jumped when I realized it was from you. I saw it was dated eight months ago," Setara said as she started sobbing.

"See," Felba said, "she started that when she first read your note. I get nervous; I tell her, quiet, don't cry, before someone is knowing our hiding place." Felba placed her hand on her sister's arm. "I ask her, 'Is from him?' I could not see in the dim lamp, trying to see. But Setara cannot stop crying and crying. She just nod."

Setara chimed in, in Dari, "Felba was asking, 'Let me see, let me see,' then she grabbed the note from me fearing it was an official notice of your death."

Felba continued in her English. "But as soon as I read, I know then why my sister was crying on your letter. You were coming for her,"

"Yes, that I would 'rotate out' on the fifteenth of the month," Eric said.

Felba grabbed her sister's hand and smiled, continuing this time in Dari. "Forgive me, but your written Dari is a little difficult to read but the part where you said you were going to marry her and bring her home to America was very clear."

"Felbie and I didn't know what 'rotate' meant but whatever it was, we knew it was happening yesterday, the fifteenth of March." Setara actually laughed, safe now that all had come true.

⚮

Felba, facing the backseat, rested her head on the back of the passenger seat and sighed as she watched her sister and the soldier hug and stroke her nephew. She was elated and so thankful as she heard her sister laugh for the first time since all this began. Once the pregnancy threatened to become obvious, she knew Setara had to leave her home; it would have been the duty of the men in their family to kill her to preserve the family honor, so she had helped her sister escape. Felba held no allegiance to this tradition and loved her sister more than her father, who at best was an authoritarian who barely managed to feed his two daughters and three sons.

While Setara was still hiding in the village, before she had escaped to the far away town where they just found her, she had begun bringing food and clothing to her sister at night and other odd times. She saw how Setara had dealt with his absence and silence by convincing herself that he died in battle, maybe even killed by one of her two brothers who went with the mujahidin.

Now her sister was happy, she saw the way Setera looked at the American, it compelled her to speak, "Eric, you should know that my sister knew that only death could separate you from her," Felba said.

Setara nodded, "I couldn't bear the thought of you dying and not knowing you had left a son or daughter." She nuzzled their son. And said a little Islamic prayer of thanks that they were all finally together.

As he looked at his son, he thought of Behzad, Setara's brother. He still chilled at the memory of how the young man looked in the crosshairs of his sniper's scope. "Setara, tell me about your brother, Behzad."

"Bezy? You want to know about him?"

"Yes, he seemed very mad at me at the well."

"You remember that?" She smiled.

"He looked like he wanted to kill me."

"Bezy? That's very funny. He is a kitten. Afraid of his own shadow."

Kalhan chimed in from the front seat, "Behzad is a poet, a lover, not a fighter. He has no bones in his back."

"Mother took them away." Felba giggled and all three joined in.

Seeing the look on Eric's face, Setara wanted to bring him into the family joke. "Behzad is still tied to my mother's pesh-daaman."

Eric tried to reconcile their description of a young man tied to his mother's apron strings with the young roadside bomber he almost shot. "I asked because I thought I saw him once while I was on patrol."

Felba laughed. "Did you see our mother as well?"

Setara felt the need to explain further. "Eric, Behzad is... is... not of proper thinking. He was very sick as a baby. He can never leave my mother. He can not operate... er, function in the world."

"So he would never be out on his own, out of your village?"

"He is not capable of that."

"It sure looked like him."

Felba chimed in, "Arman!"

Setara agreed. "Arman." She then turned to Eric, "Felbie says, and I agree, you probably saw Arman our cousin, he and Bezy look like twins. He is a mujahedeen we never see him anymore."

Relieved to his core, Eric smiled, "Then that's who I must have seen."

While Setara was paying attention to her baby, Felba shared another story with Eric. On one of their "encounters," Eric had given Setara a wire with two clips on the end that when attached to a car battery would charge the iPod in an hour or so. From time to time, Felba hooked this wire up to abandoned or damaged cars that littered the roads beyond the village. Eric's music had replaced the "filmi" music, which was imported from India, as the only music she or her sister had ever heard. Although frowned upon, this music from the sound tracks of Bollywood movies was all they had growing up in Afghanistan.

"Eric, many nights I would come to Seti and find her holding the ear pieces to her belly and playing your Western music, the music of his father, to the baby in her belly." Felba was now the one laughing.

Eric was warmed by this whole series of revelations but he still had one question, so he asked in Dari, "So Setara, how did you get to the place where we found you?"

"My dear sister, Felba, approached a woman from a British TV crew. They had just come from that place to our village and then were going back there. The woman knew of the space, one I could hide in, and told

Felba where it was and about another girl who had stayed there until her man came for her. Felba brought the TV people to where I was hiding in our village and, in the middle of the night, I got into the back of their truck. When we got there, the TV people left me with some food and water. They told the woman from this village about me. She had helped the other girl, and she helped me when the baby came and brought me food every few days. She is a very good person."

"I owe her a lot," Eric said.

After the stories, they all fell asleep as Kalhan drove through the night. They were awakened as they came to a roadblock of sorts. Men with guns, camels, and Jeeps. Kalhan explained that the tribal chief of this part of the border was very appreciative of bribes for safe passage into or out of Pakistan. Eric had about one thousand dollars on him, but knew he'd need that to get back to North America somehow. "How much?" Eric said in Dari.

Kalhan looked at the sniper rifle in the back of the jeep.

"That's worth a few grand!" Eric wasn't crazy about giving this Pashtun fighter a U.S. weapon that could be used against his guys, but on the other hand, there were millions of Russian, Czech, Chinese, British, American, and French guns everywhere in this perpetually war-torn, rubble load of a country, and the trade would preserve his cash.

"Okay, but no ammo. He'd be able to pick us off at two thousand yards!" He handed the prized rifle to Kalhan and watched as he walked over to the elder tribesman.

The older man took the weapon in his hands as if it were a newborn baby. It gave Eric guilt pangs; a sniper never surrenders his weapon, but he was no longer a Recon Ranger. He was now a father and had to think of his family first.

The next thing that happened surprised him. The old man started shelling out money. At first, Eric thought that this Kalhan guy was a real shark and good negotiator. He got their passage and cash for the rifle. There were a few more seconds of conversation and Kalhan walked back to the jeep.

Eric was amused as he nodded saying, "Nice! You got him to pay you for the rifle as well?"

"Not exactly."

The sudden look on Kalhan's face sent a chill through Eric and armed men quickly surrounded him and the Jeep. They opened the doors and ordered Setara and his son out. Two men had their guns trained on Eric.

Felba was out of the car in an instant and screaming at Kalhan. "What did you do?" When he didn't answer, she ran to her sister, who was being led away. She pushed away an armed man and he responded by slamming the butt of his rifle across her face. She went down and Kalhan ran to her. Through her cries and spitting of blood, she pounded on him, screaming in his face.

Eric looked for options. The guy closest to him had his safety on so he could probably move against him first and then take out the two others by him. The other two guys farther away were hustling Setara to a tent. She clutched the baby tight in her arms as they pulled her along. She strained to turn her head to look at him and he could see the fear in her eyes. From this distance, he couldn't shoot the men without endangering her and his son. If he still had his rifle maybe, but it was in the old man's hands and the ammo was under the trunk lid in the Jeep. Out to the corner of his eye he saw Kalhan shove Felba, still resisting him, into the Jeep and speed off in the direction from which they came. He was looking for another way to save Setara when suddenly his world went black.

21. Hunting

Owens popped the top off a beer, plopped down in his recliner, grabbed the remote, and put on ESPN. The end of a Miles Bennett commercial burned off and the next was an ad for timeshares in Florida at Golden Lakes. As he took that first long draft from the bottle, it hit him. He immediately had his cell out and was dialing.

"Miles," the voice said over the phone.

"Bill Owens here."

"Did you find her?" Miles' voice was on the verge of relief.

"Not yet, but did she ever mention a summer house or ski house or some family place she could be holed up in?"

"Wow. Umm. You know, once she mentioned that her father had a hunting cabin somewhere upstate. I can't remember where. But he's been dead for a while and she never mentioned going there. Maybe it's not in the family anymore."

"What kind of hunter?"

"Deer, I think?"

"Thanks, I'll let you know."

ID

Eric had a concussion and he was going in and out of consciousness. The stories of the last nine months Setara and Felba had told him on the long car ride were dissolving through his mental haze. He awoke in the midst of a quiet dream, of Setara with the headphones on her belly, which gave way to a pounding headache. The back of his head where the rifle butt hit him was swollen to the size of an egg. He heard voices outside and woozily got up to assess his situation. He found he was shackled to a ring bolted into the wall of the shed or whatever type of structure he was in. He wrinkled his nose and almost gagged at the smells that assaulted his senses – a mixture of urine, feces, and grease. In the room, he saw two oil drums, some chain, like the one around his ankle, and some tools on a cart well out of his reach on the other side of the room. On the dirt floor by his feet was an old frayed prayer mat, and his hands were tied together in front of him with a thick rope.

That was their first mistake.

He put his foot on the mat and pulled up on the edge, tearing off a five foot by one-inch strip down the length of the old rug. He did the same thing two more times. Knotting the three together, he tied another knot forming something like a sling around a small stone from the floor. He moved as close to the tool cart as the chain wrapped around his ankle would allow. Then he put the end of the material under his foot and using the remaining length of the strip, he swung the rock end around and around, finally letting it go.

Unfortunately, it hit the tool cart and then fell to the floor. He froze for a few breathless seconds, but the sound didn't seem to alert anyone. On his next try, he crouched down low, swinging the rock sideways. He caught the upright of the tool cart and the rock wrapped around the leg. When he pulled the cart toward him, a hacksaw was right on top. Holding it between his knees, he rubbed the rope back and forth on the saw's teeth until his hands were free. He then used the hacksaw to the cut through chain where it met his leg, and in four minutes he was free. He took a chance and peeked out of the door, seeing several men outside. He looked back in the room.

A short time later, a man entered the room, approached the American shackled to the wall and kicked him. Eric feigned awakening with the pain of his injuries. With the rope now loose around his wrists and the chain simply lying over and between his ankles, he whispered something in Urdu. "Where's my money? My ten thousand dollars?"

His ploy worked. The man, curious that there could be money somewhere, leaned down to hear the barely audible drivel. Eric swung both fists clenched together and side-cocked the man, knocking him out, and sending him over on his side. He pulled the man's sidearm from his waist and found a knife under his shirt. The knife was good – it was a silent weapon. He laid the guy out on the mat where he had been restrained and put the rope around his hands and chain between his feet. He took a position by the door then called out in Urdu. "Help."

The closest man to the shed was first through the door. Eric pounced from behind and covered the dying man's mouth as he slid the knife between his third and fourth rib, piercing his heart. He grabbed the man's rifle as he threw the body to the side and waited for the next guy to come through the door. When the huge giant of a man entered, Eric just hauled off with the end of the rifle and went for the cheap seats as he swung it into the man's throat, crushing his larynx and stifling any scream as he went down. Eric took his AK-47 and pistol as well as the man's plastic water bottle. Eric drank it empty, cut out a hole in the bottom with the knife, and grabbed a roll of tape from the tool cart.

A minute later Eric put on the man's hat, threw his kaftan over his shoulders and went outside. No one who was farther away was interested in where the other two were. Moving through the camp, he tried to figure out where the chief of the tribe was. He saw one of the

guys who was with the old man when he made the deal
with Kalhan. He was easy to spot because his Khapol
hat was a rare red color. He approached him and by the
time the man figured out that Eric wasn't one of them,
he was feeling the pinch of the knife over his heart.
Whispering, Eric asked in Urdu, "Where is the chief?"

At first, the man shook his head to say he wouldn't
tell, but when Eric pushed the knife partway into his
skin, the man flinched. Eric said, "Tell me or I go all
the way in."

"There." He pointed to a building ten yards away
with a few guys out front. Eric said, "Don't fight me or
I'll kill you." He put his other hand on the man's neck
applying pressure to his carotid artery, and in fifteen
seconds, he slumped, still alive but unconscious. For
some unfathomable reason, Eric couldn't bring himself to kill him.

The three guys outside the building weren't as
lucky. Eric lifted the rifle with the improvised silencer
on the end from under the kaftan and fired. The first
man went down, and the man next to him turned when
he heard only the thumping sound of the bullets slamming into his friend, presenting his face toward the gun
that had just fired. Eric quickly double-tapped him in
the forehead. The splatter of his blood and brain matter
brought the third man to a firing position with his AK-47.
Before he could pull the trigger, Eric put a three round
burst in his neck and he went down. The business end of
Eric's rifle smoked as the plastic bottle "ghetto" silencer
wobbled when the barrel's heat loosened the tape. He
entered the chief's lair and popped a man standing next
to the tribal leader. The sound and movement caught
the old man's attention and he turned toward Eric.

Eric could see the combination of fear and hatred in
the man's eyes. Maybe the guy he just killed was his son
or something, but Eric didn't give a shit; he wanted his
son and woman back. "Where are the woman and child?"
he said as he nudged the rifle into the man's chest.

Iℚ◣

The old guy's first thought was that he had let his greed defeat him. He didn't kill this American because he was worth much to the Taliban, who could use him for propaganda or behead him as a warning to the infidels. He had fought colonizing forces for five decades. The Soviets had sent whole companies of soldiers after him in the eighties and he survived, decimating most of their ranks while giving them only the satisfaction of taking his smallest finger. But he had never had a desperate father holding a gun on him, having just dispatched his most capable guards and nephew. For a second, he flashed on what a dirty business this was, fulfilling the devil's quota of flesh. He should have never gotten involved with this sort of human trafficking. Again he focused on defeat, how his greed now accomplished what the Russians and Americans could not. Still, the aging mujahidin was not about to cooperate with this invading godless infidel.

Iℚ◣

Eric saw the intransigence in the old warrior's eyes. Then the man's eyes made the subtlest of shifts and Eric immediately read their importance. He turned and sprayed the room, the doorway and the two men who were entering. They folded over in a bloody heap. The gun was louder now, but he hoped the sound didn't escape the walls.

All of a sudden, an armed man stormed into the room, followed by another who was training his gun out toward the compound. "Khan, the prisoner has..."

Eric crouched low and fired, silencing the first man. As he did, he saw the chief grab under his kaftan for a gun from his belt; Eric hadn't had time to frisk him. Meanwhile, startled by the death of the man in front of him, the second man was bringing his rifle around. Eric flung himself down on his back behind a piece of furniture, putting one into the chief's stomach as he landed hard on the floor. He then propped his gun on the top of the wooden chest and returned his aim to the doorway, taking out the last of the two men.

He quickly glanced around the room to be sure the threat was neutralized and then ran over to the chief and grabbed him by his kaftan, lifting his head and shoulders off the floor. He shook him as he said, "Don't die. Don't die. Tell me where my baby is!"

The old man coughed up blood, the hate in his eyes suddenly froze, and Eric dropped his body to the floor. Eric pounded his fist into his own forehead.

Then he had a thought and headed to the window in back. On the way out, he dropped the temporarily silenced rifle and picked up his sniper rifle, which was leaning against the wall.

He went back to the guy in the red hat that he had spared. He slapped his cheeks. "Wake up. C'mon, wake up!"

The man was groggily coming to. Eric had his knife at his throat.

"The woman and the baby, where are they?"

The man hesitated.

"Look, I didn't kill you before, but if you don't tell me where my wife and baby are, I'll slice your throat from ear to ear."

"They are your family?" the man said nervously.

"Yes, and I will do whatever it takes to get to them. Everyone in the camp is dead, even the chief. Everyone except you. For now."

The man looked around – nothing was moving and there was no sound. He looked at Eric.

"I didn't want to kill anybody, that's why I saved you. They fought but I won. Where is my family?" He prodded the man's neck a little with the knife.

"They are headed for America."

Eric thought he misheard the man and repeated in English, "America? Where are they now? I'll kill you right here if you don't tell me."

"On the road to Khost."

"How was the chief getting them out of the country?"

"I'd rather not say..."

"Would you rather meet Allah, you stupid fuck?" Eric prodded the knife further into the man's neck, drawing a little blood for emphasis.

He winced from the stab, "Senegalese diplomat."

"Huh?"

"By boat from Karachi."

"Name?"

"I don't know. Khan knew."

"Okay, sleep tight." Eric put the knife over his heart. Then he pulled the same trick with his artery and the guy was out cold in twenty seconds.

He found a Daihatsu pickup with the key in the ignition. He floored it and left camp in the direction he thought they were headed when they drove in.

IQ

Early the next morning, Owens rode through DiMaggio's neighborhood, circling several blocks and crossing more than a few streets, but didn't see his car. He had checked the local garages too, but no one knew DiMaggio. Wherever he was, he must've taken his car. Owens wondered if perhaps it was at an airport. He'd have to figure out how to get that search done, masquerading it as some old case hunch when he got back to the office. He walked up the steps to DiMaggio's building at five Fifth Street and scanned the names above the mailboxes and doorbells. There it was – "Apt. 5 - DiMaggio."

He noticed a woman with shopping bags walking toward the building. She pulled out her keys to unlock the door as he came up the steps behind her. "Here, let me get that for you." He grabbed the door and held it open as she entered.

"Thank you." They were inside now and she realized it. "Do you live here?"

"No, my buddy does. Do you know Mike? We're cops," he said, holding out his badge and ID.

"Oh yes, the detective on the second floor back; he is very nice."

"Do you need any help getting upstairs?"

"No, thank you, I am actually right here in the back." She walked to the rear ground-floor apartment as Owens took the stairs. He had convinced Susan to lend him DiMaggio's apartment key, but she was somewhat embarrassed to admit she had misplaced the front door key.

Inside, just as he'd hoped, he did not find DiMaggio passed out on his couch or worse, rapidly redecorated furniture with a gun six inches from a gaping wound in his head. However, he also did not find anything to indicate that DiMaggio had intended to be away from home for an extended period of time. There were just too many things that didn't add up to that possibility. He found two suitcases, a garment bag, and even a carry-on bag that you wheel through the airport. He also found DiMaggio's shaving kit and other items he'd have taken with him if he were going away for a few days. One oddity was a gun display case on the wall over the fireplace with the weapon removed. From the inscribed plate, Owen saw it was an old cowboy gun.

As he walked down the steps, he concluded that if he was still alive, wherever Mike DiMaggio was, he hadn't planned on being there.

One hundred miles north of New York City, the smell of steak sizzling over a Coleman grill filled the air of the cabin. Along with two plates and two beers, the manila folder they got from the deputy mayor was on the table and several documents and pictures were spread out between DiMaggio and Cassidy.

Cassidy was finishing up a call, "...so Julia, Debbie will cover tonight's session, and you'll cover Debbie's session with Mr. Cranston on Monday. Don't forget now, write it down." She hung up. "Okay, it's all set, Julia thinks she's trading shifts with Debbie so there won't be any one there."

"Do you think you can handle this?" Mike said as he tapped the top of the A-1 Steak Sauce on the edge of the table in an attempt to loosen the cap that had glued itself onto the bottle over the last year.

"Of course. I am just concerned about him becoming suspicious when Julia isn't there tonight."

"If it gets dangerous, use the code word; I'll be in the next room."

"Will we be safe going back there?"

"It's good we are doing this at night and I'll have Delgado meet us uptown and drive us in." He sniffed the finally opened bottle to check if it had turned into a science project. "They won't be on the lookout for a blue Caddy."

"I hope you are right," she said as she got up to flip the steaks for lunch.

"So your guy from the two-oh-two area code, is that the Secretary?"

"I never heard that term before Delgado used it."

"How does he have the same tapes you do?"

"I don't know. There's only one machine. And those are the only copies."

"That you know of..."

"Well, yes, but the originals are under lock and key in my office."

"Who made the copies under the floor?"

"Only me. I made them myself at night or on weekends when no one was around."

"And the feds put in that system?"

"Yes."

"Did you see what they installed?"

"What do you mean?"

"Were there any black boxes, wall jacks, even maybe a transmitter hooked in somewhere?"

"Actually, I didn't supervise the installation. Hannah handled that."

"Wait. Hannah, the one that set you up?"

"Yeah, the sweetheart who framed me."

"So they could be tapping your video."

"It would explain why they never upgraded the equipment." Cassidy said.

22. A Friend In Need

Through a little bit of luck, using his ranger wrist Garmin GPS, and staying to the dirt roads at night, Eric managed to get to Karachi without further incident. He had learned from a few truckers that he met at various way stations along the road that cargo and other ships headed to North America usually came out of this port. He figured that's where Setara and his son would be boarding a ship, probably under the Senegalese flag, but of that he couldn't be sure.

Walking amidst the dockworkers and seamen who populated the port, he learned there was a Senegalese freighter, Grande Senegal, destined for Muscat leaving in the morning. If Setara and his son were headed to America, maybe there was a transfer point in that Omani city.

The ship was scheduled to leave port at 7:00 a.m. Eric watched the ship all night as the loading and stowage process wound down. At 6:30, a dark limousine with red, yellow, and green flags on the fender pulled up to the ship's gangway. His heart jumped as a dark-skinned man in a white linen suit emerged along with Setara carrying the baby in her arms. He led them to the gangway at the ship's rear. Had Eric not been trained in tactical advantage, his emotions would have had him running at full clip to grab them, but the security shack to the right of the boat dampened that foolhardy instinct.

It was a commercial freighter that had a limited number of cabins for people who either liked the adventure of the sea or else were afraid of flying and hated the cruise ship environment. Or as in this case, a government official, not wanting to be seen in the more public airports.

Eric was confused. Why would a Senegalese government official be taking Setara and his son on a boat to America through Oman? What was worth all the death and destruction in the village? Why did the old warlord die to protect this particular Senegal official? As he sat on the rise, two hundred yards from his woman and child, he reaffirmed in a cooler head that even though he desperately wanted to get them back, his tactical situation was indefensible. The boat was docked at the near end of the pier right next to the Port Security office. It was also the headquarters for the Pakistani military detachment at the port and at least twenty armed men were outside with their weapons. It left him no option but to hope that the African official was present to insure their safe transit, probably under diplomatic immunity. It became clear to him that he had to work this from the other end and to do that he needed to take a risk.

ID

Being assigned to a soft desk job was a bit of a drag to Brad Hamil. He had loved the action of being on the front lines, embedded with operational units, advising and observing "in-country" tactics. So much, in fact, that he took the Special Forces training "Q" course at the JFK Special Warfare Center, Fort Bragg, just to be accepted and gain "cred" with these recon ghosts. His area of expertise was the special op, where he usually led or co-commanded a small group of operators to carry out a surgical job that needed to be done. "Surgical" was the operative word: going in micro-force, small footprint, and laser-focused on a high-value target instead of using drones or pinpoint air strikes that left messy civilian casualties. For those surgical jobs, he was usually the mission runner or case officer, teamed with a group of operators – Special Forces guys who were the mechanics of insertion, detection, execution, and extraction. Unfortunately, on his last assignment, he caught a bullet and so until his tibia knitted, he couldn't engage in any extra-curricular activity that wasn't enhanced by a crutch. To Brad's frustration, his current "theater of operation" was confined to the Consulate Office of the United States in Kabul. Although anyone with seniority knew he was on the CIA payroll, the rank and file knew him as the special assistant to the charge d'affaires. It was a nebulous enough title that allowed him much flexibility on his whereabouts and not being held to attendance records at the small U.S. diplomatic outpost. His appearance with a crutch was easily explained, saying he had fallen trying to put a satellite dish on his house, essentially to get American NFL football games which were never aired on the TV channels in the "cricket crazy" country of Pakistan.

Brad's phone rang with a code name ID he hadn't seen in a while. "Big E! How are you and why are you calling me in op mode?"

"I'm in a little trouble, B, and I need a friend in a dry warm place with connections," Eric's voice said over the encrypted phone.

"Done. Where are you?"

"Karachi. The Kebob House restaurant."

"What the hell...?" but Brad knew if Eric was in Karachi and said he was in trouble, there was a good reason for him to be there. "I can get down there tomorrow."

"Better yet, can you get me up to you, quietly?"

"I can pull some strings. Are you undercover?"

"Deep. I need extraction and papers."

"Sit tight buddy. I got some clicks in Karachi. I'll call you back." Brad ended the call. There were many questions he didn't have to ask. He knew Eric wasn't on a mission, because a mission runner would have made this extraction call. Also, he knew Eric must have burned his Army connection, since again, they would be able to get him out. No, Eric was into something off the grid. Otherwise even the call would have come through normal channels instead of directly to his secure private phone. Brad knew that he was about to tap favors, favors that could get him fired or even shot, but the bond between the two of them was stronger than his career. He sent an open e-mail to an address known to him and only him as "benny69."

Back in Karachi, when Eric finished the call, he took a deep breath. He thought he could trust Brad, but still harbored the nagging notion that since Brad was a top CIA ops case officer, he might not want to jeopardize his network or his job for Eric, especially if he found out Eric was A.W.O.L. In his heart, Eric didn't believe that, but intellectually he planned for the double-cross anyway. He set himself up down the block from the restaurant, where he could watch any advance team or activity to arrest or "neutralize" him.

23. Let's Not and Say We Did

The blue Caddy pulled up to the brownstone housing Cassidy's uptown offices. Cassidy was in a kerchief and long coat and DiMaggio wore a Yankees cap. They moved quickly from the car to the steps and in through the door.

From Cassandra's office, DiMaggio quickly scanned the street and the buildings across the street for any signs of surveillance. "I don't see anything obvious, but they could have twenty cameras on this joint and I'd never see them, so let's make it quick."

"It'll just take me a minute to change." Cassidy said.

DQ

In the observation room outside the treatment room, Cassidy returned in full regalia. Even DiMaggio took an extra look at her in a tight leather suit that was practically a second skin. Her black bustier, with yellow laces up the front, had chain link "garters" around the bottom that attached to the thigh-high leather, five-inch-heeled boots that completed the image of the Dominatrix Supreme.

"Don't overplay it until you are safe."

"I know you don't believe me, but I actually never do this..."

"This is a real shitty time to tell me, Wanda."

She picked up the riding crop. "You ever call me Wanda again and I will use this on you."

190

DQ

Burns, alerted by a sensor placed in the doorway of the brownstone, zoomed in to the replay of the video surveillance feed of the doctor's office from a minute ago. "I think we got DiMaggio."

Wallace came over and looked at the video of DiMaggio crossing the street and heading up the steps. "He's probably poking around for something he missed." Wallace picked up the phone, "DiMaggio showed at the doctor's office... Very well. The team is on the way look for them." He ended the call.

"Burns, call the team, tell 'em to get to the doctor's office now, and tell them our NYPD contact will be there as well. I don't want him getting shot."

In the middle of all this they missed another man entering the building. One they would have known.

DQ

Government bureaucrat Bob Bessen, a man of fifty was naked and on his knees, having followed the written note that read "Just stepped out for a minute, we are in 4 tonight. Julia" that was at the front desk when he found the front door and office open.

The riding crop in her hand removed all doubt of her intentions as Cassidy entered the medieval-style chamber, technically called Treatment Room Four but affectionately known as the Dungeon Room.

"Where's Julia?"

A stinging crack of the crop across his back was the only response. He adapted quickly.

"Sorry. I didn't mean to speak..."

Another painful lash left a welt.

"Permission to speak, mistress?"

"Granted, scum."

"I have been a bad boy."

"How bad, you worthless wretch?"

"How will you punish me?"

Cassidy took a big black dildo from a wooden chest and dangled it in his face.

"Depending on the severity of your offense, you will be my bitch or my slave."

He gasped as she smacked him in the face with the rubber member.

"Oh yes..."

Cassidy punctuated each of her interrogations with a lash of the riding crop across his back or bottom.

"You glorified paper pusher. Did you close down a family farm, you maggot? Did you deny a widow her social security, you human puke?"

"Worse. I made a woman have sex with me to save her grocery store."

That remark caused her to lay one on with extreme prejudice.

Bessen momentarily broke character. "Hey... that really hurt."

"Shut up, shit for brains. I got something good planned for you. Get over here, you whiny little wimp."

He crawled over to her on his hands and knees and then stood up.

"Bend over," she said, slapping the end of the riding crop against her left palm.

"What are you going to do to me?"

"Bend over or I won't use any lubricant, you insect."

She threw him down on the bed and started to administer his punishment with her riding crop. In the corner of the room, a smoke detector had an extra hole right next to the blinking red light.

ID.

In Cassidy's office, DiMaggio sat in front of a monitor hooked up to the smoke detector camera. He had the expression of someone sucking on a lemon as he watched the grainy image of Cassidy flickering on the screen, teasing and threatening Bessen with the phallus and whacking him with the crop. The sound of his screams of pain and pleasure made DiMaggio shiver and shake his head. Between blows, he saw Cassidy look at the camera.

Even though he knew she couldn't hear him, he said to her image, "I feel so dirty watching this. Don't get too much into your work now, Cassandra." He looked up to check that the VCR's record light was flashing.

ൟ

Back in the treatment room, Cassidy took out a pair of handcuffs, causing Bessen to get excited at the sight of them. She ratcheted them tightly to the wrist of her "client." Once the cuffs were secured around a metal pole with other manacles and shackles dangling from it, she dropped the rubber sex aide and removed her blonde wig. DiMaggio saw her demeanor change as she looked up at the smoke detector and nodded.

A second later, DiMaggio entered with a digital camera. He started popping shots of Bessen, who he had originally met as "Mr. Smith" in Grimes' office. He was the suit that kept pushing Grimes' button to eject him from the bureau.

"What the fuck? Who the hell are you?"

"Relax, Bessy boy." DiMaggio lowered the camera so Bessen could see his face. "I'm the guy who's going to ruin your whole fucking life like you ruined mine, you whack job."

"Get out of here! Do you know who I am?"

"Of course, dickweed. Otherwise, I would have spared myself this entire unwholesome scene. You are the son-of-a-bitch telling the cheif to stop my investigation into the crime that happened in this very place. And now I know why. "

Bent over, handcuffed and naked, Bessen quickly adapted to his situation again saying, "What do ya want, DiMaggio?"

"I want to know what you know about Judge Jenkins' death."

"Go to hell."

"Okay, asshole." DiMaggio grabbed a chain from the rack and snapped it hard across Bessen's bare backside. The man screamed and even made Cassidy wince.

"Shit! You fuckin..."

"Hmmm, that's going to leave a mark."

It was too much for Cassidy. "I am going to my office; you play too rough for me," she said as she walked out.

"Now in three seconds I am going to start wailing into you with this professional grade 'sexual aid' until your ass looks like chopped meat, so start talking. One... Two... Three..." DiMaggio hauled back the chain and rattled it for effect.

"Okay! Okay! Let me free and I'll tell you."

"Bullshit. You'll tell me now or forget about ever sitting down again, lard ass." DiMaggio slammed the chain against the wall for emphasis.

"Look, he was going to reveal the network. He had to be stopped."

"What network? Who had to stop him?"

"Are you sure you want to know about that? It would be a death sentence."

"We're already on somebody's shit list so it won't matter."

"The network is used for delivering..."

Just then, a voice startled both of them.

"Freeze!"

DiMaggio whipped his head in the direction of the voice. He was shocked to see his old boss, Chief of Detectives Grimes brandishing a .38.

"Well, well, here for your therapy too, Chief?"

"Dammit, DiMaggio you couldn't leave this alone could you? You had to fuck everything up."

"Fuck what up? Are you in on this network too?"

"How much did he tell you?"

"Everything."

"Nothing," Bessen said as he tugged at his chains.

"Doesn't matter. I am actually here to bring you your service weapon." He pulled another .38 from his waistband with a gloved hand.

"Grimes, get me out of these. I want to break this fucking dago's face for doing this to me."

"Hold on." He aimed and fired. The side of Bessen's head exploded and he jerked forward, limp, but still suspended by the cuffs, his blood gushing onto the floor.

Grimes pointed the other gun at DiMaggio.

"What did you do that for?" DiMaggio was more pissed than scared.

"What do you mean me? It was your gun." Grimes said it like he couldn't care less.

"Guns don't kill people, sick fucks like you do."

"Now Mike, the moment of truth. I can kill you now and put your prints on this clean gun or you can tell me where the disk is and then I'll give you a two-hour head start."

"Two hours my ass; you're going to kill me the second I tell you, so kindly go fuck yourself."

"Hey, Mike, they got guys who can make you confess to sinking the Lusitania. Wanna meet them or deal with me?"

"Get a lot of headaches?" DiMaggio asked and then turned his head away, averting his eyes.

Grimes was momentarily thrown by the offbeat question, and suddenly a mace came slamming across the back of his head. He crumpled to the floor as Cassidy twirled behind him, twisted around by the momentum of the solid iron, medieval weapon.

"Nice. You were swinging for the bleachers there."

"I watched the entire horrible scene unfold on the monitor in my office. I had to come up with something!"

DiMaggio sprinted off to the monitor room and returned in an instant with a videocassette. He saw Cassidy just staring at Grimes. "Oh my God, that's Kevin!"

"You know him?"

"Kevin?... Kevin?... Grimes! Kevin Grimes. He was a patient of mine," Cassidy said.

"That's my boss – was my boss."

"You mean he's dead?" she said, swallowing hard. "I killed him?"

"No, you glanced him, he's just unconscious, but we'll be dead if we don't get out of here. I know he didn't come alone or at least unseen. Is there another way out?" DiMaggio took Grimes' gun but left the other "clean" weapon in Grimes' hand.

In the hallway, DiMaggio decided the street was too hot, so they went up the stairs to the rooftop instead. They exited onto the roof and found a workman's ladder leading up to the top of the elevator equipment room. He grabbed it and lowered it over the side of the building, to the roof of a lower, adjacent building. They scurried down and he quickly carried it to the other side, placing it up against another taller building. Once they had climbed to the top, he pulled the ladder up. Hearing a noise, he ducked behind the low wall that cordoned off the roof and pulled Cassidy down as well.

When they peeked over the edge of the wall toward the roof where they had come from, they could see two men with their guns drawn, methodically sweeping the tar-covered rooftop. They watched as the men gave up the search in frustration, presumably because there was no way off the roof without a ladder. Thankful for their small victory, DiMaggio quietly opened the stairway door, which luckily faced away from the men on the rooftop two buildings away.

Even in New York City, Cassidy's dominatrix outfit drew stares as she and DiMaggio walked down the street.

Still, DiMaggio couldn't pass up the opportunity. "Do you always have to make a statement every time we go out in public?"

"I feel like an idiot. Let's get off the street."

"No. I think we'll make better time..." He abruptly stopped talking when he noticed five men frantically searching the street up ahead. DiMaggio thought one of the men might have spotted them. He turned away quickly, not wanting to confirm his suspicions by giving the guy a second chance to spot him. He looked to his right, grabbed Cassidy by the arm, and pulled her into the club in front of them. "This is perfect."

Inside the Pleasure Shack, an adult bondage and discipline club, DiMaggio was the one out of uniform as Cassidy blended right in with the patrons, who were all dressed up for either a night of participation or else voyeurism. They passed the bar and navigated through double-bed-sized cushions with all manner of men and woman in various combinations. Some were into themselves, oblivious to the others watching, while others were engrossed in the staged performance at the front of the room. Tonight's main event was a woman who was being paraded around like a prize pony, replete with a mini-saddle on her back and a tail emanating from her rear end, by another woman whose behind cheeks were popping out of her specially cut out latex suit. DiMaggio and Cassidy crossed through a beaded curtain area and entered into the "inner sanctum." It consisted of private rooms with not-so-private picture windows to allow for exhibitionism with the "air of privacy."

A quick look behind him confirmed that the searchers were now in the club. "Quick, in here!"

They went into a room with red velvet walls and a round bed in the center. As soon as they entered, a red light went on outside in the viewing corridor. A few people took notice but most were engaged in what they were watching in their current windows. DiMaggio pulled out the plug to a floor lamp, leaving only two red spotlights casting circles down from the corners of the room.

"Now what?" Cassidy asked.

"I don't know. Those guys are on our tails."

She grabbed a leather hood, "Here, put this on."

DiMaggio looked at her like she was nuts. "No fuckin' way!"

"Quick, take off your shirt or they'll know it's you."

He understood and hastily pulled off his shirt and pulled on the mask. She threw him down on the bed, feet facing the window. She then straddled him with her back toward the window and started moving like they were deep in the throes of passion. DiMaggio was motionless.

"Okay, this isn't your regular sexual routine now, Mikey. You might have to move a little so they know you are alive."

"This thing is suffocating me."

"Shut up and thrust like you don't want to die right now, lumpy-kins."

He started to halfheartedly show some movement. She began a defined and expressive circulating action; her black-leather-covered rear end was circling and undulating over DiMaggio's groin. A few spectators began being attracted to the window.

DiMaggio hazarded a glance at the window. "There are people looking at us."

"Let's keep them looking and maybe the men with the guns will keep going."

DiMaggio started to reciprocate Cassidy's every thrust, bump and grind. It began to get intense. Cassidy put her arms over his shoulders and started to actually ride him. He couldn't believe, and in fact was amazed, that he was getting physically excited.

"Ooooh. Good boy. Giving me something to work with." She dug in deeper. With that, his breathing changed as she bore down on him.

The folks outside started to huddle around the window. The peek-a-boo spectacle of the dimly spot-lit couple actually increased their curiosity.

The searchers appeared at the end of the corridor.

Cassidy was now bucking as if she were on a prized bull at the rodeo. She slapped her leather-covered ass from time to time to complete the picture. DiMaggio was back on his hands. His breathing was labored due to the mask. The combination of a lack of oxygen and Cassidy's unrelenting motion had gotten him high.

IQ

The searchers separated the crowd at the window and peered through, to the displeasure of one chain-clad patron in leather hot pants. "Hey, wait your turn."

One of the searchers just glared at him and then tried to recognize the couple simulating copulation on the bed.

He watched as the man started lifting his hips to meet the woman's as they started to breathe in unison. She was digging her nails into his shoulders while she held on and rode him. Their thrusts got more powerful and less frequent. She was audibly gasping now and he was growling through the mask.

The other searcher saw his man glued to their window and punched him in the shoulder. "C'mon. Cut the shit. They must have gone clear through the place."

He gave one last look at the riveting action in the dimly lit room and then followed the other one down the corridor. The two searchers opened an exit door at the end of the corridor that spilled into an alley. Behind them, down the corridor, the amassed crowd applauded. The searcher who was taken with the spectacle glanced back toward the cheering, wondering what had happened.

IQ⤸

Just seconds before, DiMaggio and Cassidy were nearing the crescendo of their synchronized ballet.

"Oh. Oh. Ohhhh god!" DiMaggio strained and pushed hard against Cassidy's groin.

"Yes... Yes... Oh FUCK yes!" Cassidy was panting in short breaths.

Exhausted for more reasons than one, the two performers hardly even noticed the approving sounds from their audience as Cassidy collapsed on top of DiMaggio, both of them breathing heavily. DiMaggio absent-mindedly brought his right arm up and over her back, holding her as she caught her breath.

Then, as if he was waking up from a drunken stupor, he realized where he was, what he was currently doing, and what he had already done. He lifted her up, moving her to the side as he slid out from under her.

IQ⤸

The metal door to the alleyway slammed shut as DiMaggio stepped out into the night, putting on his shirt. Cassidy had stolen a white robe.

He was pissed. "What the fuck kind of kinko, perverted, sicko, fucked up kind of place was that?"

"It worked for you," she said as she crossed her arms.

"No, it didn't."

"Did too."

"Did not."

"Did... so I suppose that's a spilled drink there."

He looked down at the large wet spot on his crotch. "Ah. Shit." He pointed his finger at her. "You... you are sick."

"Why just me? What did I do that you didn't do?"

"Hey, this is your world. Your wacko, freakazoid world."

"Well welcome to it, Mike. You just got christened into the wacko, sex-freak world of sexual deviation. And there are twenty folks back there who witnessed your 'coming' of age." She jerked her hand up and down in a familiar gesture as she spoke.

"I didn't intend for that to happen."

"Funny how that works."

"And what about you? What happened to you?"

"I came."

DiMaggio was thrown a little by the admission. "You did? Really?"

"Before you go bragging to your friends in homeroom, bucko, don't take it personal. I learned how to do that on the banister in my aunt's house when I was nine."

"You know what I like about you?"

"What?"

"Absolutely not a fucking thing." He then spun around looking up. "I can't believe that happened with... with... with someone like you."

"Okay, stop right there, Casanova, before you say something to hurt my feelings."

She turned and walked away.

DiMaggio had second thoughts. Feeling that maybe he had gone too far, he turned to call after her, but immediately pulled out the gun he took from Grimes and pointed it at her back.

"Cassandra!"

She kept walking.

"Cassandra, duck!" He fired three shots.

Cassidy whirled around with her hands reflexively covering her head as the bullets whipped past her ears. She was startled as one of the searchers fell dead in the shadows, his gun tumbling from his hand. DiMaggio rushed to her and grabbed her in his arms.

"Are you okay? Did I hit you? Did I hit you? Are you bleeding?" He started to pat her down, looking for blood.

"I'm okay. I think I am okay. Wouldn't it burn or something? I mean if I got shot? I think I'm fine. How did you see him?"

DiMaggio pointed to the strong, harsh, glaring mercury vapor light that was on the wall above and to the left of the doorway casting dark shadows into the recessed entryway. "Your white robe bounced the alley's light into the shaded corner of the doorway as you came toward him and I saw him raise his gun. We have to get out of here. You okay to move?"

"Yes. Yes, I am okay."

DiMaggio helped her up and scanned the area as they left in a hurry.

24. Just the Facts Ma'am

By now there were cop cars, ambulances, and news vans strewn at all angles in front of Cassidy's office brownstone, having been hastily parked at the crime scene. Officers strung yellow crime-scene tape at both ends of the street from sidewalk to sidewalk and parked a blue-and-white RMP sideways with its lights flashing as a roadblock on each corner as well.

"Is it true that the deceased worked for the Federal Government?" a female reporter from New York One asked as she jutted the microphone into the face of the young NYPD assistant information officer, who was trying to handle the onslaught of questions. He started to answer her, but before he could even get his mouth open, he was peppered with questions from all sides.

"Excuse me, Tiffany from Channel Two. Do you know how the naked body got in ... Bill, New York Post. There's a report that the body was found nude. Can you ... Pardon me, Daily News here. Did he fall from a window ... Excuse me, I'm with TMZ; was this a gay sex, murder-suicide ... Officer? Diane from Channel Nine. Do you have a suspect?"

The overwhelmed spokesman held up his hands to try and get control of the impromptu news conference.

Meanwhile, at the edge of the all the activity, DiMaggio casually strolled over to a double-parked detective's car on First Avenue, its spinning red light still attached to the roof. He got in, backed it up, turned, and he was off.

Cassidy, in the white robe, was standing on the corner as the dark sedan pulled up. Getting in, she picked up the red light now sitting on the seat between them.

"This is a police car! You boosted a cop car?"

"The Caddy we came down here in was right in the middle of news vans and there was no sign of Delgado. He must've run when the first ambulances and cop cars rolled up; this one was a block away. Besides, with this we can get any car we want; pick one."

Cassidy scanned the street of rolling traffic as they headed west on Fifty-Seventh Street. She saw a Mercedes SL 500. "That red one."

"You don't want to be in something that obvious. Try and pick something a little more blend-in-able."

She spotted a Bentley with a rap-star type behind the wheel. "Let's jack his ride."

"You got expensive tastes, Doctor."

Cassidy found it odd she was pleased that he had called her "doctor."

"Well then, I don't care; you pick."

The police radio in the car reported, "Be advised, one victim on scene. Central K"

"What about Grimes?"

"Probably long gone, and from the questions I heard the reporters asking, they put the body in the back alley."

"What about the man you shot?"

"I used Grimes' gun, so my guess is the body'll be reported as a mugging victim and the boys who chased us have probably already dug the bullet out so there will be no inconvenient forensics."

On Twelfth Avenue, DiMaggio looked left then right and snapped his finger as he pointed. "Bingo"

He grabbed the red light, attached it to the roof from the driver's window and then hit the lights and siren.

At Fifty Eighth Street, he pulled behind a gray Ford Taurus. There were bumper stickers proclaiming, "Jerry Garcia lives," "The Grateful Dead," "Legalize Pot Now!" and "Mushrooms aren't just for dinner anymore." The Taurus pulled over.

"Stay here. This ought to be good."

ॐ

DiMaggio stepped from his car and approached from the driver's left but stayed back behind the rear window. "License and registration please."

"What did I do, Officer?"

"Your tail light is out. Take your license out of the wallet, hand it and your registration out the window, and remain in the car." DiMaggio heard them speaking in panicked, hushed tones inside the car.

"I know – shit – what do you want me to do?" the driver said to his passenger.

Suddenly the car lurched forward and left rubber on the pavement as it took off up the West Side Highway.

DiMaggio looked down at the gravel dust that now covered his shoes. "Really?" Instinctively DiMaggio ran to the car, jumped in, and took off after the Taurus.

Cassidy couldn't believe it and said, "What the hell are you doing?"

"These guys are dirty. Otherwise they wouldn't run."

"I mean you, what are *you* doing? You aren't a cop anymore."

"Correction, I just don't have a badge anymore." He took the ramp onto the West Side Highway.

"Oh, well, that's not too crazy then... Ahhhhh!" She gasped as he nearly slammed into a slow moving VW Beetle, which crept on from the ramp at Seventy Second Street. She looked over to the speedometer as it passed ninety-five. "Once a cop, always an asshole?"

"Something like that; buckle your seatbelt and let me concentrate. They're headed for the GW, trying to make it to Jersey. Schmucks. Like we don't have radios."

"You *don't* have a radio! You can't use the editorial 'we'. For the last time, Mr. Denial, you are not a fucking c-ahhhhh-p!"

An entering Toyota fishtailed as it skidded to avoid the hurtling Taurus, which was weaving in and out of the light traffic.

On the straightaway between Ninety Sixth and One Twenty Fifth, DiMaggio floored it and pulled alongside the Taurus. "Scrunch down!"

"Huh?" At first Cassidy didn't get it, but when he pulled the gun from his belt, she reflexively slid all the way down, covering her ears and fearing the loud bang. "No! Please. Have you flipped out?"

DiMaggio saw the driver of the Taurus glance sideways, so he extended his gun toward him. He was relieved that the driver decided to live to see another day and started slowing his vehicle.

The Taurus pulled over. DiMaggio pulled in behind him, got out, popped the trunk on the detective's car, and retrieved a shotgun and a few sets of plastic wire-tie handcuffs. Approaching the Taurus, he pumped one into the chamber, a sound that immediately tightens up any bad guy's sphincter. "Real slow now, both hands out the window. C'mon. Passenger too, let me see both hands out the window. Driver, get out and get on the ground! Passenger, slide across; I want to see hands first as you come out. You, on the ground too!"

He looked back at Cassidy; he could see she was watching but obviously wasn't sure what he was doing. With his knee on the neck of one guy and the shotgun stuck into the back of the other, he slipped the wire loop over the first guy's hands and pulled. He heard the familiar small zipping sound as he cinched the restraints and then moved over to the next guy, where he performed the same procedure. He lifted the driver up by his restrained hands, bent him over the hood of the car, and patted him down. The driver had a .32 cal.

in his waistband. "You could catch a beat down for not telling me about this."

He got the keys from the ignition, walked the driver to the trunk and then opened it. He quickly counted fifteen bricks of pot in five supermarket bags.

"Trafficking, possession of an illegal firearm, broken tail light. There's enough here to send you boys away for a longtime."

"There's a hundred grand in the toolbox. Take it and let us go."

"Not the first time around for you, is it? Got two strikes on your report card already?"

"Look, man. That's my brother. He ain't in this; he's just along for the ride. That's why I didn't pull my piece, holmes. Let us go and forget about the whole thing."

"I might just do that."

DiMaggio got the brother up, after quickly patting him down, and led both of them over to a lamppost, which was set back from the roadway, and wire-tied them to the post.

"Stay put 'til the paddy wagon comes."

"Hey? What the fuck, man! We had a deal!"

He then walked back to the car, took the five bags of pot, and dodged the cars as he hustled across the parkway to the other side. He raised the bags over the edge of the river walk.

The brothers winced and protested loudly. "Whoa! What are you fucking crazy! C'mon man, not the whole... FUUUCK!"

He made his way back through the light traffic to the detective's car and spoke to Cassidy. "Get ready to follow me.

She slid over and got behind the wheel.

DiMaggio returned to the two brothers, took out a pocketknife, wiped his fingerprints off the outside as well as the blade, and placed it two feet from them.

"Why the fuck did you do that, man?"

"Wait 'til I am gone and cut yourself free. Consider this your very lucky night." He trained his gun on them until he got into the Taurus. He quickly pulled away and Cassidy followed in the detective's car.

Looking in the rearview mirror, he could see the men straining as they stretched their legs, trying to retrieve the knife with their feet.

IO

By the time all the fun and games were over in the city and they drove north, the precursor glow of the sun, still thirty minutes from rising, backlit the distant mountains. DiMaggio parked the Taurus head-in to some high brush for cover. He had left the detective's car he had appropriated some miles back at the first rest stop along the thruway, locked with the keys inside. Eventually, the state police would find it after it remained in the same spot for more than a day. His cousin's car was still at the Tepee Diner in the Bronx where they met Delgado on the way down. Cassidy was yawning as she dropped the skintight top of the mistress get up and rubbed under her rib cage as she headed for the cabin. DiMaggio opened the trunk and retrieved the toolbox, the shotgun, and the .32.

Later, as DiMaggio was seated at the wood table, stacking cash in neat piles, he heard the shower shut off and the wood-slatted, hinged barn door of the cabin's bathroom opened .

Cassidy came out in the robe toweling her hair and saw the cash. "Where did that come from?"

"Illegal drug sales most likely. I thought he was bullshitting me."

"So Mister Straight Arrow, you stole that money from them?"

"You know, I have put wise guys wearing five-thousand-dollar suits and two-thousand-dollar shoes away. I've been offered bags of cash to look the other way.

Defense attorneys have let it be known that amnesia has its rewards. But I never took a cent. Never thought about it for a second."

"Wait, you... Mr. 'How much does everything cost?' You are the most wealth-envious guy I ever met."

"Your psycho-babble aside, yes, I want more. Yes, I want to have something to depend on when I retire, something that I can give to a wife or a kid. You know what the hard truth of life is? Without money, you are nothing."

"You are wrong."

"Yeah, only people who have money say, 'money isn't everything.'"

"No. You are wrong about yourself."

"What?"

"You say you never took a dollar and I believe you. You think you're nothing without money but since you never took any, there's something you have, something you are, that money can't buy."

"Yeah, poor."

"Well I can see we made a lot of progress here." She censored herself from the next thing she was going to say and instead flipped through a stack of hundreds. "So what are you going to do with it now that you are rich?"

"Hold on to it. We may need it to start over somewhere else if this plan doesn't work."

"We?"

"Well, it could just be one of us, probably you, if I don't live through this."

She looked at him anew as he continued to count stacks of hundreds. IQ

DiMaggio couldn't sleep so he took a walk outside in the breaking light. The fresh air and altitude made each breath crisp and invigorating. He walked down to the stream and looked back at the cabin. There was a barely perceptible wisp of smoke rising from the chimney while an owl hooted in the distance. In all, a very picturesque, picture-book setting. He could see how Mr. Berkowsky, "Wanda's" dad, would need and love this place. Then he pictured the soon-to-be Cassandra Cassidy as little Wanda before she dated her aunt's banister, back when she was young and sweet, if she ever was, and how the sound of her playing and laughing must have melted her father's heart. When DiMaggio realized he was thinking about the Dragon Lady Dominatrix, the entire Norman Rockwell scene he was painting in his mind just dripped and dissolved away. After about fifteen minutes, he walked back to the cabin.

He tried not to make too much noise as he re-entered the cabin, but he couldn't see much in the dark.

"Ow! Shit!"

"Wha..." Cassidy bolted up.

"Sorry, go back to sleep."

"Are you okay?"

"Yeah, I stubbed my toe on the damn foot locker at the end of the bed."

Cassidy just turned over and fluffed her pillow, trying to get back to sleep. DiMaggio rubbed his toe and lay down with his shirt and pants on. A few minutes later, he could hear Cassidy toss and turn. Then he heard a sigh. "You up?" he said softly in the almost pitch-black room.

"Yeah, I couldn't go back to sleep. What did you do, go out for a walk or something?"

"It's nice out there; this is a great piece of property. Went all the way down to the stream."

"I caught a catfish or something ugly there once. I thought my dad was going to call Sports Illustrated he was so proud."

"He must have felt good about giving you a chance to grow up in a place like this?"

"Yeah, he was overcompensating for my mom going away."

"Look, I know this is your area, but I think he got a real sense of purpose and fulfillment as a father to be able to take you here and watch you grow."

"Wow. That's a sweet thought. You can be sensitive when you want to."

"Okay. I'm sorry it was a weak moment. It won't happen again."

"Asshole. Try to sleep; you had a busy night tonight playing policeman."

There was silence for a bit and then Cassidy spoke. "You know, not to dwell on it, but what you said before, you know, about the money and how *we* might need it. That was a rare thing in my life. I have always been alone, even here when I was a kid. And I just want you to know that I appreciated your concern. I am not used to that kind of caring from anybody – that it was a real big-brother gesture." Cassidy waited to see if he was going to say anything, but instead she heard him spring up from bed.

"That's it!"

"What? What is it?"

"Why didn't I think of this before?"

25. Off the Pigs

After five hours of sleep, they hit the road. The Taurus with the stoner bumper stickers was not out of place parked in front of RETRO FIT, a secondhand clothing store in Ulster County, a throwback to the Woodstock hippie groove. Inside, DiMaggio checked out a Nehru jacket identical to the one Paul McCartney was wearing in the poster right above the rack. He turned just as Cassidy emerged from behind the curtains of the dressing booth wearing a straight blonde wig and a sloppy kind of mid-length, earth-mother dress that came right out of the "summer of love."

It made DiMaggio smile. "Ga...rooov...vey!"

The large collection of lead detectives and precinct captains convened at One Police Plaza required the building's maintenance guys to bring more chairs into the big conference room. The usual pre-meeting hubbub quieted down as Grimes, with a gauze patch over a shaved spot on the back of his head, took his seat.

"Thanks for coming in on such short notice. The reason I called each of you individually and asked you here, instead of sending you memos, is because we need to hold this tight. It concerns one of our own."

Everyone in the room leaned in ever so slightly.

"The forensics on the Bessen shooting are in and the fingerprints on a chain and other items at the scene came up as belonging to an NYPD detective. We also have reason to believe that this detective may be implicated in the possible death of another detective by arson. I am asking everyone in this room to treat this information as 'close hold.' I have assured the commissioner that the bureau can police its own and he has given us a short window of opportunity to clean this up ourselves. Before I go further, does anybody have an objection?"

It was purely an academic question; no one who held a detective's badge would risk it by being on the other side of the chief's position. It was the same reason why no one openly asked why he had a bandage on the back of his head.

Grimes scanned the packed room "Good! The detective who is now a person of interest in the murder of Bessen is Mike DiMaggio."

From the few who personally knew DiMaggio, there was a gasp or a loud questioning, "What?" For the rest, only a raised eyebrow because they knew the name. He was a First Grade Detective, the finest of New York's Finest. Putting out a BOLO on one of their best, even just within this room, was unsettling. They all immediately understood why the Chief didn't release this as a department wide "Be On The Look Out" for a "first grade."

"Now gentlemen, if we turn up nothing by three p.m. this afternoon, my arrangement with the commissioner ends and we put out a full A&XD on DiMaggio."

The idea of putting out an Armed and Extremely Dangerous on DiMaggio sobered the room up even more than before.

"Let's get this done before three."

Grimes got up and walked out. When the detectives thought he was out of earshot, the cross-table chatter begin.

"Is he serious?"

"What happened to his head?"

"I heard he slipped in the tub, slight concussion."

"Does anybody know where Mike is?"

"What do we do if we find him?" was the main question, mixed with other expressions of shock, questions of procedure, and general attempts of the men in the room to gauge what was a rare, if not a previously unthinkable, event.

ID.

A copy of the New York Daily News was on top of the desk. Hannah read the headline again: Federal Official Found Dead in Alley. It gave her the same chill this time as when she saw it on the newsstand on her way to her one-woman office this morning. She stopped into a camera store and bought a video camcorder and blank DVDs.

She had it propped up on books on the chair in front of her desk. She got up and turned the thing on. Hannah checked the shot in the foldout monitor screen and made sure it was aimed at the chair she would be sitting in. She sat back down and took a deep breath.

"My name is Hannah Faust, I first met Warren when I worked for him at the Department of Justice. He took me with him when he moved from FBI administration over to his current position. Everything I am about to tell you is the truth and not embellished. I do this now to clear my name and my memory, since if you are seeing it ... because if... you are seeing this..." she choked up, "it means I am dead."

She took another deep breath, looked down at the paper's headline again and continued. "Nine years ago at a dinner party in Georgetown, a U.S. senator told Warren about a problem he and his wife were having. Warren and I listened and were mildly shocked. Well I was. Warren saw an opportunity..."

She continued relaying her "confession" for twenty-five more minutes. Her mouth was dry, so she stopped and took a sip of water, then continued. "So with Mumbuto handling acquisition at one quarter of a million per package, we had all the parts of the network in place..." She took another sip and noticed her hand was shaking. "But I was just an administrative assistant. I was not involved in anyway, shape or form with procurement..." She recorded for another 15 minutes. She still didn't know if Warren Rodgers was behind Bessen's death, but now she had a life insurance policy if he was. She didn't put it past him to eliminate anyone who could get in the way of him and his billion-dollar operation.

When she was done, she hooked the wire from the camera to her computer like the guy in the store said and popped the DVD into the slot. In twenty minutes she had a DVD. She wrote her lawyer's name in black Sharpie across the face of a small padded shipping envelope and wrote right on the DVD, "To be viewed in the event of my untimely or suspicious death."

DQ

The Taurus was double-parked across from the downtown headquarters of Big Brother/Big Sisters. The "hippi-fied" Cassidy got out and entered the storefront office.

Once inside, she scoped out the place and found her target, a woman in her mid-forties, long curly red hair, thin thirty pounds ago, the echo of freckles on her face long since burnt away by tanning. The woman, who looked like a sister in fashion to Cassidy's retro outfit, sat at her desk under a picture of Bill Clinton, sipping a Starbuck's Mocha Frappuccino with just a dollop of whip cream. The nameplate on the pen and pencil holder in front of her read, "Suzanne Edelstein," but Cassidy would have also accepted, "Janis Joplin."

Cassidy waited.

"Are you being helped?" Suzanne said as she looked up.

"No. Can you help me?"

"That's what I do, help people."

"Me too. It's odd to be on this side of the desk."

Suzanne beamed. "Social worker?"

"How can you tell?"

"I've been doing it for a while."

"Well you're good. Yes, I need to find someone."

"Who?"

"A young girl who was being mentored by a friend."

"I'm sorry but we are not allowed to divulge any information about our children."

"I understand." Cassidy looked down and picked at her fingernail. "It's just that... just..." Looking despondent, she slowly turned away.

Suzanne appeared moved. "What kind of work did you do?"

"Me? I did all kinds of work, community outreach, clinic, welfare, and immigration. I just can't say no to someone in need." She shifted her focus to the picture on the wall. "Now that was a president!"

Suzanne beamed for a second time. "I met him."

"No."

"Yes. I volunteered at a fundraiser. Worked for twenty hours straight and he came over and shook my hand."

"He shook your hand?"

"Well, all of us volunteers. But he smiled when he shook mine. He has the warmest eyes."

"Lucky girl." Then Cassidy leaned over the desk and said in conspiratorial tones, "I'd do him in an instant."

Suzanne just sat there with a "cat that swallowed the canary" grin.

"No. C'mon, don't tell me..." Cassidy feigned being impressed.

"All I'm saying is he is a very powerful, irresistible presence."

"Carter was like that."

"You knew Jimmy Carter?"

"Well not while he was in office; I was just a kid then..." Cassidy waited but there was no accommodation of her attempt to not age herself coming from

Suzanne so she continued. "I met him at Habitat for the Humanities later on."

"You worked at Habitat!"

"Yes. Montgomery, Alabama, West Virginia, Brooklyn, even Trinidad after Hurricane Hugo."

"Wow. What a great experience that must have been."

"Out of all the work I've done, it was the most satisfying because in the end you left them with something real, something tangible, a roof over their heads."

"If I weren't all thumbs..." Suzanne said as she placed her hand on Cassidy's.

"You are like Maggie. And she was able to contribute enormously."

She took the bait. "Maggie?"

"Maggie Reade; she's the reason I'm here. We met in Trinidad at Habitat. We bonded instantly."

"Reade... Reade." Cassidy saw a surprised look cross her face as the name registered in her mind. "Oh dear, she's..."

"Yes. A tragedy. A real loss to the world and for those who will never know her goodness and gentle way of helping others."

"Normally, I hate cops – Thompson Square and all."

"You were there?"

"Got a night stick across here." Suzanne proudly lifted her hair and displayed her now unblemished temple. She looked right and left and then uttered in a low voice to Cassidy, "Fucking pigs."

"But not Maggie, she was..."

"Yeah, I know, she was different. She was a true believer. I could never figure out how she could be a cop during the day and be such an attentive big sister at the same time," Suzanne said.

"Maybe it's because cops are actually really good people after all, who do their social work from a position of power which we, as a society, all invest in them for our mutual protection."

Suzanne was taken aback by this outburst of what she likely regarded as sheer blasphemy.

Cassidy took only a split second before she added, "NOT!"

The two laughed and Suzanne again leaned over the desk and spoke low. "So what did you need?"

"Maggie left something for her little sister, LaShana. I once promised her I would see to all the provisions of her will, her being a cop and all."

"Money?"

"A little." Cassidy took the envelope out of her purse and showed her the five thousand dollars in hundreds inside."

"A little? She was really a great woman wasn't she?"

"The best. Will you help me find the little girl?"

"Will you put in a good word with Habitat for me? I'd have loved to have met Carter."

"Done."

Suzanne was all smiles as she dug through a card file. Cassidy was suddenly wracked with guilt, her thoughts turning dour as she watched Suzanne earnestly and excitedly trying to help.

Cassidy exited the building and entered the car, slamming the door, and plopped herself in the seat, deep in disturbing thought. "LaShana Johnson, one forty six New Lots Avenue."

"What's gotten into you?"

"Just shut the fuck up and drive, will ya?"

$$IQ_\blacktriangle$$

The lights of the lower Manhattan skyline flickered through the suspension wires of the Brooklyn Bridge like a strobe as the Taurus crossed the span. Cassidy was looking out the passenger window – she had been silent since she left Big Sisters – and her face was the mask of someone in a troubled frame of mind.

DiMaggio noticed but had the wisdom to let this hornet's nest be, so he drove on without comment.

As she watched the city lights across the river below the bridge, she apparently made up her mind about something. "Let me have the cell phone."

DiMaggio fished it out of his pocket and handed it to Cassidy. He glanced to his right and saw her reach down the front of her dress and pull out the small black address book she had stashed with the hidden tapes in the cabin.

IQ.

A stone's throw from the U.S. Capitol, a phone rang in one of the classic, warm, cozy and very expensive townhouses in Georgetown. Inside the circa 1870 brick-and-stone mansion, a grey-haired man with reading glasses resting on the bridge of his nose sat behind a formidable desk. He was pouring through reams of proposed legislation. The phone rang a second time and his downstairs maid, who was dusting on the far side of his den, answered it. "Kerins' residence." She listened and then asked, "Who shall I say is calling the senator?"

The senator looked up with a wave off, as he did not wish to be disturbed.

"Well, Dr. Cassidy, the senator is indisposed right now."

Upon hearing the name, the senator vetoed his previous objection. "It's okay Hallie, I'll take the call here. Please close the door, if you will."

"Hold on, he just became free." She placed the call on hold, shutting the den door as she left.

The senator looked down at the blinking hold light for a second or two and then took a deep breath and picked up. "Doctor. I can't tell you how surprised I am to hear from you. Very surprised."

"I bet you are. I know we had an understanding, but I need a favor."

"Really now? As I remember, you stipulated and assured me that the settlement we reached was complete and final. Therefore, I don't believe I owe you any favors."

"Relax, Reginald, this is not a big deal."

"Just talking to you is a big deal; if my wife were to find out..."

"Yeah, she might cut you off from her daddy's gravy train, I know."

"You are still the she-devil aren't you?"

"I had a couple of hell-raising times with you Reggie boy. So for good old times sake, I need a warm introduction to Jimmy Carter and Habitat for Humanities."

"Come again? You? You want to volunteer to help people?"

"It ain't so far off a thought Reggie, but no, this one is for... got a piece of paper?"

"Yes." He grabbed a note pad.

"Suzanne Edelstein at Big Sisters, six four five Leonard Street in New York City. She gets the VIP treatment and we are square. You'll never hear from me again."

"That's what you said last time."

"I swear to God. I am out of your life."

"What if I didn't want you out of my life?"

"Still the passive-aggressive bad boy aren't you? Well, Reggie, you might just get the spanking you are looking for someday. Ta Ta!"

She clicked the cell phone off. The smile of satisfaction broadcasting across her face was not lost on DiMaggio as he took the Flatbush Avenue exit off the bridge. "You are armed and extremely dangerous with just a cell phone."

"I would have never hurt him; we did have a deal."

"You are some piece of work there, Doc."

IO2.

Harry had called Owens as soon as he left Chief Grimes' impromptu meeting with the heads of all the detective squads. When he finished filling in Bill on what had transpired at the meeting, Bill Owens had his doubts. DiMaggio was too experienced to leave his fingerprints at a crime scene, if he was there at all. Owens chose not to share with Harry that he had also uncovered that Cassandra Cassidy's house up in Westchester was shot up the same night Reade died. She apparently was not home at the time... or was she? Is that why she disappeared? All these questions had banged off the walls of his detective's brain as he traveled to White Plains to see an old friend, Dan Washington, who used to be NYPD but was now retired and padding his retirement as Chief of Police, White Plains. Bill entered Dan's office and was immediately impressed.

"Whoa. Is this your office or your palace?"

"Bill, you old dog, how the hell are you?"

"Nowhere as good as you, I see."

"Yeah, the good folks of White Plains only want the best for their chief. Check this out." He pointed to his own bathroom off to the side of his office.

"Now that's class!" Bill said as he gave the man a bro hug.

"Can I get you something?"

"Nah, I'm fine."

"No really, just say yes; it's worth it."

"Okay, yeah, I'll have a... a... diet soda!"

"Watch." Dan hit the intercom button, "Julie, could you bring two diet cokes..." He looked up, "Lemon?"

Owens nodded.

"...with lemon?" Dan smiled. "This is going be good. In the meantime, what's got you up in the burbs?"

221

"I came across a police insurance report on a shooting at Twelve Pine Drive. Yet, I couldn't find any criminal complaint or a write up on the incident. Why?"

At that moment, Julie entered. Well actually, Julie's breasts entered first, followed by the rest of her shortly thereafter. She was a very well developed woman in a dress that, although not sleazy in any way, was very flattering to what God had given her. Bill's eyes opened wide as Dan just sat there with a grin that was as wide as his desk.

She served the drinks and asked, "Anything else, Chief?"

"No, no. Not right now. Thank you, Julie."

"Thank you, Julie," Owens chimed in.

They waited and watched her leave; Dan's eyebrows silently asked, "Really something, huh?"

"You need an assistant here, Dan? A fella could get used to all this... plush."

"Bill, as soon as you put in for your package, you call me." He then changed tone and topic. "Why are you interested in this shooting? Actually it was a shoot up; nobody was shot."

"The doctor whose house it was is missing and along with her, Mike DiMaggio."

"DiMaggio, DiMaggio. Gold shield?"

"Yeah, first. Manhattan Homicide."

"Hot shot, huh?"

"He ain't like you and me back in East New York," Owens said.

"Hey, remember that sergeant, the one who thought you were screwing his wife?"

"Hold on. It was you he thought was screwing his wife! It's true – the memory is the first to go."

"Second! Which is why Julie is just a pleasant diversion."

"I hear ya, man." Bill turned to the doorway Julie exited from and sighed, "How did we ever have the energy?"

"Hey, hey. That kind of talk never leaves this room, partner," Dan said with a chuckle followed by a deep smoker's cough.

"Agreed. Wow, I totally forgot about Sergeant Rangle." Owens shook his head at his own lack of memory.

"Randle!"

"Right, Randle. What ever happened to him?"

"I heard he got out with twenty-five in and is now head of Security at American Express," Dan said.

"Good for him. So have you talked with the good doctor?"

"No. The feds swooped right in and took it all over. In fact, they were already on the scene when my guys rolled up. They flashed federal tin and my guys backed off and took traffic posts to keep the gawkers away. Of course, I followed up and confirmed it was a Washington play."

"That explains why there's no paperwork."

"Or anything other than an insurance report."

"So no forensics, no crime scene photos?" Owens said.

"It all went fed."

"Which agency?"

"Hold onto your seat, Bill – railroad!"

"Da what now?"

"Fucking federal rail cops!"

"New one on me."

"Me too. But the governor signed the agreement a few months back with the DOT and Amtrak to give them jurisdiction in New York State, which is the only way they could be active and not simply observers."

"Why would he do that?"

"Why any politician does anything, Bill – money. Some new federal funding from the Department of Transportation tied to a transportation security bill with lots of cash for new toys and security of the trains and buses." Dan took a sip of Coke. "How is DiMaggio involved?"

"He was on the lady doc's trail after a judge died in the same building where her offices were."

"Did she know anything?"

"Couldn't tell ya. I got to this late and they was already gone. I am following up because a 'uni' came to me with a possible cover-up – a good kid scared out of his boots. The more I'm digging, the more things just don't stack up."

"Shit. You go to IA?"

"No fucking way. This goes way up the chain. I don't know how high, but shit man, you just told me it was the feds and there's a A&XD going out on Mike for the murder of a fed."

"Sounds like a shit storm heading your way, partner."

"I got to think this through. Can I look at the house?"

"Be my guest; the feds bugged out in three days. Nobody's touched the place since. I got a car out front, so I'll call and tell 'em you're stopping by. Good to see ya, Billy boy."

Owens got up and gave the opulent office one more look around. "Dan, I want to be you when I grow up."

"See if you can do it without the ulcers."

Owens didn't find anything in the doctor's boarded-up house, except for what he found in DiMaggio's apartment – toiletries, suitcases, and other things that pointed more to a life interrupted rather than a planned trip.

On the way back, Owens replayed the meeting with Dan. Besides the cameo by the blessedly endowed, Julie, one other thing stuck in his head, *Randle at AmEx!*

26. Clandestine Meet

A day after he called his buddy from the CIA, a dark Mercedes pulled up to the Kebob House. Eric watched as Brad emerged and, with the aid of a crutch, entered the restaurant. Eric scanned the rest of the street and saw no new faces, no obvious surveillance or capture teams. He crossed the street and got to the entrance just as Brad was limping out.

"There you are. You look like shit," Brad said.

"Nice to see you too. There's a few guys in there that could be trouble; let's use your car."

In the car, Eric nodded towards the driver.

"That's Benny; he's good and doesn't speak English," Brad said.

Eric leaned close. "I have a gun pointed at your head; take me to the embassy."

The driver didn't respond. Eric sat back.

"Always were the cautious type," Brad said.

"That's why I am still the 'alive' type."

"I've worked a lot of ops with a lot of operators, Eric, and I'm telling you, you could be a first-class field operative at the CIA."

"How ya figure that?"

"You got nerves of steel and balls of brass. In the... what? Ten or so ops that we've been on, I have never seen you lose your cool; you always keep your head. You got situational awareness up the ass and you speak everything but Pig Latin."

"When you put it that way I can't help feeling I don't get paid enough. But I got to ask you, are you setting me up for some kind of quid pro quo? You know. You help me now and then get to recruit me into the Company?"

"No, Eric. This ain't a proposition. I owe you. Big time! I am just making an observation, that's all."

They rode in silence for a bit, then Brad casually asked, "Well, what have you got yourself into?"

Eric spent the twenty-minute ride to the airport and the waiting helicopter filling in Brad on Setara, his son, the Devil's Farmer and the tribal chief.

On the chopper, it was too noisy to continue, but once they got back, Brad wisely decided not to bring Eric close to the embassy or it's surveillance cameras. Instead, they sat in a teashop a mile from his office, where Brad gave it to Eric straight. "Look, Eric. It will take me a few days to see if I can even arrange for a black passport, and forget the alternate identity, because you aren't even with the CIA. And your little excursion off the reservation? That seriously complicates matters in that I'd be aiding and abetting a possible Army deserter. Other than that, thanks for dropping this bowl of steaming hot soup in my lap!"

"Any black market option?"

"You mean you want me to tell you who's forging and who's arranging for illegal transit?"

"The way you say it, it sounds so..."

Brad looked at Eric, stared actually, until just before it got uncomfortable. "Still got your military ID?"

"Yeah."

"Let me have it." He held out his hand as Eric fished it out of his wallet. "Good. Now go get a cup of real coffee and some western civilian clothes, and come back here in an hour or so."

Eric left as Brad asked for the check and as he sat waiting, he thought about what he was about to do and how it could get him fired or worse put in prison. For a brief second he wondered whether helping Eric was worth the risk. Then his conscience kicked in and he thought about why he owed Sgt. Ronson everything.

ID

They were deep in Tora Bora. Their mission was to kill a local drug lord who had intentionally given the Army bad intel on the location of Osama Bin Laden. It started when the U.S. confirmed that the DNA on a scarf he brought to the Americans was indeed that of Bin Laden's. On the basis of that, a B-52 strike was ordered on the suspected encampment. In fact, what really happened was the profiteer who brought them the story had fingered his biggest competitor and tricked the U.S. Army into wiping him out with the use of a scarf that, although it actually did belong to the most wanted man in the world, had been left behind when he was temporarily hiding out in the region.

In one bunker busting, thunderous U.S. Air Force backed play, he evaporated his biggest competitor and became the largest drug lord in that part of the mountain region. When the DNA reports from whomever it was whose remains they scraped off the wall of the cave came back, it was confirmed that it wasn't Osama Bin Laden's remains. The mission that Brad ran was to get in there and terminate, with extreme prejudice, the newly crowned drug king. He was ordered to make it messy enough to be an example to all others who would bear false witness to U.S. forces.

Eric, who had been on missions with Brad
before, was his A-team choice. Under
cover of darkness, the eight-man crew did
a midnight HALO jump that got them
seven klicks from the fortified center of
the target's operation. At two the next
morning, the drug lord met Allah. And the
operators deftly spread the destruction
and death so that there would be no doubt
he had double-crossed the big dog. Leaving a FDNY shoulder patch stuffed in the
mouth of the drug lord's severed head left
little doubt, even for the hard of thinking,
as to who got the revenge.

During the extraction, he and his eight
men walked into an ambush and lost three
guys during the five-hour firefight. At one
point, Brad was separated from his men.
With the daylight, the choppers were able
to get to a nearby landing zone. Apache
gunships, armed to the teeth, went in to
secure the LZ but there still remained a
hundred-yard patch of no cover kill zone
between them and the LZ. Brad was
between his men and the enemy. His was
the longest distance back to the landing
zone. As his five remaining men opened fire
on the enemy to cover his exit, he was shot
in the leg and went down with a busted
bone. He knew he was toast. He waved his
men on, signaling them to leave and get
the hell out. He was waiting for a sniper
or machine gun burst to finish him off. He
was more angry at himself than scared
when suddenly he saw Eric. It looked like
he was stepping on exploding earth as bullets kicked up dirt and rocks around his
feet. He scrambled over to Brad, threw a

Kevlar vest over Brad's back, and hoisted him onto his own back. Then he hustled like hell and got both of them over the small, life-saving berm. Two of the other guys then lifted Brad up and headed for the chopper as a hovering Apache was now free to use it's mini-gun on the bad guys without fear of killing Brad. The terrifying fusillade of hundreds of rounds per second shredded the enemy positions with a horrifyingly loud machine-like buzz that quieted most of the return fire long enough for the extraction to be completed. Brad blacked out in the chopper; the last thing he saw was Eric applying pressure to his severed artery.

ᴅᴏ҄

Owens knew that any official inquiry into Doctor Cassandra Cassidy would set off alarm bells with the feds, but he had an idea that it might lead him to her and possibly DiMaggio, if they were still alive. It was a delicate move and could backfire, but he thought it was worth a shot.

"Bill, Bill Owens? What the hell are you doing here?" Dick Randle said, extending his hand as he walked up to meet him at reception.

"Hey, Sarge."

"That was a long time ago, Detective. It is still Detective, right?"

"Still pounding. You, on the other hand, did very well."

"No. My daughter married well. Her college sweetheart is a VP here at AmEx and he got me the interview. That was ten years ago. So what brings you to the forty-fourth floor?"

"I need a favor."

"Well you got a lot of nerve. Don't think I forgot about you hitting on my first wife!"

"That was me?"

"Yes, that was you."

Bill was thrown. He was sure it was Dan. *Could I be getting that old?* "I don't remember being with your ex-wife."

"What? No, that was Dan who slept with her, the hard on. But you were always checking her out."

"Oh, okay then, guilty as charged. And I feel better."

"Why's that?"

"Cause it means I don't have Alzheimer's. I thought I forgot screwing her."

"I wish I could... So what is it you want?"

As they drove down Marcy Avenue past the Kosciuszko Pool, DiMaggio recalled that the last time he was on the streets of Bedford Stuyvesant was way back when he was a beat cop in the Seventy-Ninth Precinct. The place had come up somewhat from the ratty condition it was in back then. Murders were down and money slowly started trickling back into the neighborhood that, he always felt, was fighting for its survival. Bed Stuy had taken a gut punch during the times of social unrest and most people who remembered those headlines still steered clear of it, even though it was just a snapshot in time. Although, he started to remember, during his time here, a crack epidemic and gang warfare kept the neighborhood off the Michelin places-to-visit guide.

He pulled up to the curb opposite a wood-frame house that could have used a carpenter to level out the small porch and slanting steps, plus a platoon of scrappers, painters, and aluminum-siders to get it all the way back to decent.

DiMaggio and Cassidy approached the rickety screen door of the house.

A black woman in her fifties opened it and squinted into the afternoon light.

"Who whiz zit? What chew want?"

"We are friends of Maggie Reade. She was LaShana's big sister," DiMaggio said.

"She was a good woman. Spending her time with a child, not her own, like that."

"Is LaShana home?" Cassidy asked.

The woman stood straighter, as she didn't trust strangers. "Why you want ta know?"

"We have something for her."

DiMaggio flashed the envelope and the importance of the wad of cash was not lost on the middle-age woman. She yelled over her shoulder. "LAAASHAAANAAAAA git down here this minute. Some folks wants to see you."

She then flashed an ingenuous smile at the man holding the money-packed envelope. But a second later, her face was torn as her impatience contorted it. "LaShana! You git your butt down here now girl or I'll beat the black off it."

A darling little girl, in a white jumper with bows in her hair, came flopping down the stairs two at a time and took a subordinate position under her granny's arm. "Say hello to these nice people. Theys got something for you from that white girl, Maggie, who used to take you places."

LaShana lit up when she heard Reade's name.

Up in LaShana's room, Granny sat in a chair as DiMaggio, Cassidy, and LaShana sat on the bed. LaShana had spread the money on the bed and was moving it around. "You sure all this is for me?"

DiMaggio stood up, smiling. "Yes. Maggie wanted you to have it. She cared very much for you."

"Then why did she go away?"

"Ah... um..." DiMaggio was dumbfounded. He looked at Granny and she shrugged and turned away.

Cassidy jumped in. "Do you believe in God?"

The little girl nodded.

"Well, God has called Maggie back to heaven to help with things up there."

"Why?"

"'Cause Maggie was brave and helped people like you. She's up there right now looking after you and, in a way, she sent us here with the money to help you and Granny, but mostly to let you know that she still loves you. And you will never be alone because from up there, Maggie will always love you and be with you. All you got to do is keep her right here..." she gently placed her hand over the little girl's heart, "right here in your heart."

"So if she's with God, I can say hello to her every night when Granny makes me say my prayers before bed?"

"Every night." Cassidy leaned over and kissed her forehead, and the little girl melted into her arms. She held her for a long moment.

DiMaggio bent down and softly asked, "LaShana? Do you remember the last time you saw Maggie?"

"Yes."

"Did she leave something with you or forget something or give you something to hold onto for her?"

"Like what? What you looking for, mister?" Granny's suspicions started to rise.

"A computer disk."

"No, we ain't got nothing like that."

The cop in DiMaggio didn't trust her tone of voice. "Are you sure LaShana?"

"Yes."

DiMaggio looked at Cassidy. She gave him a barely perceptible shake of her head, indicating she had no other ideas, so they said their goodbyes and left.

As they got into the car, Cassidy tried to make the best of it. "It was a good idea."

"I thought for sure that was it."

She looked back at the house. "Well at least that family can use the money."

"Yeah, ain't that a kick. Maggie would've liked that."

As he started the car, Cassidy saw LaShana come out of the house and head toward the car. "Mike, hold it." She lowered the window as the little girl came up to it. "What is it, LaShana?"

She handed the zip disk to Cassidy while twisting her body from right to left and biting her thumbnail. Cassidy leaned out of the window a little and kissed her.

"This fell out of Maggie's backpack when she was here. She called and told me to hide it and don't tell nobody. She said she'd come get it but she never did."

"Then you did the right thing, LaShana," DiMaggio said.

"But I just told Granny and she said you were friends of Miss Maggie and it was okay to give it to you."

"We are friends and we are so proud of you," Cassidy said.

"Granny said to say I'm sorry, and would you like to come in for cake and coffee?"

"Thank you, LaShana. You tell your granny thank you, we'd like that, but we've got to do something," DiMaggio said.

Cassidy placed her hand on the little girl's hand that was resting on the sill of the passenger-side window. "But tell her we'll be back."

She looked up at Cassidy. "Good. I'd like that."

IOQ

Owens' hunch had paid off. After ten hours of eyestrain, pouring through the small print of AmEx statements, a purchasing pattern of Cassandra Cassidy emerged. He could see from her purchases that she spent time regularly in Aspen, East Hampton, St. Bart's, and all over New York City, of course. There were also many gas purchases, mostly along the New York State thruway. That last point was mildly interesting because he found no charges in places that far north, like if she went to Albany for instance. Then he found what he was looking for. There, buried in over twenty-three hundred transactions making up the last five years of the Platinum credit card history of Doctor Cassandra Cassidy, was one charge from four years back. Out of state, never duplicated, and out of her buying and bill-paying pattern.

He called the vendor, which was an FTD on-line service. After throwing around enough cop chat, he reached the Boca Raton florist who was able to trace the transaction to a delivery of a hundred-dollar bouquet of flowers to a Mr. Herb Bertowsky at The Palms Extended Care Facility. The card read, "Happy Birthday, Dad."

The head nurse at the facility reported to Owens that Mr. Bertowsky had died three years ago. This now explained a trip she took eleven months later to that part of Florida. From the record of her purchases, she stayed there four days, enough time for a funeral.

He then rifled through the Orange, Dutches, Sullivan, Ulster, Greene, Columbia, and Delaware County land records databases until he found Herbert W. Bertowsky in Delaware County. He owned three acres located off of a preserve where Owen had once gone deer hunting.

27. Number One

DiMaggio paid for two nights in cash and then joined Cassidy heading upstairs to their room at the Fort Lee Motor Inn. They needed to be back in the city early in the morning, so getting a room right outside New York made more sense than going back up to the cabin. From the second floor walkway, he could see the Jersey side tower of the George Washington Bridge. A pal of DiMaggio's, who was a Port Authority cop, once took him to the top of that tower six hundred feet above the river. It was the first time DiMaggio realized he had a mild case of acrophobia.

In the room, Cassidy said, "You take the bed that's closer to the bathroom."

DiMaggio laughed. "Geez, it's like we've been married for twenty years."

"God forbid," Cassidy said with a slight twitter as she entered the bathroom and closed the door.

DiMaggio found the remote and turned on the TV. He found ESPN and plopped down on the bed, crossing his legs, and turned up the volume.

When Cassidy came out of the bathroom, she said, "That's too loud; what are you, deaf?"

"No, in fact I can hear real good; it was either this or listen to you pee."

She was about to say something but then simply said, "I'm hungry."

IO.

With Cassandra still dressed in her tie-dyed peasant dress and DiMaggio in sunglasses, they felt dis-
guised enough to go out to eat in this out-of-the-way
small town across the river from Manhattan. It was
a matter of local folklore that the diner was invented
in New Jersey. So sitting in a booth, looking like they
just came from a Jefferson Airplane concert, in a classic dining-car-style establishment just enhanced the
entire retro-experience.

They were looking over the menu when DiMaggio
asked, "What are you gonna have?"

"Turkey club and a diet coke."

"You know what some guy once told me? He said
that everywhere in America, in every diner, the Turkey
Club sandwich is always number one on the menu."

She looked down again. "Oh yeah, you're right.
Number one is the turkey club."

The waitress came over and DiMaggio ordered.
"I'll have the meatloaf special and she's going to have
a number... one."

"...three! Roast beef on rye," she jumped in.

The waitress walked off to the kitchen and DiMaggio looked at her. "So what? Suddenly turkey not good
enough for you?"

"Let me put this in a way your simian brain can
process. It's a woman's prerogative to change her
mind; it comes with the tits!"

DiMaggio flipped the selections on the tabletop
jukebox that sat between them in the booth. The waitress returned. "You want a salad with your sandwich,
Miss? It comes with it."

"Oh, sure."

"Russian, thousand island, or blue?"

"Russian... on the side, please."

She left.

"Why do you do that?"

"What?"

"On the side.... Like you aren't going to use it all up anyway."

"Are we dating? Are you my husband? I have been stuck with you for a week and already you make a 'been married too long' kind of crack like that? Do you ever think before you speak?"

"I'm just saying that 'on the side' doesn't make it any less fattening."

"Are you saying I'm fat?"

"No. Not at all. I just think you are fooling yourself."

"Maybe you should stick to cops and robbers and leave the psycho-analytics to a professional."

"Why all the charades? Why don't you just go for it?" DiMaggio said as he perused the music selections.

"Okay. What's really going on here?"

"Nothing."

"Nothing, huh? How about I take a guess?"

"Nothing." DiMaggio said.

"You've never had an experience like last night before and it's bugging you. Your whole value system has been upset, turned topsy-turvy, head over heels and you need to come down on me to get your bearings."

"You don't know what you are talking about."

"Oh, don't I? Your primary, elemental way of making love and deriving pleasure has been shaken by an act of erotica, probably enhanced with the danger we were facing right then and there."

"Get bent. Deriving pleasure... I ain't no panty waist."

"Please shove your frail male ego in your holster for a second and try to follow me. You actually like what happened, but it doesn't compute with the caveman hump-hump, bang-bang, 'roll over and hibernate' way, that you are used to."

"Hey, I do all right with women."

"Sure, as long as they are emotionally wounded or have a low enough self-esteem to put up with your shit, or most likely too scared to ask for a loving, sensitive partner."

"Hey, I got shitloads of fucking sensitivity," DiMaggio said, maybe a tad bit too loud.

Some diners looked over but he glared one of them down.

"Look, don't be scared. I know evolution can hurt and it can make you feel uncertain, but the important thing is, you are not going to turn gay or into a trans-sexual cross-dresser because you had sex outside of a vagina."

"You know, I hate you."

"I know."

The food arrived. For a few minutes, DiMaggio played with his food, moving around the peas and mashing them into his potatoes. He spoke into the green and white mountain he was forming. "Does that actually happen?"

"What?"

"You know, guys turning gay after something like that?"

Cassidy slammed down her fork, "You are such a child."

As if on cue, "little Mikey" picked up his plate and was about to move to a table across the way but then he stopped. "You know, you probably have some psychoneurotic term for this, but how come there are moments when you are okay. I see good in you and I'm even impressed with the way you are. Then, like a snapping turtle, all of a sudden you turn into this ragging..."

"Bitch?"

"No, hormonal time bomb, although I don't know whose hormones you are affecting. I don't want to hate you but sometimes you make it so damn easy."

"Face it, Mike, we don't mix. If it weren't that we were forced into this, neither of us would choose to spend time with the other."

"Exactly!"

They both were about to say something but each decided just to eat.

After a few minutes, DiMaggio said, "You were great with the kid this afternoon."

"The worst thing for a little girl is to feel alone and abandoned."

DiMaggio softened and ate his dinner without further discussion.

ⅅ

Eric came back to the teashop dressed like he was going to a ball game. He had even found a New York Yankee cap in the bazaar down the street.

Brad took a sip of tea. "Look, I did some checking and what you described and the Senegalese connection through Oman sounds like the sex slave trade. Senegal is on a watch list. I'm sorry, Eric."

"Shit."

"Here's the best I could do."

Eric was amazed when he handed him ten thousand dollars in cash and Brad's personal black diplomatic passport with one difference. "The ten grand is a loan; the passport you should burn once you land."

Eric studied Brad's passport, "Wait a minute, what did you do? Just peel my pic off my ID and place it over yours?"

"A little more complicated than that, I had to reprogram the chip with your digital picture as well. The easy part was sealing it downstairs on the official machine. But I only had time to hack the picture, not the meta-data, so if some border agent digs deeper or spends more than twenty seconds on the scan of this dip passport, then you are toast!"

"So I go to the diplomatic line?"

"Not unless you like proctoscope exams. Anywhere outside the U.S., a black beauty means more scrutiny. Here's the play: you go to the regular visitors' line. If you can find some wet-behind-the-ears-looking agent, so much the better. You hand it to them. In most cases they won't be used to dealing with it and might – might – just wave you through. Sorry, but that's the best I got."

"Sounds iffy."

"Look, like every other organization, there's a pecking order. Usually only the higher echelons of immigration agents get to handle VIPs and actually discourage the lower ranks from knowing too much... a kind of job security."

"What about you? Aren't you going to catch hell for this?"

"Not as much as I will for this." Brad reached under the table and brought up a diplomatic pouch. Actually, it was more like a briefcase with U.S. State Department logos and the words "Diplomatic Pouch" emblazoned across it and a padlock-like arrangement across the flap.

He handed Eric the key. "You can put the money, and the gun I know you are carrying in here. It's actually lead-lined, not that they would x-ray a pouch anyway. It would keep Superman away, I guess. It makes a fashionable and stylish traveling companion to the basic black passport."

"They are going to can your ass for this, my friend," Eric said, slipping the money and, covertly, his gun into the pouch.

"I'll report it lost the day after tomorrow. I'll take some heat but I got enough juice and time in to survive. But then my friend, they will have a line on you so get stateside before then!"

"I don't know what to say?" Eric actually didn't. He was usually the giver and rarely the taker.

"Well, now you know how I felt when you carried me on your back through the killing zone."

"How long before you can skateboard with that leg?"

"Doc's say another month."

Eric stared at Brad's face for a second. "I'm going to find her, marry her, spoil my son, and have you over for Christmas dinner every year, because you are my family's Santa Claus."

"I'll bring the presents. Look, Eric, I checked. The ship Setara's on will make port in Muscat, Oman, in three hours. That's why I gave you mine; there was no time for me to finagle one through channels. Get going. You got maybe sixty hours to disappear."

With that, Eric left.

Brad waited a few minutes longer inside the shop so no one would see them leave together.

Walking back to the embassy with the aid of a crutch, Brad felt pleased with himself; he had achieved a kind of closure. Eric's selfless act would have won him a silver star in a regular combat unit. But because the "op" never happened, the only metal taken home that night was the 7.62 mm round they took out of Brad's shattered leg. Being able to help Eric now kind of balanced the books. As the local traffic outside the teahouse became a snarled knot, Brad started planning his cover story to explain how he lost his passport.

28. Revelations

There was a flush in the middle of the night. The bathroom door opened and the dim nightlight poured into the motel room. DiMaggio looked over at the sleeping Cassidy. She was on her stomach, one of her shapely legs and part of her right cheek jutting out from under the covers. He took a long look, also checking to see that she was actually asleep. He noticed how her hair caressed her face on the pillow. He sat himself on the edge of his bed, bent over, and once again took in the view of her perfectly shaped bottom leading to an exquisite thigh. He took a deep breath. He raised his hand. It approached the curve of her cheek where it creased into her leg. His finger was outstretched, gliding above her thigh. His hand gently snagged the edge of the blanket and he covered her. He flopped back down on his bed and started fluffing his pillow.

He lay there and rolled over a few times, uncomfortable in his own mind. No position offered respite. He ended up at the farthest edge of his bed away from Cassidy with his back to her.

◻

There must have been a noise or something, because Cassidy started to stir. For a second, she thought she was dreaming. She smelled coffee and... toast? Bacon was the next sensory discovery and she was fully awake by then. She got up and walked over to the

242

"kitchen" side of the one room "efficiency apartment" motel suite.

"Over easy? Or scrambled?" DiMaggio asked as he prodded the bacon in the frying pan over the small, two-burner, Suzy Homemaker Easy Bake stove.

"Over easy. How did you manage this?"

"Got up early, couldn't go back to sleep, so I butchered a pig, stole these eggs from a farm, milked a cow on the way out and flew down to Columbia for the coffee beans. Did my private jet wake you?"

"Didn't Superman do this for Lois Lane or something?"

"I'm sure he got the idea from me. Eggs'll be ready in a minute."

"And you even shaved!"

"I used your razor in the shower."

"You probably killed it for my legs. I'll wash up." Cassidy felt happy, something she hadn't felt for days. At least he was trying not to be such a jerk.

When she emerged from the bathroom she had only one thing to say, "This is a red letter day; the seat wasn't left up."

ΙΩ

Setara had to urinate with the baby on her lap because there was no way to ensure that he would not fall off the flat bed in the dingy cabin of the rocking and rolling freighter if she left him, even for a minute, to pee. The door to her cabin was always locked. Food in the form of some kind of gruel was served twice a day by a steward who, along with his hands, looked like he shoveled coal into the boiler when he wasn't serving. There was only one bare filament light bulb on the wall that created sharply cut shadows across the cabin that were deep and made everything look even more threatening than her situation already was. The room smelled of diesel fumes, which gave her a constant headache. Every so often, the black-skinned man with a cigarette dangling from his mouth would come in and look in her eyes and mouth and examine the baby like they were livestock. He said little, and when he did, it was in a language she didn't understand. So mostly she cried, day in and day out. She had no idea what was to be her fate and that of her son. She survived on the most basic level without hope or relief from fear. She wondered and worried about Eric. At first, he had been her forbidden lover, then her abandoner, then her savior, and finally her dashed last hope. How could Kalhan have betrayed her and her son like this? Didn't he betray Eric as well? Was Eric dead? That line of thought just made her cry more. She often thought about taking the baby's life as well as her own, the certainty of death having become more of a comfort than the uncertainty offered by the African and this room from hell.

IQ

DiMaggio parked the car in a garage on Twenty Third Street and they walked over to TekServe.

"What is this place?"

"This is the place where the geeks rule. What the rest of us mere analog mortals can't fathom, they understand and they fix," DiMaggio said.

Several other customers were inside the building – holding laptops, towers, and monitors and waiting for their numbers to be called. DiMaggio hit the lever and the ticket machine spit out the number fifty-five.

In a few minutes, a woman walked up on the other side of the counter and pressed a button, "Number fifty-four? Fifty-four?" When there was no answer, she hit the button again and the display, which was an old Mac computer, changed to fifty-five.

DiMaggio and Cassidy sat down at a desk with Amanda, a service person. "What can we help you with today?"

DiMaggio took out the zip disk. "Can you tell me what's on this disk?"

"Old zip. Sure."

She walked over to a shelf and brought back an external zip drive and power supply, plugged it into the back of the computer on her desk, and slipped the disk in. After a few seconds, she looked up and said, "Nothing. It's blank."

"What? That can't be!" DiMaggio said.

"Looking right here at the directory, zero files. Ninety-Seven point eight megabytes free on the disk," Amanda said.

'I can't believe that."

"Sorry but there is nothing on this disk."

"Was it erased or damaged?"

"No. It's initialized and it comes up. There is just nothing on it. Nothing was saved to it. Or else the files have been deleted. Let me check. I'll run Nortons."

"What's Nortons?"

"A disk diagnostic program. Sometimes a disk says there is nothing on it, but it's just the directory that's cleaned out; the files might still be there without headers... Unless someone optimized the disk."

"Sure, stinking optimizing bastards," was all DiMaggio could say.

After a few minutes, the service woman said, "Nope. She's clean." She popped the disk and handed it back.

"Thank you, Amanda. Do we owe you anything?"

"Nah. Sorry you couldn't retrieve your stuff."

"Me too."

As they were leaving, an Asian fellow approached them and handed DiMaggio a card. "I overheard your situation. Try this guy. He's the best!"

IQ

Eric discovered that Brad was right; picking the non-diplomatic line and a young kid in a uniform worked. Although he had to wait with the hordes waiting for entry, it paid off when the pimply-faced guard who looked at the passport stamped it and asked no questions. No one went through or x-rayed his pouch, so his gun was safe. No one asked how much money he had. In fact, much to Eric's amazement, the customs officer didn't even ask him to remove the Yankees cap and sunglasses in which he was now being filmed by the security camera. He knew the pictures would be reviewed once Brad reported he did not enter Oman through Muscat. Eric calculated he had fewer than forty-eight hours to pick up the trail of Setara's ship and get her to America.

Even in authoritarian and secular Oman, there were mob guys running the ports. Eric found the ship that had landed five hours before as well as a crewman walking toward the only bar on this side of the port. Inside, he sat next to the man at the bar. He threw down an American "C" note and told the bartender, "Put whatever this guy is drinking on my tab."

The sailor looked up, "Why are you doing that?"

"Most folk say thank you first?"

"Thank you. Why?"

"Because there are five more of those if you give me some information."

"What information?"

"A passenger, on this last trip – black man – a diplomat traveling with an Afghan woman and a baby."

The sailor looked around. "Keep your money. I will lose my job."

Eric pulled back the side of his windbreaker and revealed his gun in his waistband. "Or you could lose a lot more."

The sailor was suddenly in a panic. "I don't want no trouble."

"No trouble and five hundred bucks if you just answer some questions; oh, and you get to walk out of here un-punctured."

"Are you with the..."

"Mob? You don't want to ask; what you want to do is answer. And don't even try to say you don't know because I saw you on the dock in Karachi help them board your ship."

That shocked the man. "What do you want to know?"

"Name, any other clues as to where they went after they left the ship."

"The African's name was Mumbuto. Senegal diplomat, I think. I'll have to check the ship's log for anything else."

Eric put his hand on his gun. "Give me your passport and your seaman's book."

"I need those."

"I know, but I also know you'll come back for them and your five hundred."

"How do I know you won't kill me?"

"I will kill you if you tell anybody or are followed when you come back. You have one hour or I burn these and disappear. Do you understand?"

The man just nodded his head and took a long drink from his glass before he left. Eric replaced the hundred on the bar with a fifty and left.

Later he'd take a position a block away and intercept the sailor before he returned to the bar. But first, Eric went into an Internet café and logged on as Brad to his personal G-mail account. He typed an e-mail message with the heading "Mumbuto – Senegal Diplo," but didn't hit send. He just saved it to draft. That way Brad could read it from the same draft folder, but there would never be a trail of any e-mail between them. As he waited for an answer, he Googled "world sex slave trade."

His blood boiled as he read of the profusion of human trafficking and the impotent attempts and futile agreements of the U.N. and other nations to thwart the trade. Senegal was on the list of a human rights watch organization. He read that usually the children of these slaves are themselves sold off as human cargo. It made him shudder with rage that his beautiful Setara and their son could be separated and sold into slavery.

The e-mail beeped and Brad's return was in the draft folder. The message read, "Low level - attached to the ministry of interior of Senegal – currently stationed in Karachi – has served in Canada and US. Last known Canadian address, 231 Locke Street, Montreal. US – Senegalese Consulate to the U.N. 521 East 46th Street."

Eric deleted the e-mail, the cache, the cookies, the data and the history of the whole machine and left the café to meet the sailor.

Eric had watched the bar and the street it was on for at least twenty minutes before he saw the sailor walking back toward the establishment from the south. Eric didn't see anyone pre-position themselves or any cars park near him or the bar since he had been observing. He was sure no one followed the sailor. Eric intercepted him a block before the bar. "Let's go in here."

They entered an outfitter's store and stood in the lobby. "What do you have?"

"These. Radio telegrams he sent to Senegal and one to New York. Also, he booked passage on a plane to Canada. It left three hours ago."

"Where to?"

"Montreal. I over heard him confirming the reservation as I was getting their luggage."

Eric was immediately puzzled, *Why steam to Oman, just to take a plane he could have taken from Karachi?* Eric took the passport and seaman's book, with five one hundred-dollar bills folded into it, out of his pocket. "Here. I have your name. I have your address, and if what you are telling me is not true,

I will come back and kill you, here or in Karachi or wherever you are. Do you understand?"

"Yes."

"Do you still say that what you told me is the truth?"

"Yes. I swear. I am no hero."

"Good." Eric just walked away. When he got to a safe place where he could sit, he read the telexes. Some were in languages he didn't understand, but one he was able to figure out. It was a confirmation of a doctor's appointment in a hospital or clinic, he couldn't make out which, in Muscat. Five hours before they left for Canada. His first and immediate worry was that one or both of them were sick.

He taxied over to the clinic by showing the paper to the cab driver who recognized the name. It was a small operation and he spoke to the man behind the desk. "I am trying to find Mumbuto; is he still here?"

"Mumbuto?"

"Yes, he is a black, and he was here with a white woman and baby?"

"Oh, yes. He left a while ago."

"Was everything all right?"

"Yes, I believe so. Just a routine physical and examination."

"That's odd. They are just in Oman for a few hours?"

At that point, the man stopped speaking. Eric nodded for him to step away from behind the desk. At first, the man hesitated but Eric waved him on with an urgency that piqued his curiosity.

"Look I can not tell you any more, than what I have..." He stopped mid-sentence at the sight of three one-hundred-dollar bills in Eric's hand. He looked both ways and moved Eric even further away from the front desk. "It was a full screen for blood, urine, and bowels. A total work up."

"What were they looking for?"

"Anything."

"Huh?"

"They wanted to make sure it was healthy."

Eric's paternal instinct arose, surprising him, but he let the "it" go as a matter of translation.

"How will he be informed?"

"The results will be sent overnight by DHL to New York when we get them back."

"What address?"

"I have it here." The man went to the desk and came back with a clipboard. "521 East Forty Sixth Street New York, New York, 10017."

Eric recognized that as the consulate address from Brad's E-mail. He left the medical center, but he still didn't know if they were sick or if Mumbuto was just being cautious. *Why would Mumbuto care?* Then it hit him; he wanted to make sure he wasn't dealing in bad merchandise. And this Omani clinic probably kept no records and asked no questions but had the access to reliable labs and equipment.

At the airport, Eric saw that he'd have to connect in Zurich to an Air Canada into Trudeau. By then, he'd be thirteen hours behind their landing. Eric expected the black passport to work its magic again and for Eric/Brad to enjoy once again the diplomatic privileges a man could get used too.

But the concern on the immigration officer's face brought back Brad's words, *If they spend more than 20 seconds... you're toast.*

In very broken English the man said, "To wait please here." He walked ten feet to a fellow with more insignias on his epaulettes.

The superior came back with him. "Just a moment, sir."

They spoke fast and back and forth in their native tongue. The superior stared at Eric for longer than was comfortable and then grabbed the passport from his underling. He rubbed the open face of the booklet on his pants leg and then he scanned it again. The scanner beeped.

Eric didn't know if the beep was an alarm or a green light.

The superior held the passport up and looked at Eric then the picture. He then handed it back to Eric. "Everything in order. Have good travels."

Eric found a smile somewhere under his nerves and proceeded to the VIP area.

29. Crack

Joe's Shanghai Restaurant had the best food in Chinatown, and the smell of Peking duck permeated the air outside, drawing hungry patrons and tourists through the doors. Outside, DiMaggio and Cassidy were talking to Joe's (Guo) twenty-three-year-old grandson, Yau Sun Yip. He was the brilliant coder for over one hundred sites for the Chinese community, also taking care of Hewlett Packard's home page and Dell's website in his spare time.

"You want crack?"

"Whoa, no. I must have made a mistake. I need help with a computer thing, not drugs."

"No. You want me to crack encryption?"

DiMaggio didn't know what this kid was talking about so he took the disk out of his coat pocket with the card he had been given. "Beano at TekServe said you were the best."

"Five hundred."

"Whoa."

"You want a crack, five hundred bucks."

"You sure we are not talking drugs here?"

Cassidy put in her two cents, "TekServe says there is nothing on the disk. What if there isn't? Is it still five hundred?"

Yau Sun motioned for them to follow him and they went inside.

From the window of Yau Sun's computer room, two floors above the restaurant, DiMaggio and Cassidy were both looking up and down the street to make sure no one was watching or following them. A truck with Mandarin writing on the side slammed into a pothole right under them and the gunshot-like sound made Cassidy jump back.

DiMaggio looked over at the woman who'd been shot at two times in three days. "You okay?"

"Yeah, just got the jitters I guess."

Yau Sun slid in the disk, then pointed to the screen. "Look, what's that say?"

DiMaggio squinted to read the tiny print at the bottom of the disk directory on the screen. "Ninety-Eight point seven megabytes free."

"Impossible. The system on the disk is two point five megs, otherwise it cannot be read. Should be ninety-seven point five megs available. Also look here, the word megabyte is all lower case" Yau ejected DiMaggio's disk and took out his own zip disk and inserted it. "This disk clean, I know, it says, Ninety-Seven point Five megs and see how Megabyte has upper case letter M."

"I don't get it; is this blank or not?" Cassidy said.

"Someone trying to be tricky. Disk appears blank unless you're smarter than the guy who coded it and made the phony directory screen." He turned back to DiMaggio. "We are at the five-hundred-dollar point, where I tell you what is on the zip."

"Go ahead. Five hundred." DiMaggio said and watched as Yau Sun went to work. His fingers flew over the keyboard, and all of a sudden, graphics depicting the surface of the disk appeared on the screen. He kept typing different strings of characters on an entry line and with each entry the image changed subtly. "Not a polynomial supplicant variety."

DiMaggio looked at Cassidy saying, "Nah, even I could have told you that."

"This might do it." Yau Sun started another program and the computer began rifling through new entry strings at a faster and faster rate. The image of the disk surface was now blinking from the speed but still not substantially changing.

Three hours later, DiMaggio was scrunched down in a chair and nodding off while Cassidy was reading a newspaper and occasionally glancing over at Yau Sun, who was wide-eyed and focused in front of the screen.

After another seven hours, Cassidy was out for the count, face down on a couch, and DiMaggio was sprawled in the chair, dead to the world. The morning light was washing Yau Sun's face through the window that overlooked the early morning deliveries on Canal Street. Suddenly, a chime sounded loudly and Yau Sun's intensity changed as his demeanor relaxed.

The chime awakened DiMaggio. "What happened?"

"Cracked." Yau Sun took the last sip of another Red Bull and tossed the can into the wastepaper basket to join the other four.

"Good work... good work! What's on the disk?"

"Relational database."

"Come on, Yau, give a guy a break here."

"Sorry; it's a list of names, attributes and dates."

DiMaggio looked but couldn't make anything out.

Cassidy stirred and found her way to the screen. "Is that it?"

"Yeah. But what is it?" DiMaggio said.

"Names."

Both men turned and gave her the "No shit, Sherlock" look.

"Well, is the judge's name on it?" Cassidy said.

"I would have thought of that eventually. Yau, scroll down and see if there is a Jenkins on the list."

"Here."

Cassidy put her hand on DiMaggio's shoulders and moved him over. She leaned in closer to the screen. "Oh my God, many of those names are clients of mine! Looks like you were right, Mike. He's blackmailing my clients with my tapes."

"Yeah, but what's he got on the other people on this list?"

"Maybe there's another doctor in town."

"You mean two jungle rooms?"

She gave him a slight jab in the side with her elbow.

Yau clicked the mouse. "Here, I expand other fields for you." As he did, the narrow columns expanded and the whole words became visible where before they just showed the first letter.

"And if I were this secretary, why would I be interested in the age, race, ethnicity, hair color, eye color, height, and weight of the folks I was squeezing?" Mike grabbed the mouse and scrolled down the list.

Cassidy noticed something. "Mike, there are two sets of columns. See here: fifty-two, Caucasian, Irish, Red, Green, five foot eleven, one hundred eighty-five pounds. And right next to it is fifty-four, Caucasian, Italian, Black, Brown, five foot four, hundred twenty-five pounds."

"Yeah that's screwy. Why two different descriptions."

"They're all like that. You know, most of these names are men, but here it's a woman's name and the description is one hundred and thirty-five pounds. Then the one that follows is two-twenty. Mike these are men and women... coupled."

"And what do the dates here in the last column mean?"

He hit the 'G's on the list. "Kevin Grimes. That date is eight years ago... and I just figured out what this is. Cassandra, what ethnic background would you say Mrs. Jenkins is?"

"She's a wasp. English and German I'd say."

DiMaggio scrolled down to the J's. "Bingo: Horace Jenkins. His description fits and the one next to it..."

Cassidy read it out loud. "Caucasian, German/English, Blonde, Blue eyes... that's her!"

ID.

Eric paid cash for a motel room outside Montreal. He showered and changed clothes, took his gun from the bag, and headed for the address on Locke Street, easily finding the single detached home. Eric walked by a few times and even went around the block searching for any clue that someone was inside. After twenty minutes, he walked up to the front door and rang the bell. No answer. He walked around back, picked up the doormat in front of the back door, placed it over the windowpane closest to the lockset and punched.

Inside, he started looking for anything that might tell him where Setara and his son were. As he searched the house, he got the sense that no one lived here. There were no dishes in the sink or coffee cups at the ready. In fact, the kitchen looked like it was only used by professional staff. Everything was in its place, as if they just hired kitchen help on an as-needed basis. The living room felt the same way, with no homey, personal touches. It was more like a residence for visiting Senegalese functionaries. He did find a Senegalese government directory and a few items about the New York consulate. He ascended the stairs to see if the bedrooms might hold more info on Mumbuto.

In the back bedroom, he found a partially unpacked suitcase with tags that read Elster. He continued his search, poking around the drawers and closets and finally found what he was looking for – actually, his nose did. In a garbage pail in the small bathroom, he found a discarded diaper.

The next bedroom room was in the back of the house and smelled like cigarettes. He found a computer and printer. He hit the space bar to wake up the screen, navigated to the Internet browser, and looked at the history. The time stamp on the last page viewed was twenty-six hours ago and it contained the schedule of departure for a coastal freighter called the Mauritania. He quickly read the entries and saw that it had left the port of Montreal twenty-four hours earlier. He Googled the ship and found that it regularly made cargo trips through the St. Lawrence Seaway down to New York City, taking about twenty-four hours to make the trip. There was a phone on the desk that was not seated properly into its base. Eric picked it up and hit "last number dialed."

It was picked up on the second ring. "Family Services."

"Er... hello. I was wondering what kind of services you offered?"

"I'm sorry, sir. We operate by referral only."

"I'm just looking for information."

"How did you get this number?"

"Mumbuto gave it to me."

"No he..." She caught herself and paused. Regaining her composure, she quietly but firmly said, "Don't call here again!"

And she hung up.

Eric looked at the phone, then Googled "Family Services NYC." Nothing came up. Then he wrote the number displayed on phone onto the palm of his hand.

🔷

Hannah Faust was puzzled. That phone call was against all procedure. Mumbuto was usually very careful and she never had any issues with him and neither did the Secretary. Still, she'd have to report it.

🔷

Outside the house, a car pulled up and two men got out and entered the front of the house. One had a grocery bag. The one with the groceries went in to the kitchen; the other opened his coat as he climbed the stairs.

🔷

Eric turned around and saw a locked portfolio. He pulled a lock-blade knife from his pocket and pried it opened. Eric rifled through the papers he found inside the portfolio, which appeared to be official documents in an African language. He couldn't make heads or tails out of them and was getting frustrated when he thought he heard a noise. Pausing his search, he heard a distinct "thump-thump" as someone kicked their shoes off onto the floor in the room next door. Eric froze and listened for any clue that whoever it was might be coming his way. He turned with the knife in his hand just as a man entered the room carrying a towel.

The man was startled to see Eric and gave a yell. Eric deftly swung low and swept the man's legs out from under him. The man tried to get up, but Eric quickly got behind him and stood him up in a chokehold, applying pressure to the major artery in his neck. He was waiting for him to lose consciousness as his brain was starved of blood, when he heard the heavy footsteps of someone else pounding up the steps. Just as the struggling man in his grip was starting to succumb, the other fellow came through the door with a gun.

Eric quickly put his knife at the neck of the barely conscious man he was standing behind and said, "Come any closer and I will slit his throat."

The man with the gun paused.

"Mumbuto sent me," Eric blurted out.

The man with the gun relaxed his tension ever so slightly. "Why? Why would he send you? Who are you?"

"I am code name Eric. We work together in Karachi."

"Let him go," the man said, waving the gun to the right.

"Drop your gun," Eric insisted, relaxing his grip on the man's neck but not lowering the knife. "I do not wish to die before I carry out my mission for Mumbuto and Senegal. Please drop it."

When Eric released his grip on the man's comrade, he lowered his gun but didn't holster it. "Talk fast or I will kill you."

"Mumbuto asked me to find ten thousand dollars he hid under the floorboards last time he was here."

"Why would he ask you?"

"He is on the freighter headed south. He has the girl and the baby with him. He wanted the money for some reason which he didn't share."

"What baby? What girl?"

Eric was shocked that they genuinely didn't know, that meant Mumbuto was working for himself using his job as Senegalese diplomat as cover. He had to cover his play.

"Ah, now I understand," Eric said to the confused African as the other man started to stir. "I see."

"See what?"

"Last time he was here, there was a woman and now there is a child! See, he is protecting his family." Eric started worrying that he was sounding more like a South African white, so he curtailed his accent.

"From what?"

Eric was glad they were buying this cock and bull story, but he had to make a move. "Again, he did not share that with me." As the first man started to recover he stumbled momentarily, but it was enough for Eric to thrust the groggy man at the fellow in the doorway. They both went down and Eric ran and jumped over them, kicking the man on the bottom in the head, knocking him out. As the still shaky man on top tried to stand, Eric brought both fists clasped together down hard on the back of his neck and he collapsed.

Eric scrambled down the stairs and out onto the street, walking away at a brisk pace.

Forty-five minutes later at Montreal's Trudeau Airport, it was a young girl with a ponytail hanging out the back of her U.S. Border and Immigration cap at the Précontrôle line that waved Eric and his black U.S. passport right through and he headed for the next plane down to New York. Having been pre-cleared for U.S. entry in Montreal meant he could fly into LaGuardia, which was closer to the city.

Ⓓ

Testifying before the congressional budget committees is grueling on the best of days, with friendly representatives inquiring about the status of the infrastructure and whether or not sufficient funding and appropriations are being utilized. Mostly they just cared about jobs in their districts, so Rodgers led off with that. It was a true crowd pleaser and most of the DOT projects and renovations were cherry picked to occur in the home districts of the members of the committee. Still, having his private cell phone vibrate in the middle of the dance was unsettling. At some point the gentleman from Illionois asked for a 10 minute break. Rodgers took the opportunity to step outside into the rotunda and see who dared call him on a testifying day.

"Hannah, what the hell...?"

"Sorry Mr. Rodgers but there's been a breach of procedure and I felt you should know..."

Rodgers returned to his seat as the hearing resumed but he was just a little rattled and a little off his game. *Who would Mumbuto give the New York number to?* He thought as he tried to get his mind off of him. His little distraction cost the American people one hundred and six million dollars in a pork barrel highway construction to elevate the roadway to eliminate two RR crossings off U.S. Route 40 in the Texas panhandle and help to insure the member's re-election.

Ⓓ

On the plane, the captain informed the head flight attendant that she had a diplomat on board. She found a way to give Brad (Eric) a first-class seat right before the door closed. As soon as the plane took off, Eric reviewed the contents of the directory and other papers he had taken from the Senegalese residence. Mumbuto was indeed just a low level guy, yet he had traveled and taken resources and residences that were more fitting to the rank of an ambassador. His first thought was that Mumbuto was an intelligence officer, like a CIA spook, attached to embassies and doing his work under diplomatic cover. *But if that were true then why would the Senegalese intelligence apparatus be interested in a girl from some backwater Afghan village?* No. The more he thought about it, the more he reasoned that this had to be something else; Mumbuto was working for himself. The knot in his stomach returned as the words of Brad echoed in his brain – *sex slave*.

He looked up and saw the flight attendant talking to a man and looking his way. At first, he thought his cover was blown. Maybe this guy was also a Foreign Service Officer who knew Brad and knew Eric wasn't Brad. Or the Omani immigration officer finally figured out that his pant leg didn't solve the problem with the passport.

The man approached and said, "Brad Hamil?"

"Yes?"

"You are not him."

"What do you mean by that? Who's him? Who are you?" Eric said with proper curiosity.

He leaned in. "I'm the Air Marshall; I served in Iraq with a fellow named Brad Hamil."

"Oh yeah, that guy. I get his mail sometimes. Once, I got an upgrade on my way down to Orlando on Delta because he had racked up a ton of miles. I straightened it all out when I got home, but the airline said it was their mistake and didn't charge me. He works out of the Africa desk. I am strictly North America. He sounds like a great guy though. At least that's what I get from everyone who asks the same thing you did. If you want to get in touch with him, he's at the U.S. Consulate in Pakistan. I know only because that's where one of my expense checks wound up last year. If you talk to him, tell him DB says hello."

"Maybe I will." The man continued looking at Eric for a few seconds, noticing the diplomatic pouch half under the seat. "DB?"

"Dennis Bradley Hamil; my friends call me DB. I dropped the Dennis in junior high – there were five guys named Dennis in my school."

"Sorry for the interruption."

"No problem. Happens a lot: same name, same line of work and all."

Eric intentionally didn't watch the man walk away. Instead, he looked down at his papers. The marshal could radio ahead and check on Eric's story, in which case, he'd be arrested as he left the plane at LaGuardia. There was nothing he could do, so he pressed the call button and ordered a scotch from the stew.

30. The Hudson Line

It was time. He hadn't gone hunting in years, so Owens took a few personal days, loaded up his Murano with hunting gear and headed north. He had loved and missed the time alone, and the way the simple act of hunting put him in sync with the natural order of things. In the city, he felt like all the buildings, air conditioners, heat, subways, taxis, and concrete made it seem like man had conquered nature and the elements. But even after just a few hours of solitude in the wilderness, the urban chauvinism melted away and the grandeur of the world and its independence and indifference to man was abundantly apparent. Once the realization hit home that nature doesn't need human beings to keep things ticking, his mind always opened to all manner of thoughts and even philosophy. He also suspected his heart rate slowed by at least twenty beats per minute.

Aside from the Thoreau-like epiphanies, Owens practiced an almost-Zen form of hunting. He only hunted when the Fish and Game wardens decreed that the herd needed thinning. Without natural predators, deer in the wild flourished beyond the land's ability to sustain the population. That drove many to starvation, or worse, into populated areas only to be poisoned or get hit by cars and trucks. He had never forgotten his neighbor's daughter, who was only twenty-two when she hit a deer on the Taconic Parkway. It was a messy business – the animal went right through the windshield and decapitated her.

Owens liked to think of his hunting self as being an agent of nature – helping to balance the deer population. Furthermore, he felt that his particular method of hunting was more sporting. Of course, the reason for this whole trip was to check out Dr. Cassidy's father's place for any clue as to where they were; hunting was just a perk.

He didn't have any trouble finding the Bertowsky spread. It was an actual log cabin. Forty years ago, they were kit homes: really cheap and really well put together. He approached carefully, even though there were no cars, no sign of anybody there. Yet listening, he could hear the generator running. Stepping onto the porch, he knocked on the door. Hearing no response, he tried the door latch; it was unlocked so he walked inside.

He touched the coffee pot and found it was still warm. Beds were slept in and clothes were strewn about, both male and female. A picture of a man and his pretty daughter on the shelf made a positive ID that this was Doctor Cassidy's deceased father's place. The only other sound was the whirring of the refrigerator, the probable reason for the generator running. Heat was supplied by the wood-burning stove in the center of the cabin. It too was hot. He specifically noticed the old VCR and Sony TV also hooked up to the generator.

He checked out the rest of the one-room cabin and noticed that the gun rack had a rifle missing. Sitting on the bottom of the rack was an almost pristine condition Colt Peacemaker. He put his gloves back on, picked up the gun and felt the weight. It was perfectly balanced for a handgun with a seven-and-a-half-inch barrel. It was loaded. He sniffed the cylinder and there was a trace of it having been fired, maybe a week or so ago. No coincidence that there was a display case over DiMaggio's fireplace missing the exact same gun. He gently placed it back on the rack.

The VCR caught his attention again and he searched one more time. There were no tapes – no plastic boxes like Blockbuster used to have and no black VHS tapes on shelves or in drawers. *Why the VCR?*

He stood in the middle of the room and turned around in a three-hundred-sixty-degree circle. Feeling something odd under his feet, he stopped, and then turned around again. He looked down as he explored the area with his foot. The floorboard under the small rug was wobbly. He bent down, moved the rug, and found a short plank that was loose. He lifted it up and found the reason why it was seesawing. Underneath there were stacks of tapes; one tape was higher than the rest, enough to make the wood wobble.

The names on the white labels appeared to be written with a permanent marker. At first, Owens didn't recognize the special nature of the names, but it eventually sunk in – all famous and or notorious men. He turned on the vintage machinery and popped in a tape marked "Kerins." As soon as the image rolled and stabilized, he knew immediately it was Senator Kerins. He was shocked to see Kerins being restrained by a hot woman wielding a whip with many ends. As he listened to the whimpers and cries of pleasure and pain, he scanned the other names: Wilkins, Kennedy, Jenkins, Harkins, Edwards... his curiosity got the better of him and he had the urge to find out how many tapes were stashed. By the time he was finished, he had pulled out sixty-four tapes – a veritable who's who collection of the rich and powerful. When he noticed the numbers on the tapes associated with the dates, he decided to arrange the tapes by the numbers and found that the collection started at the number two. He reached down into the void beneath the floor and stretched his arm as far as he could, feeling for the missing tape. All the way in the corner, almost wedged in, he loosened and pulled out the missing first tape. It was dated more than eight years ago and the name written on the label made everything else click into place – Grimes!

Even though he felt like he needed a shower after watching it, he suddenly understood why Grimes was grilling Officer Towne on the Jenkins' case. He now knew at least one person, Reade, had already died to protect Grimes' secret and DiMaggio was either dead or on the run with the doctor for the same reason. He also knew that sooner or later someone would return here.

Owens had enough experience as a cop to practice caution in this situation, even with a fellow cop. For that reason, he decided to stay in the shadows. He knew better than to leave a note or any other clue that he had been there. It was possible he had read this whole thing wrong and DiMaggio might indeed be a bad seed. If so, he didn't want to walk right into a dangerous situation without a little more surveillance.

With his hands still in the gloves, he replaced everything exactly where it had been and went outside. After scanning the terrain, he decided the high ground was a good place to set up his camp and keep an eye on the place. He drove his car up the hill, unpacked his hunting and camping gear, which he hadn't touched in years, and then drove his car back to the ranger station and got his hunting license up to date. He decided to leave his car there and hike back. A little more than an hour later, he started to set up his tent. If worse came to worst, at least he would be able to salvage his days off by maybe bagging an eight-point buck. As the sun set, he thought of his Uncle Harrison and the days he spent hunting with him down in Alabama – remembering how Unc Harry taught him how to track, hunt, and kill cleanly. Probably why he became a detective.

$$\mathbb{D}_{\blacktriangle}$$

Phillips Manor, Scarborough, Ossining, Tarrytown, Croton-Harmon – quiet little commuter towns along the Hudson River. Miles and miles of railroad tracks edged the river, providing lots of places for animals, kids, drunks, and the depressed to die. With almost four hundred deaths occurring in the average year, one method employed to limit the number of people hit by trains along the route was helicopter surveillance. But these sleepy little towns were full of executives that had to get up early in the morning to board the commuter "troop" trains to do battle in the city, and the last thing any of them wanted was "sleepus-interruptus-helicopterus."

To that end, Metro-North security got a grant from the Federal Department of Transportation, through Amtrak under the Northern Railroad Corridor Assistance Act, to experiment with silent drones which hover high above and have all kinds of cameras and detectors to see in the dark and through clouds. Packed with thermal imaging to spot any obstruction or persons along the route, it was the next generation of railroad right-of-way security.

Since the drones were in beta-test mode and not officially on-line yet, the jurisdiction and control of the NRCAA trial program fell under the auspices of the Federal Railroad Police. So it was that a duplicate drone controller was now under the piloting control of Burns, one of the men in the makeshift headquarters in Manhattan. Burns had his hand on the remote flight stick as Wallace watched.

"The bird has a twelve-hour flight and hover time." He looked at one of the monitors. "Here, look what I found." He zoomed in and, using the infrared imaging, found two people writhing and rolling around on a footbridge that connected a college campus to the shore of the Hudson River, just south of Ossining. "They're going at it pretty good."

"What'ya figure, college kids?"

"That's my bet. Now watch this; I do an RFID scan. And bingo, I got a hit."

"What is it?"

"Crosschecking now... Ah, Nike LeBron X shoes! Expensive! One of them, wait... size thirteen so it must be the male, is wearing Nike Shoes. Bought in the White Plains Mall, two weeks ago at seven eighteen p.m.. Paid for with an Amex credit card in the name of William Payne. Two hundred sixty-nine dollars!"

"So the inventory chip that was in the shoes is still active."

"Yes, and probably will be for a while." Burns read the "provenance" of the sneakers off the screen in front of him: "Originally made in China, where the chip was manufactured right into the shoe. The first time they were scanned was somewhere in a two-hundred-acre distribution facility in Tennessee. Then this one pair was scanned and the Radio Frequency Identity chip was logged in at various points all along the distribution route. New Jersey, Elmsford and checked in at every transfer point until it was plucked off the store shelf of Runner and Track in White Plains two weeks ago. Casanova here on the drone's video feed decided to wear them tonight."

Two hours later, they checked in as the shoes' RFID located the couple at the Elmsford Diner.

"Well, this proves we got the RFID sensors tweaked; now we just have to get lucky and hope we catch a signal."

Wallace looked at a second screen. It contained the credit card purchases of Doctor Cassandra Cassidy for the last three months, the range of time when an RFID might still be active. All product purchases were flagged, and where the merchandise was RF inventory controlled, the unique number that the chip in every item emitted was printed on the statement as well.

Right now, the drone was hovering over Pine Lane. It was getting seventy hits from Cassidy's shot up house. These were elimination tags. The hits that they were collecting from products in the house were very useful because they now could cross them off the list of things she had purchased but were obviously not with her. Cassidy had made their job a lot easier by only using a Platinum American Express card.

This process narrowed down the universe of products they'd be searching for. It turned out all but eight of the seventy products in the house were on their list. Those additional eight emanating an RFID signal were probably either gifts, that she didn't purchase, or items she paid cash for instead of using her credit card. In either case, they were eliminated from the master list. That left five products remaining that she bought but weren't in the house, so the hope was that she had at least one of them with her.

The freighter Mauritania, with Setara, her son and Mumbuto as passengers, pulled into Red Hook off the Buttermilk Channel, an oddly gentle name for a place that was the very epicenter of corruption and murder during the heydays of longshoremen turf battles.

An hour later, Eric hailed a New York City cab at the airport. The driver was unusually talkative and spoke rare, unaccented English. "Short stay or coming home?"

"What makes you say that?" Eric said.

"No luggage, diplomatic bag... you a courier?"

"How about you just drive."

"Okay. Whatever you say, Sarge."

Eric was taken aback. "What did you just call me?"

"You sounded like my master sergeant."

"You served?"

"Two tours in Iraq. I got busted up with only three days until rotation and got a prosthetic leg, but don't worry; I can still hit the brakes."

"What was your MOS?"

"I was an 88 Mike, TC on an MRAP. We got hit by an IED and I was the lucky one."

"Not a lot of great P.R. for a Mine Resistant Ambush Protected vehicle is it?"

"Yep, we voided the warranty on that trip."

"How's it being back?" Eric said as he thought of the men he saved from a similar fate back on the road, the morning he went A.W.O.L to find Setara. Having a Military Occupational Specialty as a Truck Commander would have put a TC like him right over the blast.

"Sometimes it's good, sometimes it sucks. I still get a little freaked out when I pass a pile of garbage on the side of the street. I was going to do my twenty and get out, but the rag heads altered my plan. With this Mattel leg, I couldn't swing over to KBR an make some real money in the private war, so now I drive cabs instead of Cougars and Buffaloes."

"You seem like you got it together," Eric said. The driver was lucky. Big trucks like Buffaloes and the rest were amazingly vulnerable to large buried or hidden in a pile of trash explosives like IEDs.

"You caught me on a good day."

Eric watched the city go by and wondered if he'd ever get to show New York to Setara and his son. He noticed the American flag on the dashboard and it made him smile.

The driver caught him looking at it through the rearview mirror. "I had some college twerps in here and they took exception to the flag on the dash. Asked if I was cool with killing babies. I held back from telling them somebody should have practiced that on them twenty years ago."

"They say that's what we were fighting for – free speech," Eric said.

"Yeah."

Eric looked at the license and then saw from the picture that he was exactly the kind of grunt he met over and over again in the dust bowl. "So..." he read the name, "Robert, maybe you can help me out."

"Maybe."

"When we get to Forty Sixth Street, I am only going to be a minute or so, then I am heading somewhere else. I don't know where yet."

"So?"

"Can you wait and keep my stuff safe?"

"You know it's the middle of the day; I don't make as much on the meter waiting."

"I'll double whatever it is. In fact, start it now even though it's a flat rate and I'll double that too."

"Sounds like you are up to something that you're making up as you go along."

"Adapt, innovate..."

"...and overcome." The driver finished the motto, "I got it, Sergeant. And you got a deal."

The cab pulled up to the address on Forty Sixth Street, outside the Senegalese Consulate. By now, he guessed that the air marshal had probably checked his story and sounded the alarm, so he ditched his phony diplomatic passport down the sewer on the corner.

He noticed two security cameras crisscrossing the entrance to the mission. That eliminated going straight in as an option. He observed as a man left the building and started walking toward First Avenue. Eric followed him into Starbucks and watched him as he got in line to order. The man had a laminated photo ID dangling from a lanyard around his neck but it was turned around, so all he could see was the back. Eric walked up and stood behind him. When the man ordered, the barista asked him what his name was to write on the cup and he said, "Amadou." Eric walked away and opened the directory he took from the Montreal house. Amadou Sow – Administrative Assistant – Council Staff.

Outside, the man turned back down the side street with four cups of latte in a cardboard holder, Eric caught up to him. "Amadou? Amadou Sow?"

The tall black man turned. "Yes, who are you?"

"Brad. Brad Hamil with U.S. State."

"What can I do for you?"

"I hope you will help me locate Mr. Mumbuto."

"I can't help you."

He pulled back his jacket and showed the butt of his gun. "Amadou, you can be dead before the coffee hits the ground or you can live to drink it!"

Eric saw the young man's eyes dart around the busy street they were on.

"In broad daylight? You would shoot me?" Amadou said.

"I am not alone, and there is a laser dot on your forehead from a sniper across the street. This particular rifle discharges a large caliber, hollow-point slug that will only make a small hole entering but will explode inside your head and blow the back of your skull into the wall of the building behind you. We've been tracking you, Amadou."

Of course, he had no way of knowing if there actually was a spot on his forehead, but Eric had the serious look of a killer and did know his name. "What do you want?"

"Where is Mumbuto right now?"

"He is on his way to the Bronx."

"Are the girl and baby with him?"

The man was shocked. "How do you know of this?"

"Do you think we'd threaten your life, kill you, over anything less? Where in the Bronx? What is going down?"

"He is making his delivery at a place called Xtra Space Storage in the Laconia section."

"Are you lying to me?"

"No."

"You are going to sit on that stoop. You can drink the coffee but don't get up, even to piss, for an hour or my shooter will put three in your head." He poked him three times in the forehead for emphasis.

"He will also kill you if I get there and you were lying or you talk to anybody or use a cell phone. Do you still say what you are telling me is the truth?"

The man nodded nervously, causing the sweat forming on his brow to dribble down his nose.

Eric turned and walked off, adding a bit of theatrical showmanship to his ruse, by speaking into a supposed sleeve-mounted radio mic like Secret Service agents use. As he looked up and across the street to the imaginary sniper's nest, he communicated the order, "One hour. If he moves or talks to anyone before then, shoot him." He walked out of earshot toward a waiting cab.

31. Store n' Lock and Load

For their five hundred dollars, DiMaggio and Cassidy also had the whiz kid print out the list and the other documents that were on the ancient disk. As Cassidy drove up the FDR, DiMaggio skimmed through the pages. "This is unbelievable. That this kind of thing still exists... and in America no less. If I weren't looking at it, I wouldn't believe it."

"What are we going to do?"

DiMaggio double-checked two different sheets of paper and then he looked up quickly. "We are going to get off at Forty Second Street."

Cassidy drew a few angry horns as she crossed lanes to get off at the exit that was only a quarter of a mile away when she was in the left lane.

On East Forty Sixth Street, they parked the car in a spot designated for vehicles with DPL plates only. The DPL ONLY signs which peppered the immediate neighborhood of the United Nations were a bane to all the local residents who lose valuable street parking to diplomats whose DPL plates mean they are exempt from parking regulations. DiMaggio looked up and down the street, and seeing no meter maids, he figured they had five minutes.

"Okay, why are we here?" Cassidy said as she looked at the buildings on the block.

"This address was on the sheets a few times. And now I see what it is."

Cassidy followed his nod. "The Senegalese Mission to the United Nations?"

"Yes, Somehow, they play big in all this."

"What are you going to do, walk up, ring the bell, and just ask them if they are involved in human trafficking?"

DiMaggio saw a man, with a consulate ID around his neck, sitting on a stoop with coffees next to him. "Excuse me, can I ask you a question? Is the name Mumbuto a Senegalese name?"

"What is this? Are you the shooter?"

At first, DiMaggio was confused, but then he noticed the sweat on the man's head. Since it was a cool day, the sweat rings under his arms right through his suit were also unexpected.

The nervous man continued. "I just told your man all about him."

"Tell me. I want to make sure he heard right."

"He is at the Xtra Space Storage in the Bronx. Can I go now?"

DiMaggio didn't know how all this happened but he somehow needed to play along. "No." Rather than risk any further trip-ups, DiMaggio just walked away, back to the car. Cassidy had to walk quickly in order to catch up. "What did he say?"

"Mumbuto is in the Bronx."

"What? Who is Mumbuto?"

"Ever hear of an Xtra Space Storage?"

"Huh? I think they have a big sign... off the New England, around Co-op City, I think? What is going on?"

"That guy on the steps thought I was somebody else. He blabbed to me after I just mentioned Mumbuto, a name that was all over the printouts. But he was also scared shitless. Somebody got to him right before we showed up. He asked if he could go now."

"That's odd?"

"Somebody, the guy he told about the storage joint probably, told him he couldn't move and I didn't want to change that."

"Take the RFK to the Bruckner then up Ninety Five," Cassidy said to DiMaggio, now driving, as she grabbed the papers and looked them over.

The Xtra Space Storage facility was made up of seven large garage-like buildings with bright blue doors encircled by ten-foot-high razor wire topped fencing. During business hours, anyone could drive right through. DiMaggio noticed security cameras and motion detectors. He also noticed one building, way in the back, with an extra level of security – another inside fence. Parked outside were three vehicles; one was a black Chrysler 300 with DPL plates. "Cassandra, stay here. I'm going to look around." He grabbed his gun.

"Look around? With a gun?"

"Yeah... hey, I'm a cop."

Cassidy had apparently given up reminding him that he wasn't a cop anymore, so she just nodded.

DiMaggio tried to avoid the security cameras, which for the most part were pointed at the perimeter of the facility. He moved from building to building, like a soldier taking cover, assessing his next cover spot and then hightailing over to it, keeping low and listening for any sign that he had been spotted. He made it to the inner fencing; the cars beyond it were the only ones in the entire place. The gate swung freely and he managed to make it to a utility shed. He was now fifty feet from the entrance to the only building that had two floors. Since he didn't see any garage-door-type entrances to the storage rooms, he figured the rooms must all open to the inside of the building. All of a sudden, he sensed he was not alone and froze, waiting to hear another sound created by a human. Whoever it was, he realized that the other person was on the far side of the shed. He quietly stood up, placed his back against the shed, held the gun up in front of his face and listened. He turned to his left to hazard a peek around the end of the shed, when he felt the cold steel of a muzzle press against the base of his skull coming from the right side.

"Hand the gun back slowly," the voice said.

DiMaggio opened his grip on his gun and brought it behind him without turning around. A hand took the gun from his.

"On your knees."

"Are you Mumbuto?" DiMaggio said instead of complying.

"No. Knees, now."

"Hey, I don't do that."

"I can make you." The gun pressed a little more into DiMaggio's skull to reinforce his point.

"Then you're going to have to make me."

"What are you doing here?"

"Trying to find out why you guys are trying to kill me."

"Who do you think I am?"

"You're the guy who got the drop on me. And just for the record, a rare event."

"Turn around slowly," the man said.

DiMaggio turned around, instinctively putting his hands up – he knew the drill. DiMaggio recognized the look immediately. "Military! I didn't expect that."

"What did you expect?"

"Some kind of fed, a rogue G-man, hell even CIA, but not... what? A Seal? Recon Ranger?"

"Who are you?"

"I am an NYPD detective. Well, I was, 'til you guys started fucking my life over."

"How did you find your way here?"

"Are you going to shoot me? Because if you are, then I don't need the third degree. If you are going to shoot me, then stop nagging me."

"What were you going to do here?"

DiMaggio sighed; this guy apparently didn't hear him. "I was going to go in and see what this is all about."

"What do you think it's about?"

"Some kind of human trafficking." It was immediately obvious to DiMaggio that his statement resonated with the man holding the gun.

"Eric Ronson, Tenth Mountain Division. Here's your weapon."

DiMaggio took back his gun and held it at his side. "Okay, my turn; why are you here?"

"My wife-to-be and my infant son may be in there. They were kidnapped from Afghanistan and I followed them here."

"This is just a hunch but I am guessing without official orders?"

"A.W.O.L."

"So we both can't call the cops," DiMaggio said. "What do you know about Mumbuto?"

"I've been tracking him from Karachi. African diplomat who brought Setara and my son here through Canada."

The sound of a latch and opening door made both men take cover behind the shed. They watched as a black man, who DiMaggio guessed to be Mumbuto, exited the building alone. He stopped to light a cigarette and then walked to his car. DiMaggio skulked around and came up on the driver's side. Eric kept his gun trained on the door in case the others inside came to his aid.

"Out of the car!" DiMaggio said as Eric trotted over.

"What is this?" Mumbuto protested as he got out of the car.

"How many are in there?" DiMaggio waved his gun toward the building.

"I am a diplomat of the Senegalese government and as such have diplomatic immunity. I do not recognize your authority."

Eric smacked him across the face with his hand that was holding the gun. Mumbuto fell to the floor. "Look, motherfucker, we don't give a shit. Where's my wife and son?"

Mumbuto's face registered shock and he protested through a bloody lip. "I don't know what you are talking about."

"Hey, shit for brains, I saw you in Karachi board the ship with them. I tracked you here so don't even try to bullshit me. Are they in there?" Eric pulled back the hammer on the gun and pointed it at Mumbato's leg. "Five seconds, you fuck!"

DiMaggio watched; he liked this kid. He was effective and cool. Then he heard the door latch again. "Hit the dirt!" He grabbed Eric's shoulder and pulled him down as bullets shattered the windows of the car.

Both men scrambled behind the car as three men came out of the building blasting their automatic weapons.

DiMaggio and Eric returned fire. DiMaggio clipped the one who was closest and watched him go down. Eric shot at one guy who was running to get behind a dumpster for cover – he never made it. The last guy turned to run back inside and DiMaggio caught his shoulder as the door was shutting. Both men ran to the door; the injured guy's foot was caught between the door and the jam. Eric nodded and crouched low and DiMaggio opened the door. The man on the floor started shooting but high, so Eric put three in his chest.

ɪ◌₂

Cassidy was freaked out at the sounds of gunfire and didn't know what to do. She put the car in gear, inching forward to get a better view. When the shooting stopped and after a few seconds passed, she rolled down the window and was about to call out to DiMaggio. She stopped herself though when the thought crossed her mind that she might be doing nothing more than giving herself away to whoever was shooting at DiMaggio. As she carefully looked around from her new position, she saw bodies on the ground but couldn't make out who they were.

⚸

At the command center, Burns got the trip alarm from the storage building. He alerted Wallace, who immediately called the ground team. Meanwhile, he piloted the drone from its search pattern to the north Bronx location. He had to be careful; the flight paths for LaGuardia and JFK were near and he'd have to stay low. He estimated the drone would be overhead in four minutes, and the ground team was only thirty minutes out.

⚸

Inside the building, DiMaggio and Eric moved cautiously and with precision from point to point, each one covering the other as they advanced. When they came to a staircase leading down, they descended the flight and as they reached the bottom they heard a soft cooing sound. DiMaggio saw Eric's eyes well up as he ran toward the sound. DiMaggio continued his watch and kept expecting an armed man to pop up from every shadow.

When DiMaggio reached the room Eric had entered, he saw the soldier holding a woman in his arms, kissing, hugging, and crying. There was a chain on the woman's wrist leading up to a pipe on the ceiling. The length of pipe and the chain allowed her access to a bare toilet and filthy sink but she could never get near the door. Eric held his son in his arms and looked up at DiMaggio who was watching the doorway.

DiMaggio smiled and said, "Beautiful family, soldier. Let's get them out of here." DiMaggio ran up the stairs and back outside, retrieving two heavy guns from the dead men. Remembering Cassidy, he ran toward the inner gate and was relieved to see that she was all right. He waved her in and yelled, "Come on; stop here and stay with the car. I'll be right back."

DiMaggio ran back down into the room. "Eric, cover them; hold the baby's ears." Eric spoke in Dari to Setara and then wrapped his arm around her head as she covered their son's ears.

DiMaggio shot into the ceiling all around the pipe fitting, carefully avoiding hitting the metal so that the bullets didn't ricochet and injure one of them. The pulverized concrete showered down and DiMaggio reached up and pulled on the pipe. It easily broke free as the anchors, which were deep in the slab, had little to grab. He leveraged it down and slipped the chain off. He rolled up the heavy chain, which was still attached to Setara's wrist, and handed it to Eric.

Cassidy looked astounded when DiMaggio emerged with a man, a woman, and a baby.

DiMaggio ran to the car. "I'll drive."

Cassidy got out and went around to the passenger side as Eric and Setara got in the back with their baby.

As soon as Cassidy got out of the car, the sensor on the drone got a hit. "Hold on. Holy crap, I got an RFID on something on the list!" Burns said.

"Wait, where's the drone exactly?"

"It's right over the storage place... it's a pair of jeans she bought at Saks two weeks ago. Something called 'Seven' jeans. We got her tagged!" Burns said.

Wallace got up and scrutinized the video feed from the drone. He saw the three sprawled bodies, and the high quality feed was good enough for him to see the wounds and pools of blood. "So there was a fire-fight and if that's her, then that's got to be DiMaggio driving."

"The other guy?"

"Could be one of Mumbuto's guys gone soft."

"You mean like he felt bad for the girl and the asset?"

"I don't know, but let's track 'em and alert the crew. This is all going to be wrapped up soon."

"What about the scene?"

"Shit. Okay, first re-route the crew and have them clean it up. We'll keep tracking the targets with the drone and vector them in later. Then they can take out the whole car. Meanwhile, I'll make sure nothing goes out on the NYPD radios about this."

"What do I tell them to do about Mumbuto?"

"If he's alive, get him out of there. If not, they'll know what to do."

IQ

In the car, DiMaggio and Eric discussed their next move.

"We should get you to the cabin. Then we'll be able to plan a strategy," DiMaggio said.

"I'm out of ammo," Eric said as he checked his mag.

"We got some stuff back there and we can stop and get some more."

"I need nine millimeter rounds as well as .308s; the Tech Nine takes 5.65 NATO rounds and we ain't going to find those at K-Mart."

"Hey, hey, tough guys," Cassidy interrupted. "Diapers, baby wipes, Desitin, formula, and then bullets!"

DiMaggio was about to say something but Cassidy held up her pointer finger and quickly interjected. "Ah!"

He slowly closed his mouth and just shrugged his shoulders. Cassidy turned her determined face toward Eric.

Eric sheepishly looked over at the baby and said, "I guess I have to start thinking differently."

Meanwhile, four hundred feet overhead the drone silently tracked them.

32. Derailed

It was a short consist – one engine, two boxcars, and a
tank car heading for the train yard. Jack had hopped
aboard and hitched a ride in the locomotive, knowing
it would save him time. He looked at his watch and calculated that he now had time for a quick sandwich and
a restroom visit before his meeting with the Croton
West yardmaster at four. It seemed that some freight
car door seals had been broken and the man wanted
to make out a full police report, more to cover his ass
when the insurance dicks came around than anything
else. But Jack knew the drill, especially after thirty
years as a cop on the railroad.

"Did'ja hear about the derailment at Port Jervis?"
the engineer in the cab of the engine asked Jack, who
was hitching a ride.

"No, was it bad?"

"Almost. It happened right over the switch frog off
the main line. Could have shut down the whole branch
for a day. But they used a re-railer and popped her
right back on. Could have been bad though."

"Well that's good." Jack watched the rails through
the short end forward of the big black engine.

"I thought maybe you caught the inquiry?"

"Apparently not; that probably went to Chesney.
He's been working up there lately."

"You know, Frank Barnard was driving. He's a
good man. He wouldn't have hit that switch a notch
above yard speed. That switch was jinky. I hope they
don't try to pin it on him. He's a good man – got a lot
of good years in."

Jack knew where this was going. "Look, I'll call Chesney and tell him not to drill Frank if it comes up mechanical; that's the best I can do."

"Fair enough. Thanks, Jack. Frank's a good railroad man."

"Yeah, I got that. Thanks for the lift."

Jack walked outside the cab and stepped down the ladder as the engine slowed somewhat. He hopped off at about five miles an hour and hustle-stepped until he got his balance. He then headed for the diner right outside the yard. He noticed the black Suburban parked out front showing the U.S. Gov. plates with the ARP prefix that railroad police vehicles carried.

Inside the diner, he saw four guys at a table. They were the only other customers in the joint at three forty-five in the afternoon. He went to the counter, ordered an egg salad sandwich and coffee, and then hit the men's room.

A few seconds later, one of the four guys from the table entered the men's room and took the urinal next to Jack. They peed in silence and both hit the two sinks at the same time. When their hands were washed, the guy waited for Jack to take a few paper towels. As soon as his hands were dry, Jack introduced himself.

"Jack Winchell, sergeant, North East. Don't believe we've ever met?"

"Joe Adams, mid-Atlantic division."

"You guys here for Jervis?"

"Who?"

"The derail at PJ."

Joe seemed a little unsure of what Jack was talking about. "No, we are on an administrative thing?"

"No shit! Part of the Corridor Act?"

"Oh yeah. That. Look, I gotta get back; we're running late."

"Okay. Nice meeting ya. Here let me get that." Jack held opened the men's room door and watched Joe walk back to the table. Something was off. How

could a railroad dick not know what Port Jervis was?
It was the railroad connection to the Great Lakes and
the 600,000,000 tons of cargo transited through each
year. And the other odd thing – it was the mid-Atlantic
sector, not division. Jack walked back to his seat at the
counter and took out his iPhone. He opened the department app and looked down the roster of railway agents.

IQ▲

At the table, Joe sat with his back to the counter. He
put a quarter in the tableside jukebox and hit random
letters and numbers, not caring which song came on.
When the music began, he talked in hushed tones.
"The guy at the counter is a real rail cop. I think he
made me. What do we do?"

"We handle it outside; too messy in here," the guy
next to him said.

"We got to bug out. We've just been ordered to the
Bronx. A mop up," the big burly one said in hushed tones.

"He's going for his phone," the man across from
him reported.

"Is he making a call?" Joe said, while cutting his
broccoli.

"No, he's just looking at it."

"If he goes to make a call, we take him down right
here; if not, then outside," the guy next to him said.

IQ▲

Jack didn't see any Joe Adams on the roster, but he
was smart enough not to make a thing of it against
four men, so he slipped his phone in his pocket.

The four guys got up from the table and left.

"Gladys, can you wrap this to go?" As he finished
off his coffee, Jack watched them through the front
window. They pulled out and went west.

Paying at the cash register, Jack left a tip and walked outside. He was heading back across the highway to the train yard and his appointment with the yardmaster. He took out his phone to call his supervisor, and as he stepped over a spur line that was the farthest from the yard, the phone shattered as a bullet passed through and entered his head. He fell to the track, dead. The picture of the four men that Jack had taken through the window of the diner was also a victim of the full metal jacketed round.

ſ Ϙ ı

"Amtrak Security..." A dispatcher sat at a console and spoke into the boom mic as she pressed her headset tighter to her left ear, "Amtrak Security... hello? Hello?"

ſ Ϙ ı

Three hundred yards away in a desolate spot overlooking the rail yard, Joe folded the stock on the sniper rifle and turned to his team leader. "Do we mop up?"

"Too risky and we got to get to the Bronx. Besides, before the local yokels figure it out, we'll have completed our mission and be long gone."

ſ Ϙ ı

DiMaggio turned off the thruway and headed for a large ex-urban shopping mall. As they drove into the parking garage, the bird lost the visual of the Taurus.

"They are in a concrete and steel garage, so the drone can't thermo track 'em," Burns said.

"Where?"

"One hundred miles up the thruway."

"The ground crew?" Wallace said.

"Just leaving the storage mess. They successfully contained and our NYPD man, Grimes, has quashed the identities. So they're at least ninety minutes out," Burns said.

"I wish the drone was armed. One Hellfire missile and our problem would be resolved."

"We're lucky we got operational authority over this one as it is."

⚆

In all, they spent an hour and a half in the mall. Setara was in shock from the overabundance of products available in every store. Not only did they need the baby essentials, but Setara also had no clothes except those on her back and Cassidy had left her house in a hurry, so they shopped for all their essentials as well. Cassidy got a kick out of picking out a pair of jeggings for the young mom plus some tops and a new bag. It was like having a younger sister to shop with. Cassidy paid cash so as not to leave a trail like DiMaggio had pointed out.

Eric and DiMaggio hit the sportsmen shop and the K-mart and loaded up with ammo and a rifle cleaning kit. Eric found a Nightforce NSX scope and decided it was just what he, the sniper, needed.

They hit the McDonalds on the way out and loaded into the car with burgers, salads, and sodas. Eric had a moment when he held up a Big Mac in front of Setara. She looked at it warily. As he urged her to try it, she finally took a bitewhile he held it. Special sauce dribbled down her chin and she laughed as Eric dabbed it away with his finger. As she swallowed the bite, she shuddered.

"No, huh?"

Setara grabbed the salad.

From the midtown command center, Burns was carefully watching the feed from the drone hovering above the mall. He had a good view of all the cars leaving from the four possible exits. A grey Ford Taurus left out of the east side of the parking structure and Burns followed it with the drone. The car got on the thruway ramp and headed south.

Back on the road, Eric and DiMaggio discussed their options. The women went through the bags and took inventory of what they had purchased. Although Setara spoke not one word of English, she and Cassidy communicated effectively through clothes and accessories.

The radio in the Suburban crackled as Wallace informed them that the target car was now heading south, essentially narrowing the distance between them as they headed north. Burns transmitted the tracking data to the team leader's iPad and they were able to bring their own location onto the same screen. They were twenty-three miles apart on the thruway and closing.

DiMaggio took the exit onto Route 23A North to get to County Road 28. Eric looked around. "Looks like good hunting country."

"Cassandra's dad has a hunting cabin up this way and that's where we're going."

"How we doing on gas?" Cassidy said.

The gray Taurus stopped for gas at the rest stop on 87 South. Wallace watched on the drone's camera display as the Suburban came into view on the north side of the roadway, slowed in the left lane, cut across the center grass median, and came back down the south roadway to the gas station. They rolled past the Taurus but there was only one occupant – an older woman with blue-gray hair. She got out and started pumping her own gas.

"Fuck!" Wallace said as he punched the desk, spilling his tea. "What do we do now?"

"We go north, grid by grid. Once the doctor is out of the car, we'll reacquire the RFID. The signal's pretty robust and now that we know what we are looking for we can sweep fast," Burns said, grabbing a few tissues from a box and stemming the spreading liquid.

Wallace was starting to get the feeling that this whole op was somehow jinxed. It all started with the "soft push" of a single drop of liquid into a judge's drink at the bar. At that point, all he knew was that the judge threatened to reveal the network and had to be silenced before he made trouble. Of course, he found out afterward he should have been more aggressive because it turned out the judge had just stolen something he shouldn't have had on him. Had he known that going in, he would have made the judge's demise a simulated mugging instead of an induced cardiac arrest, taking whatever valuables His Honor had on him along with the disk. Then adding to the dark litany was the now-dead woman cop who drew down on them. Add to that the "not dead" detective still out there, the woman doctor, of all people, shooting back at his team from her house and then eluding them, Bessen being killed, losing one of his five wet work team members in an alley, the shoot out at the store and lock in the Bronx, and now the dead rail cop.

He was wallowing in the metaphysical possibility of bad karma besieging him and this whole affair when suddenly a bright note entered the calculus.

In addition to watching the drone, Burns was also monitoring the Port Jervis police frequencies. "They just found the body on the tracks." He smiled when he heard a sheriff's deputy on the scene surmise over the radio that "maybe it was a wayward shot from an illegal hunter."

Wallace figured, "We have at least eight hours before they even have a clue it was a hit."

"What are the odds?" Burns said.

"That we'd be discovered by one of the five real rail cops in New York State?" Wallace said.

"I don't want to be around when the Secretary hears about this." With Bessen dead, Wallace was now forced to deal directly with the mission runner in Washington.

IQ.

The other gray Taurus, with the diapers and Winchester and Remington bullets, pulled up to the log cabin. Once they all settled in, they discussed how long they'd have to hole up.

"Turn on the radio; let's see if Mumbuto has made the news," DiMaggio said.

"I think he caught one in the noggin. He wasn't looking too good the last time I saw him out of the corner of my eye," Eric said.

"Eric, can you ask Setara if she'd be more comfortable in my bed?" Cassidy asked as she brought a diaper to the mother. Eric posed the question, and at first, she shyly refused. Not willing to take no for an answer, Cassidy put her arm around her and led her to the bed. As she sat on the soft mattress, Setara said thank you or some such expression of gratitude in her native language and settled in.

The news came on the radio but the shootout they were involved in was reported as a gang war in the Bronx at the storage place. Mumbuto was called an innocent bystander who was in the wrong place at the wrong time. No mention of his diplomatic status was reported in the brief news summary in the top of the hour news.

"Whoever these guys are, they are good and they are fast, and they've got pull all the way up the chain of command to cover four dead guys," DiMaggio said.

"So we are still off the reservation, aren't we?" Eric asked as he held his son in his arms for the first time.

"Afraid so."

Eric looked at the infant's clear skin and big beautiful eyes. When he tickled his chin, the baby started to cry and the battle-hardened Ranger started to panic. He quickly handed him back to Setara with an apologetic smile. She held the baby in both hands and raised his rear end to her nose. The word "ooof" needed no translation.

Eric went back to territory that was more familiar and picked up the rifle, which he had just cleaned and adapted his new scope to fit, and headed for the door. "I'll take the first watch."

"Watch? You know I never thought about that but you are right. Someone may have followed us from the store and lock. I'll relieve you at oh three hundred."

It wasn't a major revelation, but Eric liked DiMaggio's response in military time.

IQ

"The structure must be wood since there is no metal attenuating the signal of the chip," Burns said, exhausted. It had been a long night, and he took a swig of his fifth cup of coffee.

"I don't give a fuck! Do we have them or what?"

"The SKU number emanating from the chip is a dead match for the pair of jeans she purchased three weeks ago at..."

"Yeah, all right, where's the team?"

Burns zoomed out the scan on the monitors to show a wider area and a new blip about a mile or so from the cabin.

33. Topography

At two forty-five in the morning, DiMaggio was awakened by a new sound in his life. Little Eric Junior was calling for his middle-of-the-night feeding. The last cry, which was then softly muffled as he found the natural food source his mother supplied, made DiMaggio smile.

He checked his watch and thought he might as well relieve Eric and made sure the screen door didn't slam as he walked out.

Eric was over by the car. "Catch any zees or did my son keep you up?"

"Nah, he's a good kid. Not a peep. But if you go in now, you'll catch the three a.m. feeding."

"Thanks, here." Eric handed him the rifle. "I took a walk down by the ravine and up to the rise. If I were coming to get someone in this cabin, those would be the ways."

The Suburban took a position one half mile from the location indicated by the chip's signal.

"I got no topo map for this ground," Billings, the former reconnaissance scout, said.

"Yeah, it don't make sense to scout the site at night on this uneven ground. We'll wait 'til morning when we can see the topography and where we are walking," Hayes, the contractor on the job and former infantry captain, said.

"What if they move beforehand?" Reese said in his Irish brogue.

"If the blip moves we'll hit 'em fast and take our chances. In the meantime, we'll catch some shut-eye. Reese take the first watch and wake me in two hours."

"Aye," the former Irish Republican Army bomber said as he left the car.

Once he was outside, Billings asked Hayes, "The next job, in Columbia – are you going to sign the limey up?"

"I think so; he's got the edge. Yeah, I think I will. You got any objections?"

"No. I think he'd be good. There's going to be a lot of heat down there and since we lost Kolfax in the alley, we'd be a man short."

"How's the arm?" Hayes asked as he jutted his chin at the now patched up wound from the girl cop's basement.

"It itches."

10

Once he returned to the cabin to catch forty winks, Eric had to think twice. As a soldier, he was ready to flop down on the floor, then he looked over and saw Setara on the bed. *Why not?*, he thought. He carefully lay down with Setara and the baby, cautiously bringing his arm up and softly resting it over her as he spooned. Setara let out a little moan, turned her head toward him, and kissed him. He kissed her back and exhaled for the first time in a long time. They lay there for a while and she said in a sleepy voice in Dari, "Thank you for coming back for us."

"Setara, I love you more than anything. It was hell not being with you for all those months."

"I know of the hell of those months."

He held her tighter and kissed the back of her head. "I'm never going to leave you or our son ever again."

⬡

Time passed and she started to speak but then stopped.

"What is it Setara?" Eric held her tighter as he asked.

"That man, the one you killed."

"The Devil's Farmer?"

"Yes, Dehqan. Can you forgive me?" She looked out into the dark room, her eyes filling with tears, fearing his answer from behind her.

"Darling, you were pregnant, abandoned and scared. I did that to you. You don't need to explain anything to me."

Although the words warmed her and made her fall back, resting her head on his shoulder, she felt the need to explain, to share her burden with him and possibly ease her guilt. "Felba was furious with me..." Her speech halted and her eyes welled up. "Felbie... I hope you are safe," she whispered to the sister who wasn't there.

"She and Kalhan got away. I saw them escape. They are fine."

Setara tightened her grip on Eric's arm. "Kalhan betrayed us. I don't think she is safe with him."

"Setara, I found out that Kahlan only betrayed me. At least that's what he thought. He thought he was securing your safe passage by trading me to the chief, he didn't know the Farmer was delivering you to the chief as well."

"He was a brute and a smuggler but when you did not return, I went along with the Farmer's offer. He would take my baby and find a good home in Europe or America where such children, he told me, are very desired. That was enough for me to know he would be safe, but he said he would also pay me twenty thousand U.S. At first I said no, but then Kalhan explained to Felba that with the money, I could escape my family and the dishonor placed on my family for being with an infidel." She turned her head back toward Eric. "Oh, I am sorry; I do not think you are an infid..."

"It's okay, baby, I understand." Setara was strangely comforted by him calling her a word that to her simply meant infant. "Many nights I cried myself to sleep but the only thought that gave me strength was our son or daughter living in France or the United New York States, and that was the only way I could go through the long days and cold nights." She pulled Eric's hand around to her mouth and kissed it. "Now we are together; it is the will of Allah, of that I am certain."

ID

Eric had tears in his eyes. She had been through so much; he had put her through so much. Her family turned against her with murderous intent by an ancient tradition of honor, and she was left not knowing whom to trust or where to turn. Living like an animal under a shack, pregnant no less, with no doctor, no prenatal care, no epidural to ease the pain of giving birth yet not being able to cry out for fear of discovery. And the most egregious thing of all was that she had to make a deal with the devil because he was not there for her. He vowed to himself and his God that he was going to make this up to her each and everyday of his life.

She slid her hand under the baby and moved the infant between them as she rolled over and faced him. They were both crying. They kissed; it was their first kiss without caution, the first time they could be free to not listen for intrusion and to not stifle their moans. It was the first kiss of their new life of freedom.

IOₐ

Taking a dump one hundred paces from your campsite was not only a good practice to keep animals away, but it also allowed you to stretch your legs in the morning. The last thing Owens expected to see in the rising sunlight as he was squatting was a guy carefully stepping and on-point. The man was not dressed as a sportsman or hunter and he was holding a not-very-sporting Tech Nine machine gun.

Owens froze, caught in the most compromising position a man can ever have nightmares about. He watched as the intruder looked through binoculars down at the cabin below. A minute later, the man was off and heading downhill, probably to check out the ravine that looped around the lower elevation of the cabin. Owens also noticed that a car had pulled into the cabin overnight. That meant DiMaggio and the doctor were in there. First though, he had to decide if the guy with the binocs was a good guy or an assassin. When he felt enough time had passed, he finished up and quietly and carefully made it back to his camp.

On the way back, he saw through the spotting scope he carried around his neck that at least two other guys were about one hundred yards off by an SUV. The sun was burning off the morning dew, and if they were there to hit the cabin, they'd make their move now. Judging on where the sun was and where he could position himself, he located a good spot from where he could watch and see who these guys were before exposing himself.

ᴅᴑ

Eric didn't catch the screen door as it slammed, his two hands each holding a coffee cup and the Winchester clutched under his arm. He walked up to DiMaggio who was staring at the highlands. "Here, Cassidy made a fresh pot."

"You found the Winnie," DiMaggio said without taking his eyes off the ridgeline.

"Great, old lever-action repeating rifle, and there's a sweet Colt Single Action Army revolver on the rack."

Without taking his eyes of the ridge line he said, "Yeah, that was my Grampy's Peacemaker."

Eric looked at DiMaggio. "You look like a hound that caught a scent."

"I think someone's up there." DiMaggio raised the rifle and scanned the area through the new scope.

ᴅᴑ

Billings had made his way to a spot east of the cabin. He now had the sun at his back. That added to his being harder to see while it fully illuminated his targets, who right now were standing together. He keyed his mic. "I got two men grouped in my sights."

Hayes looked through his glasses and even though Reese wasn't in the position yet where he wanted him to be, he couldn't pass up the strategic advantage of two targets inadvisably clustered in a neat kill zone. "'Take 'em," was all he said.

Billings chambered a round in his sniper rifle. He'd have a split second to recycle and get the other guy. He steadied himself against the tree he was leaning on and lined up the head of the younger one in his scope. He exhaled...

ID.

DiMaggio and Eric spun around the second they heard the groan. Fifty-five yards east from where they were standing, a man dropped a rifle and stumbled forward with an arrow in the side of his chest! He was dead on the ground before his third step.

DiMaggio and Eric hit the ground.

"What the fuck?" was all Eric could say.

ID.

Owens relaxed his stance and his grip on his hunting bow, as Unc Harry had taught him forty years earlier, and he moved from his spot to a place twenty yards away.

ID.

Up top, Hayes and Reese were in position and wondered why they hadn't heard the shots that made the two men hit the deck.

ID.

At that moment, Cassidy came out of the cabin with a skillet of eggs and bacon. She got about twenty feet when a shot rang out followed by an immediate twang of the pan flying out of her hand.

"Cassidy, get down!" DiMaggio yelled.

Eric drew a bead on the spot on the hill where he saw the rifle smoke rise from. He fired three shots from the lever-action antique.

He then scurried away from the spot he had just fired from as the return fire just missed him.

IQ

Now it was DiMaggio's turn to spot from where the shooter was firing. DiMaggio saw the shoulder of the man and pulled his sight slightly left and fired. He saw the pinkish-red plume and the body roll over in the ground cover.

He turned and saw Cassidy flat on the ground. He got up, firing up the hill to make whoever was up there take cover as he slid to a stop by her. "You hit?"

"No."

He picked her up by her arm and ran with her toward the cabin. He heard a shot ring out but didn't know who or where it came from. As he swung Cassidy around his body and through the door of the cabin, a bullet burrowed into the side of the doorjamb.

"Stay down, away from the windows." He ran to the gun case. He got two rifles, checked the loads, and handed them to both Cassidy and Setara. "Anybody but me or Eric comes through that door, blast 'em."

He then left, crouching and heading for the cover of the car.

Eric called out, "Did you bring any ammo? I'm kind of running low."

"How low?" DiMaggio called in response.

"I'm out," Eric yelled back.

"Me too! I'm out of ammo too!" DiMaggio shouted.

It was too easy. Both Eric and DiMaggio drew a bead on the man that stood up, heading toward the cabin. They both fired at the same instant and the man was pinned back as he crumpled.

"Schmuck!" DiMaggio said.

Eric just smiled.

Hayes saw Reese go down, hit from two directions, and assessed his situation. He had two men down. He needed to regain the tactical advantage, which he thought he had with the high ground. He pulled a grenade from his belt and belly-crawled to get closer to the cabin.

"Who and where's the Indian?" Eric asked from his new position behind the woodpile.

"If we get out of this, I'm buying the next round of fire-water, DiMaggio said as he pitched a box of car-tridges towards Eric.

ᴅᴏ

Owens was lying flat out in his camo gear; glad that he had kept the bright orange vest off. He was thankful they didn't manage to kill the woman. She looked like she might be the doctor. Then he saw it. A bush shook even though there was no breeze and no other bushes were moving. He took out his spotting scope and watched that patch of ground, looking for any sign of a person.

ᴅᴏ

"What are we going do?" Eric spoke in low tones to DiMaggio, who was maybe thirty feet from him behind the car.

"There's still somebody out there. How do we get him to show himself?" DiMaggio said.

"Just stand up. When he shoots you, I'll get him!"

"You know, I don't think you really thought that one through, Sergeant."

"Right, you got the scope, I'll stand up." Eric kept his eyes on the rise.

"Hold it, wait! You got a kid. That won't work."

"Back to square one. Well, I guess I got to do it old school," Eric said.

DiMaggio didn't know what he meant, but a sec-ond later when he looked over, turning his attention from the ridgeline to the woodpile, he could no longer see Eric.

Hayes was making his way toward the structure with the grenade in one hand, rifle in the other, when he heard something off to his left. He slowly turned his gun towards the rustle in the high grass. A deer sprang from the cover and hightailed it away. Hayes wasn't thinking about game animals and their behaviors; otherwise, he would have asked himself what had spooked the deer. Instead, he found out. Eric had flanked him and had him dead in his sights. Hayes, who was a trained paratrooper and didn't need much to sense a threat, fired from his elbows.

Eric dove to the right as he let a burst go from the Tech Nine he had retrieved from the guy with the arrow in his chest. The burst rippled across the other man's body and he hit the ground mortally wounded. Eric approached the dead man and then he saw it. "Grenade!" he yelled as he dove away from the smoking pineapple next to the body.

Eric shimmied low for about fifteen feet before the detonation occurred. He was pelted with dirt and rocks, and one piece of hot shrapnel tore through his shirt at his shoulder. The deep gash hurt like a bitch.

DiMaggio was up and running toward the blast site. As he passed what looked like a pile of leaves, a man fully camouflaged with branches, leaves, and face paint rose from the ground, aiming right at DiMaggio's back. DiMaggio heard the shot and when he turned his head, he saw a man who looked like a living bush arch his back and fall dead, revealing as he did a black man, crouched with a Glock 9mm in his hand. DiMaggio spun around and pointed his gun at the man.

"Mike! It's Owens. From Manhattan South."

"Bill? Bill Owens? What the hell?"

"Mike. The rifle." He gestured to the gun DiMaggio was holding on him and waved his hand down in a lowering gesture.

DiMaggio finally caught on and lowered the weapon. When Owens bent down and picked up his bow, DiMaggio got it. "I think I owe you a drink, Kemosabee."

"It's a little early, but hey, it's already been one bitch of a day, Mike."

34. End of Business

Burns and Wallace watched the whole gunfight from the drone's video camera. They were able to give Hayes some situational status information but the bounce off the bird of the VHF signal wasn't great in the mountains so they mostly watched their team get chewed up. With the crew neutralized, Wallace and Burns realized they had lost all operational ability and decided to shut down the op and get out of Dodge. Wallace just had one problem – he was the only one who wasn't a freelancer, now that his employer, Bessen, was dead. Burns and the two others in the room were security risks – specifically, they were risks to his personal security.

"Hey Burns," Wallace said, "I am going to hit the head... be right back." As soon as he was out of sight, he pulled his subcompact SIG Sauer P224 out of the holster clipped to his waistband at the small of his back. He threw off the safety, took a deep breath, turned around, and went back in the room firing.

"What the..." Burns said. Although he was hit, he quickly pulled his .32 from his waist and pumped two into Wallace before crumpling to the floor and losing consciousness.

Wallace managed to shoot Burns again and then shot the last man in the head as he fell to the floor, mortally wounded himself.

35. Early Retirement

Elsewhere in the city that night, in a very indistinct, one-room office known only by the engraved enamel name-plate on the door as Family Services Corporation, its one and only employee, Hannah Faust, was closing down shop less violently but just as permanently. She watched the blue line as it showed the progress of the secure delete feature of her computer's hard drive. This feature scrambled the zeroes and ones on the drive as well as just deleting the directories. She had seen too many cop shows where the drive was suppos-edly erased, but in reality, only the directory had been eradicated and some geek was able to rebuild its con-tents.

As a precaution against jamming the shredder, she had waited until she was finished feeding it all the paperwork – even the receipts for office sup-plies, lunch, cabs, and coffee – before she inserted the old zip disks. She had been keeping the receipts for her taxes. On the books, she made forty-four thousand a year for her services as Administrative Assistant. The "company" that paid her was a front engineered to withstand the highest scrutiny the authorities could employ, mostly because it was set up by the authorities themselves. She wouldn't need the receipts in the future because she wasn't going to pay United States taxes anymore. In fact, tonight she would execute her escape; she had already closed down her apartment and paid the last month's rent. She gave her houseplants to her neighbors this morning. In a matter of hours, she would be in Switzerland and then on to a small Greek island where she had shrewdly bought property years earlier. Her additional salary, the one she never reported and never paid taxes on, was a cool one million a year. She earned this by, in every sense of the word, babysitting. Or as she thought of it, giving the people of means the means to get the one thing that left to their own means they could never get.

As she finished off the last folder, she felt the heat coming from the overworked shredder and gave it a few minutes to cool down. She collected the three duplicate disks from her safe that were just like the one the judge had stolen from her when she went to the ladies' room during his last visit. She hadn't noticed he had removed it from the old zip drive until he was gone. That was the call to Washington she hadn't ever wanted to make.

She knew the business she had chosen wasn't the Girl Scouts but she had convinced herself that the troubling parts weren't her doing. She was essentially in sales. Fulfillment – that was another department. Her mental self-protection mechanism relegated to "lucky coincidence" the fact that the judge had suffered a heart attack during an extra-marital affair shortly after the stolen disk incident.

Hannah had started out working for the Secretary by wrangling a job at the doctor's office years ago, right atop the building where the judge's body was found. It was her work there that got her the further trust of her current employer and the sweet setup here at Family Services, the organization that she was now rapidly shredding. In fact, one of her tasks while working at the clinic was to impregnate all the doctor's computers with backdoor access. Over and over again, she had successfully used the good doctor's client list to extract hot leads on wealthy couples that needed her special brand of Family Services. Sales were good; over two hundred clients in all were acquired from the spyware, which was still on the doctor's server. As well as the transmitter on the doctor's office monitor that sent the video of whatever she was watching to Secretary Rodgers.

She jammed the first plastic zip disk into the maw of the shredder, which grabbed it with a gnarling sound as it chewed and mangled the disk, hungrily ingesting it. She turned her head, fearing that the snapping plastic parts might escape the shredder and take an eye out.

She would love to have taken her sister with her. Each having never married, neither of them had a reason to stay in the U.S. Too bad Elsa had died two years ago.

Prior to erasing the contents of the computer, she had transferred everything to a flash drive. She removed the tiny plastic USB device and slipped it into her Lorac lipstick case. She even cut a small top piece of the Leading Lady red shade and pressed it carefully into the stick. It was a metal case so she felt it was relatively x-ray proof. Besides, someone would have to be looking for it first. The now new shade of five-hundred megabyte USB "lipstick" was another insurance policy like her DVD; it contained everything on her computer and on those old disks: every name, every transaction, and every detail of the business over the last ten years, just in case.

As the last shred of plastic dangled and dropped into the wastebasket below, she pulled the plug on the shredder. She collected the four bags of confetti and put them near the door. Later tonight, she would personally take them to the garbage bins down in the basement on her way out. Tomorrow, on her way to JFK, she would swing by her lawyer's office, drop off the disk, and then go on to Greece and happily ever after.

IQ

"So I figured I'd get some hunting in while I waited."

"Well, you bagged two really bad guys. That's a good haul," Eric said.

"Mercs, posing as rail cops. You can't make this shit up," DiMaggio said.

"Somebody at the federal level's going to fry for this," Owens said.

"If he's still in the country," DiMaggio said.

"Or alive," Eric said as Cassidy taped a gauze patch to his shoulder. "What are you going to do now?"

"We're going to pay a visit to a widow and then go to court," DiMaggio said.

Eric pulled the piece of paper out of his pocket with the phone number in New York he had called from Canada. "Here, I almost forgot; this may help. Mumbuto called this number before he came to the U.S."

"You know what it is?"

"Yeah, disconnected. I tried it again a while ago. But this morning a woman answered as 'Family Services.' Then she clammed up."

"What are we going to do with the bodies?" Owens said, as the only person there who could legally have a gun.

"We still don't know who's behind this or what they monitor. I say just leave 'em for now. Nobody but crazy detectives with bows and arrows ever comes here, anyway." DiMaggio said.

"You know, I was just thinking that too. I am totally cool with leaving the bodies here. Hell, I'm out of my jurisdiction and on my day off to boot. If this ends well, then we'll call the state police and report it."

Cassidy went outside onto the porch. She looked up, noticing some birds of prey were starting to circle. DiMaggio came out and joined her.

"Is it over?"

"Hard to say."

"All this death, this violence. I am sick of it."

"I was on my way to the opera... then all this happened."

"And yet, somehow you are the reason for my being alive... at least three times," she said.

"We got lucky. Doubly so when that soldier in there came along right when we needed him. By the way, ever hear of an outfit called Family Services?"

"No. It's rather generic, but no. Why?"

"Mumbuto called them. I'll have Bill trace the number."

"Speaking about that guy, Bill, you know him?"

"Mostly by name; although we have chatted a few times over the years."

"What makes guys like you do this?"

"Whoa, you're the shrink. I couldn't even really tell you what it is we do."

"Is it a fight for justice or a battle against injustice?"

"I don't know, I guess once you decide you are going to join the good guys, you just know when the bad ones are threatening the peace, wrecking the agreement we all made to try and live together and pursue our dreams... I don't know. What I just said sounds like bullshit, now that I said it. Can we go back to the justice thing?"

She looked up as more large birds joined the circlers.

DiMaggio looked up as well. "Better cover those bodies to keep the wildlife from eating the crime scene. I saw some tarps around back."

36. Little Pre-Paid Miracles

DiMaggio and Cassidy were back at Marla DuPont Jenkins' estate, confronting the widow.

DiMaggio was treading very cautiously. "Why didn't you tell me you were trying to have a baby?"

"What's that got to do with anything?"

"It could be why all this has happened."

"I don't see how. As you know, my husband had problems in that area."

"He had a low sperm count, as well as impotence," Cassidy said.

Marla looked right at Cassidy. "Yes, you would know that wouldn't you."

"So you were going to adopt?" DiMaggio said.

"Yes. Then my husband died and... well, I didn't see the point."

"But you weren't going through the state adoption agency, were you?"

"No. Is that important to you?"

"Yes, I'm afraid it's everything," Cassidy said.

"The state agencies have lots of inner city kids, drug addict offspring, immigrant kids, and other less than desirable offerings," DiMaggio said.

"Excuse me. I have a right to choose the kind of child I want to raise."

"I guess that's the best part about being rich – you can even order up the perfect kid. One who looks like you and easily blends into your lifestyle."

"Wait, detective, are you trying to tell me all this was about my adoption?" Marla said.

"No, that's too simple. This is a ring, a... a... network. People placed orders for babies and the network supplied the perfect bundle of joy. Like Eric's kid. No questions, no hassle, and, I assume, no papers."

"That's why we were targeted, why they were trying to kill us, because we had the list of clients," Cassidy said.

"The names on that list were some of the most powerful people in the country and even the world. Most of them were wanna-be second-time-around parents and patients of Dr. Cassidy," DiMaggio said.

"Wanting a child to love is not illegal."

"Kidnapping, extortion, or just plain murder is."

Marla was taken aback by the statement.

DiMaggio walked her through the process. "I am sure most of the women they get to have these babies are paid something for their labor, but every once in a while, mother nature kicks in and these women don't want to separate from their child. In which case, they become expendable."

"Or sold into slavery themselves, like Setara would have been," Cassidy said.

"I said it before – rich people are really fucked up," DiMaggio said.

Marla shot a disapproving look at DiMaggio and walked out of the room onto the veranda.

ID

Outside, Marla looked out over the veranda to the apple orchard where she imagined a swing set would have gone someday. She had chosen not to dwell too much on the details of the "on-demand adoption." Now the reality of the seedy underside of this business was fully impacting her and her self-image. She felt weak and had to sit on the tufted cushion of the antique porch glider that she bought to be able to sit in and rock her child to sleep. Her chest fluttered as she tried to calm her breathing.

After a few minutes Marla came back into the room; her eyes were red and her handkerchief was soaked. "My husband said he knew of a way to skip all the legal issues involved. That there were babies like the one we could have had if he..."

"Yes, Family Services; we know about them now. But then your husband found out what was happening on the supply side of the operation and stole that disk. He was going to turn it over to the feds. Except someone got to him first and killed him."

"Killed? But the Medical Examiner ruled it a heart attack."

"I am sure when he reopens the case he'll find the cardiac arrest was helped along a little."

"Mrs. Jenkins, in order to be treated by me, your husband had to be checked out by a cardiologist and deemed fit for this type of treatment. I require that from all my physical treatment patients under law.

"Maybe in your husband's case some potassium chloride or other stimulant was slipped into his lunch or drink to elevate his risk. He did have a high blood-alcohol content and he had recently eaten. His clerk confirmed before he went to the doctor's office that night, he was at his regular watering hole. Everyone knew about it. It would have been easy to follow him or just wait there, ready to slip him a dash of something into his drink right at the bar."

"So then why was he in the doctor's 'treatment' room?"

Cassidy kept her tone soft. "He realized he wasn't going through with the network and the illegal adoption. It was back on him to provide you with a baby. We see...saw hundreds of men with impotence and fertility issues."

DiMaggio placed his hand on Marla's shoulder.

After it sank in for a minute, Marla looked up at him with moist eyes. "Now what do we do?"

37. Resolutions

"Owens! Since when do you just walk into my office? I don't remember calling for you."

"Well Chief, you didn't," Owens said as Marcus Towne stepped in behind him.

"So then why? Your boy Towne here get in trouble and you want me to go easy on him?"

"I'm not here as the vice president of NOBLE."

"I don't have time for games, Bill? Why are you here?"

"I'm here to place you under arrest. Patrolman Towne, would you take the prisoner into custody?"

"Hold it." Towne stopped. "For what?"

"The murder of Bob Bessen."

"DiMaggio killed Bessen. His fingerprints were on the chain that tortured Bessen before he shot him."

"No Chief, you were there. You silenced him before he exposed you and the whole network you're protecting and, I am sure we'll find out, profiting from. I got two witnesses and a video tape!"

"Who are your witnesses?"

"Me and her." DiMaggio and Cassidy entered the room.

Grimes was simultaneously shocked to see them alive and also crushed; he knew his entire world had just collapsed. He stared at the back wall for a second with the smallest twitch over his right eyebrow evident. He looked down at the picture of his eight-year-old son, who only he and his wife knew was adopted.

Towne stepped around the desk and was pulling out his cuffs when Grimes opened his desk drawer and pulled out a snub-nosed .38. Owens immediately swept away the side of his trench coat and went for his gun as DiMaggio turned and covered Cassidy with his body.

A single shot rang out.

When DiMaggio turned back to look, Grimes was face down over the desk, blood pouring out of both sides of his head, his smoking snub nose clutched in his hand on the desktop.

IQ

It was unusual for a colonel to agree to a meeting like this, but Eric Ronson had a spotless and exemplary record prior to his being Absent With Out Leave. So, when Eric called his commander at Fort Drum and explained that he wanted to come back in and that he had extenuating circumstances, Colonel Davenport drove down personally from the upper New York State Army Post, home of the Tenth Mountain Division.

DiMaggio had let Eric and Setara stay at his apartment while they were in NYC. He and Bill Owens had run over from the chief's dramatic "Single Shot" resignation and were on hand to add anything to the play-by-play or color commentary that Eric was about to describe to the full bird.

"Why do you want to come back even if it means you may wind up in Leavenworth?" the colonel said.

"Sir, I have a family now. I want my wife to be American citizen and my son to grow up as a proud American. That can't happen if I live in the shadows, sir."

"So why did you need to go off base, son?"

"Sir, I met this girl..." Eric began to recount the story and after forty-five minutes, the colonel turned to DiMaggio and Bill. "Do you to attest to his story?"

"Everything we took part in, from the shootout in the Bronx to the firefight in the woods," DiMaggio said.

"Hell, if you don't take him back, I'll sign him up at the NYPD in a second," Bill Owens said.

The colonel looked at Eric and studied him for a long minute. Then he leaned in and said, "The baby healthy?"

"Ranger tough, milk fed, bath cooled, burps like a sergeant, sir."

"You know, I can't help you with the whole State Department mess you created with the 'diplo' passport and, not to mention, however the hell you got from Afghanistan to Pakistan to Canada. I don't even want to think about what the Secretary of State will do to you for the episode in Montreal or the threatening and detaining of a Senegalese Diplomat on a Manhattan street."

"Actually, sir, I've got a friend who works with State. So it will be rough, but I think I can tough it out," Eric said.

"Yes, you would have to have a friend, a good one at State to pull off what you did, wouldn't you?" He looked over at Setara, who was cradling the little fellow in her arms. He smiled; it was a cute kid. "What's his name, soldier?"

"Bradley Michael Owens Ronson, sir!" Eric said proudly, sitting up.

"That's a mouthful, Sergeant."

"Yes it is, sir."

"I told him to drop the Owens but somehow I am now the kid's uncle too," Bill said.

The colonel stood. He walked over to Setara and the baby, gave a little wiggle to the baby's bootie-covered foot, and smiled at Setara.

"آیا دوک ناک امش داد هتشاد شاب؟" Setara said with a soft voice in her native Dari.

"Yes, I have two, a boy and a girl," the colonel said, "although I can't imagine they were once that small." The colonel headed for the door and then turned and said, "Ronson, no promises. You've done some incredibly stupid things, but you also busted a human trafficking ring. I am going to try and have this released to my authority. I can't guarantee at the end of all this you'll still be a soldier but let that be the Army's choice. No matter what, I don't want you to quit on me, Ranger."

"Thank you, sir, that is more than fair." Ronson then stood and saluted his superior.

The colonel snapped back a crisp slice through the air and left.

Ronson breathed a sigh of relief as DiMaggio and Owens made the best of it.

"Better then a stick in the eye!"

"At least he didn't shoot you."

IQ

As he emerged onto 36th street, the tall thin man with the pockmarked face pulled a prepaid phone from his pocket. He texted a message: "Done. Found a lipstick with a memory stick."

A return text almost immediately followed: "The Secretary is pleased. Arrangements have been made for payment in the usual place. Bring stick."

The man, known as Franco, then dropped the phone onto the sewer grate on 36th and Lexington Avenue, crushed it with his foot, and kicked it into the sewer.

IQ

It felt good for DiMaggio to have his badge clipped to his coat once again as he entered the revolving doors at the world's most famous building. The acting chief of detectives quickly gave provisional status of "reassigned to duty" to DiMaggio in the wake of the circumstances regarding the former chief's suicide, which was tantamount to an admission that he had been targeting DiMaggio, thus invalidating his suspension.

The phone number Eric handed over to DiMaggio had proved to be a dead end, in that even the phone company wasn't sure how it lost track of it. They couldn't explain how the number had not been billed or available for reassignment for seven years. DiMaggio knew that someone in the phone company was paid to make that number disappear. What they could tell him, however, was that according to the exchange and trunk routing, it turned out to be one of the thirty thousand phone lines that fed the Empire State Building on Fifth Avenue. He met the Verizon guy for the building and his supervisor in the lobby and handed the man in charge the warrant.

"That's a POTS line. Out of the old PBX systems," the Verizon man grunted.

The supervisor explained. "POTS means 'plain old telephone service.' It was the first service to the building. All the later stuff like T-1, fiber, and coax is computer logged. We'll have to trace this one the old fashioned way."

DiMaggio and three crime scene techs followed them to the basement.

The "POTS" number relates to a trunk number which when cross-checked with the switching schematics led the phone guy to a bank of wire terminals they called the Christmas Trees. Around the middle of the mass of colored wires was a pair with a hang-tag on it identifying the number. He then checked where he was in the mass array of binding posts that connected the wires in the basement to the seventeen million feet of phone lines that connected to the offices in the one hundred and two stories above. "Twentieth floor west end, 2039. That's a small office."

The building's manager met them in front of 2039 with the passkey. DiMaggio noticed the small "Family Services" plaque on the door. Inside, the small, two-room office was empty save for a desk, a chair, a computer and some file cabinets. The crime-scene guys went to work and in less than five minutes determined that the place was cleaned of any and all traces of the tenant. Including the computer, which was wiped so clean it didn't even boot up. DiMaggio did notice the old zip-disk drive, like the one Yau and the girl at Tek-Serve had, sitting next to the machine

DiMaggio turned to the manager, "Everyone who works in the building has an ID card, right?"

"Yes."

"Who worked here?"

The manager hit his press to talk radio and ask Lucy in his office to pull the ID for the tenants of 2039.

DiMaggio heard her response over the radio a few seconds later, "Just one card was issued to that suite, Hannah Faust."

DiMaggio knew the name; it was the women who framed Cassidy, all those years ago. "Got home address?"

ІᴰQ▲

Sniffen Court was a rarity in a city where "out of the ordinary" was the general rule. Originally built as horse stables, it was transformed in the 1930s into what was now some of the richest real estate on east 36th Street just west of Lexington Avenue. A mini-community nestled on both sides of a narrow alley with gas lamps, irregular brick buildings and carriage house architecture with curved archways that evoked a nostalgia for New York in the mid-eighteen hundred's.

Hannah lived in the fifth house on the left. The locksmith called DiMaggio over, "Look, before I touch this lock you should see this."

DiMaggio looked and saw scratches consistent with pick marks in the cylinder. "Okay, we'll do it the other way to preserve the lock. DiMaggio waved and a big bruiser of a cop stepped up and gave the century-old door one shot with a battering ram and it flew open.

DiMaggio drew his gun and stepped inside, "Hannah Faust, it's the police. We have a warrant to search your house." By the door were three bags and a trunk, all packed with luggage tags on the handles, which had Olympic Airlines logos on them. *They go to Greece,* he thought. Then his nose twitched. "Smell that?"

"Yea, smells like a hospital."

"That's ether." DiMaggio went from room to room declaring each one clear as he made sure no one was in it. Then he got to the bathroom. His shoulders slumped and he re-holstered his gun. There in the old style porcelain tub with four gold plated legs, was Hannah's naked body, submerged in blood red water. Her wrists slit, she had bled out. The bloody straight razor was on the tile floor right next to the tub. DiMaggio had been at enough crime scenes to know she hadn't been dead longer than an hour.

"Get the M.E. over here on the double," he said to one of the uniforms who were now inside the cozy, upscale, multi-million-dollar converted stable.

DiMaggio went out to her desk, put on his latex gloves and rifled through it looking for any clues. It was almost as clean as the office. He looked in the wastebasket. He reached in and pulled out torn-out pages from a book. Upon closer look they were not torn out but cut out, each one smaller than a book page. There were scores of them. He flipped through a few. It was something about Russia; there were descriptions of palaces. A character named Anna, some other Russian names, on one page was a reference to a Tsar. He walked over to the bookshelves and read the spines. There were lots of classics, a load of romance novels and a few history books. One shelf was a whole series of Greek travel books.

He turned and looked around the room to see if there were any other books and then he saw it: *Anna Karenina,* on the window sill, right by the bags stacked at the front door. He opened it. There inside the hollow of the cut-out pages was a padded envelope addressed to B. Levin Esquire. He waited for the crime scene guy to snap a picture, then opened the envelope. He found a DVD with handwriting on it. "To be viewed in the event of my untimely or suspicious death."

He then turned to the officers in the room. "I'm going to go out on a limb here and say having someone pick your lock to gain entry, knock you out with ether then stage your suicide on the day you were leaving for Europe is mildly suspicious.

DiMaggio turned on the TV and DVD player in Hannah's living room. He popped in the disk and grabbed the remote as he hit play.

"My name is Hannah Faust, I first met Warren Rodgers when I worked for him at the Department of Justice. He took me with him when he moved from FBI administration..."

He fast-forwarded.

"...mildly shocked. Well I was, but Warren, he saw an opportunity... We set up Family Services in the spring of ..."

He advanced the DVD again.

"...in Iraq, Afghanistan and in Nicaragua, all finding suitable matches for our quota system... Once found...

"This is gold." DiMaggio said as he zipped forward.

"... four point five billion dollars for the first three and half years adjusted gross profit... Warren Rodgers maintained that by including certain men with diplomatic status we could expedite the deliveries and increase our profit two-fold. I was charged with administering..."

"Can you believe she is talking about 'Administering' human trafficking? In babies!" He sped forward.

"When I returned from the ladies' room, I discovered the judge had taken the zip disk from my desk here, and left. I called Warren and he said he'd handle it. I had no further comment or input into how he did that."

"So that's how the judge got hold of the disk..." He gave it a short run forward.

"...aggio who was assigned the case and our NYPD contact..."

"Whoa, here's where I get a cameo..." He hit the rewind button and played that part over.

"We found out that it was a Detective DiMaggio who was assigned the case and our NYPD contact Grimes, who had also been a customer couldn't shake him from the trail. It was unfortunate but I later learned that another New York City Detective was inadvertently killed when Rodgers' men suspected she had the disk hidden in her home. I had no immediate knowledge of that while it was happening..."

"Hannah, you were in this up to your eyeballs, and you killed Maggie just as sure as if you burned her house down yourself." DiMaggio said to the image of the woman on the screen as she continued.

"Meanwhile, package 4,310 from Afghanistan was late, and our customer was starting to get cold feet. Warren put pressure on our man in Afghanistan and his associates to expedite...."

"Do you believe how cold this is... Expedite..." He pressed and released the FF button one more time.

"But I was just an administrative assistant. I was not involved in anyway, shape or form with procurement..."

"Talk about in denial... I've seen enough; it's all here." He ejected the disk and with his rubber-gloved hand dropped it in an evidence bag, signed it and handed it to a tech. "See the FBI gets this right now. And make sure they sign for it... better yet, go to our tech lab and make a copy first, then give it to the feds... Little miss Faust or her boss, Warren Rodgers, may still have friends in the FBI."

38. Rigor

Owens bent over. He was lining up the blood splatter with the probable trajectory of the small-caliber shooter. The room was a mess – thousands of dollars worth of computers and surveillance equipment as well as three dead bodies. The M.E. who was busily tagging and bagging estimated the scene was about four days old from the post rigor on all the vics.

Owens stuck his pen in the bullet hole in the plaster wall and got the rough angle of entry. He placed a marker, a folded tent card with the number nine, on the floor right under the hole. He then drew a circle with chalk around the gash in the wall. It seemed to indicate that the shot had entered in an upward trajectory, which meant the shooter was either sitting or else kneeling. He got up, clapping the chalk dust off his hands as he saw DiMaggio at the door behind the yellow tape. "Mike. Over here."

"Wow. It's like the O.K. Corral in here."

"Yeah, but it's all Earps. I don't see a sign or a clue of the Clantons."

"You mean that all shots are accounted for and only from the hardware you found in the room?"

"Nine for nine." Owens walked to the middle of the room and pointed to the bathroom. "As far as I can figure, this guy came out of the shit house blasting. And this one over here by the computer desk, with the waist holster, got off two .32s. One into the wall here where my pen is and the other hit the blaster in his pump."

"Aorta!" the M.E. corrected. "The slug pierced his aorta, not his heart, so although he bled out fast, death was not instantaneous."

"So he got off the kill shot to .32 shooter. Still fits."

"IDs?"

"They're all clean, but my guess is they are all work for hire."

"Hired by who?"

"That's why I called you. You know, it's almost kismet the way I caught this case on my first day back." He turned to an NYPD tech. "Harris can you get the video up again?"

The tech hit some keyboard commands and the video started on the screen.

DiMaggio was shocked. "Holy shit. I can't believe I am watching this. How did they get this?"

"Harris says that game console looking joystick thing over there is a drone controller." Owens said.

There on the screen was the gunfight up at the cabin. From a point of view high in the sky, they all saw the ground rise up and then convulse and flatten again. "Hey, that was your shot when you nailed the bushy, ghillie-suit guy. Saved my life there, buddy." He looked around the make shift nerve center, "So this is where the bad guys were HQ'd?"

"Seems so," Owens said.

"This is just a hunch, but look for any connection or reference to a Family Services or a Hannah Faust."

"Not an easy thing to do right now. All this shit is cryptic."

"Encrypted!" Harris said.

"Whatever...he figures two weeks before they can read all the data here," Owens said.

"You know, I might have a better way!" DiMaggio said.

"What's that?"

"Crack!"

Owens' squint and sour expression made DiMaggio chuckle as he fished Yau Sun Yip's card out of his wallet.

39. Almost

The Department of Transportation, or DOT, operated at an annual budget of over seventy billion a year, which visually would have been seventy thousand stacks of one million dollars each. As with all federal bureaucracies, there was no actual accounting, no examination that could possibly reach down to the penny or the hundred or even the ten-thousand-dollar level.

The DOT's yearly draw from the U.S. Treasury alone could also be thought of as seven million stacks of ten thousand dollars each. So, one could see how it would be possible to lose or misplace a few stacks. In fact, if a person misplaced twenty stacks of ten thousand dollars, it would only amount to one thirty-five thousandth of all the stacks, or three tenths of one percent. And if a person found them, let's say, in a drawer, he or she would have two hundred thousand dollars. Or enough to pay forty-thousand per man to five mercenaries. Scrounge up twenty more stacks, or a little over one half of one percent of the total seventy billion, and he or she could also get a few techs and some less-than-desirable ex-intelligence types to manage a critical mission – a mission to contain a breach that could result in that person personally losing four billion dollars a year.

At least that was the logic that Warren Rodgers, Under Secretary for Infrastructure and Planning of the DOT, thought when, ten years earlier, he first started his "side-business" of supplying desirable babies to the affluent, influential and needy wanna-be parents. They shelled out ten million each for a clean kid. All guaranteed to be under six months old, disease free, and a match to whatever criteria they desired as to gender, race, ethnicity, and even eye color. On an average year, they delivered four hundred bundles of joy that netted him a joyous four-billion-dollar bundle.

Three left, twelve right... Then that judge up in New York had to get a conscience all of a sudden. That was bad for two reasons: the obvious one and also the fact that he, like so many of his best clients, came from the patient rolls of a psychiatrist who he found when she was working with the government. When the FBI had what they wanted and were going to stop working with her, he stepped in and kept the doctor on the government treadmill, although now feeding information to only him. This data was not about crime fighting, however; this was about identifying parental candidates with deep enough pockets to shell out the ten million per kid.

Seven right, nine left... Doctor Cassidy was unwittingly responsible for almost half the sales he made. The decision to eliminate her was difficult for him. Half his referrals would cease, but that nosey cop D'Macho or DiMashio got to her instead of being neutralized. So, her death became an accepted part of his cost of doing business.

His big mistake was in trusting that pervert Bessen to bring in that idiot Wallace. It was he who picked the soldiers of fortune. Bumbling oafs who killed a female NYPD detective and nearly blew their cover with, of all things, a veteran railroad cop. On the other hand, his own choice of Amtrak rail cops as a cover agency was pure genius. They operated under his auspices, and with the new legislation he had pushed through Congress, he was able to give them all the surveillance toys and access they could want. But the men Wallace recruited were, in the end, just grunts. Not thinking, reasoning men.

...and eighteen right.

The safe opened and he cleaned it of all his cash and computer disks. Seventy thousand dollars should get him to Switzerland. Then a new identity and life, funded by the six billion in Swiss accounts that he was able to amass over the decade, after expenses.

He looked at the general accounting ledger that remained in the safe. He hesitated about whether to take it or leave it. In it were the names of all the politicians, bureaucrats, and officials he had bribed since the first day he started. Hundreds of entries with amounts paid off. Some to household names. Others, nameless faceless government gnomes. *Good leverage if I ever need it.*

Then he thought of Hannah's lipstick. She had been thinking the same thing. He'd have to remember to instruct his man in New York, who did not know him but was very familiar with his money, to make sure he destroyed whatever Franco, who dispatched her, was holding before he eliminated him when Franco showed up to be paid. It would be the last "the Secretary is aware" order he placed. With that, any and all trace of the Family Services Corporation would be erased.

He was re-hanging the painting of the Erie Canal over the safe when he was startled by his secretary's buzz and her announcement that his car was awaiting him at the New Jersey Avenue entrance. As far as she knew, he was heading to Dulles to fly to a European confab on high-speed trains. But from Dulles departures, he'd hop a cab to the private aviation side where his own Gulf Stream 5 was fueled and waiting for "Mr. Bowens," his jet-owning alias.

Sasha would be waiting for him in Zurich. In two years, after his disappearance, he would be declared dead. His kids' college was already paid for, and there were small stipends that would continue from legitimate investments he had made as well as a few stock windfalls. He had been lucky enough to benefit from whenever he learned that GM or some other company was about to have a federally mandated recall or heavy fine and he, as Bowens, cashed in by either a "put" or "call" order to his broker accordingly. His wife would get his full government pension and benefits and he'd have Sasha, the twenty-five-year-old Pilates instructor with an eye for girls as well as for him.

He closed and locked the attaché with the cash, disks, and ledger inside. After he put on his jacket, he took one more look at the picture of his wife and kids on the desk and then headed out the door. For good measure, he chided his assistant as he left. "Debra, I want to see all the reports from the Southwest project on my desk when I get back."

He headed for the elevator.

"Mr. Rodgers? Mr. Rodgers," Debra called out.

He held the elevator door open as he responded. "Yes."

"Upstairs just called; he wants to see you."

There was a small tingle starting in the back of his neck. The SecTran rarely called him into his office on a spur of the moment. He hesitated. He pressed the lobby button and said, "I'll go right up there."

When the elevator reached the lobby, he saw it in a whole new light. He was suddenly aware of the Wackenhut guards who manned the magnetometers and x-ray machines. He paid particular attention to the Spanish, or Mexican, or whatever he was, guy, whose post was the front desk as he saw him pick up the phone.

Both Rodgers' heartbeat and sweat turned up. He was only twenty feet from the door. *Twenty feet from six billion and Sasha... and her girlfriends*. He quickly grabbed the attaché as his sweaty hands almost lost their grip. Luckily, the guard didn't catch on.

The uniformed guard was still on the phone as he passed and looking right at him.

Ten feet.

"Mr. Rodgers!"

Shit! He could hear his heart pounding in his ears. He turned slowly to see one of the analysts trotting up to him.

"Glad I caught you." He handed over a file folder. "The notes on the E.U. expenditures by quarter. I thought you might like to review them on the plane."

"Oh yes, thank you, George."

"Have a good flight," George said.

"Thanks, George."

As the electrically operated revolving door deposited him onto New Jersey Avenue, the cool air hitting his face was like oxygen to a dying man. He took one last deep breath of Washington air as he got into the interagency motor-pool town car and told the driver to step on it.

In the back seat, he reached for the decanter with the scotch. He noticed his hand shaking uncontrollably. He spilled a little scotch but downed two shots before he started to feel calmer.

The town car dropped him off at the airport and he hailed a "district" cab as soon as it was out of sight. After a short drive, the cab pulled up to the entrance of the private aviation area.

Six minutes later, "Mr. Bowens" was approaching the steps of the G5 and twirling his finger into the air signaling the pilot, the universal sign to start turning the engines. Rodgers didn't want to stay in the U.S. even one second longer than absolutely necessary. The phone call from the SecTrans was ticking in the back of his mind.

As his hand grabbed the railing of the retractable steps leading to the cabin, he was startled by a man who seemingly came out of nowhere, but actually emerged from behind the steps of the fifteen-million-dollar private jet.

"Excuse me. I was wondering how much you have to make to afford your own jet?"

"What?"

"I'm sorry, Mike DiMaggio, from New York." DiMaggio raised his right hand and slammed both cuff bracelets he held in that fist onto the railing and Rodgers' wrist in one quick move. Then he nodded to the approaching black cars. "And those fellows, they're from the FBI."

Rodgers immediately felt a tightening in his chest as his legs went weak. He unsteadily sat on the step, his arm propped up as it was cuffed to the railing. "I don't know what this is all about but I am a government official and..."

"Save it pal. You know in the last two weeks I've seen a lot of tasteless, vile, despicable videos, but the most depraved was the one made by Hannah Faust."

Rodgers was stunned to hear the name.

"Yeah, that's right, she left a death-confession video, real juicy stuff. Thankfully, she's appropriately clothed during the piece, but she exposed you, your ring and your whole fucked-up network. So you had her killed for nothing, she nailed you pal, dead to rights. You must be a real charmer, Warren, if you couldn't buy someone's loyalty for a million bucks a year. What a schmuck."

The FBI agents came to the plane and DiMaggio handed them his handcuff key. They freed Rodgers and were putting him in their own cuffs when DiMaggio said, "Just a minute, men."

He turned to Rodgers, who was now standing, "And this is for having my partner, Detective Maggie Reade, a great cop and a beautiful, nurturing soul, murdered." He hauled off and punched Rodgers right in the face. He went down like a sack of hammers.

The younger agents were shocked. One of them went to Rodgers, "Sir, we witnessed that brutality, you have a right to press charges against this law enforcement officer."

Spitting a little blood, Rodgers was about to speak, when the older FBI agent said, "For what, Agent Unser? This man obviously lost his footing and fell off the steps here."

DiMaggio looked at the seasoned fed, then at the by-the-book junior agent.

"That's exactly how I saw it, sir." The young, but not stupid, agent agreed.

DiMaggio thanked the senior agent and walked off towards the terminal for his flight back up to New York.

40. The First Steps

On the steps of the Federal Courthouse in lower Manhattan, the Southern District Attorney of the United States was behind a phalanx of microphones. News reporters and camera crews encircled him and by his side was Marla Jenkins.

"This afternoon marks the end of an inhuman practice. The slave trade was alive and well and operating at the highest levels of our national strata. Seemingly benign in its intent but utterly ruthless in its execution, it is now doomed to die a death at the hands of American jurisprudence. Earlier today and yesterday, agents of the FBI, in coordination with other federal and local law enforcement agencies, have made a series of strategic arrests of the top echelon of this nefarious endeavor."

DiMaggio and Cassidy stood off to the left; she leaned over and asked in a low voice, "So that's why you went down to D.C. this morning!"

"All I did was chat with a guy about the high cost of plane travel these days, long enough for the feds to ruin his travel plans."

The United States Attorney continued speaking about U.S. vs. Warren Rodgers, Family Services Corporation and coconspirators, et. al., as he explained the depth of the network and its brutal efficiency.

The camera crews and lights made Cassidy squint. The reporters were all busily writing notes. As she listened, she turned to DiMaggio. "This is going to work, isn't it?"

"Are you kidding? The human trafficking of babies to the one percent! The press will eat this up alive. By the eleven o'clock news, the entire ring will be booked. Sunday they'll all be on a special edition of Sixty Minutes. Hopefully direct from death row. We aren't the threat anymore; they got bigger problems now."

The speaker concluded and started a brief Q&A as the press exploded into a fusillade of questions and calls for clarification.

DiMaggio hitched his head over toward the street. "Wanna go?"

They walked down the steps and then stopped on the sidewalk. As she looked at him, there was a moment of genuine sparkle in her eyes. "So what are you going to do now, Michael?"

"Take my share of the money," he patted the side of the gym bag stuffed with the rest of his half of the money they took from the druggies, "and take some time off. Go down to the islands, figure out what I want to do with the rest of my life."

"What about Susan?"

"I've learned some things about myself that don't sit right with her view of our world."

"Change can be a good thing," Cassidy said.

DiMaggio leaned in. "It's evolution that hurts!"

An awkward moment passed between the two of them. Cassidy broke the silence. "I guess I never really said thank you. So..." She put her hand on his shoulder and kissed him on the cheek. "Thank you."

"For what. Almost getting you killed a couple of times, ruining your life, your practice, and your career?"

"Yeah, you really suck for that. But I would have also been dead two or three times if it weren't for you. You are good and brave and not too hard on the eyes."

"Wow. Maybe we can go to a B&D club sometime." It was a grand day for awkward moments as this time DiMaggio broke the uneasy stillness. "What about you? What are you going to do?"

"I still like helping people. I am going to go work in a clinic."

"Starting again, from the bottom?"

"Not a bad thing." Momentarily, her eyes looked over his shoulder. "Besides I've got a new person in my life." She gestured with her head and DiMaggio turned to see.

LaShana came running toward them, her granny waiting at the cab, waving. She ran straight into Cassidy's arms. "We are going to the zoo today," the little bundle of cute said with her big beautiful eyes looking right at DiMaggio.

"Really? That is so cool! I hope you see an elephant, a tiger, and a henway!"

LaShana's nose scrunched up. "What's a henway?"

"Oh, about five pounds. How much do you weigh?"

LaShana's laughter was just the right pitch and tone as DiMaggio turned to Cassidy. "And thank you. I know my friend Reade is up there smiling right now." He kissed Cassidy on the cheek, tussled LaShana's hair, and walked off. Cassidy and LaShana watched him leave and then turned to start their day.

They didn't get fifty feet when DiMaggio trotted up behind them.

He handed the bag over to Cassidy. "You know, I was thinking. This kid should go to college. Will you take this and make sure that happens?"

"What about the islands?"

"I just remembered – I burn easy."

"You can't afford to do this."

"I'll do okay; I still got severance and will probably get my pension back in time."

"You know, Michael..."

"Yeah, I know, but let's not ruin a good healthy relationship based on mutual dislike, okay?"

She smiled. "Okay."

"See ya around sometime, Doctor."

"Yeah, sometime, Detective."

Acknowledgements

Here's something a magician would never do: reveal his sources and methods. I'll throw caution to the wind, because a lot of wonderful people gave of their talent, time and experience to guide me through the writing of lives that I have never lived. I am truly indebted to them all:

Editor Sue Rasmussen, my first audience and guide through composition and readability. Her guidance, support and insights incubated my ideas, which were destined to not make it out of the nursery.

Joe Badal, a polished and accomplished author, whose contributions to my storytelling is immeasurable. Simple drops of enlightenment that gave my work both scope and insight.

My cousin, author George Cannistraro, who is a constant champion of the little things in the book that I didn't realize could be big things.

Col. Mike Miklos, US Army Ret., who brought Afghanistan and what it is to be deployed a million miles closer to me. Mike embodies the honor and privilege of serving with comrades in defense of America.

U.S. Ambassador Mike Skol who is a constant delight both in his humor and the way he can explain foreign affairs and the nuts and bolts of the State Department so that I may weave those elements into my work.

Anthony Lombardo, Retired First Grade Detective NYPD, whose "on-demand" encyclopedic knowledge of all things guns and police procedure made it easy for me to appear like I know what I am writing about. His input into this book was invaluable.

Story consultant, Marie McGovern who gave my content the once over and made it twice as good. Her impressive story analysis helped me find the better story in my story.

To my Publisher Lou Aronica, it is his belief in my work that gives me the confidence to take risks. It's his friendship that makes the experience that much sweeter.

To Mara, Alvaro, Mary, Larysa, Leslie and all the crew at The Crooked Knife, the Manhattan restaurant that for years has always had my table (next to the plug) waiting so I can open the laptop and have a working, writer's lunch.

To Susan, Yvonne, Frances, Leddy, Angelo, Arnaldo, Lissette, Carlos, Manolo, Javier, Marcus, and all the wonderful staff at The El San Juan Hotel in Puerto Rico. The best place to sit on the beach and write, edit, rewrite and re-edit every book you've ever written.

Lastly, as I am always aware, to you the reader, for without you I am writing to myself. Thank you for coming along on this trip, I hope you had a good read. Let me know about it: Tom@TomAvitabile.com

About the Author

TOM AVITABILE, is a writer, director, and producer with numerous film and television credits. He is a retired New York ad man and professional book coach, and a member of The International Thriller Writers as well as the Mystery Writers of America. His first novel, *The Eighth Day*, the first installment of his Bill Hiccock "thrillogy," became a Barnes and Noble #1 bestseller. This was followed by two more number-ones, including the book you just read. Tom was a SOVAS finalist for best voiceover – Thriller Narration, for his first ever attempt at an audiobook, Joe Badal's *Ultimate Betrayal*. Between the pages, Tom can be found behind the drums playing jazz around the New York area.

Read the opening pages of
GIVE US THIS DAY
By Tom Avitabile

15 DAYS UNTIL THE ATTACK

*Will there ever come a morning when you wake up
and just know that you are going to die that day?*

Miles Wheaton tried to hit the pause button on
the grim internal monologue that narrated his exodus
along with hundreds of other cranky New Yorkers as
they were forced off their train against the onrush of
first responders.

*Is there a sign? Or some dark omen that you might
have overlooked?*

Big, burly cops, EMTs, and firemen laden with
emergency equipment squeezed down the narrow station steps as they funneled their way to the platform
of the Twenty-Eighth Street IRT station. The concrete, recently redecorated by the poor unlucky bastard whose head had been separated from his body by
the cold indifferent steel of the downtown number-six
train, was sprayed with blood.

*Some form of harbinger, which in hindsight was
heralding the moment when you should have hugged
your loved ones and kissed them goodbye, one last time?*

The guy had probably been sleeping or playing
Candy Crunch on his phone and missed his stop, so he
must have tried to leave the train by jumping out from
between the cars, Miles reasoned to himself. He must
have gotten snagged, so all that left the train was his
head, which met a green-painted steel column on the
platform. Miles shuddered, remembering the sound,
like a pumpkin hitting the pavement from the fifth floor.

Thinking he might jump the line and not be late
on this most important day, he instinctively reached
behind him, but caught himself and the big mistake
he was about to make, and then simply slid his ID wallet back into his pocket. He commanded himself to be

patient now, content to fold in with the horde of rush-hour, pre-caffeinated zombies lumbering and trudging their way up the subway stairs, the soles of their shoes scraping over the grimy steps as they slid sideways and snaked their way upwards.

Weaving through the throngs of descending emergency personnel, Miles ran a hand through his dirty-blonde hair and tried to shake away the haunting, slow-motion replay of the decapitation he'd witnessed a short distance down the platform from him. Try as he might to change the channel, he kept dwelling on the split-second gap between life, with all its distractions and concerns, and the serene, cold, calm of instant death.

Taking the last two steps onto Park Avenue South in one hop, the forty-two-year-old semi-pro racquetball player with an MBA and a minor in law escaped the subway, amid the wailing sirens and air-horns of still more arriving emergency services trucks.

.⑥.

The folks on the fortieth floor of Prescott Capital Management were not aware of the underground drama and he tried to not let his face be the one-hundred-dred-point headline type announcing it. He was good at concealing his thoughts and excellent at his craft. After three months of gaining trust and making alliances at Prescott, one of the top hedge funds in the nation, he would soon lower the boom. Somewhere around noon he'd have the last piece of the mosaic, and with it the end of all the probing, the seeking of connections by rotating the bits and seeing if they meshed. Soon, it would all bear fruit. He glanced down at the sixth- grade math book in his hand. In a few minutes he would receive the final piece, albeit unwittingly, from Prescott's assistant comptroller, Joe Garrison. A picture of a money-laundering scheme would snap into crystal-clear focus. Revealing the conduits of funds, which ultimately contributed to blown apart bodies, and shattered lives. *Like decapitated men in trench coats soaked red with blood.*

"Morning, Mr. Wheaton."

"Hey, good morning, Nate. Is there any cinnamon raisin left?"

"Sorry, that new girl . . . she took the last one."

"Pumpernickel then . . . and a small tea." He had no stomach to eat anyway and ordering was purely perfunctory, as it was part of his established routine. Nate put the bagel and tea on a little round platter that hung off the edge of his coffee cart, like Starbucks on wheels. Miles put down the math book, fished out a five and waved his hand for Nate to forget the change. He headed down the office hall, seeing Patricia at her desk for what would be the last time. She had her hair up and wore glasses instead of her contacts, which usually meant some big shot was coming in. The happily married woman preferred the "librarian" look to offset her model-like features when powerful men were about. Miles was going to miss her.

At around 10:45, the day was progressing as planned, except Joe Garrison wasn't in yet. Mildly concerned, Miles was about to try his extension one more time when Morgan Prescott entered his office unannounced. The head honcho had someone in tow that Miles did not know.

"Mr. Prescott, what brings you down from forty-one?" Miles asked as he hung up the receiver and stood.

"Just checking on something, Miles," the impeccably dressed and coifed CEO said, as he stepped aside to let the other, lesser-dressed man enter the room. It was obvious that being dragged into whatever Prescott was up to further diminished the man's meek, shoulder-slumped demeanor. To Miles, he looked like an inmate being forced to perform in the Folsom Prison Shakespeare Festival.

"Who's this?" Miles asked, giving the captive fellow a welcoming grin.

"I'm surprised you don't know," Prescott said.

The hairs on Miles's neck went up. The timing of this little snap quiz set off alarm bells up and down his nervous system. He looked once again at the man that Prescott had ushered into his office. He truly didn't know him. He decided to stall; he reached out his right hand. "Miles Wheaton, nice to meet you."

The man in the off-the-rack suit reciprocated and firmly shook back. "John Delano."

The slight clicking from the grasp registered quickly in Miles's brain as the sound two heavy class rings would make in a clench. He glanced down as the man's hand went back to his side, and saw a college ring set with what looked like the same blood-red stone that was set in the ring on his own hand.

Miles saw that Prescott, a keen observer of people, also caught Miles's recognition of the college rings.

Miles sat down behind his desk again and invited the men to sit in the two chairs in front of it.

"We're on a tight schedule; I just thought you two might know each other," Prescott said as he sat and picked up the elementary school math book from the edge of Miles's desk and gave it a curious look.

Miles nonchalantly glanced at his computer screen. On it an IM message appeared reading: *Working on it! Stall for time.*

Miles took a beat and feigned letting John's appearance sink in. "You know, you do look kind of familiar. But sorry, I can't place from where."

"No need to apologize. I don't seem to remember you at all, Mr. Wheaton."

Miles pointed his finger with a snap. "Wait a minute. Andover? Right?"

"Well, yes ... but I still don't ..."

Prescott wasn't looking happy. Obviously, if he suspected Miles was lying about knowing John, the clue from the ring was something he hadn't calculated.

The IM on the screen facing Miles read: *Andover Alumni—Got it!* Then it went away.

"So now, John, what was your major again?"

"I was in the economics pro ..."

"Miles, we need to get along here." His strategy foiled, Prescott was now trying to short-circuit the next three or four minutes of drivel. "Maybe you and John can catch up later."

The screen then flashed: *John Delano, Economics grad '96, Summa Cum Laude. Fraternity: Phi Delta Epsilon.* Then a picture from the 1996 yearbook popped up and showed a young John with big, bushy mustache, sideburns, and big, thick-rimmed glasses.

"Sure, Mr. Prescott. John, let's catch up later. I am dying to find out how the laser is working out."

That caused John to ask, "The laser?"

"Laser eye surgery! C'mon, I remember now. You used to wear glasses as thick as coke bottles, and now not even contacts? Or was it just eye strain from cramming your way to Summa Cum."

John was caught; now he gave Miles a second look.

Miles then turned to Prescott, to deny John a really good look at his face. "And Mr. Prescott, I was thrown at first because this guy had the father of all mustaches, big handlebar job . . . with the sideburns . . . You look much better now."

"Thanks, Miles. I'm sorry; I still don't remember you but, yeah, I got Lasik about two years ago and the face hair was gone with my first interview . . ." John said.

Miles's computer screen now showed: *1996–2001 Citigroup Global Markets Inc.—VP European Diversified Financial Group* and the rest of John's resume.

"That's right, I heard you nailed a big job at Citigroup. International banking, wasn't it?"

"Well, I started as an associate," John admitted self-effacingly to Prescott, who was clearly their superior.

Miles laid it on thicker. "Yes, but if I remember correctly, you made MD in less than five years! Have I got that right, managing director in twenty quarters? Mr. Prescott, a lot of us wandered around aimlessly after Ando, but John here did well."

Then John hitched his head towards Prescott. "Mr. Prescott thought you were a frat brother of mine."

Prescott rolled with it but his shifting in his seat was a subtle tell that let Miles know he wished John hadn't pointed that out.

"But you weren't in PDE?" John added.

"No, but the typo in the version of my resume that Mr. Prescott got says that. Actually, I was Epsilon Omega Phi. For some reason the headhunters who reworked my res screwed it up and it came up, Phi Delta Epsilon. You guys were kind of the d.o.cees."

"What's a DEE OH CEE?" Prescott asked irritably.

Both John and Miles said in unison, "Dweebs on Campus." Then they both laughed and Prescott became almost brusque as he grabbed John by the arm. "Well, we've chatted long enough; we're due in Chandler's office."

Miles couldn't let the big sigh of relief out yet, but he was reeling in his satisfaction at dodging the bullet.

As they were leaving, John stopped, snapped his fingers and said, "So then you knew Benny J. He was Epsilon Phi like you, right? Whatever happened to him?"

Blood rushing from your face is no way to win at liar's poker so Miles gave it the *"Wait, that sounds familiar, let me see"* pose then turned his head towards the screen. On the screen, a list of names popped up under the heading: *Epsilon Omega Phi—1993–1996*. Miles needed to move closer to read it so he said, "Hold on a minute, just let me stop this alarm for my eleven o'clock meeting from going off . . ." As he feigned searching for the on-screen "cancel" icon, he scrolled down the list. The fifteenth name down in alphabetical order was *Benjamin F. Jerold III—poli-sci—Minor Constitutional Law*. He then continued with his ruse. "That's it, damn annoying thing . . ."

Prescott walked around to Miles's side of the desk. "How do you stop that thing? I can never do it." Miles knew Prescott was lying and might have an inkling that somehow Miles was being coached or finding the answers online.

Miles double clicked on the clock icon and the dialog box showing his eleven o'clock meeting expanded on the screen, overlaying the IM box with its fraternity list, hiding it from Prescott's prying eyes. "Right here, sir." He clicked the cancel button as Prescott came around. "You just have to keep the panel open from the settings in the preference menu."

Miles then added his personal touch. "Anyway, old BJ 3? Last I heard he was going to run for something political. If his dad let him."

"Yeah, old man Jerold, he wanted him to come into the family firm. I liked Benny; do you still keep in touch?"

"No, we were never that close, which is why you and I never really hung out too much." Miles added a little wink to soften the still painful jab at the man's dismal college social life, which he just assumed from the pathetic picture in the yearbook.

"Well, nice catching up with you, Miles . . ."

"You too, John, see ya around sometime."

Prescott stridently marched off, his little test gone awry, and John stepped lively to catch up.

Once they were gone, Miles let out a well-heated sigh of relief. He turned to the knick-knack on his bookcase shelf that was behind and off to the right of his desk, and blew a kiss.

That could be considered sexual harassment, mister! appeared on the screen.

.₲.

In Brooklyn, on the third floor of a nondescript building, in a room with cubicles and monitors, Brooke Burrell-Morton sat in a gray pencil skirt and blue satin blouse, her suit jacket slung over the back of her chair. Her face was illuminated with the spill from the plasma display she sat behind. She smiled as she typed something else on her keyboard: *You handled that well, George."*

Miles bristled at the use of his real name but then
the name "George" was deleted letter by letter and
replaced with "M-I-L-E-S!" George Stover, US Treasury agent, aka Miles Wheaton, financial analyst/
wizard, smiled and then tried to calculate whether the
ambush test that Morgan Prescott had just pulled to
trip him up was purely innocent, or something that
could derail what was set to kick off in less than fif-
ty-seven minutes now.

Back at the Brooklyn HQ, Brooke then entered
the event in her log with the notation that all future
operations like this be armed with social as well as
academic data on all possible connections that could
blow a field agent's cover. Brooke typed in: *Mustering
now. See you at zero hour*. She unconsciously looked at
the video monitor to her right, which was showing her
the surveillance video from George's bookshelf camera. With that, she removed the headset and got up
as another agent took her place monitoring the office
in which their star undercover agent had survived for
the past three months. And, more importantly, the
last three minutes.

Brooke put on her Kevlar vest and checked her ID
wallet to make sure she had her federal creds. She slid
her Glock 23 into the Seven Tree quick-draw holster
and slipped on her jacket. From the corner of her eye,
she saw the young agent at the desk checking her out.
"Keep your eyes on that monitor, Agent Wills . . . in
case George needs more help." She pulled the elastic
from her ponytail and let her blonde hair fall; she gave
it a shake, then gathered it again and replaced the
band so it was tighter as she headed for the elevator.